BRANDED: A THREE-BOOK COLLECTION

SANCTIFIED | TURNED | BLOODLINE

DAVID BUSSELL

SANCTIFIED

1

Desk Babysitter.

It isn't actually my job title, but it might as well be.

I work for the London Underground's Lost Property Office, or the LPO as it's known in the biz.

The biz?

Who am I kidding? This isn't Hollywood. There's no glitz or glamour to this job. I man a phone, I tag lost items, I enter data into a computer. Any monkey could do it. It's a career so meaningless that the nameplate on my desk is a piece of paper folded into a Toblerone shape and inscribed in ballpoint pen.

But you didn't come here to hear me bellyaching about my poor life choices, did you? You came here for the vampire stuff: for the sprouting fangs and the stakes through the heart and the blood spraying *phut phut phut* against the walls. And spray it will. Gallons of the stuff. But this is an origin story, and you can't have an origin story without a bit of preamble.

I know. *Boo,* right?

Don't worry, you'll get to meet the vampire-killing machine who strikes fear into the hearts of the undead soon enough, but first of all, say hello to boring old Abbey Beckett.

That's me.

The Desk Babysitter.

The girl who didn't get the grades she needed for university and wound up working in a lost & found.

I know, I know, I can already guess what you're thinking...

How bad can it be, Abbey? A job's a job in this economy. Buck up and stop your whining, girl.

And I hear you. It even sounds like a cool place to work, doesn't it; London's famous Lost Property Office? You've probably read about it in one of those whimsical articles on *The Guardian*, or a *Buzzfeed* listicle if you're hard of reading. Maybe you've cycled through a photo gallery of some of the weird and wonderful things that find their way into our basement. The peculiar artefacts that people leave on the Underground, all piled up on top of each other like the treasures of Aladdin's cave: wedding dresses and false limbs and grandfather clocks and wheelchairs and water skis and burial urns and medieval swords. Last week, we recovered a stuffed swordfish mounted on a big wooden plaque. It must be at least five feet long. I mean, how do you even get a thing like that on the train, let alone leave it behind?

I'd taken delivery of a lot of strange stuff since I started working in that office. All day long it came my way, and all day long I tagged it, bagged it, and sent it down the chute to the basement for storage.

Lather, rinse, repeat. Lather, rinse, repeat.

Working at the LPO was the same as any other dull-as-dishwater office job. The kind you tell yourself you'll stick at for a month or two before moving on to something better, then before you know it, it's been a year, then two years, then some more. I started my stint there as a temp – a stopgap job before I retook my exams and headed off to uni. That was three-and-a-half years ago.

I like to tell myself that everything would have been different if I'd made it into Higher Education. What a laugh. Even if I did have my Honours, I'd still have no prospects. The job market's a joke these days, and the economy's in the toilet. It's not like having a few letters after my name was going to bury me tits-deep in diamonds.

So, there I was, twenty-one years old and already feeling like nothing. Like I belonged down the chute in the LPO's basement, stuffed to the back of some creaky old shelf, collecting dust, long forgotten.

I know, I sound like a right cheery one, don't I?

As I sat at my desk, head in my hands, the new temp hoved into view. She was peppy, eager to please, and done up nicely in zingy colours and respectable footwear. In other words, she was the polar opposite of me; dressed like Halloween and wearing makeup that had been described, on more than one occasion, as looking like it was applied by a drunk mortician.

I saw the temp mouth a sweet *hello* as she approached. What was her name again? Cathy? Debbie? Susan? I'd promised myself that I was going to take the time to remember it one of these days, but this was not that day.

A middle-aged woman trailed after the temp, grossly overweight, and moving with one of those lumbering walks that looked as though it ought to be accompanied by a tuba.

The temp spoke first. 'Hi Abbey,' she chirped, as she pulled up in front of my workstation. She'd taken the time to learn my name, and she'd only been there a week. That's a level of politeness I find genuinely hostile. 'This lady could really use your help,' she announced, beaming a Colgate smile.

I was about to protest, but before I could think of some other sucker to palm the woman off on, the temp was already flitting away. I tried calling after her, but like I say, her name eluded me. This is what happens when you don't take the time to socialise with your co-workers; you end up dealing with **ugh** members of the public.

'Are you who I talk to about lost property?' the woman barked, which, given where she was standing, ranked pretty highly among the most inane questions I'd been asked that week (the other contenders being, 'Will you be taking the full hour for your lunch break, Abbey?' and, 'Are you going to finish that chocolate pudding in the fridge?').

I painted on a smile. 'How can I help you, Miss?' I asked.

She replied with a tart, 'It's *Mrs*, actually.'

'Okay,' I said, measuring just how much of a shit I gave about her marital status and finding the scales tipping not one bit.

'I've recovered a lost item that I'd like to hand in to the proper authorities,' she went on, terribly pleased with herself.

I'd dealt with her sort before. The type of person who considers themselves a scrupulously honest samaritan, but is really just a pious old shrew.

'And what is it you'd like to hand in?' I asked, clicking on the Received tab of the LPO's computer system, which, would you believe, is called Sherlock. It's named after the fact that our office is located on Baker Street, right opposite the super-sleuth's fictitious residence, as though reuniting clueless members of the public with their knackered old brollies could be equated with Holmes solving some great, police-eluding mystery.

The woman reached into her handbag and produced a wallet; one of those old-fashioned ones with the metal clasp that the elderly love to lug around.

'Here you go,' she said, digging around in its bulging depths and fishing out a single pound coin.

I watched her place it down on my desk as if it were a solid gold nugget.

'A quid?' I said, staring at the thing. 'You came all this way to give me a quid?'

'Yes,' she said, indignantly. 'Why, what else should I have done with it?'

I could think of about a dozen alternatives, most of which involved shoving the thing up one of her bodily orifices, but instead of laying out her options, I settled with corkscrewing my hair in silent frustration.

The woman stared at me, hard and unblinking. 'You don't seem very grateful,' she noted.

'Of course I'm bloody not,' I thought back.

The woman snatched up the coin. 'Maybe I should just keep it then, if that's the way you're going to be.' She said it with the intonation of a serial killer talking to a victim she was keeping at the bottom of a well.

'What's going on here?' asked a new voice.

It belonged to Gary, my idiot supervisor. How can I describe Gary? Can I even be arsed to describe Gary? Not really. Tell you what, if you want a picture of a bloke, just imagine a man, only smaller.

'I came here out of the goodness of my heart,' screeched the woman with the pound coin, 'but this girl's been nothing but rude.'

'I absolutely haven't,' I said, and I hadn't, not out loud anyway.

Gary shook his head in my direction and apologised on my behalf, never once taking my side into account or considering that I might be the one in the right. He then spent the next ten minutes consoling the old bat and assuring her that no, *of course* she hadn't wasted a journey, and yes, *of course* her pathetic donation was appreciated. He even took the lone pound coin and placed it in a Ziploc bag, like it was forensic evidence in a murder. Meanwhile, I sat there with my arms folded, listening as Gary alternated between grovelling for forgiveness and admonishing me sideways for my lack of professionalism. Only once the woman had been reluctantly appeased and had left the building, did he engage me directly.

'What was that all about?'

'Seems like you already made up your mind,' I replied.

He jutted out his chin to make himself look more authoritative, but ended up looking like he was trying to blow a troublesome fly off the tip of his nose. 'I suggest you have a good, hard think about the way you talk to me, Beckett, because if your attitude doesn't buck up sharpish, you're going to be out of a job. Get me?' The last part he said so close to my face that I could smell the vending machine coffee on his breath.

'I get you,' I grumbled, the words like tin foil in my mouth.

'That's more like it,' he said, then did a pathetic little strut around the office, peacocking for the sake of my so-called co-workers, who sat at their desks, sniggering into their sleeves. For a moment, I genuinely thought he was going to go in for a round of high-fives. Having completed his "victory" circuit, he arrived back at my desk for round two. 'So, since you're obviously keen to carry on working here,' he said, 'I'm going to need you to step up your game. I've got sixteen bags of unsorted property over there that needs dealing with, and someone has to input the backlog into the system.'

'I'll make it my next job,' I muttered.

'Too right you will,' he replied, 'tonight. Shouldn't take more than a few hours. And don't make that face, you'll get paid for the extra time. Standard rate,' he added.

Instead of voicing my disapproval, I bit my tongue and imagined setting him on fire a bit. 'Yes, Gary.'

'Oh, and one more thing,' he said, holding up a finger, 'there's a dress code now—new company policy—so no more coming into work looking like Elvira, Mistress of the Dark.' He eyeballed my black clothes and matching nail varnish. 'It's morbid.'

It is true that I have a morbid streak. For instance, whenever I meet a new person, I always think to myself, 'I wonder what I'd wear to their funeral?' It's just a habit really, not because I actively wish the person any ill will. With Gary though, things were different. With Gary, the thought occurred every time he opened his idiot mouth, and every time I imagined standing over his coffin I pictured myself dry-eyed and dressed in my best and brightest.

'Eat a dick, Gary,' I mumbled under my breath, the moment he'd made it out of earshot.

2

Seeing as my flat in Thamesmead was a whole hour's commute away, it didn't seem worth making the long trek home just so I could drag my skin all the way back to the office again. That left me with a big slab of time to kill between the end of my crappy day shift and the beginning of my crappy night shift. A big slab of time that I ended up spending in the staff cafeteria, gorging on high-calorie snacks while I caught up on some much-overdue reading.

My boyfriend, Neil, is a novelist. I'd been lugging around his newest manuscript for days under the pretense that I'd finish the thing, but I was still stuck at the three-quarter point. Don't get me wrong, Neil's a great writer, but his stories... they just don't float my boat. While I like to read weighty hardbacks about orphaned peasant girls overcoming historical prejudice to become successful, independent women, Neil—how can I put this kindly—Neil paints in more… primary colours. His protagonists tend to be of the fantastic variety: modern-day magicians and shapeshifting monsters and generals of Satanic cabals. I mean, I love the boy, I really do, but seriously, give me a break. Just because I dress like a character from an Anne Rice novel, doesn't mean I want to sit down and read one.

Anyway, this particular manuscript was book five of Neil's *W&W Investigations* set, a pulpy, urban fantasy series about a warlock and a werewolf who run a detective agency in San Francisco. Maybe that's your bag, I don't know. To me, that's homework. Still, I only had a few chapters to go, so I took a deep breath, knuckled down, and got to reading. Or at least I *would* have if I hadn't been disturbed by the sound of a nearby conversation…

'...Oh yeah, there's all sorts goes on down there, you know?'

I looked up from the loose pages of Neil's manuscript to see Gary a couple of tables over. Apparently, he'd decided to take a break from getting on my case so he could chat up the office temp.

'...The whole of the Underground network's riddled with stuff that people don't have a clue about,' he told her. 'Like, did you know there's a hidden tunnel that runs off the Circle line and connects to a classified military bunker in St. James' Park? Fascinating, right?'

The temp's barely suppressed sigh said exactly the opposite, but Gary continued to drone on at her regardless. Over his shoulder, the temp and I exchanged knowing eye-rolls.

'If you like,' Gary continued, flashing the temp his supervisor laminate, 'I could take you on a tour of the tunnels some time. Show you some parts of London that the general public never get to see. My treat.'

The temp cleared her throat. 'That's nice of you to offer, Gary,' she replied, 'but I'm afraid I can't that day.'

'I didn't say a day yet,' he huffed back, angrily cramming his laminate back into his top pocket.

He turned, caught me earwigging on the conversation, and narrowed his eyes at me, as though I'd somehow poisoned his otherwise perfect pitch. Annoyed, he marched over to my table and used a pudgy finger to stab at the face of his Casio watch.

'About time you got to work I reckon,' he said, pressing his palms to the surface of the cafeteria table.

I stood slowly and straightened up. 'Aye aye, Cap'n,' I replied, firing off a sarcastic salute.

He gave me a stare that I think was meant to look tough, but only made him look constipated. 'Enjoy your shift, Abbey,' he said, taking his blazer from the back of a chair and tugging it on. 'I'll be going home and putting my feet up now.'

And with that, he turned on his heel and swaggered off.

What an actual prick.

It was getting on for half two in the morning and I still had a long way to go before I was finished doing Gary's dirty work. I was fuming, but more than that, I was experiencing a heavy crush of disappoint. I always thought I'd be on the road to something by this stage of my life. Instead, I was stuck in a rut and slaving away in a windowless tomb until the sun came up.

I jolted at the sound of a sharp buzz.

The office intercom.

Since I was the only one in the building, I made my way to Reception. I checked the CCTV monitor behind the front desk and saw a stocky man from the LPO's collection team using a newspaper to shield himself from the rain. Pressing the button on the underside of the desk, I buzzed him in and he fired into the foyer, shaking himself off like a wet dog.

'Bit late for deliveries, isn't it?' I said, checking my phone for the time. 'Or is it early?'

He didn't bother answering, just dumped a plastic basket of junk on the desk and thrust a device into my hand for an electronic signature. I rattled off a jagged scrawl and cast a glance to the basket. Inside, nestling among the usual assortment of umbrellas and mobile phones, was a brown leather briefcase.

'What's that?' I asked.

'At a guess, I'd say a brown leather briefcase.'

Well, ask the obvious.

'Someone handed it in at Baker Street,' he said.

The front of the briefcase was adorned with a brass plate featuring a name.

Vizael.

'Are you sure it's okay to bring this in here?' I asked. 'Shouldn't the, you know, bomb squad have looked at it first?'

To me, the name Vizael sounded—and please don't judge me for saying this—a bit… Middle Eastern.

'Fucked if I know,' replied the delivery man, making no attempt to stifle a yawn. 'Anyway, it's your problem now.'

He pushed through the exit, back into the downpour, and the door clicked shut behind him.

Wonderful.

I gingerly picked the basket up, carted it to the back office, and set it gently on my desk. With a click of my mouse, I booted up Sherlock and started logging the basket's contents, picking around the mystery briefcase like a faddy eater dodging her greens, until eventually, the case was all that was left.

Sighing, I swiped away some clutter on my desk. I pushed aside unopened letters, a couple of half-empty drink cans, and the deer skull whose eye socket I used as a pen holder (someone left it on the Northern Line a while back, and since they didn't claim it in the allotted ninety days, I made it my own. Like I say: morbid). Having cleared a space for the briefcase, I laid it flat on my desk, lid-side up. Its leather was well worn and faded, but continued to survive in the way that expensive things often do. A pair of brass clasps held the case together, each of which sported a three-digit combination lock.

I began to enter the item into the computer system:

Item #Misc205AG629. Vintage brown leather briefcase. Identifying markings: Brass plate with name, VIZAEL. Brand: Unknown. Contents: Unknown.

What was in that thing? A nail bomb? A laptop containing Top Secret files? Military launch codes? I had to know.

I took a quick glance over my shoulder to check no one was watching—despite the fact that I was the only mug still in the office—then spun the brass wheels of the combination locks with my thumbs.

Click Click.

I didn't even look to see which numbers I'd randomly arrived at, I was too distracted by the clasps simultaneously standing to attention.

'What are the chances…?' I muttered.

I carefully lifted the lid.

What I saw next came as a bit of a shocker.

Inside the case, sat in a black velvet tray, was a weapon.

Not a bomb, or a disassembled sniper's rifle, but a knife. A dagger, like something you'd see in one of those Hobbit movies. The dagger's blade was polished to a mirror finish, its handle wound with a length of purple leather, and its bottom bit—whatever that bit's called—was a finely-cut gemstone the size of a baby's fist.

'Niiice,' I gasped.

It was a beautiful bit of craftsmanship, and I couldn't help, but pick it up to test its weight.

Along with mouthing off at my supervisor, that was the second huge mistake I made that day.

The moment I picked up the dagger I knew something was wrong. The pain didn't come right away, but only because it was so intense that it took a moment for my brain to register. When it did hit me, it almost knocked me flat.

A burning sensation lit up my palm, white-hot and raw. It felt like sulphuric acid had been poured on my skin, stripping it down layer by layer, etching its way through fat, muscle and bone.

I let go of the dagger and it tolled on the edge of my desk like a rung bell.

'Jesus Christ!' I screamed, and filled a speech bubble with some more choice blasphemies.

Clutching my wrist, I turned my wounded hand over to review the damage. There, in the dead centre of my palm was a brand: a perfect circle containing a big letter Z.

'Motherfucker,' I noted.

I shot an accusatory look at the dagger and crouched down to get a better look at the thing, lying innocently on the office floor. Wrapped around the weapon's handle I found an embossed metal circle containing a symbol that matched the one burned into my palm.

'Bastard.'

I was in agony, but thankfully for me, I was also the designated first-aider for my floor, and knew exactly where to find the little green case with the white cross on it.

I made it to the staff kitchen, found the box, and rifled through tape, gauze, disinfectant, and hydrogen peroxide, until finally I laid my hands on the burn cream. I unscrewed the top of the tube with my teeth and was about to squeeze it dry when I heard another buzz.

The office intercom, again.

I checked my watch. It was three in the morning now. I ran back into the office and saw the dagger lying on the industrial navy blue carpet, outside of its locked case.

'Motherfucker,' I reiterated.

3

I should have ignored it. Should have kept my head down and let the door carry on buzzing. So of course, I let curiosity got the better of me.

The office wasn't due to open for hours, and we'd already had our last delivery for the day. Who could possibly be calling at this hour?

The door buzzed again; a long, shrill cry for attention.

I jogged back to the kitchen, ran a tea towel under some cold water, and wrapped it twice around my hand. With that done, I headed off to Reception to see who'd come calling. On my way there, striding past my workstation, I snatched up the dagger with my bandage-slash-makeshift-oven-mitt, dropped it back into its briefcase, and snapped the lid shut before swiping at the combination locks until they looked suitably randomised.

Moving behind the reception desk, I checked the monitor to see a man standing outside, braving the downpour in nothing more than a tailored suit. I squinted, but didn't recognise him. The man was tall, broad-shouldered, and—even going by the pixellated picture provided by our ancient CCTV—a looker.

I cleared my throat and answered the intercom. 'Can I help you, sir?'

He leaned in to the microphone to state his business. 'Hello,' he said, 'is this Lost Property?'

'Yeah,' I replied. 'Do you know what time it is?'

'I know, I know,' he said, apologetically. 'Look, this is really embarrassing, but I left something on the tube tonight, and I have to get it back right away.'

'What is it?' I asked, already knowing the answer.

'It's a brown leather briefcase with a brass nameplate on the front,' he replied, predictably. 'It's very valuable. I'm hoping someone might have handed it in.' He rubbed at his head like life hurt. 'I need it for work.'

Really? What line of work was this guy in exactly? What kind of job required a gilded dagger with realistic flesh-melting action? I wondered if maybe he was in the movies, and the dagger was some kind of prop. That wouldn't explain why it had made such a mess of my hand though I thought, squeezing my wrist in the hope that it might cut off the pain to my throbbing palm. Unless the dagger had a live battery inside and was wired up wrong or something. Oh, what did I know? I already told you I didn't get the grades I needed for a second-rate university degree.

I hit the intercom's answer button again. 'Can you stop by at nine when we open?' I asked, then decided to offer the poor guy some hope. 'I've a feeling we might be able to help you out if you do.'

'Please,' the man pleaded, rain whipping at his face. 'I'm going to be in so much trouble with my boss if I don't show up to work with this thing.'

Shitty bosses, eh? I knew how that went.

He spoke again. 'Is there any way we can talk about this face-to-face? It's tipping it down out here.'

My finger hovered over the button for the front door. I had his briefcase for sure, it just seemed cruel to say no to him at that point. Him out there, soaking wet while I lorded it up in my fortress, bone-dry and hoarding about twenty-thousand umbrellas.

Then again, I was there alone, in the middle of the night, and a stranger was trying to get in so he could reclaim a large, weird dagger.

'I'm begging you,' he said, looking like a very handsome

drowned rat. 'I really need to get that briefcase back. If I don't, it's my arse.'

I prevaricated for a little longer then, against my better judgment, I stabbed the button to open the door.

'Thank you so much,' the man said as he dashed in from outside, leaving puddles in his wake.

The door gasped shut behind him, closing on pneumatic hinges.

Remembering my wounded hand, I thrust it into the pocket of my cardigan to disguise the burn. 'You'll have to be quick,' I told him. 'I really shouldn't be doing this.'

I led him to my desk and his eyes immediately fell on the briefcase. 'That's it,' he exclaimed, his face lighting up.

He went to make a grab for it, but I stepped in his way. 'I have to see proof of ownership first,' I explained.

'It's mine,' he said. 'It's my case.'

'You saying that isn't really proof though, is it? For example, I could just say, I dunno, the shoes you've got on are mine.'

'Well, they're not.'

'Exactly. I would never wear shoes like that, I'd look like an absolute clown. No offence.'

'Some taken,' he said, smiling ever so slightly.

'Look, I do believe it's your case,' I said, 'but I need confirmation. For the system. If you could just show me something with your name on it...' I read off the case's nameplate... 'Mister Vizael.'

It occurred to me then that his face wasn't much of a match for his moniker. His *supposed* moniker anyway.

For a moment, his features seemed to curdle, then he brightened suddenly. 'Look, I don't have my wallet on me right now,' he said, his voice smooth as the hum of a new Ferrari, 'but I'd be more than happy to stop by later with my details. For the system.'

No wallet? Who walks around without a single piece of identifying information? A bank card, a driver's licence, Christ, I'd have taken a Blockbuster card if he had one.

'I'm sorry,' I said, 'but I can't let you make a claim without proper ID.' I felt like a tool saying it, but I just didn't trust the guy. Something about him was giving me the bad feels.

He nodded sullenly then looked away for a moment. When he looked back, something incredible happened. And by "incredible", I mean "bloody terrifying".

His eyes were two voids, a pair of black holes, bottomless, endless, drawing me in, sucking me beneath a dark tide. My blood ran cold and I felt my body go slack.

'Give me the briefcase,' he commanded, his voice thick and full of menace.

Instinctively, I felt my fist leave the pocket of my cardigan and go to pass him the case. I didn't want to, I tried to stop it, but I had no agency. It's like I was no longer a participant in my own actions. I was a witness, a puppet, acting out his will.

As I reached for the case, the wet tea towel wrapped around my hand came loose and flopped on to my desk.

The man with the black eyes saw the brand on my palm and his face twisted into a snarl. 'What is that?' he growled, his eyes snapping back to normal.

The pain in my hand disappeared suddenly as though I'd been shot with a tranquiliser, and when I looked at the brand again, I saw it glowing, the big Z lit up bright and blue.

The man seized me by the wrist, his skin so icy cold that he almost gave me freezer burn. He pulled me closer and brought my hand to his face, studying the mark upon it.

'That can't be right,' he said.

I struggled to get away from him, but his grip was vice-like.

Then something else happened.

A new pattern appeared, not on me this time, but on him. A symbol decorated the man's forehead, a glowing emblem in the shape of a letter J.

Who was this guy? *What* was this guy? I felt a cold, crawling sensation on my scalp, like a trickle of ice water.

The man scowled. 'You're no Nightstalker.'

'I don't know what you're talking about, mate. I'm Abbey, I just work here.'

Snarling, he whipped me around and tossed me across my

desk like I weighed nothing, sending stationery scattering in all directions.

I landed hard on the other side of the desk in a crumpled heap, eyes blurred, stung with tears. The man laughed before collecting the leather briefcase and removing the dagger from inside. He held it up to examine its blade then looked to me, cowering on the floor.

'What the hell were they thinking?' he spat.

He stalked towards me, pushing my heavy desk out of his way like he was sweeping aside a fold-up picnic table.

Time seemed to slow down as a mad scramble of half-conceived plans presented themselves to me—*call for help, dial 999, pull the fire alarm, go for your house keys and stab his eye out*—but the plan that won over was the one that told me to get off the floor and head away from that man as quickly as possible.

I scrambled to my feet and ran, not knowing where I was going until I got there. Within moments I found myself in the staff toilets. I don't know why, but somehow the idea of being in a place with lockable doors trumped the more intelligent notion that playing hide-and-seek in the bogs would mean backing myself into a dead end.

Too late to turn back, I dashed into the farthest cubicle, threw the latch, and climbed on top of the toilet to hide my feet. Dumb, I know, but that's the situation I put myself in.

The outside door to the Ladies creaked open. Terrified, I held on to my breath and found myself entirely rethinking my liberal stance on gender-neutral bathrooms.

Footsteps bounced off the cold ceramic walls. My skin prickled as the steps grew louder, the intruder doing nothing to disguise his presence. I was drenched in sweat, and my heartbeat rang in my ears, loud as a Keith Moon drum solo. I felt like I was stuck in a dream—an incredibly vivid dream—every detail painted just right, every character cast to perfection. Except I knew I was awake. I knew this was really happening.

'This little piggy went to market,' the man cackled, as he kicked open the nearest cubicle door and sent it crashing flat.

'This little piggy stayed at home,' he went on, as he put his foot through the next door along, edging ever closer to my cubicle.

'This little piggy had roast beef,' he roared, kicking down the neighbouring door.

'And this little piggy,' he said, pausing for effect, '...had none.'

Eyes fixed on the gap at the bottom of the cubicle door, I saw his foot separate from the ground as he readied to make his kick, and that's when I made my move. Pressing my back to the wall behind me, I kicked out the door as hard as I could, sending it the other way and smashing it into the intruder's face.

He howled in pain.

I paused, open-mouthed, surprised by my own strength. I'd hit the door so hard it had come right off its hinges.

Shocked, the man held a hand to his pulped nose, which streamed twin rivers of blood.

'You little fu—' he started, but before he could finish his thought, I smacked him in the face with a toilet brush, painting the red brown.

Without giving him a chance to recover, I slid between his legs and took off.

I ran for the way out this time, but when I got to the reception desk and found the button that opened the front door, I saw it had been ripped from its housing.

I was stuck with this fucker. Trapped.

I ran for the basement, hoping I could find something down there to defend myself with, but the intruder had me cut off.

'You're not going anywhere,' he said, taking a goalkeeper's stance.

There was another way down though. He saw my eyes dart to it. The chute. The one we used to deliver logged items from the office floor to the building's storage area.

He ran for it, but I was closer, and quicker too.

I jumped feet-first into the chute, which was only just big enough for my frame. Seriously, if I'd had a slice of Janet's 40th birthday cake that day, I'd have wedged it.

I banged down the chute, metal rushing by me in a blur until I landed in the padded basket at the bottom, which was thankfully parked where it ought to be.

Looking up, I caught sight of the intruder leering wolfishly down the chute at me. He snarled, and as his lips shrank back from his teeth, I saw his canines sprout, long and sharp and impossible. I wasn't stuck in this place with a psychotic, I was stuck here with a monster. A genuine monster!

I didn't stick around to find out what the hell was going on. Instead, I leapt out of the basket and sprinted off deeper into the storage area, trying to stop my brain from fixating on how preposterous this all was, and tasking it with keeping me alive.

Passing between two towering metal racks, I scanned the shelves for something—anything—I could use as a weapon. I saw lost scooters, cellophane bags full of footballs, towers of shoe boxes, but nothing that would be any use in a fight.

Then I saw the broadsword.

Thank Christ for this lunatic city and its scatterbrained residents.

I went to snatch the weapon off the shelf, but before I could lay my hands on it, I felt a familiar icy grip close around my wrist.

The fanged intruder smiled and bony ridges rode up beneath his drawn skin, now white as freshly-poured milk. 'This is where you die,' he remarked, matter-of-factly.

Dagger in hand, he stabbed the point of the blade in my direction. I batted him away and swerved aside just in time to avoid the thrust, and the knife embedded itself in the belly of a giant gorilla plush toy.

I tried for the broadsword again, but the fanged man barred the way. Before I could move out of his reach, he landed me with a stinging backhand that lifted me off of my feet and deposited me halfway up a rack of shelves. I hit the rack so hard that the metal crumpled as I tumbled down it, then the entire unit teetered and toppled, crushing me under its weight.

I struggled to pull myself free, but I was pinned like a framed butterfly.

'No!' I cried.

The intruder giggled and clapped his hands together, the nails now long and ragged.

I wriggled helplessly. I couldn't free myself. I was done for.

The fanged man was going to get me, kill me, and there was nothing I could do about it. Why me? I shouldn't even have been pulling the night shift, and now there I was, trapped with a monster from a horror film who was about to put a violent end to my disappointing life.

It made me… angry. I hadn't done anything. I'd barely tasted life. I'd spent too much of it cooped up in this stupid, boring place, and now it was all going to be taken away from me. Taken away before I could do anything to change things for the better. It wasn't fair.

It wasn't fair!

I winced as my hand throbbed, and looked down to see the brand on my palm glowing blue again, burning bright as the sun.

And as the brand came alive, so did I.

Power flowed through me like a raging, frothing waterfall. Muscles I didn't know I had tensed and sprung up, strong as steel cables. With a furious yell, I worked my knees under my chest, bucked my spine, and levered the shelves up and off me.

The fanged man stopped in his tracks. I couldn't say I blamed him. Whatever it was he'd witnessed was more than just a spike of adrenaline, and we both knew it. He switched his grip on the dagger so the tip of the blade was pointing down, then came at me like I was a block of ice he was setting a pick to.

I scurried backwards, panicking, feet propelling me across the floor, but ended up backing into a dead end at the farthest reach of the aisle. The fanged man stepped forward and lifted the dagger, and as he did, my hand instinctively went up to protect my face. The dagger came down and I acted without thinking, catching the man by his weapon arm.

As my fingers closed about his flesh I felt his skin go from polished marble to fine china. Bones ground and popped as I tightened my grip, and the fanged man yowled and pulled free of my grasp. He scurried away, face pinched with pain.

'You little bitch!'

The dagger slipped from his crumpled paw and I snatched it up, forgetting what had happened the last time I took it in my hand. On this occasion, I found the weapon cool to the touch, so I kept hold of it and turned it in my attacker's direction. The blade glowed cobalt blue as if lit by some inner fire. I liked the way the dagger felt in my hand. The weight. The possibilities. It felt... *right.*

The fanged man hissed at me and my heart kicked into a higher gear. I bounded up on spring-loaded legs, landing on my toes with perfect poise. My muscles were singing and my blood sizzled and popped like a can of Red Bull in a paint-shaker. Knock-kneed Abbey Beckett with the toothpick arms was no more. In her place was an amazon. A nuclear-powered valkyrie, ready to kick monster arse.

'Come on then,' I said. 'Let's be having you.'

The fanged man looked dismayed. 'No,' was all he had to say for himself.

Pulse jacked and acting on instinct, I lashed out with the flaming blue dagger and left the fanged man clutching a six-inch gash in his shoulder. It wasn't deep—just a scratch, really—but it gushed like a busted water pipe.

'You stupid cow,' he snarled, his voice a cable about to snap.

Spotting the broadsword, still on its shelf, he snatched it up and launched himself at me, swinging the weapon with both hands. Jaw firmed, I brought my own blade up to intercept his, and our steel met in a shower of blue sparks.

I fought back reflexively. Confidently. No thought, no strategy, just letting my body move how it wanted. The dagger felt natural to me, an extension of my arm.

My attacker came at me again and I swung the dagger in a powerful half-moon. It sang as it cut the air, and a long, horizontal gouge appeared across the fanged man's midriff. He rocked back on his heels in shock, blood blossoming beneath his torn dress shirt like a big red flower.

The fanged man's surprise turned to rage. He dumped the sword with an ear-splitting clang and came at me with his bare hands. He moved fast—too fast—like a scratched DVD, skipping from one frame to another and losing the moments in between. I thrust the dagger at his throat, but before I could get there, he deflected my forearm and knocked me aside.

His fist connected with my jaw and the pain threw green and

purple splotches into my eyes. After that came his other fist, knocking a fresh helping of pain into my guts.

When I regained my senses I found myself dangling in the air, feet tracing tiny circles above the floor. The dagger lay on the ground beneath me. The fanged man was holding me up by a fistful of hair, a rictus grin on his face. I raked at him with my fingernails, but he held me at arm's-length, just out of reach.

'I'll earn my stripes for this,' he said, smiling so wide that it made it look like he was unhinging his jaw to swallow a baby. 'Earn my stripes and then some.'

As I gasped for air, his hand went for my face and I felt his fingers slither between my lips. I gagged as he forced himself into my mouth, his graveyard flesh invading my throat, ripe with corruption. I tried biting down on his knuckles, but he just smiled as blood trickled from his hand and into my gullet. I hacked and spluttered, desperate for one ragged intake of breath, but there was nothing I could do.

As I fought, terror turned into hopelessness, then into resignation. My body, clenched and rigid, sagged and went limp. The fringes of my vision darkened and my body grew numb. I was drifting away. Slipping gently into a deep, hot bath. All I wanted was to close my eyes, to tip back my head and slide beneath the black water.

But no.

I had to stay awake. A voice in my head told me so; a nagging, insistent demand that I open my eyes, plant my feet, and get back into the fight.

With my last ounce of strength, I kicked up a foot and swung a Doc Marten at the space between the fanged man's legs.

Oof.

He folded like a lawn chair as the steel-tapped toe connected with the jelly of his balls. I felt my feet touch back on the ground. Without taking a pause, I threw my shoulder into my attacker's chest and sent him stumbling backwards. He lost his balance and keeled over, and as he did, I saw a long, silver knife sprout through the centre of his chest. It was so coated in blood that it took me a couple of seconds to realise what it actually was…

The business end of the five-foot long stuffed swordfish.

A pink mist of blood shotgunned from the fanged man's mouth and his body went stiff as a board. All at once, he changed. It was like watching a time-lapse video of a man decomposing, only played in fast forward. His eyes became hollowed-out sockets and his lips turned blue. His skin went tight like he'd been vacuum-sealed, then turned brittle and papery. Steam spat from his mouth with a kettle's scream, then *BADOOF!* he exploded in a cloud of soot.

I watched incredulously as the black confetti spiralled down, cinders mixing with the red pool on the ground, like pepper shaken into a bloody mary.

I was alive. Alive! A monster had tried to end me, and instead I'd ended him. I should have collapsed with relief. Instead, I realised I was grinning wildly.

I looked at my palm and saw the symbol had gone dim now, the glowing blue letter Z returned to a dull, pink cattle brand.

'Hello there,' said a voice over my shoulder. I whirled around to see an elderly man stood before me, smiling beatifically. His eyes went to the dagger. 'I believe you have something that belongs to me.'

4

The old man was short and dressed in a crumpled white linen suit, his belt hoisted to chest-height. He had on his person a wooden, ivory-handled walking stick, on top of which wobbled a frail white hand. If you were to call Hollywood Central Casting and say, *'Send me a sweet old man type,'* you'd have ended up with this guy.

I grabbed the dagger from the sticky red floor and brandished it in both hands. 'Who the hell are you?' I inquired. 'And how did you get in here?'

He smiled wider and held up a hand in surrender. 'I mean you no harm,' he said.

'Yeah, sorry, but that's pretty much the same story the pile of ash tried to sell me.'

'Don't worry,' the old man replied, 'I'm on your side.'

'Oh yeah? And whose side is that?'

He cocked a fluffy white eyebrow. 'Why, the side of the angels of course.'

I was in no mood for riddles. To tell you the truth, I never am. I'd sooner inject myself with bleach than do a cryptic crossword.

'Tell me what you're doing here,' I demanded, punctuating the sentence with an air-stab.

'I told you, you have something of mine,' the old man replied. 'That dagger you're threatening me with, in fact. It belongs to me. My name is Vizael, but you can call me Viz. What do I call you?'

I studied his eyes. I saw no malice there, maybe he was on the level. Then again, I'd given Mr Fangs a pass too, and look where that gotten me.

'I'm Abbey,' I said, even though I wasn't really obliged to give any answers. 'Now it's your turn. Tell me this, if the knife belongs to you, who was that guy?'

'An imposter,' the old man explained. 'An imposter who wanted my dagger very badly.'

What was so special about that hunk of metal that a man was prepared to kill for it?

'Let's say I believe you and this knife really is hot shit. How did the dead guy know he'd find it here?'

The old man shrugged. 'My best bet is that you alerted him to the dagger's presence when you logged it on to your computer system.'

I suppose Sherlock was technically hackable, but getting into it would require some serious, Matrix-level I.T. skills, wouldn't it? Then again, the amount of time I'd spent using my machine to fart around online, its system could be loaded with all kinds of spyware.

'And the guy pretending to be you?' I said, pointing to the ashy puddle on the ground that looked so nasty a dog wouldn't lick it up. 'Who was he? Scratch that, *what* was he?'

'A vampire,' the old man replied, as though it were the most obvious thing in the world. 'Surely the fangs gave it away?'

'A vampire? As in, well, a vampire?'

'Quite so.'

It hardly seemed worth arguing with him. In the last half hour I'd been burned by a magic dagger, demonstrated superpowers, and killed a man with a stuffed swordfish. Whether or not the guy who attacked me was a vampire seemed immaterial at that point.

'Is that why he asked permission to be let in?' I asked. 'Because vampires need to be invited into places?'

'No,' replied the old man. 'He did that because there was a locked door in his way.'

As is so often is the case, it turned out the solution was simply the most obvious one.

'And what about this?' I asked, showing him my palm. 'What's the big Z stand for?'

'It's not a Z,' he replied, rotating his hand ninety degrees clockwise and encouraging me to follow suit. 'It's an N.'

'Okay, so what's the big *N* stand for?' I stared quizzically at my palm, but kept one eye fixed on the old man.

'It stands for Nightstalker,' he explained.

'Nightstalker? Isn't that what they called that serial killer in the Eighties? Something Ramirez?'

'Richard, yes. An unfortunate coincidence. We were using the title first though, so take some comfort in that.'

I'd wandered off topic. The only thing that really mattered at this point was, who was this guy and what was his game?

As if sensing my uncertainty, the old man shuffled over on his cane and held out a hand. 'Please,' he said.

Trustingly—*too trustingly*—I took his papery hand in mine, dagger at the ready in case he tried anything funny.

Just like when I'd touched the imposter, something appeared upon the old man. It wasn't a letter J this time though, it was a halo. A corona of silvery light hovered above his head, accompanied by the faint sound of choral music.

I withdrew my hand and took a couple of steps back. He hadn't been joking before when he said he was on the side of the angels.

'No way,' I said, wide-eyed.

'Oh yes.'

'You're actually shitting me.'

'I'm actually not.'

'You're a… well, a…'

'An angel?'

I laughed, my free hand slapping over my mouth to keep the crazy in. 'Bullshit. No. No, no, no. This is all a bit much.'

'I imagine so.'

'Vampires and magic and now a bloody angel! Have I gone mental? It's this place, isn't it? The long hours and the tedium have finally broken me.'

'You're not mad, I'm afraid, you're just seeing me as I see you.'

'And what are you seeing?'

'I see a good person, destined for greatness.'

I snorted. 'Okay, now I know you're talking out of your arse. I'm a straight C student who lives in a high rise in a shitty part of town. I can show you about a billion people doing greater than me.'

'Doing what exactly?'

'I dunno. Climbing the career ladder. Getting their degrees. Wearing clean underwear every day.'

'A degree won't save them from the vampire apocalypse,' said the old man, and it was hard to argue with him there. A degree is a pretty flimsy defence in any kind of apocalypse.

The old man elaborated. 'They're waking up from hibernation, Abbey. The vampires. In their hundreds.'

'Are they now? Right, sounds a bit bad. Can I go home now? I reckon if I get a solid eight hours, all this will be forgotten.'

'I'm serious, Abbey.'

I pushed the heels of my hands into my eye sockets, grunting with frustration. 'Fine,' I said, 'where are these vampires waking up from?'

'They've been rising in small numbers for hundreds of years of course—'

'—Oh, of course—'

'—But now we're facing an epidemic.'

'I see. And why now?'

By way of an answer, the old man crossed to the far wall and pointed to a framed map of the London Underground network. 'Plague sites,' he went on. 'All over the city.'

'You mean... from the Black Death?'

'Yes, exactly.'

'And the plague sites, they're the pits they threw all the diseased bodies in, right?'

'That's right,' the old man replied, impressed. 'Very good.'

The bubonic plague was my favourite thing from History at school. Again: morbid.

The old man carried on with his story. 'At the start of the

outbreak, parishes did what they could to provide proper burials for their parishioners, but they soon ran out of space. Bodies were buried on top of each other in mass graves, layers upon layers, like some kind of horror lasagna.' He went quiet for a moment, then, 'Do you have anything to eat?' he asked. 'All this lasagna talk is making me peckish.'

'Are you serious?'

'Or a sandwich, if you've one spare. Cheese and pickle would be lovely.'

'I can't believe I'm saying this, but can we stick to the vampire apocalypse, please?'

'Of course,' he replied, slapping his forehead. 'Sorry, my mind's not what it used to be. One of the drawbacks of being over six-thousand years old.'

Did I hear him right? Did he just say he was six-thousand plus? Before I could ask him to repeat himself, he went on with his story.

'The burial sites are being disturbed by modern developments, shaken up and unearthed. Because of that, the bodies are rising,' he dotted a finger all over the map. 'Imagine it: legions of vampires, stirring from their slumber, every single year. And these aren't ordinary vampires, either. These are a new breed.'

'Right.'

'Do you understand what I'm telling you, Abbey?'

'Yep. Got it. Vampires, disturbed, new breed, it's a hell of a story,' I said, even though it actually sounded like piss-poor Buffy fanfic.

'I've fought them for about as long as I can remember,' he went on, 'but I'm too old for that now. That's okay though, because I finally have a successor in you, Abbey.'

There was a bit of a silent pause at that point. 'Come again?'

The man smiled, his watery blue eyes twinkling.

'No. No, no and no again. You've got the wrong person, mate. You want Jason Statham, or Bruce Willis before he went crap, not a girl who works in an office and whose diet is seventy-percent cheap cheese.'

'It's you, Abbey. It has to be. You have been chosen. The

hallowed dagger does not make mistakes. I've seen you fight, and I believe you are the answer to the vampire menace.'

I laughed. 'So, that's it, is it? No interview? *"You got the job; when can you start slaying bloodsuckers?"* Simple as that?'

The old man pointed to the puddled remains of the fanged man. '*That* was your interview.'

I shook my head. 'And what if I say no?'

'I understand your concerns, Abbey. This is a lot to ask.'

'Avert an apocalypse? Uh, yeah, kind of a biggie.'

'I'm afraid the choice has already been made. The dagger has made its choice. You have been Sanctified. You are the one who will destroy the vampires before they bring about the End of Times.'

The bloke was off his nut. Abbey Beckett was going to save the world? Abbey Beckett, the girl the kids at school used to call "2D" on account of her being so stick-thin she was in danger of slipping between floorboards? That Abbey Beckett?

The old man smiled. 'I understand this is a lot to take in,' he said, and reached inside the front pocket of his jacket to produce a calling card. 'Look me up when you're ready to get to work. The card will evaporate by next nightfall though, so don't leave it too long.' He turned to leave.

'That's it? You're just going to go?'

'Yes,' he said. 'I've taken up enough of your time already. Besides, you have some cleaning up to do before the morning shift arrives.'

He was not wrong; the storage area looked like a bomb had gone off in a slaughterhouse. As I examined the state of the place I felt this morning's bowl of Frosties preparing to hit the ejector button.

'Ugh, that is nasty,' I groaned.

'Goodbye, Abbey,' said the old man, smiling, tipping an imaginary hat, and shuffling out the way he came. 'I'll see you soon.'

'Actually, you won't. Bye-bye for good.'

I looked down at the dagger. 'Wait,' I said, snatching it up and calling after him. 'You forgot your knife.'

'Keep it,' he insisted, not turning back. 'It's better off in your hands.'

I looked at the dagger again, then down at the remains of the vampire, and then at the trashed room.

'Well, shit.'

5

It took some serious elbow grease to clean that place up, but clean it up I did.

I was at it for hours, pushing a mop, back and forth, back and forth, until the basement was gleaming. By the time I was done making the place spotless the sun was threatening to rear up and spit its yellow venom.

I snuck out before the morning crew arrived, and headed for Baker Street station to catch the first train home. It was cold as the witch's tit outside, and the pavement was sugared with frost. I pulled up the collar of my leather jacket and breathed into my hands as I walked. It was gearing up to be another bastard of a winter.

The journey to Thamesmead left me with plenty of time to think, but I failed to make much sense of my scattered thoughts. Not only was there the mysterious old man's info dump to trawl through, there was also the fact that I'd killed a guy. I had ended someone's life. That was kind of a big, horrible deal. Okay, he was, apparently, a vampire, and it was very much done in self-defence, but still, I'd killed someone.

I found myself circling back again and again to the comforting thought that it hadn't happened after all, and that I'd just gone momentarily loopy. I must have been imagining things. *Must have.* There were no such thing as vampires, and angels belonged in Sunday School, not the real world. The tiredness must have gotten to me, that's all. I always figured it would take more than a double shift at the office to break my brain, but there I was, convinced that I'd slain a bloodsucking creature of the night and been recruited by a divine being. Mum had lost her marbles when she was fairly young, and there I was jumping on the crazy train with her. *Choo choo!*

But then there was the brand, and the dagger too: cold, hard proof that the events of last night had actually taken place. I reached for my backpack—a spiky black rubber thing that looked like a hedgehog on its way to Torture Garden—unzipped it, and stared down at the weapon inside. The quicksilver shine of its blade gleamed back at me, impossibly bright. If only Neil could see what I'd just seen, he'd cream his jeans. All that make-believe he wrote about in his goofy novels wasn't just a product of his brain, it was actually happening!

The train pulled into Abbey Wood Station and I made my way to the high rise council flat I called home.

From a distance, Thamesmead looks quite impressive with its dramatic tower blocks thrusting from the bank of a shimmering, silver lake. On a nice day, it looks like the future. It's only when you get closer that you find out the lake's choked with rubbish and the towers all stink of piss. If you ever want to get a feel for Thamesmead without actually going there, check out the dystopian masterpiece, A Clockwork Orange, which was shot right on my doorstep. There's a scene in it where Malcolm McDowell and his gang of droogs are strolling through Thamesmead's concrete hellscape, when he suddenly turns and kicks one of them in the crotch for no good reason. It's a sensation I feel every time I arrive home.

The tower's lift was out of order as usual, so I had to haul myself up nine flights of stairs to reach my apartment. By the time I got there I was shattered. I stared at the brand on my palm accusingly. Apparently, my new-found superpowers were good for vampire killing, but not much use when it came to the everyday task of negotiating steps.

I twisted my key in the lock and let myself into the flat quietly, doing my best to keep the volume down so I didn't wake

Neil. Of course, I'd be well within my rights to have given my boyfriend a shake considering the night I'd had, but it was only six in the morning and I couldn't bring myself to kick him out of bed just yet. Besides, I had to yo-yo back to the office again in a few hours thanks to my shitty supervisor, and needed all the sleep I could get.

Most of all though, I just wanted my brain to turn off; for the picture inside my head to turn still and black, and for all the things that had happened to me that day to shut up and go away. And who knew, maybe when I woke up I'd find out that the trauma I'd been through had been a dream after all, like the ending of a kid's first creative writing assignment.

But before I got my head down, I needed food. I slipped off my Doc Martens, tiptoed to the kitchen, and opened up the fridge. I hoovered up the leftovers of a chicken korma then stripped off my blood-stained clothes and popped them in the washing machine for a spin. I checked my naked body for any signs of injury, but found my skin smooth and unblemished. Ordinarily, I bruise like a peach at the slightest knock, but I'd been bashed about like a Chris Brown special and didn't have a mark to show for it. Weird.

I reached into the laundry hamper, found a t-shirt that didn't smell too rank, and tugged it on. Switching off the lights, I made my way to the bedroom. The curtains were drawn and I couldn't make out much, but the sight of the room always depressed me, so I really didn't mind. I padded over to my side of the bed without difficulty, there being very little to trip me up. The room was so sparsely furnished that it looked like a San Fernando Valley porn set. Picture a lonely, malnourished pot plant sitting on a dresser beside a tacky, reproduction painting, and above the bed's headboard, a string of fairy lights, tacked to the wall with push pins for a pathetic bit of cheer.

Neil lay in bed, snoring soundly. He wore a breathing mask that was hooked up to an oxygen tank by his side. Neil was born with an incurable genetic disorder called cystic fibrosis, or CF for short. The extra O_2 being piped into his system helped with his breathing. Everywhere he went, that tank would go with him. Without it, he was out of breath. Too long without it, and he was in real trouble. Neil had an estimated life expectancy of about forty-one years old. I tried not to think about it. I tried every day.

Neil and I met during our A-Levels when we were both seventeen. Back then, his condition wasn't as serious as it is now. I tell myself that even if I knew how bad it was going to get, that I'd still have gone out with him. Whether or not that's true I really don't know, but I like to tell myself it is.

Neil had learned to live with his condition, and coped with it brilliantly. He was limited in what he could do physically, but I'd never known a freer mind. The things he came up with, the places his brain went… where it all came from I did not know. The boy was no slacker either. If I suffered like he did, I'd have given up on my dreams a long time ago. Not him though. He soldiered on, working into the wee hours, tapping away at his books and paying his half of the rent from the royalties, no matter what. Which was just as well. While I'd have been more than happy to pay Neil's way, the money just wasn't there. Even with our combined wages, the two of us were piss poor. I'm talking washing our hair with Fairy liquid and wiping our arses with leftover kitchen towel poor. Taking care of Neil's condition was expensive, even on the NHS, so we were constantly boot-strapping. The disability benefit he got helped a little, but not much since the Tories slashed the fuck out of it. Maybe it wouldn't have been so bad if either of us had parents to fall back on, but with Neil's folks both in the ground, and mine pissed off to Spain to live with their mistress (Dad), or fallen off their rocker (Mum), we had to make do with the pittance our jobs brought in. Without a steady wage coming in I'd have ended up selling manky roses in the middle of the motorway, which was precisely why I couldn't afford to tell my boss to swivel, and why I really had to get some shut-eye in time for my next bullshit shift.

I slipped under the covers beside Neil, worried that I wouldn't be able to sleep with all the crazy going on inside my head as I played and replayed my epic battle with an honest to goodness vampire. Instead, I conked out the moment my head hit the pillow.

6

Much to my surprise, I managed to wake up after just two hours of sleep, and when I did, I felt completely restored. Can you believe I actually bounced out of bed?

Bounced.

That was a lifetime first. Even after a good eight hours' kip I usually woke up feeling like death warmed-over, but instead of leadenly rolling off the mattress and stumbling for the toilet, I came to life feeling like I'd been hooked up to the mains. Seriously. Within seconds, I went from being completely unconscious to fully alert, firing on every piston and keen to take on the world.

But before that, I had to eat, and my nose told me something was cooking. The sizzle of bacon and butter tickled my nostrils, drawing me to the kitchen.

'Morning,' said Neil, cramming a mountain of rashers between two doorstops of buttered white bread and setting it on a plate. 'I made breakfast.'

He smiled and threw in a wink for good measure. Unruly bed hair sat high on his round head, and a cute little pot belly poked between the folds of his blue towel dressing gown.

I responded with a delighted, 'Morning,' kissed him on the cheek, and tore into the bacon butty. 'God, that's good,' I said, using the back of my wrist to wipe grease from my lips.

'Take a seat.' He aimed the spatula at a chair. 'I'll be with you in a second.'

'No can do,' I sighed. 'I've got to get going.'

'What? Where to?'

'Back to work. Gary's got me working another shift.'

'That actual prick.'

'You are not wrong,' I agreed, between hurried mouthfuls of fluffy white bread.

I set the empty plate in the sink, only remembering at the last minute that I had a big N sizzled into my palm. I didn't have time for that conversation, so I hid it quickly, placing my hand behind my back before Neil could get a look at it. Whatever had happened to me last night was a conversation for another time. I headed for the bathroom.

'Hey, do I get a goodbye hug at least?' Neil asked, jutting out his bottom lip cartoonishly.

'Of course, you big twat,' I said, and threw my arms around him quick enough that he didn't notice the brand.

After that, I showered, threw on some clothes, and slipped on a mitt to disguise my palm; a fingerless, black leather-and-lace number that I picked up in Camden Town one time. I couldn't find its partner though, so I left the flat looking like some kind of drag Jacko.

I arrived at the office, dreading what I might find there. If my memory of last night's events were to be believed—and at this point, I really couldn't be sure that they could—I'd gotten into a tangle with a vampire, wrecked the basement, and reduced my attacker to a pond of bloody ash. I'd covered my tracks though, or at least I hoped I had. After the old man had given me his calling card, I spent hours mopping up the place, re-hanging the toilet cubicle door, and removing every last trace of my... well, homicide, I suppose. I mean, if you want to get technical about it. Justifiable homicide though, to be sure.

I hung my coat and sat down at my desk, which I'd already returned to an upright position and reset to its usual, messy state.

I needed something to occupy my mind. For a moment I thought about doing my job, but quickly reconsidered. I mean, why break the habit of a lifetime? So, instead of getting any work done, I pottered around the web for a bit until I arrived at a cool idea.

I opened a tab for eBay.

So long as I wasn't going to be this Nightstalker thingummy —and I absolutely, positively wasn't—I had a perfectly decent magic dagger in my backpack going to waste. I wondered what I could get for that at auction. Surely there must be a line of neck-beards waiting to cough up for an honest-to-goodness enchanted artefact? A nice big bundle of money would have been a total game changer. We had to escape that shitty, spirit-killing flat. The pair of us had been there too long already, and the mould sprouting from the walls couldn't be doing Neil's condition any favours. What if selling that dagger was our ticket out of there? What if opening that briefcase was a good idea after all?

'Why are you looking at eBay?' came a voice over my shoulder. It was Gary of course.

I shut down the tab and switched to Sherlock. 'No reason,' I said.

He harrumphed and steepled his fingers in that way only arseholes do. 'You managed to polish off less than half of the backlog last night, Beckett. Are you going to make up for that, or am I going to have to take away your web privileges?'

The gall of that guy. Every time I walked by his desk he was reading the Daily Mail or smack-talking on some Alt-Right forum. And he was threatening my web privileges?

'I'll make up for it,' I told him, doing my best to keep the edge out of my voice.

'Good,' he said. 'And don't let me catch you shopping around for any more of your Fields of the Nectarine albums.'

'Actually, it's Fields of the *Nephilim*.'

'Don't be such a pendant.'

'I think you'll find the word is *pedant*.'

'See, this is exactly what I'm talking about, Abbey.'

I wanted to throttle him with my bare hands, but knowing my luck, someone would miss the dumbshit. 'Sorry, Gary. I didn't get much sleep last night.'

He folded his arms imperiously. 'About that... did something happen here last night? Something downstairs?'

'What? No, nothing happened here,' I insisted. 'Nothing at all.'

Were there cameras down in the basement that I didn't know about? Did I leave behind some clue? I racked my brain, trying to figure out where I might have gone wrong. Did somebody find a trace of leftover vampire? Did I fail to wring all the blood out of that mop? Did I blink and miss the fanged man's head popping off and rolling under a shelf? Was I about to be escorted from the premises in handcuffs?

'Ash,' said Gary. 'I found ash all over the surfaces downstairs.' He mimed wiping a finger along a horizontal plane. 'Tell the truth, Abbey, Were you smoking down there?'

What? Of all the things he could have noticed, that's what caught his eye? A man had been killed, a room turned upside down, and the only thing he cared about was the possibility of someone using the basement for a cheeky cigarette break?

There were about a hundred things I wanted to say to him, most of them expletives, but I was smart enough to know when to play dumb. 'I don't know anything about that, Gary,' I said with a polite shrug. 'I don't smoke.'

He glowered at me and somehow I resisted the urge to lift him over my head and bounce him off the nearest wall.

He went to leave, but before he did, he fired off one last FU.

'I thought I told you there was a new dress code, Beckett. Get rid of the glove. You look like that dead paedo with the pet monkey.'

7

There has to be more to life than this. Has to.

Over and over the thought went, nagging at me, needling me, daring me to do something about my sorry lot in life. Of course there was an obvious solution to the problem, but since it meant acknowledging the events of the previous night, I chucked it in the fuck bucket.

The chucking did not work.

I took off the glove and stared at the brand on my palm.

'No,' I said, like my hand was a cat trying to swipe the last of my lunch. 'Forget it. Not happening.'

I thought about how powerful I'd felt before. How… flowing I'd been in battle. Well, apart from the bits where I was getting my arse kicked, or I was running away.

'I said no!'

The temp looked at me, startled, as she passed my desk. I avoided her stare and pretended to work until she was out of sight.

I looked down at the brand on my hand again, tracing the letter with my finger.

N for Nightstalker.

What was I doing? Why was I playing so hard to get? I'd been offered the chance to be something more than a Desk Babysitter, and I'd said no out of hand. Shouldn't I at least hear the old man out? What if he was telling the truth and I was meant for something better? What if I really *was* special?

No, it was absurd and it was dangerous. My mind was made up.

It did not stay made up for long.

My shift finished at three o'clock; Gary's meagre concession for making me work back-to-back shifts. I was travelling south on the Bakerloo Line, heading for home, when I felt myself standing up and exiting the train early. I couldn't do it. I couldn't carry on with this shitty life I'd crafted for myself, knowing that I might have passed up something great. Something... something extraordinary.

Standing on the platform, commuters jostling me from left to right, I reached into my wallet for the old man's calling card. There it was, black text on plain white stock: his name, Vizael, along with an address in Bethnal Green.

The card will evaporate by next nightfall, so don't leave it too long.

I remembered the old man's words and checked my phone for the time. It was winter and had just gone three-thirty, which meant the sun was about to go down on the day.

Nightfall.

I felt something happening to the calling card as I held it between my forefinger and thumb. The material it was made of had turned brittle as a thin skim of ice, and was beginning to crumble before my eyes.

'No, no, no!' I cried.

I went to take a picture of the card with my phone before it disintegrated, but when I swiped the camera open, my ageing handset froze. I knew from experience that it would take a good ten seconds to get its act together, by which time the card would be dust.

I hurriedly dived into my backpack and whisked through its contents in search of a pen. Snatching hold of a half-empty Biro, I pulled up my sleeve and frenziedly copied the details of the crumbling card on the inside of my forearm.

'Come on, come on!'

I managed to get it down just in time. As I scrawled the last letter of Vizael's address on my flesh, the card turned into a fine powder and was carried away by the gust of an oncoming train.

'Shit the bed,' I sighed.

The exertion of transcribing the address had really taken it out of me. What a laugh. The great Sanctified one, rendered breathless by a hurried spot of shorthand. Apparently, there was a vampire apocalypse coming, but not to worry. The world was in capable hands.

I checked the blue dot on my phone's map again. Yes, this was definitely it, I was in the right place. Google said so, and Google didn't lie.

The address on my forearm had led me to an abandoned industrial park in an ungentrified part of Bethnal Green. I had to sneak under a rusted chain link fence to get access to the place, and when I did, all I found were a couple of decommissioned gas towers surrounded by vacant warehouses bearing the name of companies that didn't exist anymore.

Who the hell lived in a place like this? Homeless people? Angry punks from an Eighties movie? I must have written the address down wrong, that was the only explanation. Then I saw a thin crack of light coming from inside the larger of the two gas towers. Someone was home after all.

I considered shouting a *hello*, but since there was a distinct possibility that I was trespassing, I decided to keep it buttoned. I made my way to the old gas tower and headed for the lone sliver of light. I could see now that one of the panels had been peeled back from the cylindrical wall of the tower to form a makeshift entrance. From the looks of things, someone had decided to break in there and claim squatters' rights.

Through the gap I could see that the structure had been converted into a living space with partition walls, tatty bits of furniture that looked as though they'd been dragged from a skip, and a makeshift roof to protect its inhabitants from the elements. There was even a circular staircase leading up to a mezzanine. I turned sideways to step through the gap, but no sooner had I set foot on the other side, than something hard connected with my face.

The blow knocked me to my knees, and before I could recover, I felt something wrap around my throat. As the spots cleared from my vision I got a picture of my attacker, or the rough shape of them at least. It was a young woman, dressed in a hoodie, and without getting racial about it, she was black.

The woman whirled around to the back of me, and as we switched positions, the thing around my neck tightened. By this point I was getting pretty fed up with strangers trying to throttle me, so I hooked my fingers under the noose and attempted to free myself. I found it cold and hard to the touch. It wasn't a noose, it was a chain.

I tried to take in a breath, but couldn't. The chain was too tight, cutting off my air supply, choking me out, wrapping the world in black. Throwing an arm behind me, I managed to get a hand under my attacker's hood and grasp a fistful of her afro mane. With the last of the fight I had, I yanked hard and tore the hair out at the root.

The woman screeched and the chain around my throat went slack. Gulping down a double-helping of air, I twisted around to face my assailant, fists bunched.

Blood ran from her scalp, only it wasn't red, it was royal blue.

She wiped away the slick of blue blood with the heel of her palm and snarled like a feral cat. In her other hand was a short wooden shaft, at the end of which was a chain terminating in a spiked metal ball.

'What the fuck is that?' I croaked. 'Did something go wrong with your nunchucks?'

'It's called a morning star, you cretin,' hissed the woman, and came at me again, chain-and-stick-thingie swinging.

I didn't have time to dig around in my backpack for the dagger, so I met her with a fist instead. It was the first real punch I'd ever thrown, and it fell *way* short of expectations. The punch connected, but when my knuckles made contact with her chin I felt a shock-wave travel up my forearm and explode in my elbow like dynamite.

'Shit!'

I yelped in pain and the cry ricocheted madly off of the tower's curved wall.

The woman clicked her jaw back into place, surprised by the force of my punch. 'Good Lord, girl, are those hands or gorilla feet?'

Before I could respond with a witty comeback, she swung her weapon and smashed me in the gut with the metal end, knocking the air from my lungs. Winded, I wasn't able to defend myself against her next attack, and she hit me again, catching me hard in the left tit.

'Ow!' I clutched at my sore breast, jaw clenched so tight I thought my teeth might implode. Anger surged through me like poison, slicing, burning, screaming for release.

Kill, kill, kill!

I felt my fingernails digging into my palms, deep enough to draw blood.

'You bitch,' I hissed, and the brand flared hot and pulsing blue.

The woman saw the enraged look on my face and her expression turned from triumph to trepidation.

Like a volcano erupting in one ferocious red cascade, I threw myself at her, my hands catching her under her arms like a forklift and hurling her through the air. That's not poetic license either, I literally picked her up, hoisted her over my head, and sent her on her way.

The woman sailed across the room and slammed into the tower's outer wall before dropping to the ground like a rock.

Crack!

She lay perfectly still, leaving me to wonder for a moment if the impact had snapped her neck.

'Shit. Uh, are you okay?'

As I looked down at her crumpled body I saw something I hadn't seen before: a nimbus of light floating above her head, just like the one the old man had worn. It was a halo, no mistaking it. Was this woman an angel, too? Because she sure as shit didn't behave like one.

It was just as I was weighing up the karmic implications of

slaughtering one of God's holy messengers, that the woman groaned and peeled her face from the floor.

Phew.

I figured she must have had enough by this point, but somehow she managed to climb shakily to her feet and throw back her head. 'I don't know who you are,' she said, 'but when I'm done with you, you're going to be shitting teeth.'

She snarled, snatched up her flail and unleashed a battle-cry, then—

'Enough,' said a new voice.

The old man in the white suit stood framed by the tower's doorway, propped on his ivory-handled walking stick. It was Vizael, the mysterious owner of the magic dagger. 'Abbey is here by my invitation,' he told his fellow angel. 'No harm will come to her.'

The look on the woman's face told me that she hadn't been made aware of any invitation. She shot the old man hate rays then turned her attention back to me, looking me up and down, grimacing at my head-to-toe black ensemble and living-dead makeup. 'This is her?' she asked. 'She looks more like one of them than they do.'

'And who the fuck are you, if you don't mind me asking?' I fired back.

Since all the punching and strangling had stopped, I could see her properly now. I had to admit, though I wasn't exactly taken with her at this point, she was a sight to behold. Her big Disney princess eyes and obscenely full lips were married to a flawless bone structure. Her ebony skin was like black silk draped over fine cut glass, and unusually, her eyes were blue; seriously blue, almost sickeningly so, like a summer sky on a perfect, cloudless day. The woman was an absolute stunner. I'm not going to lie, if I swung that way, I definitely would. Or at least I would if she wasn't a total Bitch word.

'I am the archangel Gendith,' she replied, puffing out her (of course) ample chest. 'Bringer of Light, Scourge of the Damned—'

'—Talker of shit,' I said, dotting in one last sobriquet. Yes, I did just use the word "sobriquet". Who needs a university degree, eh?

'How dare you speak that way to me, mortal?' she roared, and shoved me hard in my bruised chest.

I was fully ready to lamp the cow. It was girls like her who picked on me something rotten at school, and I wasn't about to go through all that again. Not now, not ever.

I shoved her and she skidded back on her heels, keeping her balance, but losing a couple of feet of ground.

'I said enough!' cried Vizael. It came from his lungs in a deep, throaty roar that was totally at odds with his small, wizened frame.

The pair of us froze.

He took a breath and resumed in his usual, avuncular tone. 'We're all on the same side here.'

'You keep saying that,' I said, 'but I don't even know you, and this loony bint tried to throttle the life out of me, then hit me in the boob.'

'I apologise for the unfortunate reception, I truly do,' he replied, with a look of anxious misgiving. 'Allow me to make proper introductions. Abbey, this is Gendith, a colleague of mine. Gendith, this is Abbey Beckett, the new Nightstalker.' I saw his colleague's lip curl at the last part. 'Welcome to our home,' he said, extending a hand. 'Please, take a seat.'

I wasn't exactly in a handshake mood at that point, so I declined his hospitality and reached for my backpack. 'I never agreed to any Nightstalkery stuff, okay?'

'And yet you are here, as I knew you would be.'

'Yeah, and now I'm going to go. Here, you can have your dagger back.' I handed it to him, but he wouldn't take it.

'Beautiful, isn't it?' he said.

I couldn't argue with him there. 'Yeah, it's pretty cool.'

'It's forged in witchfire, you know, and the blade is made from the thirty pieces of silver that Judas was paid to betray Jesus.'

'Judas? Jesus? Like, from the Bible?'

Gendith snorted and shook her head. 'You have got to be joking with this bitch.'

'Yes,' said Vizael, smoothing over his companion's rudeness. 'From the Bible.'

I looked towards the exit, but curiosity got the better of me again. 'Okay, what does Judas have to do with anything?'

Vizael smiled, a twinkle in his eyes. 'Judas has everything to do with this. Judas is the vampire master.'

'Right. Totally. That would have been my first guess.'

He gestured for me to take a seat and, unable to help myself, I took one. How could I not? Folks have been trying to make sense of the Good Book for thousands of years, and there I was, in the presence of an honest-to-goodness angel who was ready to spill the beans on life, the universe, and everything.

The two of us sat opposite each other around a small, cracked coffee table.

Viz turned to his companion. 'Gendith, would you be a lamb and make us a brew?'

His fellow angel mumbled something unkind under her breath before marching off to the part of the tower that had been partitioned off as a kitchen.

Vizael sighed softly and whispered to me. 'A formidable warrior, but not blessed with much of an understanding of social niceties.'

I found myself smiling back at him. 'Go on then,' I said, 'cough it up.'

The old man sat forward in his chair and his eyes settled into a ten-mile stare. 'Judas is the father of all vampires,' he said, 'cursed by God for betraying his only son and condemned to haunt the earth for all eternity. Condemned to live with his guilt and never be granted the sweet release of death.'

'Oh yeah? And how's that working out for you?'

Viz offered a crooked smile. 'Not too well,' he admitted. 'Instead of waiting politely for Judgment Day, Judas had other ideas. He created progeny.'

'Like... kids?'

'Not exactly. Those he took a liking to he made as himself and recruited into his army.'

'An army of vampires.'

'Exactly.'

It was a hell of a story, and rife with so much religious mumbo jumbo that it would have sent Dan Brown running for the Kleenex. 'So why doesn't God step in and do something?' I asked.

'He did,' Viz replied. 'He sent me to Earth to destroy Judas.'

I tried to imagine the old man taking on a Bible character with a vampire army at his back, but my imagination wasn't up to the task.

'I was younger back then of course,' said Viz, sensing my doubt. 'This was all the way back in the Fourteenth Century.'

Wow, he really did have some years on the clock. No wonder he was a bit dotty.

'So what happened?' I asked.

'I fought Judas and won,' Viz replied. 'But it wasn't enough.' He looked to his toes. 'At the end of our battle the vampire master fell into the Thames, dead. What I didn't know then was that his body had infected the source of most of London's water.' He let out a long exhale. 'Millions perished.'

I thought back to History class, and to the conversation about plague sites that we'd had before. 'You're saying Judas was the big germ that started the bubonic plague?'

Viz sighed. 'All because of me. All my fault. I've been living here on Earth ever since, my punishment for failing God.'

'He really holds a grudge, eh?'

'Oh, you have no idea.'

'And now the vamps are everywhere,' I said. 'So what's the Lord Almighty doing to stop them?'

The old man offered a shrug. 'I don't know. Perhaps nothing. We're not exactly on speaking terms these days.'

'So, that's it, is it? The dead are walking the Earth and God isn't picking up the phone?'

'I see things,' he said. 'Visions and portents. Whether or not they come from Him directly, I cannot say, but I know them to be true. In any case, my mission endures. I failed once, I will not fail a second time. I cannot.'

I shook my head. None of this made any sense, but there was one thing that had been *really* bugging me since we'd sat down. 'You keep going on about a vampire army, so why aren't I seeing bloodsuckers running about everywhere, flapping around like bats and sinking their fangs into everyone?'

'You've seen what they're like, Abbey, you've met one in the flesh. They aren't the creatures Bram Stoker wrote about. They don't sleep in coffins, and they don't care a whit for crucifixes or cloves of garlic. They're far more sophisticated than that.'

It's true that the vampire I'd seen didn't fit the Halloween costume. When I thought of vampires I'd always imagined pale, Draculoid men in frilly blouses and Napoleonic jackets. The guy that assaulted me was nothing like that, at least until he popped his chompers and went into monster mode.

Viz fixed me with a hard stare. 'The Judas Clan aren't like other vampires, Abbey. They're far more sinister than anything you've read about in a horror novel. Far more powerful.'

'And there's a whole army of them? So, what do you do? How do you fight that?'

'I don't,' he replied. 'Not anymore.' The old man straightened his crooked back and leaned across the table. 'I don't have what it takes to defeat a threat like this, Abbey. I'm out to pasture. What humanity needs to win this war is new blood.'

I looked down at the brand on my palm.

'Why me? What about your angel friend next door? Why not make her the Nightstalker?'

A shadow fell across me as two slopping mugs of tea came crashing down on the coffee table.

Gendith loomed there with a face of thunder. 'Good question,' she said, tartly. 'As a matter of fact, I'd like to know the answer to that one myself. Go on then, old man, why exactly are you passing me over for this... stick insect?'

Viz looked at her with a cold gleam in his eyes. 'Behave yourself, Gendith.'

'No,' she seethed, 'answer the question. Tell her how it is that I've been training for this moment for ten years, and now *she's* the one wearing the brand.'

Ten years? Jesus, she could have gotten three university degrees in that time. No wonder she was pissed off.

'I didn't choose her,' Viz barked back, 'the dagger did.'

It's like I was watching the scene from a movie where the hero is struggling with her conscience, only in this version, she wore an angel on both shoulders, and the pair of them had given up dispensing advice and turned rabid on each other.

Gendith folded her arms. 'The dagger chose her, did it? That's a good one. Why don't you tell her exactly how it *chose* her?'

'Gendith—'

'Tell her!'

Viz chewed at his bottom lip. Only once the pregnant pause had reached its third trimester did he finally speak. 'I left it on a train,' he confessed.

'He left it on the train!' Gendith spat, turning to me. 'That's why you got the brand. Not because of some divine right. Not because you were chosen. Because some demented old codger walked off a train without his briefcase and you got nosey.'

'That's not true,' Viz retorted. 'It is written—'

'Written?' she bleated, and marched over to a heaving bookcase to pluck a dusty old tome from its shelf. 'Written by *your* hand. Prophecies and predestinations that only *you* see.' She rustled through Viz's texts, thrusting his words at him. She landed on a page written in an old man's spidery scrawl, the heading of which read: The Sanctified One. 'These words are not sacrosanct,' she went on. 'The only way we will stop the Clan is through strength and cunning, and this waif you have dubbed "Nightstalker" has neither.'

'Guys—' I said, trying to cut in.

'There's more at play here and you know it,' Viz barked. 'Fate guided the weapon to Abbey, and the blade chose to sanctify her.'

'Guys—' I tried again.

'Senile nonsense,' Gen snorted. From beneath her shirt she plucked a necklace; a string of teeth, all canines, long and sharp. She shook them at Vizael and the sinister grin chattered at him. 'I should be the Nightstalker and you know it!'

She swept an arm along the rickety bookshelf, sending a row of Viz's tomes tumbling to the floor in a swirling grey blur of dust.

The old man clambered to his feet. 'You embarrass me like this and you wonder why you are not fit to wear the brand?'

'GUYS!' I screamed, and finally they shut up. 'You're fighting over nothing. I have one shitty boss already, I don't need two more.' I stood up from my chair. 'Find someone else to do your dirty work, because I'm going home.'

'There is no one else,' said Viz.

'Of course there is,' I replied, throwing up my hands. 'Call the police. Call the army. Call the frigging coastguard for all I care.'

'That would create pandemonium,' he replied. 'No, ours is a secret war. A battle that won't be recorded in the history books.'

'Why not? Why not get the law involved?'

'Because normals aren't equipped to fight vampires,' he said. 'They'd be peashooters against battleships.'

'That's what you call us, is it? "Normals"?' I shook my head. 'Jesus, what am I even doing here? Angels and demons and holy weapons? I don't even believe in God!'

'And He probably doesn't believe in you either,' said Viz. 'So show Him why He should.'

I paused for a moment, but barely. 'I'm nothing special. I'm not cut out to stop an army of undead bastards. I'm sorry,' I said, heading for the door. 'I'm bashed to bits and I'm working on about two hours sleep. I need my bed.'

Viz stood up now, wobbling on his cane. 'The reason you're not getting your eight hours is because of what you've become,' he said, then, as though it were obvious, 'it's one of your blessings, to be able to function on a bare minimum of sleep. You are the Nightstalker after all.'

'That wretch is no Nightstalker,' said Gen, cementing her position on the matter for about the hundredth time. 'The dagger belongs in my hands.'

As I made for the door, I snatched up my backpack and threw it over my shoulder. 'Just for that, I'm keeping the knife.'

'Give that back right now,' she demanded, reaching for her morning star.

'Leave her be,' sighed the old man, placing a hand on Gendith's elbow.

She begrudgingly stood down, shaking with pent up aggression. 'What did I tell you?' she told Viz. 'She's no saviour. She's nothing special. She's the same as the rest of them.'

It stung, but not so much that I stopped moving.

8

My head was at war with itself.

All I'd ever wanted in life was to stand apart from the crowd. To be significant. To reach my potential. And yet what had I ever done to achieve those goals? I stood out all right—so long as I wasn't at a Sisters of Mercy concert anyway—but that's about where my quest for individuality ended. I wasn't unique. I wasn't extraordinary. Gendith was right. Fish hook earrings and ripped fishnets don't make a person special, just a different kind of nothing.

But then wasn't that just the way of things? Weren't we all just pretenders, acting like we were something more than worker ants, but showing up at the ant-hill all the same. Saying no to something more didn't make me a failure, it just made me human. Another Desk Babysitter among millions more.

I still couldn't shake that feeling though. The feeling that I'd been shown a way out of the ant-hill—a true, special calling—and I'd gone the other way. As I strode to catch the last train home, I looked at the brand on my palm. There was magic in that thing. A blessing from on high. Was I really going to let that go to waste?

I felt my phone vibrate in my pocket, accompanied by the theme tune to Tales of the Unexpected. I didn't need look at it to know who was. Neil. He'd called three times already, and he'd call again. I just couldn't face talking to him though. The argument I was having in my head was all the conversation I could handle.

By the time I arrived home it was just short of midnight, and Neil was not a sunny bunny.

'Where were you?' he demanded. 'I must have called you ten times, Abbey.'

'I'm sorry, okay. Some work people went out for drinks and asked if I wanted join them.'

I hated lying to him, but what could I do? I was hardly going to tell him that I'd been hanging out with a couple of angels. Neil wrote fantasy stories, but that's all they were to him: stories. If I came through the door banging on about real-life vampire cults and magic daggers I'd have looked fucking mental.

'You could have at least texted me,' he said, hurt.

'I tried,' I said. 'I guess my phone must have run out of battery.'

'You guess?' He took the breathing tube from his nostrils and leaned in to sniff my breath. 'I don't smell booze on you, Abbey. Tell me the truth.'

I felt like a reverse alcoholic being castigated for her sobriety.

I tried a joke. 'You know the pubs in this town, always watering down their drinks...'

The gag went down like a turd on a wedding cake. Neil replaced his breathing tube and looked back at me, forehead knotted, a dimple forming a crease between his eyebrows.

Then he saw my palm.

'Whoa, what the hell is that?' he said. I tried pulling my hand away, but I wasn't fast enough. 'Did you hurt yourself? What happened?'

'I'm fine, I said. 'It's just a… um… I got a body mod, that's all. Tattoos are such old hat, aren't they?'

He traced a finger gently along the grooves of the brand. 'What does the Z stand for?'

'It's not a Z,' I explained, turning my hand sideways. 'It's an N for… um… Neil! That's right, I got your initial burned on to my palm, so… surprise.'

He held my hand softly in his, looking at the brand and wincing.

I felt terrible bullshitting him like that, but there was no walking it back now. 'So then... do you like it?'

He looked up at me with the sad eyes of a Basset Hound. 'Sure,' he said. 'I love it.' Then he had a sudden thought. 'Hey, I don't have to get one though, right?'

Lying to Neil and telling him that I'd willingly had my hand seared to a crisp wasn't exactly my finest hour, but it beat telling him the truth. Besides, what did the truth matter now? I'd said no to being the Nightstalker – closed the door on that for good. The events of the last couple of days had been insane and dangerous. The smartest thing I could do was leave that stuff well alone, even if I couldn't stop looking at my hand and wondering *What if?*

I woke the next morning to a grim sky the colour of a detuned TV. It seemed only fitting, I supposed. I couldn't have it both ways – either I chose to live in a world full of magic and mystery, or I carried on with my boring, humdrum way of life. Oh well, at least this way I wouldn't get my throat torn out by some bloodthirsty hellspawn. At least this way I got to see a new sky each morning, even if it was a grey one.

But something had changed. The planet had shifted on its axis. The world I thought I lived in was a lie. I knew that now. Knew the truth. Monsters walked the streets, magic was real, and no one but me had a bloody clue about it.

Now I saw danger everywhere. Peril, lurking around every corner. Menace, squatting on its haunches, ready to pounce. I saw it in the smallest of things. I saw it in the sideways look I got from a stray dog as I exited my flat. I saw it in the creepy, spidery veins of an old woman's calf as she threw bread crumbs to a flock of mangy pigeons. I saw it in the gaunt-faced drunk with the rotting teeth, chewing on a strip of—what was that?—raw meat?

I'd never been the most trusting of people, but now that mistrust had been turned up to eleven. It was as though my eyes had been opened, and now there was no closing them. I was witnessing the world in a whole new way, noticing unforeseen details, seeing through the grand illusion. My surroundings looked like the picture from a brand new telly, still configured to its presets, the colours a bit too rich, the picture so sharp it looked like something from a bad soap opera. I wasn't just observing the world anymore, watching the narrative unfold around me like it was someone else's story. I was the story now, and the story was menacing and weird.

I blinked a couple of times to clear my senses, then took a breath and pointed my eyes straight ahead.

Get a hold of yourself, Beckett. You're going to work, that's all. Nothing weird there. Nothing weirder than Gary anyway. Focus on your little life and ignore the bigger picture.

Brown frosted leaves crunched underfoot as I cut through the park. I wasn't far from Thamesmead station now, but I'd have to take a detour to get there. The whole site was undergoing construction, and the developments had severed the direct route from my flat and forced me to start my daily commute with a grinding hike over the grubby flyover that dominated most of the area. I passed between the concrete outer wall of the overpass and a line of traffic cones, choking on the exhaust fumes of passing cars until I reached the stairs that lead to the station.

Winding my way down the steps to street level, I ran into a stick-thin man dressed in a pinstripe suit. He was standing halfway down the stairs, feet a shoulder-width apart, his posture stiff and unnatural. He wasn't doing anything. Wasn't checking his phone, wasn't listening to headphones, wasn't reading a newspaper or begging for money. He was just standing there like a crazy person doing absolutely nothing.

I carried on by, expecting him to at least move slightly as I passed, but he didn't move a muscle. Even his eyes stayed still, fixed on the horizon, not tracking me in the least. I wondered for a moment if he was a human statue—I even checked to see if he had a box of change at his feet—but no, he was just a man… waiting. Waiting for what I had no idea, and I didn't care to stick around and find out. His stillness made me uneasy. It was the stillness of a cat about to pounce. Of a big red button, ready to be pressed.

As I made my way past him, I felt a strange tingle, as though I'd grazed something charged with static electricity. I trotted down the next flight of steps, spurred on by the queasy feeling in my stomach. Reaching the bottom of the stairwell, I couldn't help but cast a look back to see if the man had moved at all—

Only he wasn't there anymore.

Had he headed up to the overpass? Had he dropped something and ducked behind the concrete balustrade to pick it up? I got my answer when I turned around to continue my walk and found him stood right in front of me.

'Morning,' said the skinny man.

He stood the exact same way he had back on the stairs, legs a shoulder-width apart, back ramrod straight, a store mannequin's pose.

I was too stunned to reply, so I nodded instead and headed for the train station, which was still a walk away.

What the hell was that? Did the guy have a twin brother? A twin brother who just happened to be wearing the exact same outfit? Was this some freaky performance art, and if it was, what the hell was it doing out here in Thamesmead at seven o'clock in the morning?

I quickened my step, thankful that I'd chosen to dress in accordance with the LPO's new dress code that day. Because of Gary's edict, I was wearing a sensible pair of flats instead of a towering pair of platform knee-highs, so I could manage a decent clip.

I glanced over my shoulder as I hurried off and saw the pinstriped man again. He still wasn't moving, and yet in the time I'd taken my eye off him, he'd somehow managed to close a significant distance between where I'd left him and where I was now.

He gave me a wink and I felt my heart rear into my neck. Was I the butt of some sick joke? Were a bunch of lookalikes working in tandem to put the scares on an unsuspecting member of the public?

No.

I wasn't being punked, I was sure of it. I was being hunted.

Turning from the pinstriped man and breaking into a jog, I sped by a row of graffiti-covered hoardings and hung a right at the far end—

Only to be confronted again by the pinstriped man.

He stood the same as before, cutting me off, feet planted, chest puffed out. 'Don't I get a hello?' he leered.

'Get away from me,' I said, taking a step back.

He hadn't touched me, and yet I felt like I'd been mugged. This wasn't right. I'd taken the safe path, I'd said no to the angels, and yet there it was, the impossible, waggling its tongue at me still.

The strange man smiled at me. He wore his black hair slicked back to his scalp in a way that might have been fashionable in the last century. His features were pale and cruel, and there was something wicked in his eyes. Something nasty.

I darted around him and carried on past, but as I brushed by the pinstriped man, something happened.

A letter J glowed on his forehead.

J for Judas.

I looked about for help, but there was no one around.

'So, you're the new Nightstalker, huh?' he said, chuckling. 'What are you, a diversity hire?'

Twin fangs shot from beneath his upper lip as he assumed his true form.

It was daylight... just about anyway. What the hell was a vampire doing out at this hour?

Instinctively, I went for the dagger that I'd been keeping in my backpack, but stopped short when I remembered that I'd left it at home. Shit.

Pinstripe lunged for me, nostrils flared, his breath hot and reeking of something animal. His fingernails dug into my shoulders like the talons of a bird of prey, but instead of carrying me off to his nest, his head came forward and his fangs flashed for my neck.

I only just managed to stop him from breakfasting on my throat. The moment I realised I wasn't packing the dagger, I found my hand reaching into my jacket pocket and returning with my house keys between my knuckles. The vamp was fast, but even so, I managed to get the pointy end of my door key between my jugular and his bite.

I jammed the metal into his face and caught him between his lower eyelid and the soft flesh of his eyeball. He yowled and recoiled, and when he looked up again I saw a ruby red teardrop running down his cheek.

'I'm going to open you up and dance on your guts,' he growled, wiping the blood from his face.

I didn't stick around to find out whether he meant that literally.

I ran as fast as I could, my heart going two-hundred beats a minute, my panicked breath firing in hot spurts. I could hear the vampire running after me, his footfalls heavy, slapping hard against the pavement as he drew ever closer. I picked up the pace, my thighs burning as the adrenaline screamed through my body, daring me to run faster still.

I felt his fingers snatch at my long brown hair (yes, a lesser-spotted brown-haired goth!) and felt my head dip backwards as he took hold. A scream squeaked through my scorched throat, and then I tore away, leaving him with a fistful of curls.

I made it to the train station and threw myself across the ticket barriers and into the foyer. Commuters scattered as I sprawled across the tiled floor, my legs kicking out in fright, face lit with fear, eyes wild and darting.

Pinstripe was gone.

No, he'd just stopped chasing.

I could see him beyond the barriers, not a crease in his suit, not a bead of sweat upon his candle-white skin.

He smiled a razor blade smile, then lifted a lock of my hair to his nose and inhaled deeply.

'See you soon, Abbey,' he mouthed, then melted into the crowd with his prize.

There was no getting away from this. The moment I'd touched that dagger, it was too late to go back. The monsters, the magic, the mayhem – it was all out there, whether I liked it or not. It didn't matter that I wanted nothing to do with it, *it* wanted something to do with me.

9

I called in sick to work. I was hoping the temp might pick up the phone so I could relay my excuses to her, but my clown shoe of a boss took the call personally.

'Sick how?' he demanded. 'How exactly are you sick?'

'Put it this way,' I replied, 'it's coming out of both ends.'

I find that phrase tends to shut down any further questioning, and it worked a charm on this occasion, as it always did.

'You can't keep taking days off like this, Abbey. It's not on.'

'Go back and check your records. I haven't taken a sickie since a pony broke into my house and I had to spend all day chasing it out with a spatula.'

Sometimes, just to keep things interesting, I like to switch out grossness for absurdity. Tactically, I find it just as effective. After all, who makes up a story *that* unlikely and *that* specific? Only a true diabolic, that's who.

'We need you here at the office. You have responsibilities.'

'Right,' I replied. I was tempted to ask him to remind me what those were exactly, but he told me anyway.

'You perform a valuable function at the LPO, Abbey,' he said, using my name like a politician. 'We need you here.'

I couldn't help myself. 'I'm sure the system will survive one day of me not logging a few knackered umbrellas.'

The line went quiet for a moment while he thought of a comeback, then: 'Are you saying your job's not important, Abbey?'

'No, but—'

'You're the designated first-aider on your floor and your backup is on leave in Corfu. What are we going to do if someone suffers a work-related accident?'

'I already told you I'm sick, Gary. How about instead of worrying about some potential mishap, you show a bit of compassion for mine?'

More radio silence. 'You know,' he finally said, 'if your job's really as dispensable as you say it is, maybe the post isn't necessary.'

Jesus Christ. For a bloke who looked like he bought his clothes in Mothercare, he sure did like to act the big man.

'I'll be in tomorrow,' I told him, and hung up the phone.

I went back to the flat after that. My plan was to return to the angels, but not without collecting the dagger first. After my run-in with Pinstripe, I didn't feel safe without it.

Neil would still be home of course, working on the latest novel in his Wizard & Warlock series, but I was counting on being able to sneak in and grab the dagger without him noticing. Just because I'd made the decision to run away with the circus, didn't mean I had to take Neil with me. Viz had said the war against the vampires was a secret one, and I intended to honour that. Besides, Neil's day-to-day life was tough enough without me throwing monsters into the mix.

I'd hidden the dagger in a rarely used kitchen drawer under a bundle of old shopping bags, and was confident that I could get to it without Neil picking up on my being there. When he wrote, he liked to listen to music—movie soundtracks mainly—and I figured the theme to Gladiator would mask my footfalls nicely.

By the time I arrived at the front door of the flat I'd begun to think of swiping the magic dagger from under Neil's nose as my first Nightstalker assignment. A stealth mission. The Great Dagger Robbery (only, you know, robbing my own property from my own property).

I took out my key, cleaned a smear of vampire blood off of it, and inserted it into the lock with as much finesse as I knew how. I worked the tumbler ever so slowly, turning it until it produced the gentlest *click,* and the door popped free. Pleased to find the hinges nice and quiet, I pulled the handle in one smooth motion—

Only to find Neil waiting on the other side with the dagger in his hand.

'What's this?' he asked.

'Ah.'

'And why are you home already?'

I tried to turn it back on him. 'What are you doing going through my stuff?' I asked. 'My private, very personal stuff, hmm?'

'I wasn't. I found it accidentally while I was looking for the tin opener.' He waggled the dagger at me. 'So, come on then, what's it for?'

'It's… um… a present…'

'For who?'

'For… for you, silly!' I couldn't let a normal know the truth. Christ, did I just call my boyfriend a "normal"? Very nice, Abbey.

'Who's it really for?' he asked.

'I told you, I bought it for you. And now you've gone and spoiled the surprise, you big… bastard.'

'You bought me a giant knife?'

'Yeah. I know how you like all that swords and sorcery crap, and I thought it would make a nice paperweight for your writing desk.' In fact, *writing desk* was a bit of an overstatement. Neil's workstation was a titchy IKEA thing in the box room with a folding chair underneath. 'Plus, it's good for self-defence,' I went on. 'You never know what's going to go down on the mean streets of Thamesmead.' I was kidding, but given that I'd just had to fight for my life out there, not kidding at all.

Neil considered the dagger and offered a half-smile. 'Well… thank you then,' he said. 'It is really nice looking, and it will go great with my collectible Hufflepuff wand.' He gave me a hug. 'Thanks, I'll go put it on my desk now.'

My stealth mission had backfired spectacularly. If I was going to be the Nightstalker I couldn't have that dagger collecting dust on Neil's tiny desk. Served me right for only thinking one move ahead; now I'd trapped myself... unless...

'Oh, would you look at that,' I said, snatching the dagger from Neil at a speed that surprised even me, 'right there, on the blade, there's a mark.'

'I don't see a mark,' said Neil, trying to retrieve his present, which I'd since jacked up behind my back.

'Yup, a great big mark,' I said. 'Can't have that. Going to have to take it back to the shop and get a replacement. Right now in fact.'

'It's fine, really. I didn't even notice it.'

'That's nice of you to say, but it'll play on my mind. What kind of a human shit gives a dinged dagger to the love of her life?'

I backed out of the door. 'See you later then,' I said, waving goodbye with my free hand.

Neil looked back at me, utterly befuddled. 'Wait... you never said what you were doing back from work.'

I pretended to misunderstand him. 'Probably won't be back until late,' I said, tapping a pretend watch. 'Don't wait up.'

I closed the door behind me and dabbed some sweat from my forehead. So much for stealth missions.

10

By the time I elbowed my way off of a packed train in Bethnal Green I was questioning everyone around me.

Who were these people? What were they doing milling around at that time of day? Were they like me, or were they something other? Which of them was human? Which of them was a vampire? Was I about to be set on again? If I turned my back, would I feel another hand grab me by the hair and tug back my head? Would a vampire's claw slice through the soft flesh of my throat and ink the pavement with my blood?

'See you soon, Abbey,' I recalled Pinstripe saying.

My pulse quickened and I broke into a jog which quickly turned into a sprint. I felt as though death was coming in at all sides, stabbing me from every direction.

Go go go. Run run run.

Eyes straight ahead, I caned it a half-mile to the industrial park, ducking the chain link fence and racing full-tilt for the gas tower, throwing myself through its entrance—

And crashing pell-mell into Vizael.

For a little old man on a walking stick, he took the collision remarkably well. Though he looked as brittle as dry bone, Viz was rock solid. I hadn't appreciated it when he told me about his vampire fighting days, but cannonballing into him just then gave me a good sense of his martial prowess. The old man was a tough nut, no doubt about it.

'Can I help you?' he asked, calm as a cucumber. Cool, I mean. Cucumbers are calm by default.

'...Being chased,' I panted, stabbing a thumb behind me, '...vampires everywhere...'

But there was no one there. I'd run all this way, fuelled by nothing more potent than paranoia.

Viz placed a hand on my shoulder and smiled warmly.

'Come on in,' he said. 'Let us begin.'

Gendith was there too, sat in a tatty armchair and eying me coolly as I entered.

'Look who returned to the fold,' Viz announced, brightly.

Gendith nodded in my direction, eyes half-lidded. I'd expected her to shoot daggers my way, but instead she regarded me with the jaded indifference of a house cat, which was at least a step in the right direction. Clearly, she and Viz had had a sit down since my last visit, and reached some level of understanding

'I'm not promising I'll join the cause,' I said, 'but so long as you're offering training, I could stand to lose a few calories. Cheaper than the gym anyway, right?'

I was putting on a show, feigning an air of nonchalance. The truth was, I was scared and desperately needed their help to learn how to defend myself.

I told them about the man in the pinstripe suit who attacked me, and the angels nodded along as though I were presenting a 9 a.m. slideshow.

'I'm sorry, am I boring you?' I asked.

'Not at all,' Viz replied, 'it's just... well, we already know this story.'

'What? How?'

The old man hesitated a moment, cleared his throat, then spoke. 'I was there,' he said. 'During the incident.'

'Are you serious?' I cried. 'You stood there and watched while I got chased through Thamesmead by a vampire?'

'Yes,' he admitted. 'I've been shadowing you, Abbey. I needed to keep tabs on the dagger. We couldn't afford to have a thing like that falling into enemy hands. You understand, don't you?'

It seemed to me that my life was worth less to these people than the hunk of metal in my backpack.

'And you never thought to step in and help?' I asked. 'Even when you saw I didn't have the dagger on me?'

He shrugged. 'I didn't see the need. You acquitted yourself very well, Abbey. My assistance was unnecessary.'

I was pissed off to the core. 'I could have been killed,' I spat through my teeth. 'The vampire who attacked me, he was jumping around, blinking from place to place...'

'Yes,' Viz replied. 'One of his powers. Vampires of the Judas Clan are known to possess a host of different abilities. Thankfully, you have skills that are more than a match for theirs.'

'Powers? Like what?'

'You already know, don't you?'

I understood what he was saying. 'The brand, it makes me strong. And fast. And I can see things too. Things I couldn't see before.'

'That's right,' Viz replied, pleased at my observations. 'And you have many more powers besides, though it's only through training that you'll learn to harness them properly.'

'Okay. Powers. Actual powers. That's pretty cool.'

'Pretty cool,' Viz agreed, smiling.

'So what are we waiting for?' I asked. 'Let's do this. Train me up, Mister Miyagi.'

He nodded and looked at me with the calm eyes of a monk. 'Show me the dagger.'

We started off in the dojo, or at least that's what Vizael called it. In reality, the "dojo" was a portion of the gas tower that had been converted into a small training room, complete with a punching mannequin made of high-strength rubber, a heavy bag strung to a rafter by a chain, and a compact target range.

'Put the dagger in the bullseye,' the old man instructed, pointing to a round, pockmarked target at the end of the range.

It wasn't far away, five metres at most, but I still didn't fancy my chances. 'I'm not much good at throwing,' I confessed, remembering my disastrous try-out for the high school netball team.

'Of course you are,' Viz insisted. 'You're the Nightstalker.'

I looked at the big N on my hand. 'Right. Yeah. Of course. I'm the Nightstalker. Okay.'

I drew a breath, pulled back my arm, and brought the blade up to the side of my head.

'Just throw it?' I asked.

'Just throw it,' Viz replied.

Focussing on the concentric circles of the target, I took aim at the middle spot, ratcheted my arm back to its rearmost point, and sent the dagger flying. The metal scythed through the air, turned over once—

—and embedded dead centre of the bullseye, shivering with spent energy.

'Holy shit!' I said, leaping off the floor and doing a fist pump. 'Take that, Mrs Thompson!'

'Who's Mrs Thompson?' asked Viz.

'Old gym teacher... doesn't matter...' I stabbed a finger down the target range. 'Did you see that shit? I'm a bloody natural.'

'I did see that "shit", as you say.' He pointed to the dagger planted in the bullseye. 'Now pick it up and show me again.'

He didn't have to ask me twice. I started toward the target, but he barred me with his walking cane.

'No,' he said. 'Pick it up from here.'

'What? How? Wait, can my arms stretch like Plastic Man? Is that it? Stretchy arms?'

Viz gave me a look.

'Okay. I don't have stretchy arms. That would be pretty awesome though, just saying.'

'The dagger and the brand share a bond,' said Viz. 'They

belong together. You need only ask them to become one.' He brought his hands together and laced his fingers.

I was skeptical to say the least, but I figured there was no harm in giving it a go. I held out my throwing hand and concentrated on the dagger, willing it to return to me. Willing it to reunite with the brand.

'Imagine an elastic band, Abbey. An elastic band connecting your hand to the dagger's handle. Imagine it snapping back fast and tight towards you. Picture it. Feel it. Make it so.'

I reached out, fingers twitching, teeth clenched. At first, nothing happened. I was about ready to give up, and that's when I saw the jewel at the base of the handle judder slightly, and realised something was happening after all. Something I was making happen. I was so pleased with myself that I forgot all about the manifest properties of elastic bands, and almost didn't notice the blade pulling free of the bullseye and winging its way back to me, fast as a bullet.

I threw up a hand just in time, seizing the dagger by the handle right before it blasted into my face, halting its progress centimetres from the spot between my eyes.

'Very good,' said Viz, offering a single, small clap.

'Yeah, thanks,' I replied, sweating, trying to ignore how close I'd just come to stabbing myself in the face.

'Now let's see how you do against a live opponent. Gendith, please assist the Nightstalker.'

Gen came forward. She was wearing thick body padding, the kind K-9 trainers use when they're bite schooling their animals. 'Do your worst,' she challenged.

'I'm not chucking a knife at her,' I told Viz.

'What are you worried about?' asked Gen, a mocking chuckle to her voice. 'You really think you'd hit me?'

'I hit that bullseye easy enough, didn't I?'

'Yes, you sure showed that static target,' she said. 'Now all you need is persuade your enemies to stand perfectly still while you line up your throwing arm.'

I very nearly gave her the finger. Two of them in fact.

'Girls,' said Viz, 'let's keep this civil.' He positioned Gen to the end of the range and returned to me. 'Gendith knows what's she's doing,' he assured me. 'All you need to concentrate on is hitting her.'

I didn't want to hurt her, but I sure as hell wanted to shut her up, and I supposed they must have known what they were doing. Besides, she was wearing an awful lot of padding.

'All right then,' I said, and pulled back the knife. 'As long as you're sure.'

I threw my hand forward and sent the blade winging Gen's way. Despite the extra weight she was carrying, she moved out of my firing line and side-stepped the dagger effortlessly.

'Nice try,' she said. 'Again.'

I recalled the dagger to my hand. This time it was a reflex. I was learning.

'Go on,' Viz urged. 'You heard her.'

I hurled the knife at Gen a second time, and it tore right after her, straight as an arrow. Instead of dodging on this occasion, she whipped her morning star from her belt and smacked the blade aside, leaving it lodged in the outer wall of the tower.

She yawned and rolled her eyes at me.

Infuriated, I called the dagger back, caught it, and let it fly again in one smooth move. Gen tried to deflect the missile, but was caught off guard and ended up with the blade lodged in her shoulder.

Shit.

She screamed and tugged off the body armour, which fell to the ground with the blade still embedded in it. 'Bitch!' she screeched, as she put a hand to her shoulder and came away with blue blood on her fingertips. 'I didn't tell you to throw! I wasn't ready!'

She was marching towards me now, weapon in hand and murder in her eyes. I called back the dagger to defend myself, but no sooner had I plucked it from the air than she'd grabbed my fist in her hand and smashed it against the wall. The dagger fell to the ground, along with one of my black-painted fingernails, which lay next to the blade looking like a shucked beetle shell.

It hurt like buggery.

I hadn't meant to almost kill Gen when I threw the knife—at

least I don't think I had—but now I was ready to go the whole hog. I lunged at her, fingers twitching for her throat, but Vizael's walking stick appeared between us.

'Break it up,' he said, staring us down like a lion tamer handling a pair of disobedient wildcats. 'The forces of evil are arrayed against us and you two insist on fighting like children.'

Gen bared her teeth at me, then a new face arrived on the scene, breaking the tension.

A squat woman stood in the dojo's entrance, her face gaunt, her eyes gluey and pink from crying.

'Please,' she begged. 'You have to help.'

11

The woman wasn't human.

On closer inspection, it was clear she was something else entirely. Her teeth were pointed, but not like a vampire's, more like a piranha's – two rows of tightly-packed, pearl-white needles. Neither Viz nor Gen questioned this. Whoever the stricken woman was—*whatever* she was—they followed her without question.

'Where are we going?' I asked, trailing behind them as they pursued the woman from the industrial park and out on to the streets. 'Who is this person?'

'A friend of ours,' replied Viz, hobbling along on his stick. 'An eaves.'

'A what now?'

'A race of Uncanny. They get their name for the talent they have for eavesdropping on conversations.'

'Doesn't sound like much of a talent to me,' I said, 'earwigging on other people's business.'

'It is when you rely on that talent for sustenance,' he explained. 'The eaves exchange their knowledge for magic, which is a sort of food to them.'

Before I could unpack that, the woman we were following arrived at a door set into the brick wall of a railway overpass.

'In here,' she said, 'quickly,' and pushed open the door.

It led somewhere it shouldn't have.

Through the doorway I could see an empty, cobbled alleyway in a part of the city I didn't recognise. An outdoors on the inside. An impossibility.

'Hop to it,' said Viz, as he hurried me through.

I stepped inside (well, outside, really), and the world warped out of shape for a moment. I felt my insides flutter as my foot set down on the cobbles, which were splashed with bright sunshine. It was a different time of day here. A different world. Behind me, I saw the doorway was gone – vanished into thin air. I'd seen some freaky stuff since I made the mistake of opening that old briefcase, but what I was seeing now would make David Blaine shit a brick.

Gen saw my bafflement and gave me a withering look before shaking her head and heading off after the eaves. 'Idiot.'

Viz was a touch more understanding. 'It's confusing at first, I know, but just go with it for now.'

And I did, following the eaves blindly towards a new doorway. This one opened out on to a rooftop that must have been a good twenty storeys up. Again, I followed, only to arrive at yet another doorway—a hatch in the ground this time—which led to a ladder that dropped into an underground sewer.

Impossibility after impossibility after impossibility.

'I don't know about you,' I said, 'but I'm totally lost.'

'It's by design,' Viz replied. 'When your stock in trade is telling tales, it behooves you to maintain a certain degree of obscurity.'

He explained that the eaves liked to hide their nests where no one could find them, way off the grid, and accessible only through a complex and ever-shifting maze that they fashioned using the magic given to them in exchange for information. That way, even if a person had visited one before and thought they had its location memorised, in truth, they knew fuck all.

I followed Viz some more, his cane clicking on the cobbles with each stride, until the eaves woman arrived at a final door. This one belonged to a dilapidated, two-storey Victorian house on an anonymous street in who knew where. Its front door was scratched and dented and marred by years of water damage. The eaves pushed on a large brass knob dulled with greasy fingerprints, and the three of us stepped through and followed her up a flight of narrow, crooked stairs.

The house looked like a crack den: a decaying slum that hadn't known the sound of a vacuum cleaner in decades. The odd sparse bit of furniture we passed was scuffed and moth-eaten. Only a few scraps of wallpaper clung to the building's walls, tenaciously refusing to disengage, despite the creeping damp beneath. It made my toilet of a flat look like a palace by comparison.

The eaves led us quickly across the landing and into a large room that served as some sort of communal area. Piss-coloured light leaked in through ragged drapes and fell on warped walls, bellied inwards. Above us were sagging oak rafters, and beneath, a floor; jagged, lumpy, and glistening wet and red.

The floor was piled high with dead bodies.

Carpeted with them, wall to wall.

Like a game of Twister gone horribly wrong.

Eaves. A whole crowd of them, slaughtered like cattle. No, not like cattle, cattle were treated better than this. These bodies were torn up and broken. Carved up and snapped. Slaughtered in horrible, unthinkable ways.

The ones on their backs stared skywards, blue-lipped and blank-eyed, the floor beneath them rusted red with their blood. The smell was horrific, and had already attracted a swarm of buzzing, fat-bellied flies that meandered lazily about the carcasses.

'What happened?' I gasped.

'I don't know,' cried the eaves. 'I came home and found them like this. Please help.'

How in God's name were we meant to do that?

I was staring down at the floor, hand clamped over my mouth, when I saw something twitch among the bodies. 'There, what is that?' I asked, my blood curdling.

A small arm poked between the mess of corpses, its pudgy little hand splayed and clawing at the air. A high-pitched wail followed.

'My baby!' screamed the eaves, and dropped to her knees to dig between the bodies and scoop out the infant.

A baby girl. Alive. I felt an overwhelming sense of relief. Somehow, something had survived this slaughter. A living creature left lying on the meat market floor, spared the butcher's cleaver.

'I'll call an ambulance,' I said, digging around for my phone.

'No,' said Vizael. 'That won't be necessary.'

'What are you talking about?' I replied, turning to the blood-soaked baby. 'She needs to be checked over by a professional.'

I may have had a first aid certificate, but my training fell woefully short of this.

Vizael approached the mother. 'Give her here,' he told her. 'For her own sake.'

The eaves resisted at first, eyes streaming, drawing the baby tight to her bosom, then her head slumped as she arrived at some sort of understanding. She handed over the child.

'Be kind to her,' she said, as Gendith led the woman away to somewhere private.

'What's going on?' I asked.

Viz wore a grave expression as he cradled the baby in his arms. 'They left the baby alive to send a message.'

She looked so sweet. Pudgy hands, dimpled cheeks, like a little girl's best doll – the kind you don't play with. 'What kind of message?' I asked, leaning in to get a better look at the child.

'Careful,' said Viz, and I immediately found out why.

The baby's face transformed in an instant. Her skin turned almost translucent, like some cave-dwelling creature, and shrank tight to her tiny skull. Eyes like two ink spots glared out from cavernous sockets, and she opened her mouth to reveal a mess of fangs, two of which projected further from her gums than the rest.

I managed to pull back just in time as she lunged and snapped at my neck. Her fangs grazed my throat and snapped together with an awful sound that put my own teeth on edge.

'What the fuck?'

Viz wrestled the baby to the ground, placing a hand on her chest and pinning her to the floorboards. 'This is what they do,

Abbey. The vampires. They kill, they maim, and they turn good people into them.'

'There has to be some way to fix her though, right? To make her better?'

The baby hammered her fists on the floor, screeching like torn metal. Viz used his free hand to reach for his ivory-handed walking stick, then snatched it up, gave it a twist, and drew a slim blade from its shaft

'It's too late. There's nothing that can be done for this one,' he said, eyes watering, 'but we can help others. With you on our side, we can stop this from ever happening again.'

'What are you going to do?' I asked, certain that I already knew the answer but hoping beyond hope that I didn't.

'You should turn away for this part,' he said.

I wanted to but I couldn't. I finally got how this was about more than just me. I'd been told it from the start, but only now was I really hearing it. I was a part of this, and that meant bearing witness to all of it, no matter how ugly. No matter how terrible.

Viz pushed the blade through the baby's heart and she turned brittle and black, then crumbled to dust.

Who could do that to a baby? Infect her and leave her in a pile of dead bodies, knowing we'd have to kill her ourselves? I felt a searing hatred bloom in my chest.

'What do we do now?' I asked, my jaw aching from how hard I was gritting my teeth.

Viz wiped away some tears and slotted the blade back into his cane. 'We spend a day recuperating,' he said. 'After that, we take you out into the field.'

I looked down at the small pile of ash that had once been an innocent child. My days of eating cheap cheese and binge-watching Netflix were over. There was evil in this world, real evil, and I was going to put a stop to it.

12

I made it into work the next morning after another, shall we say, *tense* evening with Neil. He knew I was hiding something from him and bugged me non-stop about it. Not that I could blame him, or get angry about it. He was right to be suspicious, right to be worried, and I was wrong to snap at him every time he tried to broach the subject. But hey, what else could I do? It's not like he'd believe the truth if I told him. He'd just think I'd gone loopy like Mum.

I was tired. So tired I felt like I was wearing a lead-lined coat. All I wanted was a bit of peace and quiet, a chance to collect my thoughts. Instead, what I got was the temp, tiptoeing over to my desk with her head cocked to one side.

'Are you all right, Abbey?'

There she went knowing my name again; the nerve of that woman. 'I'm fine,' I said, with an edge that made it very obvious I wasn't.

'I feel you, babe,' she replied. 'I saw it too.'

'Saw what?' I asked, stiffening.

'Bake Off,' she replied. 'You're upset about Tom getting the boot, right?'

My shoulders sagged. 'Yeah, that's it. Because of Tim and everything.'

It was surreal. There we were talking TV, and just hours

before I'd been knee-deep in gore and fighting off a vampire baby. My days had become divided, split in two between the mundane and the horrific. I'd always hoped for a different kind of life, but did it have to be *this* different? At least, couldn't there be, I don't know, *zero vampire babies*?

'This isn't about Bake Off, is it?' asked the temp, sensing that my turmoil might amount to more than a contestant being eliminated from a cake-based reality show. 'What is it? Boyfriend stuff?'

'Yeah,' I said, reflexively. I guess I must have needed to talk about it, because it all came out after that.

I told her how I hadn't been able to spend any time with Neil lately, then I told her about last night.

'What happened?' she asked.

'We had a fight.'

'A big one?'

'Yeah.'

She cocked her head to the other side, willing me to go on.

I sighed and did just that, only in a coded way. 'Well, I was off sick yesterday...'

'Gary mentioned.'

'I'm sure he did. Anyway, I'd had a really shitty day, and all I wanted was get some sleep, but Neil wanted to talk.'

'About what?'

'About how we hadn't been spending any time with each other.'

'Right,' she said. 'So what did you tell him?'

'I asked him if it could wait until the morning, but he wasn't having it.'

The temp chewed on the end of her pen. 'What did he say when you told him you didn't want to talk?'

'He said I was tired of him. Said I was trying to run our relationship into the ground.'

He knew something was up—the dubious absences, the erratic behaviour, the phony gifts—and he'd added them all together to spell out "CHEATER". I wanted to tell him he was being daft, but I had nothing better to offer, and his guess beat the truth.

'Do you think it'll work out between you two?' she asked.

'I honestly don't know,' I replied, feeling defeated.

'I'm so sorry to hear that,' she said, 'but if it all goes tits up, don't worry, I know a bloke who's just your type.'

'Is that right?'

'Yeah, he's a total goth-looking weirdo, just like you!'

'Thanks very much.'

'You're so completely welcome!' she replied, and there was no hint of sarcasm there, the simple thing really meant it. The temp's forehead wrinkled. 'There's just one thing I don't understand, Abbey.'

'What's that?'

'Where *have* you been spending all your evenings?'

Ah yes, that. I was groping around in the back of my brain for something to say when our mouth-breathing supervisor elbowed his way into the proceedings.

'All right, ladies, let's break up the knitting circle, shall we?' said Gary.

Saved by the very annoying bell.

The temp bowed her head and scampered away to her desk.

Gary turned to me. 'I'm not paying you to sit around and chat all day,' he said, hanging over me like an unwelcome scrotum.

'I was multitasking,' I told him, and technically I was: I was at work, and at the same time I was doing bugger all. That's two jobs for the price of one.

Gary continued to glare, so I placed my hands on my keyboard, jogged the space bar to magic away the screensaver, and tapped out a few random keystrokes. I did it to trick him into believing that I was working, but it was also meant as a testament to his awesome management skills. Gary values delegation as his greatest asset, and there's no denying that when it came to passing the buck, Gary was Number One. The best of the best. Then again, Charles Manson was pretty good at delegation too, and no one gave him a Christmas bonus for it.

'What's that about?' Gary asked, looking down at the missing fingernail on my right hand. 'You're coming into work beaten up now, are you? What did you do, join a fight club?'

I balled my hand into a fist. If a missing fingernail was

enough to get him in a tizzy, imagine if he'd seen the cattle brand on the other side of my mitt.

'Get it together, Beckett,' he said, 'because if you don't sort yourself out soon, I'm giving your post to someone else.' He shot me a hard stare. 'I've got people lining up to do this job.'

I was about to answer him back—perhaps to point out the unlikelihood of there being a queue outside, begging to work for minimum wage under the supervision of a jumped-up jobsworth with a Napoleon complex—but kept my mouth shut. Though I'd have given just about anything to quit that shitty job, Neil and I wouldn't survive without my puny income. I had enough problems dealing with a vampire uprising, without having to eat out of a fucking food bank.

13

I arrived home that evening expecting the worst. I'd sent Neil a text to let him know that I'd be home on time, but hadn't gotten a reply. Not even an emoji. Not even a *poop emoji*.

When I pushed open the door to the flat I was braced for an ice-cold reception, but what I got was just the opposite. The smell of cooking tickled my nostrils; hot bread and garlic and sweet, life-giving cheese.

'Hi, hon,' said Neil, appearing from the kitchen wearing a greasy apron. It was illustrated with a pair of twenty-sided dice where boobs would be, along with the tagline, *Yeah, They're Natural*. He bounded over and gave me a bear hug.

'What's all this for?' I asked, feet dangling above the ground.

'I felt bad about last night. I'm sorry, that was out of order, what I said.' He set me back on the hallway carpet. 'Just, lately… it sort of feels like we've been drifting apart, and I guess I started to think the worst.'

I can't say I blamed him. If the situation were reversed and he started disappearing every night and coming home with weak-sauce excuses, I'd have given him more than a talking to. I'd have had his nuts off.

Then there was Neil's lifestyle, sitting around at home all day, going stir crazy while I went gallivanting about town. It was bad enough for the guy at the best of times, without me playing hide and seek on him. Is it any wonder he got it into his head that I'd been shopping around for another man? I'd played right into the worst of his insecurities; Neil, the way he saw himself when his moods were at their blackest: the poor, sick weakling with rubber tubes up his nose, trapped at home while the world moved on without him. Left to rot while the love of his life banged some side piece behind his back.

I felt more than a little terrible. I went to make my apologies, but Neil cut me off.

'Don't say a word,' he said, and escorted me to the kitchen. There, on the dining table, was a feast fit for a queen. 'I cooked all your favourites.'

And he had. Lately he'd been exploring his inner chef and had become obsessed with one of those meal kit services. You know the type; you sign up and they send you boxes of raw ingredients you're meant to cook yourself. Airfix dinners, I call them. Luckily for me, he'd thrown all that out and gone with the classics.

'Pizza baguettes and Alphabites, Madame,' he said, sweeping a hand across the table to show off his culinary masterwork. 'And for dessert, Sara Lee's finest Double Chocolate Gateau.'

My mouth began watering immediately. Forget about dinner in a box, this was the real deal: pizza toppings on a half-loaf of French bread and fluffy chips shaped like letters, followed by a defrosted chocolate cake.

Neil had obviously been busy. No wonder he missed my text message.

He gestured for me to take a seat then laid a square of kitchen towel on my lap and poured me a glass of box wine. After that, he sat down opposite me and we had a long-overdue catch up. We talked, we laughed, we stuffed our fat faces. When I circled back to the fact that I'd been so distant lately, he brushed it off like it was nothing.

'It's fine,' he said. 'I was being a big Jessie. Anyway, it's not like I've been all that available lately either, sat at my desk writing all the time.'

Writing.

'Oh, that reminds me,' I said, sitting up straight, 'I finished reading your latest.'

I'd managed to polish off the last few chapters during a lunch break.

He sat up straight too. 'So… what did you think?' he asked, tentatively.

I stroked my chin. 'You know, I think I actually loved it,' I replied, and meant every word of it.

I'd always known Neil was a good writer, but I'd felt a certain detachment from his books before. Wizards and werewolves… I mean, what did any of that stuff have to do with me? Of course, now I understood. Now I found myself wrapped up in vampires and angels and impossible magic portals, it all made sense. I finally got where Neil was coming from.

'What did you like most about it?' he asked, leaning closer, elbows on the table.

'I liked all of it,' I replied, 'but the bit that got me the most was the fight at the end. You know, when the werewolf and the warlock combine their powers to defeat the demon overlord. That was badass.'

'Ah, yes,' he said, nodding enthusiastically, 'you mean when Azzerad the warlock uses transmutation magic to enlarge Dirk's wolf paws, and then off he goes, tearing through Darkblaze's demonic shock troops like a hot knife through butter?

'That's the bit.'

'They have a name for that move, you know. They call it the *Combine Harvester*.'

That beautiful, sweet nerd. I leant across the table and planted a kiss on Neil's mouth. As we parted, his brow creased.

'What's wrong?' he asked, seeing the tears streaming down my face.

He was right to be concerned. I'd never been much of a crier. Not then, not ever. One of my other nicknames at school—and I had plenty—was even less kind than the one about my puny weight. "The cyborg", they called me, in reference to my general lack of emotionality. The name caught on to such a degree that when a bunch of us went on a camping trip, the other girls started referring to my waking up as, "Coming online". The shits.

Something about the sweetness Neil was showing me just turned on the waterworks though. For someone to be that kind after the way I'd treated him...

'I'm fine,' I told Neil. 'Just happy.'

I took his hand in mine and watched him trace a finger along the brand on my palm.

'I think I'm growing to like this, you know,' he said. 'Makes you look like a character from one of my books.'

Yeah, it did. More than he knew.

I swiped away the tears and smiled. After everything I'd been through—after being attacked, after seeing those dead bodies, after watching Vizael put down that poor baby—a bit of loving normality was exactly what I needed. Because now I knew that there were monsters out there. Monsters that wanted nothing less than to rise up and wipe out humankind. And for the first time since this all started, here in my little oasis, I felt safe. Level. Ordinary.

If only for one evening.

14

I woke up early the next morning, knuckled the sleep from my eyes, and headed out to the gas tower to prepare for my first hunt.

It was a Saturday, so I didn't need to make excuses at the office. When Neil asked what I was doing up so early, I told him I was attending a self-defence class I'd downloaded a Groupon for (which was about as close as I could get to the truth without lying completely).

I crossed the flyover on my way to the train station, and was heading down the concrete steps to street level when I ran into a familiar figure. The moment I saw him my heart started racing so fast that I felt the pulse in my neck. There he was, the skinny human statue in the pinstripe suit, same place as he was before, only now he gripped a tuft of my hair in his slim white hand.

'Good morning,' he said, offering the thinnest of smiles. I instinctively went for my dagger, but he held up his hands in surrender. 'Easy there, tiger. I didn't come here to fight.'

'Then you should have stayed in your coffin,' I replied, tugging open the zip of my backpack and reaching inside for the dagger, trying to sound braver than I felt.

'You're embarrassing yourself,' he chuckled, and as he said it, a passerby came up the steps heading in the other direction: a woman in her forties, accompanied by a little girl.

'Morning,' she chirped as she headed up to the overpass.

'Morning,' I replied, holding the dagger inside the bag, concealing its blade until the two of them had passed.

'Come on then,' I told the vampire, hoping he didn't notice the tremble in my arm as I gripped the dagger's handle. 'What are you waiting for? I'm right here.'

Pinstripe chuckled, then nodded over his shoulder. Below us was a group of kids, huddled around a phone and rapping along to some grime music. I'd been so focussed on the man in the suit that I was only just now hearing it.

'Too many witnesses,' he said. '*Ours is a secret war*. Don't you know that?'

I saw a baby, turning to ash. 'I don't care if they see me kill you,' I told him. 'It'd be worth it to see the look on your face.'

As if triggered by my threat, a bead of blood appeared from Pinstripe's right eye and ran down the crag of his cheekbone, an after-effect from me stabbing him with my house key. I grinned, but my smile soon faded as he mopped up the leak with a lock of hair that used to belong on my head.

'Consider yourself lucky they're there,' he said, nodding back to the youths. 'You wouldn't stand a chance against me, with or without the brand. I've lived too many lives. Seen empires rise and fall. I have powers that you couldn't even fathom. Do you really think a trembling little girl is going to put an end to me?'

'Can we cut through the treacle, please?' I said, feigning boredom. 'I've got a lot of vampires to murder today.'

'You're scared,' he replied, not intimidated in the least. 'And you should be scared. You're trafficking in someone else's world, Abbey. A world you don't belong to. A world of apex predators, and you, girl, are the bottom of the food chain.' He took a step in my direction and met me nose-to-nose. 'Give it up. You're no Nightstalker. You have no place in this war. Return the dagger to the angels and go back to your ordinary existence. Do it now. Because if you continue down this path, I promise I'll see to it that your life is ripped to pieces.' He grinned like a Cheshire cat. 'You cannot defeat us. We are eternal. We are darkness.'

And off he went. One second he was with me, the next he was gone.

The world returned to normal.

I heard the traffic from the flyover, thundering above my head. I heard the kids rapping below. I pulled my hand from my backpack, leaving the dagger tucked inside, and when I looked down at my palm I saw the brand, glowing dim and warm, like cooling lava.

My hand was shaking.

15

I wasn't giving up. No way. The dagger had chosen me to kill the vampires, and kill the vampires I would. Besides, if those toothy shitbags really were the walking apocalypse, what good would it do to hide from them? How is it that quote goes again… you know the one…. *"The Only Thing Necessary for the Triumph of Evil is that Good Men Do Nothing."* Yeah, that. Although, you know, broaden it out a bit to include us chicks.

I pictured that baby being pulled out of a pile of corpses again. It played over and over in my mind's eye like a gif I couldn't scroll past. That tiny, crying mass, its life barely begun, its life already over.

No. I wasn't giving up shit.

I arrived back in the gas tower, where I was met by Vizael and congratulated on accepting the mantle of Nightstalker. To say thank you, he gave me a tan leather sheath for my dagger, which came with a harness I could wear under my jacket. He helped me into it, fussing at its fasteners like a proud father getting his daughter ready for her first day of school. For a moment I thought he was going to take a photo for posterity: me stood by the door smiling meekly, dressed in a crisply ironed blouse, my skirt a little too long, but I'd soon grow into it.

'There,' he said, taking a step back to drink me in. 'Fighting fit.'

I didn't mention my latest encounter with Pinstripe – I was too embarrassed to admit that I'd let that rotten bastard get the better of me a second time. I knew Gen would love that. Besides, today was about killing vampires, and holy shit, was I about to kill me some vampires.

The place Viz sent me to wasn't at all what I'd expected. When he said I'd be visiting a vampire nest, I imagined some gloomy, coffin-filled hole in the ground covered in cobwebs and stinking of rot and death. Instead, I was posted up outside the Lloyd's of London building, a cluster of gleaming silver towers in the city's financial district, the Square Mile.

I wasn't alone. Viz had instructed Gen to shadow my inaugural dust-up, a prospect she was about as enthusiastic about as you might expect.

'Makes a change seeing you out in the daytime,' she said, observing me through hooded eyes. 'I half-expected you to burst into flames under sunlight.'

I ignored her and concentrated on the matter at hand, staring up at the giant, interlinked monolith. The sky reflected from the building's polished metal surfaces, clean and blue. The Lloyd's of London Building was a peculiar structure that wore its services on its exterior, showing off its pipes and ducts like it had been turned inside out by some science experiment gone wrong.

It was around noon. The weather was cold, but I felt hot beneath my jacket, so I unzipped the leather and gave it a flap to let some air in.

'There,' said Gen, pointing up to a glass lift descending down the outside of one of the towers. 'Visual acquired.'

I squinted and could just about make out two suited figures standing inside.

'Those are our vamps?' I asked.

Gen replied with a curt nod. 'You catch on fast.'

'What are they doing out here?'

'What did you expect? This isn't a Hammer Horror, girl. The

Judas Clan aren't castle-dwelling boogeymen, feared by simpleton peasants.'

'Then what are they?' I asked.

'They're leeches, not just of blood, but of riches. The Clan are sophisticated, corporate monsters, profiting from mankind's misery, draining society dry.'

'So… bankers?'

'Precisely.'

It's funny, but of all the insane things I'd learned these last few days, that was easily the most believable. Stock traders and hedge fund managers were bloodsucking vampires? That tracked just fine.

Gendith went on. 'The thing that really makes the Judas Clan vampires is the toll they take on humanity. Ever since they began to rise from their slumber, the Clan have been using their powers to infiltrate the financial sector and bleed the system. They are master mesmerists, and unlike other bloodsuckers, they can survive in sunlight, which gives them the ability to influence the living world in ways the rest of their species can only dream of.'

'So what's this then...?' I said, gesturing to the building. 'Vampire Incorporated?'

'This is only one part of their operation,' Gen replied. 'The Clan's organisation is made up of many cells. Wheels within wheels. Thousands of vampires, covertly working in conjunction with one another, maximising profits. Together, they make billions each year.'

'Sorry, did you just say *billions,* with a *B*? Holy shit. What do they need all that money for?'

Instead of answering, Gen held up a finger and shushed me. A finger would have been fine, the shush was overkill.

Following her finger, I looked back to the tower to see the two suited men exiting the ground floor of the building and making their way across the forecourt. They looked normal enough, a couple of cutthroat city boys in Gordon Gekko suits, faux-hawks and spray tans.

'What do we do?' I asked.

'We follow.'

So we tracked them. Tracked them at a distance as they

crossed the road and took a side alley to head in the direction of Fenchurch Street. After that, we followed them for another mile, tailing them right to the edge of the district. They were taking one hell of a lunch break.

'Do you know where they're going or what?' I inquired.

'Instead of asking so many questions, why don't you try using your eyes?'

I turned back to the two vamps to see them entering a Starbucks.

'I don't get it,' I said, 'they already walked by two Starbucks to get here.'

Gen smiled. Well, half-smiled. 'So, you were paying attention after all.'

We discretely followed the vamps inside then watched them approach the counter to place their orders. From the opposite end of the shop, we observed quietly as the taller of the two vamps approached a barista; a perky young blonde with an apron tied around her pinched waist.

'Can I get a name?' she asked.

'Vlad,' he replied.

I almost laughed out loud. 'That's a joke, right?' I whispered to my companion.

'No, it's a code.'

"Vlad" paid in cash, and a couple of minutes later the barista returned from a back room and set down two short paper cups. I watched as the vamps took their drinks and supped the contents through the holes of the cup's plastic lids. Each gave satisfied gasps as their faces came away from the drinks, and as they did, I noticed dark red smears on their lips.

'Blood,' I said, stating the obvious.

'This is where they come for their afternoon pick-me-up. All the Clan in the neighbourhood flock to this place.'

I could see it now. Looking around, I noticed letter J's on the heads of most of the coffee shop's patrons. Even the baristas were Clan members.

'There's so many jays in this place I'm surprised Snoop Dogg isn't here,' I said.

Gen looked at me quizzically. 'What?'

'Weed joke. Don't worry about it.'

She shook her head and returned to the matter at hand. 'If you can see the Judas brand without having to physically touch the subject, that means your powers are growing. Good, you'll need them for what comes next. Who knows, maybe you'll even make it out of this alive.'

I was about to ask what that meant, but went hush as the vamps passed us by and exited through the shop door. We tailed them as they headed back to their office with their blood macchiatos, doing our best to remain nondescript as we lagged a short way behind. After a while, they took a turn into the same deserted side alley they'd cut through the first time.

Gen stopped me at the entrance. 'This is where it happens. You'll need to act fast.'

'Just me against the two of them?'

'Yes. The Judas Clan can tolerate sunlight, but it weakens them physically. It's solar noon right now, which means the sun is at its highest point and the vampires are at their most affected. They shouldn't provide much of a challenge, at least not to the Sanctified one.' She regarded me coolly. 'Why, are you having second thoughts?'

'No. Course not.' I said, more out of belligerence than anything else.

'Good. Then get in there and start stabbing.'

'Okay, but only because I want to, not because you said so.'

16

I slid the dagger from its sheath, took a couple of deep breaths—which completely failed to calm my jangled nerves—and went pacing off after the vampires.

As I did, a strange, unseen weight seemed to descend on the alley. My ears popped as though the air had become pressurised, and when I turned back to Gen, I could see a shimmering wall separating us, flecked with shifting threads of gold.

'I've cut them off at the other end too,' she said, her voice muffled by the force field, 'but I can only hold them for so long.' She was making this happen. Manipulating the surrounding light and forming it into solid walls. I had to admit, that was pretty impressive. 'Go now. I'll make sure you're not interrupted.'

I was amped but terrified, my fingers flexing around the handle of the dagger. Was I really going to do this? Was I *really* going to take down a couple of stone-cold Nosferatus? I could die. I could die, big time. Die here, in this alley, and then what? Would the angels tell Neil what had happened to me, or would they leave him to think I'd just disappeared, never to return home? I could picture him there, waiting and waiting, growing more and more worried. Unless my body showed up, I felt sure he'd come to the conclusion that I'd finally gotten tired of him and ghosted out of his life. I don't know, maybe that was for the best. Better than knowing I'd been torn apart by vampires anyway.

I found myself dithering, my feet not wanting to carry me any further into the alley, my heart beating so hard I thought it might crack open my rib cage.

Was I really going to do this?

I thought back to the house of dead eaves. Back to what Viz had told me. About how he needed me, and how more people would die without my help. And I wanted revenge. Revenge for that poor baby. Revenge for every person who'd ever suffered because of those bloodsucking freaks.

I could do this.

I had to do this.

I felt the brand pulse in my hand and saw it glow hot and bright.

Yes.

Yes, I could do this.

I was *meant* to do this.

Any fear I had evaporated as my powers ignited, burning new pathways into my brain, endowing me with abilities I never thought possible. I was alive – truly alive. Every cell in my body was dancing, fizzing, popping like a flood of champagne bubbles.

I was ready to erupt.

I shook a few last nervous tingles from my muscles and had at it.

'Hey, fuckers,' I shouted, and the two vamps turned as one. They saw the silver dagger in my hand. 'That's right,' I told them, 'Game. Fucking. Over.'

I ran at them, screaming, supercharged. I had this. I'd taken down one vampire already—the one who came by my office—and that guy had the jump on me. I'd make mincemeat out of these two. One little scratch with my magic knife and they'd be bleeding like stuck pigs.

As I closed in, the vamps took off in the other direction, but were quickly halted by Gen's force wall. Trapped like rats in a maze, they spun about to face their attacker, shoulders hunching as they went into monster mode. Immediately, their skin turned a cadaverous, bluish pallor, stretched tight and webbed by spidery black veins. Sinews stood up beneath the skin of their necks, as if thick worms had tunnelled beneath their flesh. They threw back their heads and hissed to reveal gleaming sets of white fangs, slick with saliva.

One of them fell right away. Without hesitating, I drove the silver dagger deep into his neck, right up to the hilt. His eyes bulged wide as air bubbles frothed in the blood escaping from his jugular, and I roared and twisted the knife until his eyelids fell shut and his body slid from my blade.

'Next!' I crowed.

Cornered, his friend saw no option but to fight. He came at me, his movements sleek and fluid, arms outstretched and grasping for my throat. Refusing to get choked out by another of those dirty bastards, I lashed out with the blade and drew a long, red line along his forearm.

He shrieked and recoiled, and as he went to staunch the flow of blood escaping his wound, I closed my hand into a small, bony fist and clobbered him in the jaw.

Crack.

He staggered backwards, floundering, but not quite capsizing.

Blood hummed in my veins. Electric. Volcanic. I swung the dagger again and slashed him across the chest, sending half of his necktie fluttering to the ground. A fresh wound bloomed beneath his shirt. More blood.

'Come on, then!' I screamed.

Enraged, he came at me again with impossible speed, evading my next cut and closing the distance between us in one long stride. Grabbing me by the shoulder of my jacket, he gathered a bunch of leather in his fist, hauled me towards him, and threw a punch into my face.

I felt a hot spike of pain as the blow landed and my nose flattened flush with my skull. Stars exploded in front of my vision and blood shot from my nostrils and splashed to the ground.

Like a hungry shark drawn to fresh chum, the vampire went into a frenzy, pummelling me, raining fists upon my body, each of them heavy as a van full of anvils. I threw out a couple of sloppy swings to defend myself, but it was no good. He was all over me.

My knees gave out and I crumpled to the pavement, curling up into a foetal ball as he continued to kick at my face. The tip of one of his Oxfords connected with my jaw, and I felt blood pooling in my mouth. As I lay there, taking blow upon blow, my mind went to another place. I began to wonder, once all this was over, what they would write on my tombstone.

"Died of a vicious beating"?

Nah, they'd never write that. The dead always died gentle deaths. They departed this life, died in their sleep, fluttered away to reunite with their loved ones. They never got kicked to bits in a grubby alleyway by some scumbag murderer.

Things began to go dark as the purpled flesh of my face puffed up and squeezed my eyelids shut. Any powers the brand gave me were depleted now. I wore my nerve endings on the outside of my body. My cells were empty. The champagne had gone flat. I cried for help, but the only thing that escaped my shattered jaw was a hollow gurgle. It didn't matter. Nothing mattered.

I was dead.

17

Actually, let me walk that back a bit. "Dead" is a bit strong. Sure, I might have *felt* like death, but I survived my encounter with the two vampires, just about anyway. Sorry if I left you feeling a bit cheated there. My bad.

I woke up in a ratty cot back at home base. Back in the gas tower. Sweat cooled on my face, a face that I expected to be puffed and painful, but instead felt almost normal. I yanked out my phone and reversed the camera so I could get a look at myself. On the screen I saw—much to my surprise—not a mashed-up, broken mess, but an almost-normal looking me staring back, wide-eyed. There was a little light bruising, and my bottom lip was a little fuller than normal, but otherwise, you'd hardly know I'd taken about two dozen boots to the face.

I looked at the brand on my hand. It had to be down to that. To my "powers". They hadn't won me the fight, but they'd helped me recuperate fast.

It turned out, since I'd managed to fall flat on my face, that Gendith had been forced to intervene. It was an act that I had mixed feelings about. On the one hand, my catastrophic performance had demonstrated perfectly that I didn't have what it took to be the Nightstalker, which was regretful, to say the least. On the other hand, without Gen stepping in and battering my attacker to death with her morning star, my remains would be pasted all over that Square Mile back alley.

So, swings and roundabouts, really.

Jesus, I'd really made a fool of myself. I wasn't cut out for this gig and Gendith knew it. My first mission was meant to be a doddle, but I'd botched it big style. Survived it by the skin of my teeth. Of course, Gen was only too happy to relay this information to Vizael in her debrief, which she delivered with enough conviction to wake me from my stupor.

Having forced my eyes open and crawled out of bed, I staggered from the room and on to the mezzanine balcony. The angels stood below in the main living area, having a heated conversation. I looked on secretly, spying on them from the shadows.

'...You made a mistake,' Gendith said. 'The girl was never meant for this life.'

'She wears the brand,' Vizael replied, not meeting her eye.

'And look where it got her,' Gen cried, her voice like a blade on a leather strop. For a moment I thought she was about to attack Viz's library again, but instead she took a calming breath and continued in measured tones. 'Just because she wears the brand, doesn't mean she's fit to use it. Do the right thing, Vizael. Please.'

The old man let out a long sigh. 'Abbey was Sanctified. That *means* something.'

'It means nothing. Let me do this. I don't need the brand. I don't need anything. Just give me the dagger and cut me loose.'

Viz was about to answer her when he saw me in the corner of his eye. 'You're awake,' he said. 'Good, there's work to be done.'

I traipsed downstairs to join them. 'What are you talking about?' I asked. 'I just got the crap beaten out of me.'

'And yet you endure.'

'Only because I interceded,' Gendith noted.

'She's right,' I said. 'I was done for back there. If Gen hadn't jumped in...'

'You need more practice,' said Viz. 'That's all. These are dangerous creatures, it's arrogant to assume, just because you have taken up the Nightstalker mantle, just because you wield a great power, that you could brush them aside as though they were nothing. Respect your enemy, Abbey, otherwise they will break you in two, power or no power.'

Gen snorted. '"Power"? I certainly didn't see any "power" back in that alley. What is it with you and this girl?'

Viz shot Gen a hard stare and she threw up her hands before plopping down in a moth-eaten armchair, silenced.

'This is my fault,' said Viz, turning back to me. 'I shouldn't have thrown you in at the deep end like that. You must learn to walk before you can run.'

Mixed metaphors aside, I knew he was right. I had what it took to fight these things, I could feel it in my bones. When the brand was doing its job I was a powerhouse. A vampire-killing machine. And I needed to be. Because if somebody didn't step up, the whole of London and beyond was going to start looking like a slaughterhouse kill floor. I just needed more practice, that was all.

'So, what's next on the docket?' I asked. 'And just so you know, I'd be very up for anything that doesn't involve a large foot connecting with my nose.'

Viz smiled back at me, eyes glittering. 'Tell me, Abbey, what do you know about ghosts?'

18

What did I know about ghosts?

Well, I knew Patrick Swayze and Demi Moore were in a movie about one in the Nineties, I knew Scooby and the gang were always getting into scrapes with the things too, and yet I had a sneaky suspicion that neither of those factoids was going to help with what came next.

Before we went any further, Vizael decided to edify me on a few more things about the Uncanny.

'There,' he said, handing over a telescope. 'Do you see?'

We were up on the roof of the gas tower, sat on a couple of pieces of old lawn furniture. I aimed the scope across the industrial park, following the line of Viz's finger to spy on a woman stood on a street corner over the other side of the canal.

'All I see is a woman in a short skirt. A hooker maybe? Not that I'm slutshaming anyone.'

'Not a woman,' said Viz. 'A succubus.'

'I see.'

'Do you?'

I nodded. 'Absolutely not.'

'A succubus is a female demon that drains men of their life force through sexual intercourse.'

'Sounds like a real Angelina Jolie,' I quipped. 'Again, not slut-shaming.'

Viz frowned and found me a new target. 'What about him?' he asked.

I found the person he was pointing at, a big brute of a man standing around seven feet tall. He was ugly as sin and had the sort of waxy, warty complexion that made me think you'd catch septicaemia from shaking his hand.

'Yuck,' I grunted.

'Well?' said Viz. 'What do you think *he* is?'

I shrugged. 'No idea.'

'Guess.'

'I don't know. A really unsanitary basketball player?'

Viz shook his head. 'An ogre.'

'Huh, how about that? I have a quick question.'

'Go on.'

'What's the point of all this?'

Viz took the telescope from me, compacted it, and replaced it in the pocket of his linen jacket. 'The point is that there are more than just vampires and eaves running around this city. There are phantoms and demons and werewolves and trolls, and they each have their own agenda.'

That certainly was a whole mess of monsters. It's a wonder we weren't tripping over the bastards, really.

'So, London has monsters out of the arsehole?' I said. 'Is that the lesson?'

'That's certainly one way of putting it.'

'What do we do about it then?' I asked.

'We remain vigilant,' he replied, 'because the situation out there is only getting worse.'

'Why? What happened? Was it Brexit? It was Brexit, wasn't it?'

'It wasn't Brexit,' he replied. 'Though it was a departure of sorts.' He straightened up in his deckchair and assumed a posture I'd learned to recognise as his storytelling pose. 'In days gone by, a coven of witches looked after this city. The group, who called themselves the London Coven, used their combined magic to protect us against the creatures of the Nether.'

'Then what happened?'

The old man let out a long exhale and looked to the floor. 'The

Coven aren't around anymore,' he replied. 'They're gone forever. Now it's up to us to look after things.'

So, the city was crawling with all kind of beasties and baddies, not just vampires, and it was up to me to keep them all in check? No pressure. Nope.

'Well then,' said Viz, staring at me intently, 'are you ready for the next item on the docket?'

I told him yes, hoping his eyesight wasn't strong enough to see the sweat forming on my forehead on a cold winter's night.

19

For my second mission I'd been tasked with a single, bite-sized undertaking: to go eyeball-to-eyeball with a ghost and send it back to wherever it is that ghosts come from.

Viz was light on the details, and Gen certainly wasn't about to dazzle me with any science, which was probably for the best, all things considered. So long as I was only confronting the ghost to send it packing, the thumbnail version would do just fine.

I focused on the task at hand as we made our way to the site of the haunting. I had to get it right this time. Had to prove that I was cut out for this job, to myself as much as anyone else.

'Let's see if you fare any better in the spectral world,' huffed Gendith, accompanying me for a second time.

The mission didn't take us far. As a matter of fact, it didn't even take us outside of the industrial park where the gas tower stood. After a short walk, we came to a halt at the padlocked entrance of an old circuit boards factory. A chill wind whistled through its crumbling facade, and moonlight chromed the building's battered edges. It looked like exactly the kind of place a Scooby-Doo monster would lurk.

'It happened a couple of decades back,' Gen explained. 'A factory worker fell into one of the acid vats they use for copper plating. They say the fumes overwhelmed him and he lost his footing.'

Yikes, I thought. It'd take more than an appointed first-aider to square that circle.

'The company called it an accident,' Gen went on, 'and the courts agreed. Evidently the victim felt differently, as he keeps manifesting here on the anniversary of his death.'

'And what does he do when he shows up?' I asked.

'So far, nothing. For twenty-one years, the revenant has materialised on this site, but every time he has, we've put him out of commission.'

'Revenant?'

'A malevolent phantom. Otherwise known as returners, ferals or wraiths.'

I thought back to my performance with the vampires in the alley. 'And what happens if the revenant isn't, like, *put out of commission*?'

Gen shrugged. 'Best guess: it will make a bid for freedom, mindlessly terrorise the area, and maybe kill a local or two.'

'I see,' I said, letting out a scared little laugh. 'So what can I do? Kill it?'

'Oh, it can't be killed.'

'Right. Good. So what is it we're doing exactly?' I asked.

'We're banishing it.'

'Uh huh. And I suppose there's a difference between the two?'

Gen sighed and explained it to me like I was an American politician. 'We can't kill that which is already dead. All we can do is keep driving it away when it manifests.'

'So… kind of like a game of whack-a-mole?'

Gen sighed again. It was really getting on my nerves. 'Look, when you see the ghost just stick it with the pointy end of that dagger, okay?'

And with that, she reached out, grabbed the padlocked chain securing the warehouse door, and ripped it free with her bare hands.

The space beyond was pitch black. I stepped inside and scrabbled around for a light switch until my hand found a frayed cord dangling from the ceiling. I tugged on it and a bulb fizzed to life, briefly throwing up a few spooky shadows before popping and plunging the warehouse into darkness again.

Remembering the blue glow the dagger gave off, I drew it from its sheath and used it to light up the warehouse's interior. The cobalt bloom illuminated the shop floor, which was laced with cobwebs that billowed gently in the cool draught from the open door. Among the webbing, huge broken-down machines lay dotted about like the aftermath of some giant robot battle.

I made my way inside, brandishing the blade above my head like a treasure hunter holding aloft a flaming torch. I looked about for any sign of paranormal activity, but the only movement I saw came from motes of dust, kicked up by the breeze from outside and sent spiralling before me.

'Hello? Mr Ghost…?'

'Shhh,' hissed Gen.

As I progressed further into the building I saw deposits of bird shit piled up on the floor like ancient stalagmites. I covered my mouth with my sleeve, but the pungent air sat damp and heavy in my lungs. Breathing it in was like swallowing something solid. Like swallowing wet chalk.

I heard a sudden drumming sound and my muscles went tense.

'What is that?'

It was nothing, just rain striking the roof above. A storm had appeared overhead, sending pellets of water bouncing off of the corrugated iron canopy and making a noise like two skeletons going at it with a tin can condom.

Trickles of fresh rain water poured through the roof's many cracks, mingling with stagnant puddles on the warehouse's concrete floor. I stepped over a pool of water and rounded a corner to see an errant shaft of moonlight puncturing the roof some twenty feet above, its silver glow pooling on a large metal vat.

Rust and time had gotten the better of the vat's support frame, and now it lay on its side, toppled flat. The mouth of the tank opened up before me like the cavernous maw of some fearsome beast, enormous, and impossibly black.

'This is it,' said Gen, her voice echoing about the vacant space. 'This is where he died.'

'Okay. So what now?'

Gen pulled up a sleeve of her hoodie and checked her watch. 'Now we find out if you're really the Nightstalker, or whether you're about to faint like some anaemic woman in a penny dreadful.'

I heard a sizzling sound coming from within the bowels of the vat and my head snapped to one side to find the source of the noise. Inside the pit I saw a flicker of light, then a white hole flared open like a lit cigarette burning through the night.

A shimmering mist drifted out from the white void, accompanied by a soft whispering sound. As the white hole closed behind it, the entity became clearer, focused, and the whisper turned into an eerie, rasping voice as the diffuse entity congealed into a humanoid form.

The revenant.

At first, it was no more than a distortion of the light, a rough human cut-out made from a substance that didn't belong in this world. Then the apparition became more substantial. More complete. It was a man, arms held out like a sleepwalker, feet hovering a few inches from the ground as he floated out of the toppled vat.

I saw his face as he came for me; the hollow sockets of his eyes as empty as his gaping mouth, which was wide open and blacker than squid ink. I couldn't believe what I was seeing. That was my first mistake. You can't fight something you don't believe in.

Suddenly, a terror gripped me. This was a ghost. An actual bloody, leap out of your bathroom mirror and grab you around the throat, ghost! I tried to scream, except my throat was too dry, so instead, my vocal cords made a peculiar clicking sound, like a stick being dragged over a washboard.

The revenant floated towards me with an anguished howl. I didn't have it in me to step aside. Instead, I stood rooted to the spot as he drifted through my body, putting ice in my veins and leaving me cloaked in a chill sweat.

'So... cold...' I chattered.

'Here we go again,' said Gen, watching me choke for the second time. 'Come on, we can't let it get away.'

She spun on her heel and took off after the revenant, only for it to pass through the wall of the warehouse and escape outside. My instinct was to stay exactly where I was, but I knew that wasn't an option. If I couldn't take down one lousy spook, what good was I against a vampire army?

I needed to get my shit together. I felt the ice in my blood thaw and my body came to life. I was going to get that ghost and I was going to prove to Gendith that I had what it took to be the Nightstalker.

Third time's a charm, right?

I blasted through the warehouse's exit, hot on Gen's heels. The storm lashed down, stinging my face and plastering my forehead with loose tangles of hair. I gripped the dagger tight as I took off after the revenant, rain sizzling as it struck the blue fire of its blade.

Up ahead, I saw Gen powering after the revenant, trying to close the distance, only her quarry was too fast. It made it to the edge of the industrial park and phased through the chain link fence, off into the city beyond. Undeterred, Gen continued her pursuit, snatching up a length of old scaffold and using it to pole vault the fence and continue the chase.

Not being the gymnastic sort, I charged the fence instead, juggernaut style. Whether it was because the rusted barricade had already had its day, I don't know, but it came down under my shoulder and smashed flat to the ground. The soles of my Doc Martens pounded over it as I kept up the pace, tailing the fleeing revenant by a good fifty metres, but drawing closer with each footfall.

As I sped down the street, arms pumping, running faster than I ever had, I saw a sweep of headlights as a car slowed down to drive alongside me. Without stopping, I snatched a look over my shoulder and saw an overweight man leering from the driver's window of a second-hand Audi.

'Where are you rushing off to, Morticia?' he shouted over the sound of his purring engine. 'Late for a funeral?'

He was making a crack about my outfit, of course. We goths get that a lot...

'What's another name for a goth girl? A crow-ho!'

'How do you get a goth out of a tree? Cut the rope!'

'How many goths does it take to change a light bulb? Three. One to change it, and two to talk about patchouli oil and creative uses of laudanum.' (Okay, that last one we get less often).

Mostly, I let it glide off me. I don't know about you, but in a world full of Kardashians, I take pride in being an Addams. This guy though, this guy caught me on the wrong day.

'Get to fuck, you bloated shit-juggler,' I called back, still not breaking my stride.

'What did you just say to me?' he cried. 'Come 'ere!'

He put his foot down, but I accelerated too. 'Catch me if you can, numb-nuts.'

I picked up the pace, running faster still, my adrenaline pumping so hard I felt like my eyes were going to burst out of my skull. It was as if I'd found a way to turn that dickhead's catcall into pure rocket fuel. His idiocy was my power. The juice that I needed to catch that revenant and send it back to Hell.

I shot down the rain-slick street like a bullet from a gun. I don't know how fast I was travelling exactly, but it was fast enough that I heard the driver have to shift into second to keep up with me. He howled obscenities from his window as he gave chase, but I didn't look back, just kept pumping my arms as I sprinted onwards, eyes fixed straight ahead.

A little way in the distance I saw the road narrow, pinched off by a couple of traffic-calming bollards. For a pedestrian, the obstruction wouldn't prove a challenge, but for a driver?

The car continued to hurtle along in my rearview. My pursuer wasn't giving up. He was going to carry on chasing me, no matter what. Going to take his chances with those concrete bollards, confident that he could slip between them unscathed.

I flew through effortlessly as the driver shifted into third and attempted to thread the needle...

SCREECH!

A sound like Freddy Krueger petting a kitten – the sound of

rending metal as the car clipped a bollard, glanced off it, and ground to a sudden halt.

I looked over my shoulder to see the crumpled vehicle inserted between the two concrete posts, nose to tail and belching engine smoke. The collision had caused it to spin and become wedged lengthwise across the road, completely immobilising it. The sound of my laughing masked the curse words flying out of the shit-juggler's mouth as I carried on running after the revenant, leaving the world of dickhead catcallers in my wake.

A moment later I was running by Gen's side, raindrops popping on my shoulders as the deluge from above thrummed against the pavement below. Our prey was only a short way ahead of us now, but having drawn closer, I could see that something about it had changed. The revenant was transforming; losing its translucency, turning solid, becoming flesh. No longer drifting above the ground, its feet had touched down on the pavement, shuffling at first, then moving with purpose. Scorched clothing clung to the revenant's body, and beneath the tatters I saw burned skin, dripping from its bones like melted candle wax. Its fingers dangled from the bone in long sloughs that swung from side to side as it ran, accompanied by more molten flesh, flapping beneath its underarms like the wings of Icarus.

'What's happening?' I asked Gen.

'The longer the revenant exists on the physical plane, the more corporeal it becomes,' she replied.

Without slowing one bit, our quarry arrived at the entrance to Bethnal Green Tube. It headed down the stairs and into the station, taking the steps three at a time, not letting up. Gen and I followed suit, barging past terrified commuters and landing in the ticket hall. Our wet feet skidded perilously on the slippery floor as we chased the revenant deeper into the station, through the parting crowd and over the ticket barriers.

'We have to catch it,' shouted Gen. 'If it makes it into the tunnels, we've lost it for good.'

I couldn't let that happen.

No way.

20

The last of the revenant's tattered rags shed from its body as we gave chase, revealing smooth marble skin beneath, healed and tight. The ghost had been reborn to the land of the living, given form, made athletic. The revenant was completely solid now, muscles bobbing on its frame as it ran. The only thing that separated it from an ordinary, naked man was the eerie, radioactive glow it gave off, and the eyes I saw as it cast a glance over its shoulder; a pair of frantic black scribbles.

The revenant was almost at the escalator now. If it made it down there and reached a platform, it was only a hop skip and a jump into the tunnels, where we were bound to lose sight of the thing.

I knew what I had to do.

Pulling back my arm, I drew the dagger alongside my sight-line, took aim, and sent it flying.

The dagger's metal caught the station's sickly striplighting as it spun towards its target, flashing yellow as it turned over and over, then extinguishing like a snuffed flame as it sank between the revenant's shoulder blades.

'Yes!' I cried, punching the air.

But my celebration had come too soon. Without breaking its stride, the revenant shrugged, causing the dagger to slip from the wound and clatter to the ground in its wake

'It's too strong,' said Gen. 'Even the dagger won't hurt it now.'

I called the weapon back to my hand and chased the revenant down the moving escalator. The creature carried on, shouldering commuters aside as it made its way deeper into the station. It was too fast. Too powerful. I wasn't going to catch it, and even if I did, I had no idea where to go from there. The revenant was going to escape and I'd be forced to hand over the mantle of Nightstalker to someone more deserving. Another defeat to add to a long list of failures. A lifetime of fielding the question, *What's that big N on your hand for, Abbey?*

"Nobody". That's what it stands for. A big fat Nobody.

Then I saw it.

A woman hung over the handrail of the escalator, barged aside by the fleeing revenant and left paralysed with fear. Around her neck was a long woollen scarf, which I snatched from her as I sped by. She tried to protest, but her objection came out as little more than a stifled squeak.

Below me, the revenant had hit a panicked swell of commuters, and was struggling to force its way between the throng.

I'd only get one shot at this.

I looped the end of the scarf in on itself, turning it into a rudimentary lasso, then, just as the revenant was about to step off the bottom of the escalator, I tossed the thing at its head.

The lasso closed around its neck and went taut. Score! I pulled sharply on the scarf, yanking the creature off its feet, then quickly threw my end of the scarf to the ground.

The discarded end disappeared beneath the metal teeth of the escalator, which gobbled the neckwear up like a mouthful of spaghetti.

The revenant threw out its arms for something to grab hold of, but found only the sheer walls of the stairway's balustrade. Its nails screeched against the metal as it tried to find purchase, only to be drowned out by an even more distressing sound as its head met the escalator's metal teeth.

The stairway made short work of the revenant. Bones crunched and popped as the creature's freshly-regenerated body tangled with the people-mover's unforgiving machinery, and within moments it had disappeared completely into the guts of the stairway, leaving behind only a wet red stain.

Silence as the escalator ground to a halt.

I looked around to see dozens of dumbstruck Londoners staring in my direction, each of them a witness to a paranormal bloodbath. So much for our so-called *secret war*.

I turned to Gendith, who had arrived by my side. 'Um, what do we do about that?' I asked.

The angel stared at the stunned crowd, then turned back to me. 'The dagger,' she said, taking it from my hand.

Turning it upside down, she raised the weapon's jewelled end in the air, told me to shield my eyes, then spoke something in Latin.

I cupped a hand to my eyes as a blinding flash of light swamped the station, so bright that I could see my finger bones through my skin. When I lowered my hand, I saw the dagger's jewel go dim, and all at once the scene around us returned to normal. The commuters carried on as though nothing had happened, going about their business as they had been before we showed up and started garroting ghosts.

'What the hell just happened?' I asked.

'I used the dagger's magic to blank their memories,' Gen replied, slipping the knife discretely back into the sheath beneath my jacket. 'No witnesses.'

'Cool,' I said. 'So, it's kind of like the flashing stick thingie in *Men in Black*?'

'I have absolutely no idea what that you're talking about,' Gen replied, and headed for the up escalator.

Of course she didn't.

21

Much to my surprise, Gendith insisted we do something to celebrate my first success as the Nightstalker.

Pleased to hear we were in agreement for a change, my immediate thought was to hit the nearest boozer and down a few pints, only Gen had other ideas. Never one to make things simple, the pub she insisted on was all the way across the other side of town in Ealing, and quite unlike any pub I'd ever set foot in.

The Beehive seemed to be going out of its way not to advertise itself. As a matter of fact, the old cobbled backstreet that it was located on didn't even exist. Not really. The only entrance to the alley was through a solid brick wall, which conveniently parted at Gen's behest. Even once we were past that, the only evidence of the pub was a small, flaky picture of a beehive painted on a stout, oaken door. No swinging pub sign, no welcoming music, just a tiny, barely distinguishable mark, left there like a clue to some mysterious puzzle.

'So what is this?' I asked. 'One of those speakeasy places?'

'You could say that,' Gen replied, pushing her way inside.

As I passed through the threshold after her, I felt a warm tingle wash across me. It was as though my body had punctured some kind of bubble that separated this place from the ordinary world outside.

What The Beehive lacked in friendliness, it more than made up for in quirk. Unlike most of the pubs in London these days—the Wetherspoons', the O'Neills', the All Bar Ones'—The Beehive wasn't part of some chain. It was barely part of planet Earth in fact.

Judging by the rattling old fan on the ceiling that stirred air as thick as gravy, The Beehive had elected to disregard the smoking ban, and if the baby—*the actual baby*—sat drinking at the bar was anything to go by, the premises played fast and loose with just about every other licensing law.

'Is that baby drinking a pint of bitter?' I asked.

'Take a closer look,' suggested Gen.

I did, and noticed a tiny pair of white bird wings sprouting from the infant's pudgy little back.

'Is that…?'

'—A cherub,' Gen cut in. 'Don't worry, he's well over the drinking age.'

'He looks about two.'

'Trust me, he's been on this rock a lot longer than you have.'

I followed Gen deeper inside the establishment, sticking close to her heels and doing my best to remain nondescript. As it turned out, looking nondescript in this place would only make me stand out all the more.

The bar's patrons were a colourful lot, and I'm not talking bunch-of-lads-on-a-stag-night-dressed-in-matching-Smurf-suits colourful. I'm talking Star Wars cantina colourful. As we passed the gawping locals on our way to the bar, I saw a werewolf, a cyclops, and something I can only imagine was a gnome (at least if the little white beard and pointy red hat were anything to go by). The cyclops paid close attention to Gen's behind as she pushed by him, then turned and gave me the… well, *eye*.

'What do you think of the place?' asked Gen, slapping her wallet down on the bar.

'It's definitely got ambience,' I replied.

Too scared to turn my back to the bar's patrons, I cast a nervous glance over my shoulder, only to find the werewolf licking his black lips and looking at me like I was a microwave with five seconds left on the clock.

'Is this place, you know, safe?' I asked.

'In a manner of speaking, yes,' Gen replied. 'The Beehive is a neutral zone. People who come here know better than to start trouble. For the most part, anyway.'

'What stops them?'

Gen didn't need to reply. I got my answer the moment I clapped eyes on the pub's proprietor, a rafter-scraping man-mountain named Lenny. The Beehive's landlord was a giant—an actual giant—standing at least eight feet tall. His shoulders were square, strong and burly like a lumberjack's, his face shaggier than an unshorn sheep.

He placed his hands palms-down on the bar and I saw the thick cords of his veins knotting beneath the skin of his forearms. 'What'll it be?' he asked in a voice that sounded like he was gargling gravel.

Without batting an eyelid, Gen ordered a round of beer, and Lenny went about pulling a couple of pints.

I cast another look over my shoulder and saw the cyclops still ogling us beneath his monobrow.

'Shouldn't we be, like, slaying everyone in here?' I asked my companion.

'Not all Uncanny are evil,' Gen replied. 'Just because they're not like you, doesn't mean they're dangerous. You see that gnome over there?'

'Yeah.'

'He's an actor. Been in just about every George Lucas film there is. The werewolf: he works for an animal charity when he's not busy howling at the moon.'

'And what about the one-eyed guy?'

'The cyclops? Oh, he's a royal shit, but we can deal with him another time.'

The giant barman returned and set two beers down on a pair of cork coasters. Gen thanked him and we took our drinks to a nearby seating area positioned beneath a stuffed unicorn head. The leather booth burped a *whoof* of cigarette stink as I set my arse on it.

Gen and I chatted between sips of beer. I don't know if I'd have called what we did "bonding" exactly, at least not at first, but it was something. I suppose you'd call it more of a ceasefire than anything else. Smalltalk without the edge. A polite exchange of light conversation that didn't end in either of us trying to bludgeon the other to death.

'So, why *do* you dress like that?' Gen asked.

'Like what?'

'Like you're grieving.'

'I don't know. I suppose I just dress the way I feel.'

'Okay,' Gen replied, rolling her eyes. 'And how do you feel right now?'

'Pretty great, actually,' I said, stretching my legs out under the table. 'I just kicked my first ghost butt.'

'Yes,' Gen conceded. 'Eventually, anyway.'

'What's that supposed to mean?'

Without hesitating, she put her hands in the air, started shaking, and did her best impression of yours truly. 'So... cold...' she chattered, throwing her limbs about in a shiver.

'Hey! It just wasn't what I was expecting, that's all.'

'And what were you expecting?' she asked. 'A white bedsheet with two eyeholes punched in it?'

'No. Okay, maybe.'

'You succeeded in offing a single ghost. I wouldn't try walking on water just yet.'

I smiled and went for another slug of beer, only to discover that I was getting perilously close to the bottom of my pint. I checked my phone and cursed under my breath.

'What's the matter?' Gen asked.

'The time,' I sighed. 'I really want another pint, but I have to be up at the crack of dawn for work. Christ, I hate my boss.'

'I know how that goes.'

'With Viz?'

'No, the boss I had before him. The one who fired me.'

'Who was he?'

'God.'

'Right,' I said. 'Of course,' as if it were the most natural thing in the world to be speaking to someone who'd answered directly to The Great Almighty. 'So, why *did* God fire you?' I asked. 'I always thought He was supposed to be a good guy.'

Gen offered a wry smile. 'You didn't hear it from me, but the man can be a bit of a dick.'

I laughed. 'I'll drink to that.'

I went to clink glasses, but her face soured all of a sudden.

'We're a long way from that,' she said.

'Come on, Gen. Why do you have to give me such a hard time?'

'Why? You know why.' She reached out, took me by the wrist, and turned over my hand until it was palm-side up. 'You stole my birthright when you got that brand. That was my destiny. That was my whole purpose in life, and you took it from me.'

She might have been a dick to me most of the time, but I can't say I didn't feel a little tickle of guilt.

'I'm sorry, okay, but I can't take this back. If I could, I really would. Honestly. I mean, maybe. Actually, maybe not, you've no idea how shit and unexceptional my life was.'

'My heart bleeds.'

I held the brand up to her. 'This means I get to be something. You were already an arse-kicking angel, I was just me. A skinny goth in a temporary job I'd already been stuck in for years, and was probably still going to be stuck in a decade later.'

Gen leaned back and yawned in an overly dramatic fashion. I was ninety percent sure it was a fake yawn.

'Whatever,' I said, 'it happened, and there's nothing either one of us can do to change it now. Can't we just work together? Can't we be friends?'

'Friends? You and me? This isn't going to be some... ebony and ivory thing, you know.'

'Wait a second... you know Stevie Wonder?'

'Of course I do.'

'And yet you've never seen Men in Black?'

Gen sighed and settled back into her seat. Unless I was mistaken, she was wearing the slightest hint of a smile. 'Why don't you fetch another couple of pints and tell me all about it?'

22

By the time the pair of us staggered out of The Beehive, it was going on ten o'clock. Or at least I think it was, I was having trouble making the numbers out on my phone. Things had gotten a bit smudged by that stage, to the point that I could already feel tomorrow's hangover creeping around the corner.

I wasn't about to let that get me down though. Christ, no. I was living it up. I'd looked the boogeyman in the eye and sent him back to Hell. I'd earned my fun all right. Earned my fun and then some.

'You're drunk,' Gen noted, as I succeeded in tripping over my own Doc Martens. 'I'll have to escort you home.'

'Oooh,' I said, entirely too loudly. 'Are you trying to get inside my knickers, missy? What kind of an angel are you?'

I prodded her playfully in the chest. She grabbed my finger and shoved me back, almost knocking me on my arse.

'Oh, calm your tits,' I slurred. 'I'm just mucking about.'

I followed this statement with a rousing karaoke rendition of Stevie Wonder and Paul McCartney's classic, Ebony and Ivory, complete with mispronounced lyrics and badly screeched instrumental solo.

Unsurprisingly, Gen failed to join in, leaving me to sing the duet alone. Not that I minded. I was perfectly happy to sing solo, and very very loudly too. As a matter of fact, I must have reached a good hundred decibels by the time we passed by another pub and a bunch of normals spilled out.

One of them I recognised right away. It was Gary. As in my boss, Gary, the 4Chan forum that got hit by lighting and became a real boy.

'Abbey?'

'You?' I belched back. 'What are *you* doing here?'

He was accompanied by two other men. Friends, I guessed, that or I was seeing triple. Actually, that seems more likely in retrospect.

'I'm leaving a pub quiz,' he said. 'Victorious, I might add.'

'Ooh, look at me,' I chirped. 'I'm Gary and I'm dead clever and that.'

'We were just heading home,' said Gen, putting an arm around my shoulder and trying to steer me away.

I was feeling gobby though, and had decided that this was the perfect forum to tell Gary exactly what I thought of him. Batting Gen's hand away, I wobbled my way towards my supervisor and all but pressed my nose into his.

'You know what you can do, Gary?'

'What?' he asked, fanning the air between us to banish my beer breath. 'What would you like me to do?'

'I'll tell you what you can do, mate. You can stick your job up your arse is what you can do.'

'Okay, that's enough of that,' said Gen trying to guide me away again, but forgetting that I had Nightstalker strength (not to mention a powerful, drunk belligerence).

Gary said, 'If I were you I'd go home and sleep this off before you get yourself in real trouble.'

'But you're not me, are you, Gaz?' I countered triumphantly. 'You're just a stupid office supervisor, and I'm a professional monster hunter.'

'What are you banging on abou—?' he started, but I was already spinning the other way and flipping him off over my shoulder.

'Fuck you, Gary,' I said as I swaggered away singing Ebony and Ivory.

Roughly three minutes later, after I'd staggered into a side street and fallen on my face, I puked my insides into the gutter.

Gen was kind enough to hold my hair back. 'Sing with me!' I insisted between retches, but the girl was decidedly reluctant. Angels can be snotty like that.

There was a bit of an old blackout after the puking, and the next thing I knew I was waking up on a train in Thamesmead. Gen helped me out of the carriage and on to the platform, then led me to my tower block.

'You didn't have to come all this way,' I slurred, 'I'm absholotely… absoslutly... I'm fine.'

I gave her a thumbs up to prove just how okey-dokey I was, but managed to jab myself in the eye doing it. This did little to convince her of my sobriety.

We pushed our way into the building, and eventually, after a nine-storey hike, we reached the front door of my flat.

It was hanging wide open.

That sobered me right up.

I lunged inside. 'Neil? Neil!'

No answer.

I felt as if I'd taken a sudden dip in an ice bath. I checked the flat from top to bottom, but there was no sign of him. Everything was just where it was supposed to be—no overturned furniture, no missing valuables—but Neil was nowhere to be seen.

Panicking, I ran back to Gen. 'He's gone. Neil, my boyfriend. Even his oxygen tank.'

'So he went out, what's the big deal?'

'Neil doesn't really go out, not with his condition, and especially not at this time of night.' My heart hammered under my chest. Terrible scenario after terrible scenario whipped through my mind, each of them featuring men with large, pointed teeth.

Gen had started prowling around the flat, sniffing at certain areas and grimacing before circling around, back to the front door.

'Was it them?' I asked. 'Did they take him? Gen, have vampires found my home and taken my boyfriend?'

Gen stayed silent.

'Fuck! Why? Why would they do that?'

'You've taken two of theirs already, it was only a matter of time before they fought back. This isn't a safe world you've wandered into, Abbey. This is for keeps.'

I was about to respond when I saw a twitch of movement behind Gen and noticed a pair of rheumy eyes staring out through my neighbour's letterbox. It was the old man who lived across the hall, Mr Munford.

Munford was the chair of the block's Residents' Association, a nosy old sod who wielded way to much power around these parts. Ordinarily, Neil and I walked on eggshells around the bloke knowing he could cause us any end of grief if the mood took him, but tonight I wasn't worried about the terms of my tenancy agreement. Tonight I only cared about saving Neil.

'Munford,' I said, catching his eye.

Realising he'd been spotted, he quickly retreated into his flat, leaving the flap of his letterbox to slam shut with a metallic clang.

I marched over to his door and pounded my fist against it. 'Open up,' I shouted.

After a few moments hesitation, the door opened a crack, secured by a short, brass chain. An old man in a ratty dressing gown stared back at me with a face so ancient you could have taken it on the Antiques Roadshow. Unruly whiskers sprouted from his ears, and a bald spot shone through the remains of his hair like a big red bulls-eye.

'What do you want?' Munford demanded.

'You saw, didn't you?'

'Do you have any idea what time it is?' he croaked.

'I don't care. Tell me what happened to Neil.'

Munford frowned. 'He left about an hour ago. Buggered off with some young fellas.'

'What, they kicked the door in? Dragged him out of there?'

Munford snorted. 'What are you banging on about, girl? They

walked out of there like best friends. Or maybe more than friends, if you catch my drift...'

I was considering busting Munford's door down and throttling him when Gen placed a hand on my shoulder and whispered in my ear. 'They must have used mesmerism,' she said, 'a vampire trick.'

'Yeah, I pretty much worked that out myself,' I hissed back.

'People shouldn't be coming and going at this time of night,' Munford grumbled. 'Clomping about in their size-twelves and waking up the whole building. It's a bloody disgrace.'

'What did they look like?' I asked. 'The other men?'

'There were four of them,' he said. 'Done up in suits.'

'What kind of suits?'

'I dunno. Black. Grey. One of them was wearing stripes I think.'

I felt my blood go cold. 'Pinstripes?'

'Yeah. A nice suit, actually. Used to have one like it myself once. Very sharp.'

Gen cut me a sideways look. I'd only briefly mentioned Pinstripe before, embarrassed that he'd waylaid me, roughed me up and snatched a lock of my hair in the process.

'This pinstriped man?' she asked. 'He's the one who attacked you?'

I swallowed hard and ignored her. 'What else?' I asked Munford. 'What else can you tell me?'

He was running out of patience now. 'What do you want to know, girl? Nice shoes, expensive haircuts, tall.' Then something else came to him. 'Except for one of them. He was a big lad, but only sideways. A proper porker, he was. Had a right old birthmark on his face. You know, one of them... whatchamacallit... port-wine ones.'

'Is that it? Is that everything?' I felt spittle spray from my mouth.

'Thank you, sir,' said Gen, dragging me away from the old man's door. 'You've been very helpful.'

Munford muttered something unsavoury and closed his door, latching it from the other side. 'It's a bloody disgrace,' I heard him say.

'What are we going to do?' I begged Gen. 'I can't let those bastards hurt him.'

'Don't worry, if they took your boyfriend with his oxygen tank, it means they want him alive.'

'Okay, great. That's good, right? Right?'

But Gen's eyes said otherwise.

23

'Why Neil?' I asked, as we raced down the tower block stairs.

Gendith powered on ahead of me, not pausing for breath, not answering my question.

I racked my brain, my thoughts tumbling over each other as quickly as my feet. Gen had said the Clan wanted him alive, but what for? Was it a symbolic victory for them, capturing the boyfriend of the enemy? Neil would make for a good trophy after all – the Nightstalker's loved one, stolen from under her nose, from inside her home no less.

But there had to be more to it than that. Of course there did. The Clan weren't about to mount Neil in a glass case, dust off their hands and say, *'Well done, boys, job done.'* They were going to use him, most likely as leverage. They'd threaten him, torture him, maybe even kill him, just to get to me.

'It won't do you any good trying to figure out their plan,' said Gen, as if reading my mind.

I threw up my arms as we arrived on the ground floor. 'Well, then what should I do?'

'For now, don't worry,' she said, pushing through the building's exit. 'I'm sure we have plenty of time before they do anything to him.'

'Don't worry?' I cried. 'A gang of vampires just shanghaied my boyfriend, Gen!'

'I know, I was just trying to make you feel better so you'd focus. We really don't have a lot of time at all.'

'Good. Great.'

I cradled my stomach. The leftover beer I was carrying had been sloshed and shaken during my sprint down the stairs, and burned like battery acid in my gut.

Gen put a bracing hand on my shoulder. 'The pinstriped man. Tell me who he is.'

I fought back a belch. 'He's the ringleader, I think. He ambushed me a couple of times, tried to warn me off of becoming the Nightstalker.'

'And yet you went ahead and did it anyway,' she said, almost impressed.

'Seemed like a giggle,' I replied, somehow laughing and crying at the same time.

If I was expecting Gen to hand me a tissue, I'd only be disappointed.

'What do you know about Pinstripe?' she asked, all business.

'Not a lot... well, except that he likes fancy suits.'

Gen arched an eyebrow, struck by something. 'I have an idea. Give me your phone.'

She snatched my mobile off me and used it to order us an Uber. The cab was with us in minutes. Gen bundled me into the back and strapped on my seat belt seeing as I was too shell-shocked to work the clasps.

'Where are we going?' I asked.

'Not now,' she replied, putting a finger to her lips.

Given that we weren't able to discuss vampire business within earshot of our driver—at least not without zapping him with the jewelled end of the dagger, and who knew what lasting effects that might have—I stayed quiet for the drive. I found myself doing something I hadn't done since I was about six. I offered up a silent prayer. A prayer to God to save my boyfriend. *Neil doesn't deserve this,* I pleaded. *As if he hasn't had a hard enough life. As if he hasn't suffered enough, now this? Taken by monsters and served up like some sacrificial lamb.*

No.

I unclasped my hands. Neil wasn't a victim. He didn't see it that way, and I wasn't going to think of him that way either. Fate might have dealt him a rough hand, but he never once complained about his lot in life. Never once said, *Poor little me.* Even on the days his condition left him hardly able to breathe, he always found a way to stay positive. Always appreciated what he had. I owed it to him to be that way too. To keep the faith, no matter what. Neil was alive, and so long as he stayed that way, I was going to find him and save him and mess up anyone who stood in my way.

The cab bounced over a speed bump, jostling me from my thoughts. I looked out of the window. We were across the other side of the River already and heading into town. A short while later we were passing by Trafalgar Square, then we were on to Mayfair.

'Pull over here,' Gen told the driver, as we rounded the corner of Savile Row, London's golden mile of tailoring.

The car stopped outside an establishment called Hawkes & Ravenscroft, which boasted, in hand-painted cursive, *Bespoke tailoring and alterations ~ Made to measure suits and custom clothing.*

We got out of the cab and the driver pulled away, making off to his next fare.

'Best suits in the City,' said Gen.

It must have been two in the morning at least. 'What kind of tailor is open at this time?'

'A vampire tailor, that's who.'

Without further ado, Gen pushed her way inside, setting the shop bell tinkling.

The establishment was exactly as fancy as you might expect, all waxed wooden floors and polished brass fittings. The aroma of expensive cologne hung heavy in the air. A pair of Bose speakers played classical music; Mozart or Bach, or some other dead white bloke. It was stirring stuff, and reminded me of one of Neil's movie soundtracks, which only put more fire in my belly.

In the centre of the shop stood a man in his boxers with his arms held out by his sides. Crouched at his feet, measuring his inside leg with a length of yellow tape, was a second man with a crop of salt and pepper hair. They turned as one as we barged inside, their eyes wide. The tailor spat pins from his mouth in surprise, while his customer ran for the door, not bothering to collect his clothes first.

I shot an arm across the doorway, blocking his path, and he cowered before me like a dog wincing at the threat of a rolled up newspaper. He obviously knew who I was. I studied his features and saw he wasn't wearing a letter J on his forehead. He was a vampire though, no mistaking it. Waxy skin, dark, predatory eyes and pointy, coat hanger shoulders.

'Let him go,' said Gen. 'He's not Clan, and we're on a clock here.'

She was right. Finding Neil had to take priority. I reluctantly stood aside and the vampire darted off into the night.

It was just us and the proprietor now, a silly little man in a silly little waistcoat that made him look like he was running late for a snooker match.

'We're looking for a Clansman,' Gen told him, sliding shut the lock on the shop's door.

'One of those American fellows with the pointy white hats?' he asked, trying for jovial but coming off awkward and sweaty. 'Afraid I don't tailor for those boys. No sense of style.'

'That's Clan with a C, you piece of shit,' I said. 'As in the Judas Clan.'

I got up in his business, fixing him with my best drill sergeant stare. Just like the runaway customer, the tailor's forehead was also letter-free, but this guy was as alive as I was, with a healthy pallor to his skin that didn't match any vamp I'd laid eyes on.

I turned to Gen. 'I thought you said he was a vampire tailor.'

'I meant that he tailors for vampires, not that he is one.'

'I'm a businessman,' the tailor stammered, 'that's all.' His expression was pinched, his mouth turned down. 'I serve people who appreciate fine clothing, whoever they might be.'

'Even if they're vampires?' I asked.

'With all due respect, *especially* if they're vampires.'

'What's that supposed to mean?'

'Vampires make excellent customers. They enjoy the finer

things, dress well, and need new outfits regularly on account of them… well, getting bloodstained all the time.'

This fucking guy. I picked up a wooden measuring stick from the shop counter. 'You know what you are?' I said. 'You're Hugo Boss, except instead of making Nazis look pretty, it's vampires.'

I struck him across the side of the face with the stick, making a loud *thwack* and leaving a red welt on his cheek. The brand throbbed with satisfaction.

'Please!' the tailor begged, hands held up in surrender, 'I don't want any trouble.'

'Well, you've got some, mate...'

I raised my arm to strike him again, but Gen stopped me. 'The man we're looking for has a thing for pinstripe suits,' she told the tailor. 'Now, are you going to tell us where we find him, or do I let her smack you around some more?'

'Pinstripes?' he said. 'Yes, yes, I know the man.' Without making any sudden moves, he reached under the counter for an old-fashioned Rolodex. He quickly rifled through the contact cards until he arrived at the one he was after, tore it out, and handed it to me, shaking like a shitting dog. 'He comes in here all the time. Likes his suits delivered to his home address.'

I snatched the card from his soft, pink hand. 'You'd better not be lying to me,' I warned him.

But the look on his face told me he wasn't. It was the look of a man who knew his life depended on giving me the right answer.

24

Getting the skinny on Pinstripe's location felt a little too easy for my liking, but I was ready to run with it. Given the way the evening had gone so far, I figured it was due something going my way for a change.

Pinstripe's address was a couple of miles from where we were, which meant calling another Uber on my phone.

'So, how does this Nightstalker stuff work then?' I asked Gen as we waited on the cab. 'Do I keep my receipts and expense all these fares?'

'Being Sanctified doesn't pay,' Gen explained. 'At least not like that.'

'Of course it doesn't,' I sighed. 'Another unpaid internship for Generation Y...'

'Don't you think maybe we have bigger things to worry about than the state of your bank account?'

She was right, I was dodging the real issue. Keeping myself distracted, steering my thoughts from the horrible reality of my situation. Neil was at the mercy of a bunch of bloodsucking fuckers, ready to do who knew what to him. I could only imagine how terrified, how utterly bewildered, he must have felt.

This was all my fault. I thought I'd been protecting him, but I'd only been protecting myself. If he'd known what was out there, what I was working against, maybe he could have prepared himself. Maybe he could have escaped before the vampires took him. Maybe he wouldn't be about to die wondering whose nightmare he'd wandered into.

All these maybes were driving me crazy. I shook my head violently, trying to will them away, but it didn't work.

The cabbie pulled up beside the address we'd given him, a house on a street bordering Green Park. 'Nice gaff,' he remarked.

He was not wrong.

The place was a palace. Carefully manicured ivy grew upon the walls of the stately dwelling, which loomed proudly behind a pair of ornate iron gates. At its threshold stood a delicate marble fountain, gurgling melodically. It looked like the kind of house Lara Croft might live in.

'This place must have cost a fortune,' I said, stepping out from the back of the car.

Gen joined me by the roadside. 'The Clan buy up property like oligarchs, strip-mining the City for profit and driving up house prices all over town. London is their Monopoly board.'

'Are you telling me the reason I can't find a two-bed for less than half a million quid is because of vampires?'

Gen nodded. God damn it. As if I wasn't pissed off enough already.

'Do you think he's home?' I asked.

'The lights are on,' Gen replied.

But then they weren't.

As the house lights switched off, the front door opened, and out stepped a stick-thin man in a tailored suit.

Pinstripe.

We ducked behind the property's surrounding wall and peeked through a gap in the brickwork to spy on him.

'That's him,' I whispered.

Pinstripe's patent leather shoes crunched over gravel as he made his way across the mansion's impressive driveway and stepped into the plush leather interior of a silver-grey Mercedes. The engine fired up, and with a stab of another button, the outer gates swung slowly inwards.

'What now?' I asked. 'Do we tail him?'

'Tail him in what?' Gen asked.

Our cab was gone. We were pedestrians now.

'We can't let him get away,' I said. 'He knows where Neil is.'

The Mercedes was rolling, heading for the gates.

Gen saw me getting twitchy and said, 'Don't do anything rash. Let's think about this…'

But I couldn't help myself.

It was like something was doing my thinking for me. The brand was *burning*. It knew what I wanted. Knew I couldn't just hide and let our only link to Neil get away.

I jumped out of my hiding place and stepped into the gateway, right into the path of Pinstripe's oncoming car. He saw me and jammed on the brakes, bringing the vehicle to an emergency stop. The parked car sat there, purring softly. For a moment, the two of us just stared at each other, then a grin split Pinstripe's face as he revved the engine.

He shifted into gear and stepped down on the accelerator, sending the back wheels spinning and kicking up a spray of shingle.

I held my ground as the car bore down on me, picking up speed, engine screaming.

'Move!' yelled Gen, but I wasn't going anywhere.

I felt sure of myself, my fists clenched, teeth bared.

Pinstripe wasn't getting away.

Just as the car was about to plough into me, I leapt in the air, toes pointed forward like a human missile.

I hit the windscreen feet-first and landed in Pinstripe's lap with a shower of glass. My Doc Martens kicked the air out of the vampire's lungs and his hands left the wheel, sending the car into a spin.

'Where is he?' I hollered, my fingers digging into Pinstripe's throat.

I was a woman possessed. I clung to him tight, giving him no room to manoeuvre. He tried to buck me off, but I wasn't going anywhere.

Just then, the spinning car clipped the marble fountain and

went into a roll. The ground and the sky switched places, over and over, the car throwing us about like a tumble drier. I saw the property's surrounding wall fill my vision as we headed for it on a collision course—

Then we were somewhere else.

The two of us were free-falling through an impossible tunnel of swirling, strobing yellow light. I clutched on to Pinstripe like a tandem skydiver as we tumbled down and down, screaming against the wind shearing my face.

When I opened my eyes, the tunnel was gone and we were back on solid ground. We weren't in the car though. We weren't on the grounds of Pinstripe's palatial mansion. We weren't even on planet Earth for all I knew.

We were indoors now, lying in the middle of a packed night-club dance floor. Men in tight vests and muscle tops rollicked and writhed to the tune of a Scissor Sisters song. Where the hell was I?

'Get a room, you two,' roared a dancing beefcake in a crop top as he spun around to find Pinstripe and I, embracing like lovers on the floor.

The vampire took the opportunity to break away from me, pulling himself to his feet, using the beefcake as leverage and dashing off into the crowd. Screaming bloody murder, I took off after him. I couldn't let him get away, no matter what.

Before he could make it any further I launched a rugby tackle at him, grappling him around the ankles and bringing him smashing to the floor—

And off we went again, hurtling through the strobing tunnel, onwards and downwards, away to the next destination of our magical mystery tour.

This time we were transported to the site of a pansexual orgy. The tackle I'd thrown in the nightclub carried us into a carpet of sweaty, squirming bodies, packed so tightly that at first I thought they were fused together.

This was Pinstripe's doing. He was leaping from place to place like I'd seen him do before, only this time he wasn't chasing me, I was chasing him. Or at least I was so long as I kept my hands on the creep. For some reason, being in physical contact with him meant that I was taken along for the ride each time he tried to shake me.

Pinstripe crawled across the heaving mass of naked bodies, trying to break free of my grip, but I wasn't letting go.

'Where is he?' I demanded. 'Where's Neil?'

'Somewhere you'll never find him,' he called back.

And suddenly we were tumbling through the tunnel again, heading for another of Pinstripe's seedy haunts.

We landed in a rural car park at the edge of a forest this time. A number of men with their jeans around their ankles stood around the back of a Campervan, admiring a middle-aged woman being serviced by a tattooed skinhead. As we crashed the proceedings, the doggers scattered like cockroaches from the light, running for their cars and peeling out of the car park.

Pinstripe managed to get an ankle free of my grip and kicked back at me, catching me in the jaw with the heel of his leather shoe. My hand went reflexively to my face, and as it did, he wriggled off and made it to his feet. He hurried out of my reach, panting hard and slick with sweat. Dusting himself down, he flashed me a shit-eating grin, ready to make off without me—

But when he engaged his superpower this time, he got less than he bargained for. A lot less. Instead of vanishing, Pinstripe stayed right where he was, rooted to the spot. The only sign that his power was doing anything at all was the slight flicker he gave off, as though I were watching him from between the cars of a passing train. He staggered backwards, holding his head, looking like he'd run the five-minute mile.

'What's the matter?' I asked. 'Battery dead?'

I drew the dagger and lunged for him, but he was quick, and succeeded in grabbing hold of my arm.

'Oh, I don't know,' he said, 'I think I've got one more left in me...'

—My stomach climbed into my throat as we began to plummet once again, plunging headlong down the strobing shaft. I wondered briefly where we'd end up next, but there was no "we" about it this time. This time, he succeeded in shaking me, elbowing me hard in the temple and throwing me loose.

I fell away.
Away from him.
Away from the tunnel.
Away and away to who knew where.

25

When I landed, I landed alone.

I awoke to a hot blaze of pain.

'Ow,' I groaned, rubbing my throbbing skull.

For a bloke who looked like he'd be carried away by a stiff wind, that pinstriped bastard really knew how to throw a punch.

So where was I?

I was utterly in the dark, both literally and figuratively. I lurched to my feet and took a look around, using the dim blue glow of the dagger as a torch. It didn't give much away. Ahead of me stretched a corridor. Behind me too. I saw no furniture, no decorations, no windows even, just plain white walls, as far as the eye could see.

Given that I had nothing to navigate by, I decided to head in the direction I was facing. After a few steps, I began to feel a tingling sensation on my palm, and when I unfurled my fingers I saw the brand glowing like the burner of an oven, only in bright, searing blue.

I carried on, and with each step I took, the pattern grew a little brighter. Wherever it was I was headed, the mark on my hand had something to say about it. If only I'd known what it was trying to tell me. Was it a warning? An alarm bell of some kind? Was Pinstripe about to make a sudden reappearance, leaping out from behind me and slashing me from ear-to-ear, sending blood spurting from my jugular like a high-pressured water sprinkler?

Phut phut phut.

I thought not. It seemed to me that the last trip Pinstrike had taken us on was a real Hail Mary leap. Judging by the look of him before we parted ways, he was out of juice, at least for a little while. For the present at least, I was here, and he was somewhere else.

The brand was raging now, throwing off angry, electric sparks. Was it playing a game of Hot and Cold with me? Letting me know that I was getting warmer? That I was closing in on some important goal? Was this where the Clan were keeping Neil? Was he somewhere at the end of that corridor, waiting to be rescued? It sort of followed. All the other places Pinstripe had tried to panic-escape to were obviously places he liked to frequent; what if this was where he'd been getting his kicks tormenting my boyfriend?

I hurried on, and by the time I reached the end of the corridor, the brand was spitting like a malfunctioning firework. The blade of the dagger freaked out in sympathy, seething with a light of its own, painting my surroundings an eye-scorching azure blue.

Soon, the corridor opened out and I found myself standing in a vast, marble room, so big that the light I was giving off couldn't find its corners. Couldn't find its centre even. There was a quiet in that space so vast that it almost seemed loud. The chamber felt cold and characterless, like I imagined a bank vault might feel, except there was no bullion there. This room was protecting something far more precious than that.

As I reached the middle of the room I saw it: a large, complicated-looking machine, something like an iron lung, only not quite. Hooked up to the state-of-the-art contraption were hundreds of rubber tubes, which emerged through a port in the ceiling of the room. They were cable-tied together and grouped in twisting bunches, like sinews combining to form muscle. The tubes were transparent, revealing a thick, red liquid that pumped inside of them.

Blood.

Hundred of litres of it, draining into the machine in the centre of the room.

The brand was going absolutely berserk now, but if it was a warning, I wasn't listening. Not if that strange machine had anything to do with Neil.

I approached the contraption to get a better look and I must have tripped a sensor, because suddenly the room was lit up by dazzling overhead lights. When my eyes adjusted to the brightness, I saw that the pod part of the machine—which had obviously been built to accommodate a person—was covered by a glass hood.

'Neil? Are you in there?'

I rushed over to get a better look, only to find the glass hood coated in condensation, obscuring whoever was inside. I reached out a hand to swipe the condensed vapour away, then leapt back at the sound of a sudden, pneumatic hiss.

The pod came to life, rotating on its central axis, standing up to greet me. A second hiss followed as the hood swung open, revealing the pod's contents.

It wasn't Neil.

The man inside was old and withered and dried up like a mummy. His skin was paper-thin, so much so that it was translucent in places, revealing the pale organs beneath. With the pod open now, I could see that the tubes feeding into the machine terminated in large hypodermic needles, which pierced the old man's body all over, coating him like a porcupine's quills. I stared at him for any signs of life, but he was perfectly immobile inside of the apparatus, his eyes shut tight.

Who was this poor man, and what were the Clan keeping him alive for? What could he have possibly done to deserve this kind of treatment?

Just then his eyes snapped open, amber and bright.

I pulled back in horror. His body may have been emaciated and weak, but his eyes were strong. Furious. Terrifying.

The brand flared and something lit up on his forehead.

It was a letter J.

The biggest J of them all.

And just like that, I knew exactly who I was looking at.

This was Judas.

26

'Welcome, Abbey,' he said, in a voice that left me all but paralysed.

It couldn't be. Judas Iscariot. From the Bible. The father of the Clan.

'No, I thought... you're dead,' I stammered.

Vizael had told me so. He said he'd defeated the vampire master in battle and left him lying at the bottom of the Thames.

'Is that what those angels told you?' Judas replied. He stretched out as if waking from a long slumber. 'I was inactive for a while, that much is true, but stories that I met my end have been, as you can see, greatly exaggerated.'

He stepped from the pod, left foot first, right foot following. A smile that made me shudder stretched across his face. A smile that didn't quite reach those ancient eyes.

I clutched the sacred dagger in both hands, warding him off. 'Stay away.'

'Ah, good, I see your blood's pumping again. Speaking of which, you're probably wondering where the blood in those tubes is coming from, aren't you?' He gestured to the knotted pipeline dangling from the ceiling. 'It comes from far and wide, from hidden sites dotted all about the city, each of them connecting to this room via a vast subterranean aqueduct. Impressive, no?'

I'm not sure if that's the word I would have gone with exactly, but it was certainly an absorbing story.

'I didn't come here to listen to your master plan,' I managed to say. 'I came here for Neil.'

The master vampire was walking towards me now, tubes trailing behind him like the stingers of a Portuguese man-o-war. 'I'm afraid he isn't here,' he said.

'Then where is he?'

'Why don't I show you?'

In a flash, he leapt forward and seized my head between his skeletal hands, clamping down on my skull like a vice.

Suddenly, I was having an out of body experience, only it wasn't my body I was looking down on, it was Neil's. He was strapped to an altar of some kind, surrounded by a circle of suited vampires. As I watched, he struggled to break free of his bonds, but they only dug deeper into his flesh the more he toiled.

'Abbey!' I heard him scream. 'Abbey, please help me!'

I heard Judas in my head, talking over the scene like the narrator of a movie. 'Your boyfriend is about to make a valuable contribution to the cause,' he said. 'Every drop of blood he donates will bring me one step closer to achieving full strength.'

As I continued to look on, Pinstripe entered the frame carrying a hose attached to a hypodermic the size of a knitting needle. He tilted his head to look up at me and grinned. I tried to grab him, but I had no hands to grab him with. I had no anything. I was a spectator, nothing more; a helpless, disembodied witness to the events unfolding beneath me.

Pinstripe held the needle aloft to show me its cold, metal gleam, then plunged it into Neil's heart.

'No!' I yelled, but no sound came out.

The hose went at Neil like an extractor pump, sucking the blood from his body by the pint-load. He screamed and screamed as the needle went to work, his cheeks sinking into the hollows of his skull as his face collapsed in on itself, until finally, death pinched off his cries. There was nothing left of Neil now. My boyfriend was gone, and all that was left of him was a dry husk. An empty, soulless bag of bones.

Even though I had no body I felt myself go foetal. Felt my breath turn shallow, caught in my non-existent throat in tiny, hitching gasps. It was all over. Neil was dead and I was done.

Just then, the hand I didn't have became warm. My right hand: the one with the big N on it. N for Nightstalker.

When I looked down, I saw that my hand was there after all, as was the rest of my body, lit by pulsing blue fire.

The brand blazed bright – so bright that it burned through the fabric of my surroundings and showed them for what they really were.

An illusion, nothing more. A silly bit of puppet theatre, meant to scare me. Meant to push me over the edge and make me forget my mission.

I was back in the big marble room again, face-to-face with Judas. 'Nice try,' I said, voice trembling, 'but you're going to have to do better than that.'

The stretched smile faltered momentarily. 'You think you know fear, girl?' he growled. 'You do not. But soon… you will.'

I was gone again.

When I came to my senses I found myself in a maze.

Another illusion, I told myself, but the brand wouldn't burn this nightmare away. This nightmare was real.

The walls of the maze were made of an impenetrable dark grey stone, and towered a good thirty feet above me. The sky was dark, and the air cold and shocking to my throat. As I stood there, wondering what to do next, I heard a great, savage howl.

When I looked behind me I saw pack of vampires—ten of them at least—only they were unlike any vampires I'd encountered so far. They were running on all-fours like attack dogs, eyes fiery and red, their mouths huge, their teeth like the jaws of a bear trap.

My legs took a few small backpedals then gradually sped up. I turned and ran. Ran as fast as my skinny legs would carry me, deeper into the maze. I didn't look over my shoulder, but I could hear the vampires coming after me, barking, snarling, hungry for blood.

I sprinted through the labyrinth, taking corners at random,

trying to shake my pursuers. I had no idea where I was going. Each stone wall I passed seemed identical to the next, and there was no reason to think that taking a left would serve me any better than taking a right. The only thing I knew for sure was that there was no turning around. No getting past the creatures gnashing at my heels.

I carried on running, my heart pounding, my panicked breath thundering in my ears. The retreating sound of the vampires' slathering growls told me I was putting some distance between us, but for how long? I couldn't run forever. I had to find a way out of that maze. Had to escape those monsters.

I rounded another corner and found myself in an opening that measured about twenty feet square. I'd arrived in the centre of the maze, and in the dead centre of that centre was a wooden frame shaped like an upside down L.

A hangman's gallows.

And a whisper...

Do it, Abbey. Do it before they do it to you. Put your head in that noose and leave this world on your own terms. Take your life before it's snatched away from you.

I saw the brand on my palm glow dimly, then I heard the braying howls of the vampire beasts gaining on me and the brand sputtered out, snuffed away by the drench of my sweat. Fear stole into my mind like a deranged thief.

I was scared out of my mind, but my feet started moving anyway. I ran, past the gallows and down a fresh path of the maze. Stone walls raced by me as I hurled myself forwards, desperate to outrun the murderous creatures at my back. I took a corner, then another, bouncing off the hard stone with my shoulder as I threw myself this way and that—

Only to find myself back at the centre of the maze.

It couldn't be, and yet it was.

The gallows creaked and the noose swung tantalisingly before me.

Do it, Abbey. Do it now. Do it before it's too late.

I tried to extinguish the voice in my head but it carried on, insistent, deafening.

They'll be here soon, Abbey, and when they get here, they'll tear you to pieces. Don't let them have the last say. Go quietly. Step up to the gibbet and do what needs to be done.

My legs broke beneath me and I collapsed to the ground. I was all out of running. I tried to gather my senses, but fear crowded out my thoughts. Crowded out everything. Whichever path I took through that maze, I'd always return to the hangman's noose. My only choices were to die at the end of a rope, or perish inside the gnashing jaws of those relentless hellbeasts. No soul had made it out of that terrible place, I was certain of it. Not with their heart still beating.

I looked to the gallows.

And upon those gallows, transposed over the image, I saw something else.

I saw the rafter of a wooden shed knotted with a length of garden twine.

I saw someone hanging from that twine, hanging by the neck.

I saw Mum.

Just like me, she'd tried to outrun her demons, and just like me she'd failed. When Dad walked out on us she tried to keep it together, but after a while she just couldn't hack it anymore. She gave up. Stopped taking her medication and hit the bottle. There was nothing anyone could do about it, least of all me, I was just a kid. She'd made up her mind, and there was no turning her around. And now there was no turning around for me either.

I sheathed my dagger and forced myself upright on trembling limbs. The gallows beckoned, and I responded to the call, stepping up to the gibbet, my feet leaden on its wooden planks, but driven by purpose. I'd made up my mind. I was going to follow in Mum's footsteps. I was going to put an end to the pain, once and for all.

I placed my head in the hangman's noose and drew the knot tight to the nape of my neck.

'Sorry, Neil. I can't do this anymore.'

I wasn't the Nightstalker. I was no one's saviour. I couldn't even save myself.

The trapdoor beneath me sprung open and I plummeted through the hatch.

Crack.

The rope snapped taut and I found myself unable to breathe. There was no pain though, no discomfort. I was just hanging there, drifting away. For the first time in a long time, I felt at peace.

At least for a little while.

As I swung from the yard-arm, my bowels cramped and gave a terrible liquid wretch. I felt both exhaust ports twitch, set to a hair trigger. My body was doing everything in its power to expel my lunch from both ends, just like I'd told Gary it had when I phoned in sick to work that day, only this time, the sensation was very much real.

Except... was it real?

Like, *really real?*

A giant maze and a bunch of monsters chasing me around like Pac-Man? It definitely didn't sound real. It sounded like a dream. Like a nightmare.

The rope of the noose dug deep into my throat, cutting off the oxygen to my brain. Whatever was happening to me, I'd die if I didn't do something about it.

The noose dug deeper still, seemingly alive, as though it were obeying the tune of some homicidal fakir. The rope drew even tighter, pressing down on my windpipe like a pair of thumbs, strangling me, choking me like the vampire who invaded my office and tried to take my dagger away. The vampire who forced his fingers into my mouth, whose fingers slithered between my lips, whose graveyard flesh I could still taste in the back of my throat.

That fucker.

Fuck that fucker.

Fuck all of these fuckers!

I danced on the end of the rope, my feet frantically pedalling the air as I reached for my dagger. Getting it from its sheath was harder than I'd anticipated. My brain was scrambled from the lack of air, and my hands were numb and turning blue. My forefinger grazed the weapon's handle a couple of times as I swiped for it, but the dagger hung at an awkward angle and I failed to get a grip on the thing. Finally, after my third or fourth try, I managed to close my hand around the dagger's hilt. It caught in its sheath on the first couple of pulls, until finally, with one last, desperate flail of my arm, I yanked it free of its holster and sliced the noose in two.

I landed hard on the ground. Hard enough to have knocked the breath from my lungs if I'd had any left.

The gallows were gone now—vanished into thin air—but a new threat had emerged.

Appearing from the many paths of the maze came the vampires, their dagger-like teeth eerily incandescent in the darkness. I was surrounded, frozen to the spot, breathing hard and trying to refill my lungs as my limbs trembled with exhaustion. The monsters advanced on me, some of them moving slowly, deliberately, others scuttling along the walls of the maze in a chaotic spider crawl.

Too late, Abbey. You could have taken the easy way out, but they're here now. Here to rip you limb from limb.

The voice in my head again. Telling me the end was nigh and that there was nothing I could do to stop it. Unravelling my mind. Trying to drive me mad. Trying to send me off my rocker, just like Mum. Just like she was before she went to the garden shed and strung herself up to that rafter.

But I wasn't her. I was built of stronger stuff. When Dad walked out I kept it together. I made my own way then and I'd make my own way now. I was getting out of that maze, even if I had to make my own exit to do it.

The vampires formed a pack, coalescing into a teeming, toothy mass. My thighs twitched, fighting the impulse to whirl around and sprint off in the opposite direction, but no. This time things were going to be different. This time I was facing my challenges head on.

I took a step toward the monsters and they froze in place, watching me with a mixture of horror and anticipation. I slid the dagger back into its sheath and balled my fists.

'I'm getting out of here,' I said.

Fury swept through me in ferocious waves, and the brand responded by burning bright, so bright that it caught on fire, coating me in a flickering tongue of blue flame.

The monsters took a couple of steps back as I ignited, their snarling faces lit by cobalt fire. They were angry, but I was angrier. I was anger itself. I'd embraced my inner psycho, swallowed my Pac-Man Power Pellet, and now I was going to eat my ghosts whole.

Jaw set, I gritted my teeth and charged the chattering mass.

The vampires howled and bared their claws, but I blew through them like a one-woman wrecking crew. Like a big, blue fireball, burning up everything in its path. The monsters screeched in dismay as I cannonballed through their ranks and sent them scattering, not stopping, not letting up, even when I hit the wall of the maze and smashed through that too, busting through stone as if it were peanut brittle. I powered on, picking up speed, blasting through another wall, and another, and another, until I was clear of the labyrinth's bounds and floating.

Floating in a sea of white.

My vision adjusted to the light and I felt my body go heavy.

I was back in the white marble room.

Back with Judas.

The ancient vampire reeled backwards a couple of steps, his expression both annoyed and impressed. I'd fought his mind game and won. Refused to give in to his deception. Chased away the dread and found my way back to him.

'Very good, Abbey,' he said, his words loaded with acid. 'But you should have taken the noose. Soon you will be dead, and your lover too. Come dawn, his blood will be syphoned from his body and delivered down one of these tubes; another donation to my glorious cause.'

The withered old bastard was acting like he'd already read the script and knew how the movie was going to end. It pissed me off. It pissed me off something fierce.

'You know,' I said, 'there's still a few hours left before this night's over.'

'And?'

'And I'm the Nightstalker.'

I whipped out my dagger, showing Judas its silver gleam, reminding him what its metal was made of.

'Have your thirty pieces back,' I told him, and went to plunge the blade into the vampire master's heart—

But with a casual wave of his hand, Judas banished me from the marble chamber and dumped me right back where I started.

27

I found myself standing outside of Pinstripe's stately dwelling, a few metres back from his mashed-up Mercedes Benz. The front end of the vehicle poked through the smashed brick wall surrounding the property, crumpled like a balled-up paper bag. A crowd of passers-by had gathered around the wreck, taking photos on their phones and posting the snaps to Instagram.

I saw Gendith with her back to me, looking on helplessly at the demolished vehicle.

'Hey,' I said, putting a hand on her upper-arm, 'I made it out.'

She jolted and whirled about at me, eyes wide with shock. 'What? How in the hell…?'

'Pinstripe. He blinked me away. Blinked both of us away.'

'A long-range teleporter. That's interesting. We've not encountered a vampire with that power before. Something new for Vizael to add to the bestiary.'

'Something else you might want to let Vizael know about: Judas Iscariot.'

Gen looked at me curiously. 'What of him?'

'He's alive,' I told her. 'I've seen him.'

She snorted. 'Don't be ridiculous.'

'It's true. When Pinstripe magicked me out of that car we went hopping all over the place. When he finally managed to shake me off, I ended up in some kind of room, or tomb, or something, and he was there. Judas was there!'

'No. I'd know. Vizael would know…'

'I'm telling you it's true. I saw him with my own eyes. Judas is alive and he's getting stronger every second. The Clan are feeding him, and when he's good and full, he's going to climb out of that tomb and fuck shit up.'

Gen's stared into my eyes, looking for any hint of a lie. Of a mistake.

'I'm telling the truth, Gen. He's alive. Judas is alive.'

Finally, she blinked, gritted her teeth, and swore. 'If what you're saying is accurate, we're in even more danger than we thought. The Clan are dangerous enough, but with Judas leading the charge…' She trailed off. For the first time since I'd met her, Gen seemed uncertain. Scared even.

I checked my phone. It was almost four in the morning, and my weather app told me the sun would be coming up at just after 8 a.m. Dawn was closing in, and with it, Neil's death.

'Four hours,' I said. 'Four hours and Neil's done for.'

Gen nodded. 'Okay. We need to find out where he's being kept captive.'

'Pinstripe is still our best lead, right?'

'Yeah, but he could be anywhere right now.'

I thought back to our conversation with my crotchety neighbour, Mr Munford. 'Oh! One of the other vamps who took Neil, he had a birthmark on his face. Maybe we could track him down?'

'A birthmark? Not exactly a lot to go on.'

'It's something at least,' I said, the frustration almost bending me double.

'Wait...' Gen's face brightened. 'Maybe it is. I think I know someone who might be able to help us find him.'

'All right!' I held my hand up for a high-five, but it remained decidedly un-fived. 'No? Okay.'

'Give me your phone,' Gen insisted.

I gave her my mobile and she ordered us another Uber, and within a space of minutes a cab was shooting us through the empty roads to Whitechapel.

'Just here,' Gen told the driver.

The cab slid up to the curb next to an all-night cafe, ingeniously named Cath's Caff.

'What are we doing here?' I asked. 'Is this where the person we're meeting is?'

'You really ask a lot of questions,' said Gen, as she stepped out of her door and made off into the greasy spoon.

I thanked the cabbie and chased her inside, following her across the linoleum floor to an empty table.

The cafe was about as East End as it got; a grubby stop-off for cement-caked builders and late-night lorry-drivers. The furniture was cheap and laminated in easy-wipe vinyl, the decor simple, worn, and, perplexingly, decorated with posters of West End musicals that its patrons wouldn't be seen dead at.

Ambling over to our table came a sixty-something woman with crumpled features, peroxide hair, and mascara like two tyre skids. 'What're you 'avin'?' she asked, her voice as rough as a badger's arse.

Gen glanced up at a nearby blackboard, browsed the menu, and ordered two fried eggs, baked beans, and a double-helping of bubble and squeak.

'What about you, love?' asked our waitress, who I assumed was the titular "Cath".

'I'm not really hungry,' I replied.

It turns out that being completely terrified for the life of your significant other sort of robs you of an appetite. Still, the hard look Gen gave me suggested I order something all the same. I scanned the blackboard, didn't see anything I fancied, and briefly considered ordering off-menu. Something told me that asking if they served mashed avocado on rye bread would be answered by a swift smack in the mouth though, so I opted for black coffee and white toast instead.

Minutes later, we were served our food along with a steaming jug of jet-black coffee.

'What's going on?' I demanded. 'You said we were going after Neil, now I'm watching you feed your face? We only have a few hours left.'

'We're here to meet Carlo.'

'Carlo?'

'He's sort of our man in the street. He can come in handy.'

'Well, where is he then? How long are we going to sit here waiting for your man while my boyfriend's tied up somewhere and about to have his blood fed to Judas?'

A couple of heads turned.

'Keep your voice down, you idiot,' said Gen. 'Not everyone in here is like us.'

'Well, excuse me if I lose my shit a tiny bit,' I said.

I wrapped my hands around my coffee mug, taking in its warmth.

'Just be patient,' said Gen, tucking into her fried eggs. 'We still have time to save your boy, all being well.'

I took a sobering swig of coffee and gasped at a sudden recollection. 'Did I really tell my boss to stick his job up his arse?'

Gen smiled. 'Yes, you did.'

'Great. Fantastic. Well, this is the worst night of my life, and I'm including the one when I got drunk for the first time and managed to puke and poop myself in front of Dalton Myers.'

'Who is Dalton Myers?'

'Only the best looking boy in school, Gen.'

She nodded. 'I see.'

I groaned and buried my face in my mug.

'There he is,' said Gen, glancing at the door.

I looked up to see a young man bearing down on us. He was skinny, dressed like an extra from an Eighties rock video, and wore a skunk stripe of white in his lank black hairdo. As he reached our table, he swept a lock of hair aside and I saw something on his forehead. A glowing letter J.

My fingers closed around the closest available weapon, a stainless steel butter knife, which I snatched up and thrust at the vampire's heart—

Only for Gen to seize me by the wrist and force my hand flat to the table.

'This is Carlo,' she explained. 'We don't kill Carlo, even if we sometimes want to kill Carlo.'

'I thought you told me she was cool,' said the vampire, backing off.

'She is,' Gen assured him. 'Isn't that right, Abbey?'

I loosened my grip on the butter knife. 'Why are we talking to one of them?' I hissed. 'I thought we killed them, not exchanged small talk with them.'

'She's a feisty one, eh?' said Carlo.

'He's not with the Clan,' Gen explained. 'Not anymore.'

'So what, he's a snitch?'

The vampire slid under the table beside Gen. 'I prefer to think of myself more as a valued informer, your man on the inside, your Rosetta Stone, if you will.'

'Sounds to me like you're a prostitute without a pimp,' I replied.

Carlo considered this then nodded. 'Well, yes I suppose, but let's not split hairs, eh?'

'Why do you do it?' I asked, pulling away from him. 'Why do you sell out your own people?'

He cocked an eyebrow. 'Have you met my people?'

Fair point.

'Carlo isn't like the rest of his bloodline,' Gen explained. 'He's... different.'

'Unique, you might say,' Carlo grinned. 'Live and let live, that's my motto. Just because you're a monster, doesn't mean you have to act like an arsehole all the time.'

'He helps us out from time to time. Tells us things about the Clan.'

'So, a Judas from the Judas Clan,' I said. 'That's a bit bloody rich.'

Gen shrugged. 'So long as he carries on feeding us information we can use against them, we offer him immunity. Of course, if he should do anything to renege on that deal, you can stab him with that butter knife as many times as you like.'

'You know, words hurt, Gen,' said Carlo.

'Yes, but not as much as a butter knife to the heart.'

'On that note,' he said, chuckling nervously, 'how can I assist you lovely ladies?'

'My boyfriend was taken,' I told him. 'By your lot.'

'Not my lot, please and thank you,' Carlo corrected. 'I parted ways with those scumbags a long time ago. I'm a lone agent now.'

'I don't care. You're going to tell me where they've taken my man or no amount of immunity is going to save you from this knife, or fork, or any other utensil I choose to stick you with.'

Again, a couple of heads turned.

'All right, all right, dial it down a bit, will you?' Carlo whispered. 'I'm here to help. Jesus. Just tell me what they looked like. Give me something to go on and I'll be only too happy to point you in the right direction.'

'The man we're looking for had a birthmark on his face,' I told him.

Carlo's eyebrows shot up. 'One of those gross lumpy purple ones?'

I nodded.

'Big fat lad?' he asked, puffing out his cheeks and bracketing his sides with his arms.

'Yeah.'

'Ah, now him I do know.' He pulled out a pen and scribbled an address on the back of a paper napkin.

I went to take it, but he snatched it back.

'When do I get paid?' he asked, returning the pen to his pocket.

'Paid?'

Carlo turned to Gen. 'You mean you didn't tell her?'

Gen stared into her plate of bubble and squeak.

'What?' I said. 'What didn't you tell me?'

'Blood,' said Carlo. 'When I rat on the Clan I get blood. Gossip for you, a lovely bit of claret for me.'

'I'm sorry?'

'Just a little nibble,' replied Carlo, grinning.

I stared slack-jawed at him. 'Yeah, no, not happening, sorry. Gen, give him some blood and let's get out of here.'

'Angel blood?' said Carlo, making a face. 'I might as well drink bleach.'

'It's true,' said Gen, 'my blood would kill him outright.'

The two of them stared at me across the table. 'No chance. I'm not giving him my blood, not even a little bit.'

'It's in the covenant,' said Gen.

'I don't care what weird promises you've made to this freak, I'm not letting a vampire chew on my neck. And you really should have let me in on that part of the arrangement before we got here.'

'You only would have said no,' she replied.

'No fucking shit I would have, because I'm not mental.'

Carlo sighed and screwed up the napkin. 'Then if you don't mind, ladies, I have to feed before sunrise or I'll… well, starve to death.'

He stood up and smoothed down his denim waistcoat.

'Abbey,' said Gen, 'we need that information. That's our lead. Without it, Neil is dead. Do you understand that? He's dead. It's up to you.'

I stood and walked away, grunted and walked back, teeth clenched. 'Okay, wait,' I said. 'How much blood are we talking?'

Carlo tried to stay poker-faced, but I could make out a smile quirking his lips. He sat back down. 'Less than you'd give the doctor for a routine check-up,' he replied. 'I wouldn't ask, but without your kind donation I'd have to resort to less… savoury means.'

I sighed, closed my eyes, and saw Neil smiling back at me. *Shit.*

'Okay,' I said, reluctantly. 'Fine. You've got a deal.'

Gen relaxed as Carlo unbunched the napkin and slid it across the table to me.

I took it and gave it a read. The address he'd written was some place in Kensington I'd never heard of. 'You're telling me that if we go to this place we'll find Neil?'

'I can't say for sure,' Carlo replied. 'He could be there, or he could have been passed up the chain. That's if he isn't already dea—'

'In any case,' Gen cut in, 'it's the best and only lead we have right now.'

I grunted, placed some cash on the table, and tugged on my jacket. 'All right then,' I said. 'How do we do this?'

Carlo grinned. 'This way, madame.'

Then he led me outside to an alleyway untroubled by lamp light or casual passers-by.

28

Giving Carlo his donation was like losing my virginity—one little prick and it was gone—and just like losing my virginity, the experience meant a *lot* more to him than it did to me.

It turned out that the blood of the Nightstalker was like crack to Carlo; a powerful, irresistible narcotic that knocked him on his arse almost at once. By the time his needle-like fangs withdrew from my wrist, his breathing was shallow, his pupils the size of saucers, his limbs as soft as silly string. The man was high as a kite.

'Pleasure doing business with you,' he purred, his spine sliding down the alley wall until he was left squatting among the smelly relics of week-old takeaways.

I watched as Carlo's eyes rolled back into his skull. His jaw went slack and drool ran down his chin, pooling on the dirty ground. It was a sorry sight to behold, watching the junkie get his fix. I had to look away. I never thought I'd feel sorry for one of those bloodsucking freaks, but I actually left that alleyway feeling bad for the guy. Sympathy for the devil, and all that.

'I'm not going to catch anything, am I?' I asked Gen, spitting on the pin pricks in my wrist and giving them a rub.

'No,' she replied. 'The Sanctified one is immune to all vampiric diseases.'

'What about turning into one of them?' I asked.

'That's not how it works, but you shouldn't worry, the brand gives you immunity to that too.'

Good to know.

I checked my phone. It had gone five and was edging its way to half past. 'Come on,' I told Gendith. 'We'd better get going.'

We hailed another cab, this time to Kensington.

The night had grown long—very long—and I was sick and tired of having to ping pong all over the map. Honestly, I'd seen more of London in a single evening than I had the whole time I'd lived there.

We'd already been subjected to a half hour of Heart FM before the cab finally rolled into Kensington. I wiped some condensation from the window beside me and peered out at our surroundings. The streets of Kensington may not be paved in gold, but in terms of real estate, they might as well be. Everywhere I looked I saw money: brightly lit shops full of fancy hats and pricey doodads. The kind of places that only the cream of society have a need for. A playground for visiting sheikhs to run up bills on their black credit cards. A haven for the chinless, toffee-nosed, tax-dodging aristocracy.

We took a couple of corners and parked up next to a grand, red brick mansion block with a view over a well-tended communal garden.

'You think Neil's in there?' I asked Gen, after the cab had left us.

'Let's find out, shall we?'

I went to push past her, but she barred my way.

'This time we do it my way,' she insisted. 'No more charging into places like an angry bull.'

I nodded, remembering what had happened when I stepped in front of Pinstripe's Mercedes.

'Very well,' Gen replied, then checked the coast was clear, put a finger to her lips and gestured for me to follow her lead.

She effortlessly hopped a wrought iron fence and took a circuitous route through the mansion block's front garden, avoiding the motion detectors that triggered the building's floodlights. Watching her go was like watching a puma—a greased puma—slicing through the veld. I shadowed her with as much grace as I could muster, and together we snuck into the mansion block's front porch.

'Are you ready?' Gen whispered.

'Of course I am,' I shot back, though my stomach was doing cartwheels.

'The man we're going after won't give us what we want willingly, you understand that, right? This isn't going to be like putting the squeeze on the tailor. Vampires are tough. They can take a lot of pain.'

'I get it.'

'So you're willing to do whatever it takes to get the information we need?'

Her meaning was clear, and sounded all the more sinister coming from an angel.

'They took my boyfriend, Gen. If I need to staple his testicles to his forehead, that's what's going to happen.'

Gen dipped inside the front pocket of the gilet she was wearing and produced a leather wallet full of small, complicated-looking tools. She selected a couple of slim metal picks from her collection and inserted them into the door's keyhole, jiggling them to and fro. Moments later I heard a *click*, and the door was undone.

I followed Gen across a mosaic floor, then on to the hall's runner carpet and up a flight of stairs. We crept on to the next floor until we reached a door with a number matching the address on our napkin, then I watched Gen jimmy it open with as much ease as the first.

The lights were off, but I could hear the soft burble of a television coming from an adjoining room. I decided to take the lead, slowly drawing my dagger from its sheath and tiptoeing past Gen in the direction of the next room. On my way I passed a beautiful cast iron fireplace in its original cornice, and a generously-sized sash window overlooking the private garden below. All of this—all of this luxury, all of this privilege—stolen from under our noses. My fingers tightened on the handle of the dagger, a white-knuckle death grip.

I angled my head around the door frame of the TV room and

took a peek inside. Sat in the centre of the darkened space was a plush leather armchair facing a giant flat screen TV, and in that chair I saw a man, sat watching a film. Not a horror film, as you might expect, but a documentary on Minimalism. Something you might find on Netflix, add to your list with the best of intentions, then never actually get around to watching. I couldn't believe it. This gross fucker, surrounded by all of his wealth, all of his expensive material possessions, was sat there schooling himself on the joy of having less.

Holding my breath, I moved inside the room, padding across the polished hardwood floor, creeping towards the chair. I heard a sniffing sound and saw the nostrils of the chair's occupant twitch. He turned to look over his shoulder, but before he could rotate his head fully, I slipped the blade under his chin and brought its edge to the wattle of his fat throat.

'Make a noise and you go from being undead to dead-dead.'

Gen switched off the TV and dragged a lamp stand across the room, aiming it at his face before turning on its hot, bright light.

I could see the man clearly now. See the fangs in his mouth. See the livid purple mark on his cheek. This was our guy.

Birthmark was fat as a well-fed tick. The swollen stain that covered half his face stood proud of his skin like a bubble of blood fit to burst.

'Do you know who I am?' I breathed into his ear.

He nodded ever so slightly, setting his jowls a-jiggle.

'Then you know what you took from me,' I said, 'and you can probably guess what I'm going to do to you if I don't get him back.'

He nodded again.

'Good. So let's talk.'

'He's not here,' he whispered.

'Then where is he?'

He swallowed and his Adam's apple bobbed beneath his three chins, scraping the edge of the blade and making a nasty rasping sound. 'I can't tell you,' he said.

Gen pushed the lamp closer to his face, dazzling him, making him sweat. Up close and personal now, I saw tiny beads of blood ooze through the pores of his fat forehead.

'Tell us where you took him,' Gen demanded.

'I can't.'

'Wrong answer.' Gen lifted up a foot and ground the heel of her boot into the fat man's groin.

Birthmark squirmed and cried out in pain, but I clapped a hand over his puffy fish lips to stifle the noise.

'Why don't we try that again?' suggested Gen, placing her foot back on the floor. 'The boy you took, where is he now?'

'I can't tell you,' he said. 'If I say anything I'm a dead man.'

Gen picked up the TV remote and turned up the volume to mask the sound of what was to come. 'You did this to yourself,' she said, shrugging.

What followed was the most savage beating I'd ever witnessed. Layers of blubber rippled and danced as Gen batted the fat vamp about the place, bringing to mind a waterbed being subjected to a vigorous bone-sesh. By the time Gen was finished punishing the guy, his downstairs neighbours must have thought he'd turned his front room into a mosh pit.

'Please,' he begged, splashed across the parquet floor, broken and bloody. 'Please... stop.'

I looked down at the sorry bastard, lying there like a beached beluga whale. He was ugly enough before Gen had laid into him, but now he was grotesque. His eyes were swollen over with two purple blooms that matched his birthmark, and a stream of bloody spit drooled from his broken jaw.

From between his split lips came a pitiful moan. 'Please…' he begged.

Gen wiped some blood from her knuckles. 'Just tell me where he is and this stops.'

'Can't…' he wheezed, 'they'll… kill me.'

Despite the ferocious beating he'd taken, he still wouldn't squeal.

'And what do you think I'll do?' Gen raised a fist, ready to go at him some more, but now it was my turn.

'Let me try,' I whispered.

I straddled Birthmark's great, fat body, and set my rear down on his stomach.

'I know what you're thinking,' I sighed, resting my elbows on his copious man bosoms. 'I sympathise, I really do. It's like you're opening an umbrella in a phone booth, right?'

'What do you mean?' he groaned.

'I mean, whichever way you turn, you're going to get it in the eye.' I placed my free hand on his shoulder. 'Thing is, with your lot, you have a chance. You've got money, you can go underground, drop off the map. With me, there's no running.' I showed him the brand on my palm. 'Do you know what I did before I got this?' I asked.

'No.'

'I worked in a lost property office,' I told him. 'The big one on Baker Street. You know it?'

'Yes,' he wheezed. 'Saw it on... BuzzFeed.'

'That's the one. And it's all true you know? You wouldn't believe some of the stuff that made its way to us—prams, stuffed animals, telescopes—all kinds of junk. Most of it found a home eventually, either the owner would show up, or we'd auction it to the highest bidder.'

'Why are you telling me this?'

'I'm getting to that,' I replied. 'Now where was I? Oh yeah, the rest of the junk. The stuff we couldn't find a home for. That would just sit there in the basement, collecting dust, at least for a few months.' I tapped him on the shoulder. 'I bet you're wondering what happened to it after that, aren't you? What we did with the things that no one wanted.'

He grimaced, which I took for a yes.

'We destroyed them,' I explained. 'Stuck them in a great big crusher and flattened the lot. Because that's what we do with useless things. We get rid of them.'

I leaned in close enough that he could feel my breath on his face. Close enough that I could smell his aftershave failing to mask the stench of his leaking bladder.

'Are you catching my drift here?' I asked.

He nodded.

'So what's it going to be, big man? Are you going to tell me where Neil is, or do I crush you like an unclaimed dildo?'

'Fuck you,' he croaked.

'What's that now?' I replied, using my dagger to draw a thin red line across his jugular.

'I said, fuck y—' The vampire's flabby jaw clenched as I pressed the tip of the dagger against his neck, the point slowly sliding into his skin.

'The Admiralty Citadel!' he cried.

'Come again?'

Gen leaned in. 'Did you say the Admiralty Citadel?' He nodded and Gen turned to me. 'It's an old Ministry of Defence building near St. James' Park.' She turned back to our prisoner. 'You're telling us that the Citadel is where they're keeping Neil?'

'Yes,' he said. 'Or what's left of him anyway.'

'What did you just say?' I asked, returning the point of the dagger to his neck.

'Your boyfriend is as good as dead,' he hissed, his face lit with fury. 'You don't stand a chance of getting inside the Citadel. You never did and you never will. Because you're weak. Weak little humans. Nothing but blood bags for the master. Cattle to be cull—'

He didn't get to finish his sentence on account of me plunging my dagger into his heart and turning him into a hill of ash.

'Jesus!' cried Gen, taken by surprise.

'What, I should've left him alive? This is what we do, right? This is why I was given this brand; to kill vampires.'

She brushed some ash from the sleeve of her hoodie, placed her hands on her hips, and smiled.

'Damn, girl, maybe you've got some Nightstalker in you after all.'

29

It was a touch shy of seven in the morning and the sun was due to come up in just over an hour. Thank God it was winter and the nights were long, because there was still so much left to do.

Having snuck out of Birthmark's flat, Gendith insisted we contact Vizael and bring him up to speed with the mission. Since the gas tower was way across the other side of town and Neil was about to be very dead, we'd have to deliver the news by phone.

'Give me your mobile,' Gen insisted.

I handed it over. 'I've been meaning to ask, Gen, why don't you have a phone of your own?'

'Oh, I do,' she replied, 'it's just cheaper to use yours.'

Viz picked up after a couple of rings and we huddled around the phone, the glow of its screen illuminating our faces like a campfire. After a frustrating few minutes of trying to explain to the old man how to put the call on speakerphone, we were able to fill him in on the bullet points of what he'd missed.

'Judas is alive?' he said, flabbergasted.

'Yes,' I said, 'but we can't get stuck on that right now. We need to find a way into the Citadel so we can rescue Neil.'

'Of course, of course,' he replied, trying his best to sound professional but sounding quite rattled.

We waited impatiently while Viz fetched some research materials from his bookshelf. I heard him leaf through some dry, old pages, then he said, 'I'm afraid there isn't much to go on. The Admiralty Citadel was constructed during the Second World War and occupied by the MoD until they sold it to a third party around ten years ago. Seeing as how that lined up roughly with the emergence of the Clan, I made a note that they might have purchased the property. I don't have any evidence to back that up though.'

'Neil's there,' I said, feeling the brand throb on my palm. 'That's where they've taken him, I know it.'

'In that case,' said Viz, 'the only question is, how do we get you inside? The place is a fortress.'

He was not wrong. I'd already taken a minute to Google the Citadel before making the call, and seen pictures of a stone building shrouded by creepers and surrounded by high, squared-off hedges. It looked pretty formidable. Impenetrable, even.

'They built the Citadel to protect the military's top brass in the event of a bombing,' Viz said. 'It's heavily fortified, and I have no clue what you'll find inside, even if you do figure out a way to get in there.'

Something about the way he said those last words gave me an inkling of an idea. Yes, the Citadel was bomb-proof, and no, we weren't about to scale its walls and lay siege to the place, but there had to be some other way of gaining entry. A back door, or a secret entrance, or maybe an underground—

'I'll call you back,' I blurted, stabbing the phone's red button.

'What are you doing?' asked Gen.

I held up a finger to shush her then swiped through my contacts and hit Call.

The phone rang a few times then, 'What do you want?' demanded a croaky voice on the other end of the line. It was Gary, my clown shoe of an ex-boss.

'Listen, Gary, this is important—'

He sucked in a deep breath and I could practically see his pigeon chest puff full of hot air. 'Abbey, if you've called to apologise about what you said last night—'

'I don't give a shit about that,' I assured him, taking the wind out of his sails. 'What I want is to know what you were telling the temp in the cafeteria.'

'What?' he spluttered.

'The other day, when you were trying to chat her up...' He started to protest, but I cut him short. 'You were banging on about a hidden tunnel that ran off the Circle line and led to some army bunker.'

'What's this about, Abbey?'

'I want you to tell me the name of that bunker.'

'And what if I don't want to?'

'If you don't, I'm going to come by the office, stop in at Human Resources, and tell them how you made unwelcome advances on me.'

'That's not true—'

'Sure it is, at least until I told you I had a boyfriend and you started lumping me with double-shifts and telling me how to dress. And you know what, since I'm popping by, I bet I can get some of the other girls to talk to H.R. too, because this isn't your first offence, is it, mate? There's a reason the girls all call you Pepé Le Pew, and it's not just because you fucking stink.' I buffed my nails on my jacket and examined my cuticles. 'So, what do you say, Gazza? Wanna help me out?'

I heard a fit of coughing followed by a long pause, then he finally spoke. 'Fine. Whatever. The bunker's called the Admiralty Citadel. Happy now?'

'Very.'

I hung up the call and spun around to Gen.

'I know how we can get in there,' I said. 'There's a tunnel that connects the Citadel to the Underground network. We'll find our way in there, bust inside, and come up right under their noses.'

Gendith didn't seem so sure. 'We don't have any schematics of the building, and there's no telling how many vampires could be holed up there. This is the sort of thing you plan for, Abbey. Tactically speaking, running this mission now makes no sense.'

I shot her a cold look. 'Ever since I got this brand, you've been telling me I don't have what it takes to be the Nightstalker, now I find you a hive of vampires and you go gunshy? Are we in this fight or not?'

My phone rang. It was Viz. 'Where are we at?' he asked.

I answered the call on speakerphone. 'I've found us a way in,' I told him, 'and I'm going to take it.'

'I see,' he replied. 'And Gendith, does she approve of this course of action?'

I looked to Gen, who wavered on an answer. Finally, she bobbed her head. 'Yes. Okay. Let's do this.'

'Excellent,' said Viz. 'But listen, if you're going to do this, you'll have to do it as a team. The only way the two of you will survive that Citadel is by working together. No more squabbles. No more pettiness or hurt feelings. You must put aside your differences and combine your efforts to succeed.'

He was right, even if it did feel an awful lot like mansplaining.

I turned to Gen. 'Come on then, what do you say? Girl Power?'

I held up a hand for a high five, but once again it remained disappointingly un-fived.

Finally, she made a long, frustrated sigh and gave me some skin.

'Girl Power,' she groaned.

30

Using my LPO pass, which had yet to be cancelled, we blagged our way into Westminster Underground before the shutters opened for the day.

Gendith followed as I made my way speedily through the ticket barriers and down the steps to the Circle Line. The station was bare except for a skeleton crew of staff sipping coffees from a shared thermos, readying themselves for the day ahead.

We arrived on the eastbound platform, which was quiet and chilly, like a crime scene waiting on a murder. Together, we walked to the platform's end and stopped at the mouth of the tunnel next to a lightning bolt sign that warned, NO PASSENGERS BEYOND THIS POINT.

'This is the way,' I said, flicking on a torch that Viz had given me.

I aimed an ear into the tunnel and listened. All was silent. I held up a hand to check for a breeze, but the tunnel was still and didn't give off the telltale push of air that warned of an oncoming train. I stared into the maw of the tunnel, a great grey snake, coiled beneath the city. The beam of my torch shone pale and feeble, lost in the beast's insides, swallowed whole.

I sucked down a steadying breath then stepped off the ramp at the end of the platform and into the tunnel beyond. Gen followed, and our footfalls echoed off the shaft's curved wall like ghostly cries. Soon we'd left the safety of the platform behind completely. The real world was lost to us now. Now it was just the two of us in the pressing, claustrophobic darkness, a couple of foolhardy adventurers with nothing more than a fragile lance of torchlight to light our way.

Desperate to bring some warmth to our grim surroundings, I struck up a conversation. 'So what exactly goes down if the baddies manage to pull this thing off?' I whispered.

'Pull what off?' asked Gen.

'Their whole resurrection scheme. If the vamps get the blood they need to restore their master to full power, what then?'

'Oh, you know, the Seven Seals crack open, crows blacken the sky, the rivers turn to blood. Basically The End Times: Judas Iscariot and his children, kicking in the doors of heaven and laying waste to paradise.'

I laughed, I'm not sure why exactly. 'Okay, so no pressure then.'

We journeyed deeper into the city's twisting, subterranean network until we rounded a bend and I saw a passageway branching off from the main tunnel. It was barricaded though, cut off by a muscular metal gate decorated with a stern NO ENTRY sign.

'This must be the passage to the Citadel,' I said.

I grabbed the gate's iron bars and tried to wrench it free. It wouldn't budge, not even an inch. The entrance was welded shut. I rolled up my sleeves and had another go, but even after I saw cords standing up on my forearms like knotted garden hose, nothing gave. Gen stepped in to assist me, but there was no shifting the thing, even with the two of us working together.

So much for Vizael's parting advice. Girl Power, my arse.

'Can't you use your magic to bust it open?' I asked.

'Magic?' Gen replied.

'Like you did with those force fields back in the alley.'

She shook her head. 'It doesn't work like that. I can only manipulate sunlight, and there's not much of that down here.'

I heard a noise. A buzzing sound echoed down the tunnel.

'What's that?' I asked.

'A train?' Gen suggested.

The buzzing noise was getting louder. Shit, what now? I thought about pressing myself to the wall to evade the oncoming train, but it wouldn't have done any good, the tunnel was too tight.

'Wait a second,' said Gen, 'that's not a train.'

I swung the torch down the tunnel and picked up a flash of movement ahead.

Something flitted through the air. Some tiny creature. I took it for a stray bird at first, but it turned out to be something far more exotic. It was a miniature woman, around six inches tall, elfin-featured, and borne upon a pair of gossamer-thin butterfly wings.

'Is that… a fairy?' I asked.

'Yep,' Gen replied.

As I watched in rapt silence, the fairy performed a lavish aerial display, spiralling through the tunnel like a shooting star, leaving a trail of glitter in her wake. I couldn't believe my eyes. Yeah, I'd seen vampires and angels and werewolves and gnomes already, but a real-life, no-fucking-around fairy?

The creature performed a couple of graceful loop-the-loops then hovered just beyond my reach, regarding me with her dewy brown eyes. I was utterly hypnotised. It was as though she were staring into my very soul. I outstretched an arm, inviting her to take a seat on my palm, but just as she was about to set down, Gendith struck out a hand and seized the fairy around the waist.

'What are you doing?' I asked.

Just then, Gen's diminutive captive hissed and bared a mouthful of razor-sharp fangs.

'What the hell?' I cried, as the demonic fairy seethed and spat, thrashing around in the angel's grasp.

In the blink of an eye, the creature had transformed from Tinkerbell to a rabid, snarling animal, screaming like an untapped firehose full of scalded babies.

'Vermin,' Gen replied, tightening her grip. 'Lurking beneath the City like rats.'

'But she was so cute!'

'There's nothing cute about them. Have you any idea how these little monsters reproduce?'

'Well, given that up until a couple of days ago I thought fairies belonged on Christmas trees, I'm going to say no.'

Gen squeezed, and the fairy rasped in pain. 'They lay eggs,' she explained, 'on the surface. Not in nests, but in the safest, warmest places they can find.'

'What, like heating ducts?'

'Like people.' She gave me a moment to let that sink in. 'Homeless people usually, asleep, out in the open. The fairy lays its eggs inside of them—you don't need to know how—and then they wait.'

'Wait for what?'

'The egg has an effect on the victim. Puts thoughts in his head. Soon enough, he gets an idea that he needs to go underground, so he heads into the sewers, and that's where it happens.'

'He lays the egg?'

'No,' she said, tightening her grip on the fairy to such a degree that her eyes bugged from her perfect little skull. 'The victim doesn't give birth, at least not like that. The egg hatches inside them and its contents chew their way out.'

I felt a wave of nausea wash over me. 'That's... I mean, Jesus wept.'

'A fresh batch of monsters, bursting from their host's stomach and leaving his husk to rot, only so they can grow up, lay more eggs, and repeat the whole, sick cycle.'

Gen brought the fairy to her face, opened her mouth, and bit down, tearing the creature in half.

'What the fuck!' I cried. 'Couldn't you have just stamped on it or something?'

Gen finished chewing and swallowed. 'I didn't do that just to kill it. I did it in preparation for what comes next. Fairies are full of magic. Eating them gives us a boost of power, like a magical energy drink.'

'Right. Okay. Wait, did you say "us"?'

She held out the remains of the fairy and gave me a nod. 'Tuck in.'

'Oh no. No way. I'm not touching that.'

I felt a breeze on my face as wind streamed through the

tunnel, clutching scattered pieces of rubbish and twirling them in the air.

A train.

There was no mistaking it this time.

I swung my head around, frantically looking for a way out, but there was no chance of outrunning the oncoming train. No chance of stepping aside. The only way we were going to survive it was by busting through that metal gate and getting into the safety of the passageway beyond.

I grabbed a metal bar and pulled at the gate with all my might, but the result was the same as before. I just didn't have the strength.

'Are you going to help or not?' I yelled at my so-called partner.

'I'm trying to,' Gen replied, waggling the rest of the fairy at me.

I saw lights sweep around the tunnel ahead and felt the ground beneath me vibrate. 'Stop dicking around,' I begged.

'If you eat this you'll have that thing down in no time,' Gen assured me.

I heard the train tracks rattle as the rolling stock rounded the bend. Shivers rippled across my body as the tunnel shook, loosening dust from above.

'Okay, fine!' I turned to Gen and snatched the remains of the fairy from her. 'You know, you really don't act much like an angel.'

She gave me what I can only describe as a very non-saintly grin. 'No, I do not.'

I sank my teeth into fairy meat and swallowed it down like I was trying to win a Bushtucker Trial.

An awful lot had happened in the last couple of days. I'd found out God was real, donated blood to a vampire, and now I'd chowed down on a fairy. Funny how these things go sometimes. To think, it was only a little while ago that I thought I was missing out on new experiences by not going to university.

The effect of the fairy kicked in quick and hard. At first I felt hot—uncomfortably so—but then that shifted as time slowed down and the buzz really hit me. Bells rang in my ears. Sparks danced upon the hairs on the back of my arms. Raw power flushed through my system, invigorating, thrilling. My brand went supernova and turned retina-searingly bright. I bunched my hand into a fist to dim the glare, but rays of light razored between my fingers, burning like flaming swords. I felt like I could sprint a mile in lead boots. Burn holes through brick walls with my eyeballs. Punch my way to China.

The train roared towards us, deafening, furious, sounding its horn and applying its squealing brakes, but it was too late to stop.

I grabbed the welded-shut iron gate with one hand and tore it off its hinges like it was nothing.

31

We threw ourselves into the passageway and the train hurtled past us, skimming our heels as it flew by.

When Gen climbed to her feet she was laughing. Hysterically. A full-throated belly laugh. It was a sound I'd scarcely imagined possible.

'What's so funny?' I demanded, dusting myself down.

She wiped a tear from her eye. 'Lighten up,' she said. 'This is the good part. We made it into their nest. Now we go vampire killing.'

I could have done without that little pantomime back there, but I had to admit, I did feel pretty amped. The fairy magic burned hot inside me still, pumping me up like a gallon of steroids chased by a bucket of Red Bull. I don't know that I found the situation quite as amusing as Gen did, but wiping out a hive of vampires did sound like a pretty good way to let off some steam.

'Let's finish this,' I said, drawing my dagger and filling the passageway with its flickering blue glow.

Gen produced her morning star, drew its chain taut, and performed a quick flurry of whips and spins. Having warmed herself up, she nodded and we set off down the corridor, into the lion's den.

The crumbling passageway was dark and sinister, and infused with a sickly-sweet butcher shop odour.

'This is definitely the way,' said Gen, nostrils twitching.

I checked the time. We had fifteen minutes until sunrise. A quarter-hour to save my boyfriend's life. I prayed we were on time. Any moment now, night would turn to morning, and Neil would be done for.

We carried on into the bunker proper, following the source of the smell down several winding corridors until we reached a set of double doors leading to the Citadel's inner sanctum.

It wasn't what I'd expected at all.

Instead of a dingy chamber decorated with candles and a pentagram painted in blood, we found an antiseptic room with green tiled walls. I had to keep reminding myself that we weren't dealing with chanting cultists dressed in robes and brandishing wavy knives and upside-down crosses. Vampires were surgical, white collar killers, so it was only fitting that their sacrifice site looked more like an operating theatre than the setting of a black mass.

The room was bright. Bright enough to perform brain surgery by. Blazing overhead lamps illuminated stainless steel trolleys lined with sterile surgical implements, and in the centre of it all, an aluminium table supported a semi-naked man attached to breathing apparatus.

'Neil!' I cried, dashing to his side and wrapping my arms around him. He didn't respond. Instead, he just lay there with his eyes shut, stock still. 'What did they do to him?' I asked, tears stinging my eyes.

I pressed my ear to his chest and was grateful to hear the soft beat of his heart.

'He's alive but sedated,' said Gen, pointing to the IV drip in his arm.

Neil looked so fragile on that cold metal counter, dressed in his boxer shorts, his ribcage showing through his pale white chest. Surrounding him was an inch-deep gutter that ran the perimeter of the table. The gutter lead to a drain that connected to a downpipe, which presumably funnelled vital fluids into the blood viaduct that Judas had told me about. I was pleased to see that the table was spotlessly clean, unmarked by even a drop of blood.

'Thank God,' I said, breathing a long sigh of relief.

'Oh, so *now* you're religious?' said Gen, raising an eyebrow.

I shot her a withering look and carefully removed the needle from Neil's forearm. He was fastened to the table by four thick straps securing his wrists and ankles. 'Cover my back while I get him out of here, will you?' I said, unfastening his bonds.

I was just about to hoik Neil over my shoulder and take off when I heard a slow clapping sound. Turning around, I saw Pinstripe strolling into the chamber.

'*Fools rush in where angels fear to tread,*' said Pinstripe, quoting from an old song. 'Or not, as the case may be.'

I placed Neil gently back on the table. 'Please don't do this,' I said.

'What was that?' asked Pinstripe, cupping a hand to his ear. 'Do I hear the dreaded Nightstalker pleading for her life?'

I snorted. 'Oh, God, no. What I mean is, can we please just cut to the chase? You know, do away with the witty banter and the whole staring match thing?'

His expression darkened, betraying a mixture of disappointment and anger. 'What are you talking about?'

'Don't get me wrong, I'm up for a ruckus, but it's been a long old day and I'd really like to get home and finish watching that new season of Stranger Things. I hear Steve Harrington's hair is *incredible* in this one.'

His eyelid twitched and a bead of ruby red blood emerged from his wounded tear duct and tracked down his cheek, forcing him to dab at it with a handkerchief to restore some masculinity.

He tried for a smile. 'What exactly is it you think is going on here, girl?'

'What do I think? I think you tried to turn my boyfriend into your boss's personal blood bag, and now you're going to get your head kicked in.'

This time he succeeded in smiling. 'You honestly think I went to all of this trouble for *his* blood?'

I didn't like the sound of those italics. Not one bit.

Pinstripe fixed me with a psychopath's stare. 'Whatever gave you the idea that I'd supply the master with the anaemic swill pumping through that boy's veins?'

I saw Gen's face drop as the pair of us arrived at the same realisation. This was a trap, and Neil was just the bait.

A dozen suited goons entered the room, each of them wearing the mark of Judas upon his forehead. The last two closed the doors behind them, sealing us all together in the windowless, subterranean chamber.

'This weakling's blood would be a mere drop in the ocean for our purpose,' said Pinstripe. 'But the blood of the Nightstalker…' He kissed his fingertips and tossed them joyfully into the air. 'That would be worth a thousand sacrifices.'

Of course it would. This was never about some symbolic victory. Pinstripe didn't kidnap Neil just to make me feel bad. He didn't kidnap him to bolster his reputation. He did it to lure me here and drain me dry.

'Now,' said Pinstripe, turning to his men. 'Get that pathetic lump off of my table and strap her down.'

I drew the dagger. 'I'd like to see you try.'

'I'm so glad you said that,' he replied, drawing a barber's shop razor from the pocket of his jacket and unfolding the blade.

With a nod of his head, the goons came for us, their complexions white, their flinty eyes ringed with kohl-black circles. Each of them drew a matching weapon, a large, serrated hunting knife. It was the kind of knife a yuppie might carry if he wanted to look tough during a hike across the Lake District, only these boys meant business.

My dagger looked decidedly small by comparison.

'Flick it,' said Gen, as the goons continued to advance.

'Pardon me?'

'The dagger. Flick it.'

Not sure what I was doing it for, I shrugged and snapped the dagger with my wrist. Much to my surprise, it extended like a police baton, transforming from a knife into a full-blown sword.

'What the hell, Gen?'

'Cool, huh?'

'It turns into a frigging broadsword? I *really* feel like you should have led with that. I can't believe I've been fighting with a toothpick this whole time!'

I wasn't about to waste another second, so I got stuck into our attackers right away.

As the first of the vampire goons stepped into my range, I swatted his dumb knife aside and swiped off his head with one clean stroke. The decapitated noggin flew off like a champagne cork and thudded to the ground.

It was a hell of an opening statement.

The goons went still as they took in the sight of their companion's head rolling across the floor at their feet.

'What are you waiting for?' screamed Pinstripe. 'Kill them both and make a mess doing it!'

The mob obeyed, charging as one.

The second vampire who entered my kill-zone didn't fare any better than the first. I buried the sword in his stomach, which burst like mouldy fruit and spilled a pile of fetid guts on the ground.

Meanwhile, Gen set into the rest, throwing herself into the vampires' midst with her morning star and tearing through them like a wheat thresher. She struck out at the attacking vampires, landing a tattoo of weltering blows upon them and earning at least three notches on the handle of her weapon as she beat a path through the undead horde.

I fought hard and I fought angry. Vampires fell left and right of me, hitting the ground like bags of wet cement. It was as though the sword was wired into my central nervous system. I didn't even need to engage my brain to use the thing, the blade found its mark as easily as my eye fell upon it.

One of the vampires lunged at me with a clumsy stab, but I sidestepped his attack and landed a blow to his side. Abbey Beckett for the win! The blade bit into the goon's midriff and carved off a great, slippery flap of flesh. As his eyes rolled back into his head and his knees unhinged, I moved on to my next target, slashing him across the throat. The vampire's head tipped back suddenly, revealing a gaping neck wound that vented a spray of blood, painting my face crimson.

Oh, it was on. On like Donkey Kong in a thong smoking a bong.

A second vampire went to avenge his murdered brother, but the semi-decapitated goon—head draped over his back like a hunchback's hump—hadn't cottoned on to the fact that he was dead yet, and came out swinging, accidentally sinking his bowie knife into his would-be avenger's gut.

As yet another vampire met his maker, I saw a new goon coming my way, locked into a full charge. Unfortunately for him, he managed to slip on a fallen comrade's spilled innards, and found himself sliding helplessly in the direction of my sword tip. With only a slight tilt of its blade, I was able to skewer him through his screaming mouth, piercing his head like a cocktail stick through an olive.

Across the room I saw Gen, battling the vampire heavies like a woman possessed, smashing one in the head so hard that his skull cracked open like an egg. The fight was going decidedly in our favour, at least until I felt a punch to my stomach that folded me in half and sent my sword spinning across the deck. One of the vamps had sensed my distraction and landed me in the gut with a fist like a cannonball.

I keeled over backwards, hugging my abdomen. Immediately, I felt four bodies pile on top of me, their claws digging into my flesh, fangs snapping at my neck. My surroundings went dark as the scrum of torsos and limbs knotted together and blotted out the light above. The sound of battle turned muffled and quiet as the vampires pressed down harder, suffocating me, starving my brain of oxygen. I struggled and fought, but couldn't worm my way free of the tangle.

My resolve faltered fast. I didn't belong here. Not "here" at the bottom of a pile of vampires, but "here" at all. How had I gotten myself into this mess? How had I wound up in this place? If I hadn't mouthed off at my boss and been stuck with the night shift, some other chump would have picked up that dagger. Someone else would have been given the brand and named Nightstalker. This was never *my* destiny. I had no business battling the forces of darkness. I should never have been allowed a look behind the veil. I was an ordinary person, a regular member of the public. A wage slave, a normal, just like everyone else.

I tasted blood in my mouth, coppery and thick... and that's when I realised something. That was my blood. The same blood that had been pumping through my veins when I fought off the vampire in my office. The same blood coursing through my arteries when I jammed my keys in Pinstripe's eye. *My blood.* And not one of those fanged fucks was getting a drop of it.

I went off like a landmine, exploding to my feet and sending the vampires flying in all directions. In a flash, I snatched up my sword, swung it in a wide arc, and took the throats of the whole pile. Four vampires fell to their knees clutching their necks. They might as well have tried tapping a fire hose with toilet paper for all the good it did.

The Desk Babysitter had flipped her desk and gone absolutely berserk.

32

Only two more vampires remained now, one last goon and the final boss himself, the man in the pinstripe suit.

I saw Gendith overcome the goon with zero difficulty, clobbering him so hard that he hit the ground looking like a horse had stepped on his face. Now it was just her and Pinstripe. She charged at him, weapon swinging, and was almost upon her mark when—

Pinstripe vanished into thin air, reappeared behind her, and brought his cut throat razor to her neck.

He laughed and turned to me. 'Oh, I'm sorry, did you forget I could do that?'

Gen drew a couple of ragged breaths. 'Don't worry about me,' she croaked, 'just take him down.'

'How very noble of you,' said Pinstripe, keeping the blade at her throat, 'but I'm afraid neither of you is leaving this room alive...'

I saw his arm tense and knew I only had one chance.

I hurled my sword at him, and as it pinwheeled through the air, it compacted, changing back into a dagger. The blade turned over a couple of times, dead on target, but just as it was about to sink into Pinstripe's face, he pulled his head aside and the tip of the knife buried itself in the wall behind him.

'Oh, so we're throwing things now, are we?' he mocked. 'Well, if that's the way we're playing it…'

He raised his free hand, fingers splayed, and as he did, the surgical implements on a nearby trolley levitated into the air and swivelled to face me, pointy ends first.

Whoosh.

I dived to avoid them, but I wasn't quick enough. A pair of scalpels darted through the air and struck me in the hands, piercing my palms and pinning me to the wall. The scream that came out of my mouth was so loud I almost popped my own eardrums.

Before Gen could retaliate on my behalf, Pinstripe clubbed her across the back of the skull and sent her sprawling to the ground, unconscious.

'Gen!'

I tried to pull myself free from the wall, but struggling only acted like a magnifying glass for the pain, enlarging it and bringing it into sharper focus.

I was in agony.

Pinstripe shrugged and offered a devilish grin. 'Did you really think this was going to go your way, girl? Did you honestly believe I'd let you beat me?' He ran a hand through his crow feather black hair. 'I've been here before, many, many times. You won't be the first person to die in this room, my love, far from it. As a matter of fact… you won't even be the first *Nightstalker* to die here.'

But for all the malice in his voice, his speech sounded empty and rehearsed, like an ageing magician's tired old patter. It was true that he'd been here before. True that he'd repeated this little diatribe of his, over and over. He was half-arsing this. Going through the motions. Treating me like another item on his to-do list. And that, more than anything else, was the thing that really pissed me off.

The anger acted like petrol poured on a bonfire. I screamed and threw my arms forward, wrenching my hands free of the wall, and as I did, the scalpels pinning me there dragged through the meat of my palms.

A lance of pain pierced my skull and threw colourful spots

before my eyes. As I fell to my knees, nursing my wounds, Pinstripe chuckled. 'Still got a little fight left, have you? That's what I like about you fearless vampire slayers, you always add a little spice to the kill. So many humans just wilt away as I cut short their lives and take what's mine.'

He began to move slowly towards me, relishing my fear.

'Stay back!'

He laughed as he continued his approach, licking his lips. 'Oh, Nightstalker, I bet you taste wonderful.'

'Sorry,' I said, 'but I'm not on the menu.'

I threw out a hand, willing my errant dagger to return to my bloody grip. It did its best to obey, but sadly for the dagger—though not for me—it ran into some resistance along the way. The nature of that resistance was Pinstripe, who happened to be blocking the weapon's path in a most unfortunate manner.

'Oh,' said the vampire, right before he found himself stalling the dagger's momentum with the back of his head.

Blood erupted from his mouth as the weapon pierced the nape of his neck and ejected through his face. For a moment, the lodged blade sat beneath his tongue, making it stick between his lips in futile mockery, then the dagger disappeared through the hole and landed back in my grip.

Pinstripe stood dumbly for a moment, blood pumping from his wound, *phut phut phut* against the walls—just like I promised—then he collapsed face-down on the ground, vomiting great scarlet gushes.

I wiped the dagger on my jeans and returned it to its sheath. Job done. Clambering to my feet, I hobbled over to Gen, praying she was all right. Thankfully, she was already starting to come around by the time I made it over there.

'Did you get him?' she groaned, rubbing the back of her head.

It made my face ache to do it, but I sketched out a smile. 'It's like you said, Gen: Girl Power.'

But we weren't out of the woods just yet.

The room began to shake uncontrollably. I saw an aluminium trolley go skittering across the floor as if it had a mind of its own, and watched as flakes of masonry floated down from above. Neil jerked from side to side on his metal table. For a moment I thought he was awake, but it was only the tremor throwing him about.

This was Pinstripe's doing.

I looked over to see him on his knees, blood soaking the front of his suit like a big red bib. How he was alive still I had no idea, but he was using his fingers to trace the air with some sort of complex invocation. Blood foamed from his mouth, gushing forth and collecting on the ground, but instead of pooling, it tracked along like a river.

As Gen and I watched, more rivers appeared as blood drained from Pinstripe's dead goons, forming a crisscrossing delta that ran towards a single point in the centre of the room.

'Blood magic,' Gen hissed.

I went to get up so I could stop whatever it was Pinstripe was doing, but no sooner had I found my feet than I was knocked sideways by a sudden gust of wind.

Pinstripe grinned, blood gumming his shattered teeth. 'Good-night, Nightstalker,' he said, then tipped forwards and died face down on the floor.

The contents of the room swirled and eddied about at a rate of knots—scalpels, forceps, aluminium trays—skimming my flesh, dashing off the room's walls. At the centre of all this din and strife—at the heart of the howling mass—a figure began to emerge, a human silhouette growing ever more distinct. Ever more alive.

'What is that?' I screamed over the roar of the tempest, battling for my voice to be heard.

'A blood golem,' Gendith called back, her voice crumpled, her face lined with defeat.

I had no idea what a blood golem was, but it was obvious that something from another world was taking a toehold in ours. Something powerful. Something fearsome.

The figure at the eye of the hurricane was almost solid now, and growing still. It was the figure of a giant man, built like a gorilla, arms outstretched as if pushing through some invisible curtain.

'How do I fight it?' I screamed.

'You don't,' Gendith roared back, 'you might as well try fighting the sea.'

'Then what do we do?'

'We die.'

As I fought to stay upright against the tempest, a scalpel tore by my face, narrowly missing my eye and painting my cheek with a blusher of blood. I cried out in pain, but the sound was lost in the gale. Shielding my face, I cast my eyes to the ground and saw the rivers of blood draining into the golem had almost dried up. Soon the monster would belong to this world entirely.

Unless…

Something about the situation we'd found ourselves in made me think of Neil's book, specifically the part where the Wizard and the Warlock combined their powers to defeat the big bad. And that made me think of something that someone had recently told me...

I turned to Gendith. 'You're right, I can't fight this thing,' I shouted. 'But *we* can.'

'What are you saying?'

'Do you trust me?'

'Yes. Well, mostly. Why?'

'Good enough. Give me your hand.'

Gen glanced to the golem, which had almost grown to full height. Without further hesitation, she placed her hand in mine, uncertain what for.

We stood there, hands linked, united as one.

'Okay, so what now?' said Gen shouting to be heard over the noise.

'You know, you ask a lot of questions,' I said, grinning. Then I turned her hand over and sliced her across the palm with my blade.

To say she looked betrayed would be selling it short.

'Motherfucker!'

As Gen stumbled back, the cut opened up, spilling blood—royal blue angel blood—which slithered from the wound in throbbing gushes to join the rivers of red tracking across the chamber floor. The golem's lifeblood; the raw materials of its existence.

At first, the blue met the red like oil in water, then the angel blood began to infuse with the vampire blood, hissing and spitting. The golem shuddered, its entire body convulsing, and then it let out a tortured howl as the Yang met its Ying.

'*Ebony and Ivory...*' I sang.

Then the monster exploded, knocking me and Gen to the floor as we were showered in a geyser of cold, lifeless gunk.

I sat up, laughing and wiping blood from my eyes.

I did it. *We did it.*

The golem was gone.

The fight was over.

Gen sat up and looked around, bewildered, then winced as she clutched at her lacerated hand, cursing my name in some dead language.

'Hold still,' I told her, shuffling over on my knees and applying pressure to the wound with one hand as I tore off one of her sleeves with the other.

'What did you do?' she bleated.

'I killed the big bad.'

'I can see that, but why did you cut me?'

'I remembered what Carlo said about angel blood being bleach to vampires, and I guess I just ran with it.'

'It hurt like hell.'

'You'll live,' I told her.

A couple of minutes later I'd managed to stem the flow of blood by tying it off with a tourniquet.

Gen inspected my handiwork and flexed her fingers. 'Not bad,' she admitted.

'Yeah, well, I am my office's resident first aider.'

Gen looked at me coldly then laughed. 'Maybe you're not so terrible,' she said.

I looked around at all the dead bodies, at the room drenched in blood, and had to agree. I crouched down by Pinstripe's body, checked his pockets, and found the lock of hair he'd stolen from me.

Yeah. Not so terrible.

33

The first rays of sunshine kissed the gas tower as the grey light of morning bled through the streets of Bethnal Green.

Vizael had called us back to base for a debrief, and while Gendith gave him her report, I spoke with Neil.

'So… vampires are real?' he asked, still trying to make sense of the situation he'd found himself in. We'd begun the conversation shortly after I'd destroyed the blood golem (once he'd stopped screaming at the sight of all the dead bodies anyway), and the discussion was still in effect.

'Yeah, vampires are real,' I replied. 'Real arseholes.'

I fessed up to the lot. The monsters, the angels, the whole stopping the apocalypse shebang.

'And that N on your hand,' he said, tracing a thumb along the zig-zags of the brand, 'I'm guessing that doesn't stand for Neil after all, right?'

'No,' I admitted, 'it stands for Nightstalker.'

'Oh,' he said, smiling, 'cool name.'

Viz hobbled over to us on his ivory-handled walking stick. 'Pardon me,' he said, 'but may I speak with you alone?'

'Okay,' I said, worried where this was headed.

Gen cleared the room, taking a very tired and confused Neil with her.

Viz gestured for me to take a chair, and we each took a seat across the same cracked coffee table we'd sat at the first time he tried to convince me to become the Nightstalker.

'Well done, Abbey, ' he said, reaching over to place a hand on my shoulder. 'I always knew you were worthy of the brand.'

'Thanks,' I said, and meant it. I meant it so much I began to cry; great, heaving sobs that wracked my body from top to toe.

'There, there,' said Viz getting up from his seat and taking a knee before me.

He wiped a smear of blood from my face and pecked me on the forehead, warming my heart like a baked potato, fresh from the oven.

I smiled back at him. 'Can I please go home now?'

'Yes,' he chuckled, 'of course.'

'Thank Christ,' I gasped, wiping some sob snot from my nose.

Viz helped me to my feet—or I helped him, it didn't seem to matter—and patted me on the back. 'You just passed your biggest test so far, Abbey, so go home, rest, enjoy a normal life for a day or two, because our fight—the fight to end all fights—has only just begun.'

By the time I'd finished filling Neil in on the missing details, the two of us had found our way back to Thamesmead, back to our flat. My stigmata had healed by then, and the pair of us were already feeling much better. Sure, we'd suffered a harrowing ordeal at the hands of a terrifying vampire menace, but we were home now, and home had never looked so good.

I had reservations about returning to the scene of Neil's kidnapping, but Viz had assured me we'd be safe there, at least for the time being. The Clan had suffered a humiliating defeat, and wouldn't be mounting another attack tonight. We'd disrupted their bloodletting and purged the sacrifice site. They'd be too busy licking their wounds to pick on me any time soon.

So we celebrated. Me and Neil, the moment we got home. How exactly did we celebrate? Why, we braided one another's hair and softly kissed each other's foreheads of course. Just kidding. We banged like mad rabbits is how we celebrated. I mean, we *really* went to town on each other. I set into Neil like I'd just been released from prison after a ten year stretch. Like it was Christmas Day and he was the biggest present under the tree. I didn't even bother to take off my makeup before we got down to it. I'm telling you, by the time we were done, he looked like he'd been beaten up by a clown. I felt sure we'd be getting a note slipped under our door by nosy old Mr Munford about the racket we made, shortly followed by a noise abatement letter from the council, but that was a problem for another day.

'I love you,' Neil told me, and I said it back to him, meaning every word, every syllable.

I'd been guilty of taking Neil for granted—of treating him like a comfy, loose-knit jumper, all worn in and snug—but he was so much more than that. When those vampires took him away, they left behind a hole, an emptiness where Neil belonged. It made me realise that a future without him was no future at all. It had been a valuable lesson, even if I did have a criticism or two regarding the overall syllabus.

The sun had been up for a couple of hours already, and it was absolutely, most definitely, time for bed. I was so shattered that I barely had it in me to draw the curtains. My eyelids refused to stay open, except on an individual, one-at-a-time basis. I climbed into bed beside Neil and felt my body go limp. He rolled over to put on his breathing mask, and I nuzzled into the nape of his neck. We said our good nights and I draped an arm across his torso and closed my eyes. The worries of the world vanished as sleep descended on me, heavy and warm.

When I woke up, it was getting on for noon. A few threadbare streaks of daylight trickled in through the crack between the curtains. The room was nice and toasty, and smelled of last night's sex; sickly and sweet.

I wouldn't get up for hours yet—God willing—but before I nodded off again I gave Neil a hug and sniffed his back. He felt cold, so I pulled the duvet tight around his neck and patted it down. That's when I noticed he wasn't wearing his oxygen mask.

'Neil?' I said, feeling a surge of panic.

He needed that mask to breathe, yet there it was, lying on the carpet beside the oxygen tank, pumping air into nothing. It must have slipped off of his face while he was sleeping. It had happened once before a couple of years ago, and that had almost been the death of him.

'Neil?' I screamed, rolling him on to his back.

He looked like death. His eyes were closed and sunk deep into their sockets. His skin was the colour of curdled milk. At first I thought he wasn't breathing, but when I whipped the sheets off him, I could see his chest rise and fall ever so slightly. Breath quivered from his lips in short, shallow gasps.

I dived astride him and scooped up his oxygen mask, pressing it to his face and forming a seal around his mouth. 'Come on, Neil. Wake up. Wake up!'

His eyes opened to puffy slits and he broke into a shiver. His expression was glassy, not altogether there. 'I don't feel well, Abbey,' he said, his voice a reedy whisper.

'It's okay,' I said, 'We're going to get some air in you, then I'm going to call the hospital.'

He coughed with such force that I had trouble keeping the mask on his face, then he went into a spasm. His heels kicked at the mattress so hard that I was almost thrown off him, then his jaw clenched tight as his body convulsed some more, writhing and bucking beneath me like a prize bronco.

He went still.

'Neil?'

I checked his breathing but couldn't feel a thing. His skin was ice-cold to the touch. I went to grab my phone and call for an ambulance, but I knew in my heart that it was already too late. By the time an ambulance got here, by the time the paramedics made it up those nine stupid flights of stairs, Neil would be gone.

What had I been thinking, bringing him home after everything he'd been through? He should have been in a hospital bed under the watchful eye of a doctor, not here. Why had I listened to him when he said he felt fine?

Without warning, Neil's eyes snapped open and his lips peeled back like a corpse decomposing at speed.

My limbs flexed in shock. There, on Neil's forehead was a mark.

A mark I recognised all too well.

The mark of Judas.

The Clan had turned Neil into one of their own.

A pair of long white fangs ejected from Neil's gums and glistened in the murky midday light.

'No... not you, Neil...'

'Hello, Abbey,' he rasped, his tongue flicking across his new teeth. 'I'm really hungry.'

To Be Continued...

TURNED

1

My boyfriend was a vampire.

It sounds like the title of a dodgy B-Movie, but now it was my reality. Now it was my Sunday.

Rewind...

Neil and I were splashed out in bed, dog-tired and ready to sleep off an evening of intense carnal celebration. Too much information? Not very ladylike? Yeah, you can stop clutching your pearls and get off your fainting chair, princess. I'd earned my bit of fun and then some; I mean it's not every day you rescue your boyfriend from a sacrificial altar and save the city from an unholy vampire uprising, is it?

It really had been a hell of a night—both inside and outside of the bedroom—and I was all set to conk out. I wouldn't be asleep for long though, oh no. One of the many, many crappy things about being the woman chosen to guard the frontier between civilisation and an undead apocalypse is that I don't get much sleep. And I love sleep. *Love it.* Before I got the Nightstalker gig, my ambition in life was to basically be in a coma. Now I'm lucky if I manage to snatch a couple of hours. I'm telling you, it's not easy being London's heroic and incredibly modest saviour.

But let me backtrack a little further. Not all the way back to me getting Sanctified (because shame on you if you're not up to speed with that already), but to the moment right before my boyfriend sprouted fangs and went for my neck like I was made of prime Kobe beef.

Yeah, *that* moment.

The two of us were marinating in post-coital bliss when things took the unexpected swerve. Actually, it was less of a *swerve* swerve than a *full-blown, skidding on the chicane, smashing through the guardrail, and plunging headlong over the edge of a cliff* swerve.

I first realised something was wrong when I woke up and noticed that Neil wasn't wearing his oxygen mask. Straight away, gooseflesh went creeping up my arms. Neil suffers from a condition called cystic fibrosis, which means he needs extra O_2 to raise his low blood oxygen. It's a bitch of an illness, but he gets by, at least he does so long as he wears his respirator, which at that moment was lying beside him, breathing air into nothing.

What followed was a blur. A giddy little waking nightmare that ran the gamut from Neil being dead, to Neil being alive, to Neil being something halfway between.

When I saw the colour of his fishbelly white skin I obviously thought the worst, but when I rolled him over and saw his eyes staring straight at me, I felt a huge wash of relief. *He's just sick*, I thought, *that's all*. But he was more than that. Much more. He was one of them.

'Hello,' he growled, his tongue flicking across his razor blade smile. 'I'm really hungry.'

Then he was lunging for me, canines gleaming, eyes blood-red. I thrust out my hands and held him at arm's length as he chomped at my throat, thirsty for the taste of my hot blood. Two pearl daggers scraped my flesh, eager to gnaw through skin and sinew to get at the juice beneath. Claws sprang from his fingers, shredding the bed sheets as he swiped at me, turning the quilt into confetti.

'Neil!' I cried. 'It's me, Abbey, your girlfriend! You know… the one who never remembers to unload the dishwasher!'

Then I saw it: the mark of Judas on his forehead, a glowing letter J, visible only to me. He'd been turned by my sworn enemies, the Judas Clan, the same people I'd just rescued him from. That did not fill my heart with smiles and cupcakes, let me tell you.

The Clan had made Neil into one of their own, and now he was doing their bidding, trying to sink his chompers into me and snack on my red stuff. Well, lucky for me, I have a letter of my own: a big letter N seared into the palm of my hand that makes me a vampire's worst nightmare (well, daymare, I suppose).

The brand turned hot and bright, throwing darts of blue light about the bedroom. I felt a tremendous surge of adrenaline as my powers kicked in, snarling inside of my belly, filling me up with impossible strength, making me powerful beyond the limits of my puny frame. Something had woken inside of me. My own kind of monster.

In one smooth move I seized Neil by the wrists, flipped him on to his back, and pinned him to the mattress. He bucked beneath me, a trapped animal, growling and thrashing and throwing his weight from side to side. The headboard beat a frenzied tattoo against the bedroom wall, only now the noise didn't signal pleasure, now it was the noise of a man trying to throw me across the room and tear out my jugular.

'I know you're in there, Neil,' I said, pressing down on him, 'and I'm going to get you out. Somehow.'

One of his arms momentarily broke free of my grip and he caught me with a wicked punch to the jaw. *Ow*. Not so long ago, a knock like that would have left me with a lump the size of a gobstopper. Not anymore though. Now I'm the Nightstalker, I heal about as quickly as I wound.

Neil let fly an awful, pterodactyl screech, loud enough to make the bedroom windows rattle. If he carried on like that he was going to wake Mr Munford across the hall, and then I'd really have a problem. It was bad enough that the love of my life had transformed into a bloodthirsty Nosferatu, but the last thing I needed was to give the Residents' Association any more of a reason to turf us out.

Wasting no time, I gathered Neil's wrists in one hand and used the other to whip off a string of fairy lights tacked to the bed's headboard. As my vampire boyfriend fought and fussed, I tied him up with the lights and looked for something to gag him with. The only thing in reach were the socks I was wearing, so using all of my yoga training (by which I mean the one time I tried yoga), I arched over backwards, hooked one off, and stuffed it into Neil's screaming mouth.

'It's for your own good,' I assured him. 'Now, hold still.'

Of course he didn't, and how could I blame him? I certainly wouldn't have enjoyed having a smelly old sock stuffed into my gob, and I hadn't had the misfortune of being turned into a bloodsucking hell beast. He spat the sock out, and before I could stuff it back in and secure it with a bit of tape, managed to use the F word as a verb, a noun and an adjective, all in the same sentence.

My boyfriend was a vampire, and he was making a real pig's ear out of my weekend.

2

I had to get Neil to the angels, which, believe it or not, wasn't a euphemism for putting him down like a sick dog, but an actual thing that I needed to do.

Vizael and Gendith were the ones who'd dubbed me the Nightstalker, and knew just about everything there was to know about vampires and their kin. If anybody was going to help me flip Neil's condition, it would be those two. Until then, I had to deal with what I had, and what I had was one *extremely* pissed off bloodsucker.

Vampire Neil thrashed and flailed like he was undergoing an exorcism, sending the mattress bouncing up and down on its frame and causing a terrible, creaking din. Clearly, he had no intention of going quietly, which meant I had to figure out a way to get him out of the flat without anyone seeing him. How exactly I was going to manage that I did not know. I had a few dozen neighbours, lived nine storeys up, and the lift to the tower block I called home had been out of order since Thatcher took office.

I tried to marshal my thoughts but couldn't hear myself think over the racket Neil was making, so I tied his ankles to the bed's footboard and sat on his stomach. It didn't shut him up entirely, but it stopped him using the mattress as a bouncy castle. I set my mind to the task at hand. How in the name of sweet Siouxsie

Sioux was I going to smuggle this boyfriend-turned-beast out of the building and get him across the River to the angels?

Come on, Abbey, think. Think, think, think.

Seizing on an idea, I went in search of something I could use to keep Neil in check while I manoeuvred him to the ground floor. It would have to be something that kept him constrained as well as concealed, because the sight of a girl towing a non-cooperative, half-naked guy down nine flights was likely to raise a few eyebrows.

I considered my options. I could use the bed sheet Neil was lying on I supposed – tie up the corners like a knapsack and sling him over my shoulder. Or how about the living room rug? I could roll him up in that and carry him downstairs like a man burrito. No, that wasn't going to cut it either, he'd make too much fuss and be seen. I needed to disguise him better than that.

Think, think, think.

I could always knock him out of course, but where would I start with that? This wasn't a movie. I wasn't going to fetch him a quick tap to the skull and drop him peacefully on to the pillow, only for him to wake up later at my convenience. Nor did I have the nerd credentials to put him out with a subtle Vulcan nerve pinch, which meant I'd be smacking the guy over the noggin with no rhyme or reason, and even though that was tempting—given that he'd just tried to rip out my windpipe—I knew my boyfriend was still in there somewhere. Punching the poor guy out carried the distinct risk of permanently damaging him, or worse, killing him.

So no, I couldn't just club Neil over the head and drag him to Bethnal Green by the roots of his hair. Not unless I wanted to get felt up by the law, and that was the last thing I needed. The war I'd been drafted into—the war against the Judas Clan—was a secret one. The cops weren't equipped to deal with an ancient sect of vampires descended from Judas Iscariot himself. Christ, they were barely equipped to kettle a few demonstrators armed with harshly-worded placards. Let them look after the real world. This other world—the world of the Uncanny, the world of bloodthirsty monsters and things that went bump-slash-devour in the night—that was a job for the Nightstalker.

If only the Nightstalker could figure out how to haul her boyfriend out of bed and get him out of this place...

Think, think, bloody well think!

Then I saw it. A suitcase stored under the bed, edged out by Neil's thrashing and sent halfway across the room. It was a large one—the largest you could check into a plane without paying the excess—and made from a solid clamshell of hard plastic. We'd bought it a couple of years back thinking we'd use it for a holiday one day, only Neil's health had taken a turn for the worse and we'd had to spend our vacation money on antibiotics and mucus thinners to offset his cystic fibrosis. I know, what a life, eh? Christ, I feel like a bitch even joking about it. Neil's life kind of outweighs a week in Tenerife. Two weeks, even. With a free hotel bar thrown in.

Wrestling Neil into the suitcase wasn't going to be easy, but I'd fought harder battles already.

'I'm going to untie you now,' I told him, 'so please behave.'

The moment the fairy lights slipped off his wrists he made a lunge for me, but I was ready. Wrapping myself around his torso, I pinned his arms to his sides then keeled him over sideways and forced him into the suitcase. His ankles were still tied, so I could only get his top half inside, but it gave me a chance to flip the case's lid shut on his waist and protect myself from his claws and fangs while I undid the rest of his bonds. With one foot pinning the lid shut, I went to work on his ankles, and once I had those free too, I was able to bundle Neil's legs into the suitcase and snap the thing shut.

Was he going to be okay in there? Neil's respiratory condition meant that he rarely left the flat for fear of coughing up blood trying to climb the stairs back to the ninth floor – what chance would he have trapped inside an oxygen-deprived suitcase?

Then again, he seemed to be doing fine. Well, maybe not *fine*, but he was certainly full of energy. His breathing tank was across the other side of the room, yet the suitcase he was trapped in was bouncing around on the carpet like a jumping bean. Whatever the drawbacks to being a vampire were, the transformation had done wonders for his lung disorder.

Always a silver lining, hey?

I threw on some clothes—black drainpipe jeans, black Bauhaus tee, black leather coat (black's kind of my thing)—and wheeled the twitching suitcase to the front door. I took a deep breath and steeled myself. Was this really going to work? Was I seriously going to ship a vampire all the way to Bethnal Green in broad daylight without anyone noticing? It was a stretch. Truth told, it was about the biggest stretch since Stretch Armstrong and Plastic Man got into a dick-measuring contest.

Still, what choice did I have?

I snatched the luggage up by its handle in one sharp tug. Neil resisted, throwing his body against the walls of the case, trying to dislodge himself from my grip, but I had him locked in my claws like a hungry bird of prey. I opened the drawer of my bedside cabinet and grabbed the Nightstalker's dagger; fifteen-ounces of hallowed silver, guaranteed to ruin any bloodsucker's day. The blade glowed cobalt blue as it met with the brand on my palm, and the two throbbed in synchrony. Using the tip of the knife, I punched a couple of breathing holes in the wall of the suitcase —*stab stab stab*—just big enough to stop Neil from suffocating, but not so large that he'd be able to use them for a mouthpiece.

Time to go. I slipped the dagger into its leather sheath, hid it under my jacket, and made for the front door. I lugged the suitcase to the top of the stairwell and started to descend, slowly at first, then picking up the pace the more sure-footed I became. Neil groaned and fidgeted, but his protestations soon fell away as he began to run out of steam. I carried his dead weight down five flights of stairs, edging ever closer to the exit, ever closer to the idea that I was actually going to get away with this, when a familiar and most unwelcome figure appeared.

I screeched to a halt in front of Mr Munford, local busybody and long-standing Chair of the Residents' Association. Munford was a constant thorn in my side, and one that I'd only recently taken it upon myself to aggravate when I all but kicked in his door looking for my kidnapped boyfriend.

'You,' he said. 'I take it you found your man then?'

He scrunched up his ancient face and peered at me over the rims of his cheap, two-for-one spectacles.

'Yup,' I replied, being extra careful not to let my eyes stray to the suitcase I was holding, else he realise that the man in question was inside of it. 'He showed up at the flat in the end, wouldn't you believe. Men! What are they like, eh?' I offered him a silly little laugh, as authentic as I could make it.

Please don't let the old bastard catch me kidnapping my own boyfriend, I think my irony bone might snap.

'Where did he get to then?' Munford asked, stabbing his hands into the pockets of his ratty old overcoat. 'And who were the blokes he took off with?'

'Oh, um... poker buddies,' I tried. Best I could come up with at short notice.

'Poker buddies?' he sneered.

'Yup. Texas Hold 'Em. Don't understand the attraction of it myself. "What's wrong with a nice game of whist?" I tell him, but it's poker or nothing with that one.'

'Hmmm,' the old man replied. 'Is that right?'

'Yup,' I replied. 'And look, I'm really sorry about knocking on your door last night, that was... well, that was about as out of order as our lift is, eh?'

My attempt at camaraderie must have dislodged something in him, because his face creased into something that might just have been a smile. 'Tell you what, so long as you don't go waking me up again gone midnight, I suppose I can let last night go.'

'Thank you,' I said through gritted teeth. 'That's very understanding of you, I promise it won't happen again.' *Now fuck off out of here before my vampire boyfriend gets free of this suitcase and opens up your carotid artery,* I added, though only in my head.

At that moment the suitcase jolted in my hand and knocked against Munford's thigh.

'Stone the crows,' he said. 'What have you got in there?'

Searching for an answer, my eyes landed on the blue plastic bag he was carrying. Inside was a carton of milk, a loaf of bread, and a couple of cans of something or other. Shopping. Maybe I could tell him I was going shopping too. Yeah, that could work.

What are you thinking, Abbey? Shopping with a giant suitcase? You'll have to do better than that, girl.

The case shuddered and Neil let out a wolfish growl.

'It's a dog,' I stammered.

'A dog?'

'Yeah. I'm, um... taking him to the vets.' Neil growled again. 'He hates the vets.'

Munford cocked an eyebrow. 'You know we don't allow dogs in the building, Miss Beckett.'

'Oh, he's not my dog,' I explained, punching the side of the case, playfully I hoped. 'I'm just looking after him for a friend.'

The old man wasn't having it. 'The rules are clear: no animals on the premises for any reason. I'm afraid I'm going to have to report you for this.'

I didn't have time to debate the finer points of my tenancy agreement—not while Neil was ready to bust out of my suitcase like the world's least child-friendly Jack-in-the-box—so I sucked it up and let Munford have this one. 'Okay then,' I said. 'You know best, after all.'

'I don't like that you've put me in this position,' he replied, tutting. 'I really don't.'

As Munford grabbed the bannister and continued up the stairs, it was all I could do not to whip out my dagger and sink it into his back.

I'm the Nightstalker, you old coffin-dodger. You're giving me shit because I knocked on your door in the middle of the night? What if next time it's a clan of vampires kicking the thing off its hinges? A clan of vampires looking to strap you to an altar and feed your blood to their dark overlord? Maybe then you'll be thankful that you live opposite the goalkeeper standing between human civilisation and an undead apocalypse, so how about you ease up on the finger-wagging and stay the hell out of my way?

I don't know, just a thought.

With Munford gone, I raced down the last few flights of stairs, hustled through the lobby, and made my way outside. It was another dull winter's day in Thamesmead; grey buildings squatting beneath an ugly, bruised sky. The chill air lapped at my face as I picked my way across a minefield of broken chicken bones and stepped-on nitrous canisters. Standing on the edge of the pavement, I fired up Uber and ordered myself a ride to Bethnal Green.

The thrashing inside the suitcase had stopped, but I could still hear laboured breathing beneath. Good. Neil was alive, he'd just tuckered himself out with all that howling and trying to kill me stuff.

He stayed quiet the whole time I waited for the Uber to show up. Meanwhile, I hopped from foot to foot in the cold as I watched the little car on my phone screen draw nearer. If I could just get Neil in the back of a cab, I'd have a straight shot across the River to the angels, and then I could get him fixed. At least I hoped so. God, I hoped so. I'd just have to believe that was possible for now, because the alternative would have sent me to the ground.

The cab pulled up and the driver popped the boot then stepped out to help me load the suitcase.

'Let me get that,' he said.

He was a big bloke—the kind who had to take a door sideways—and his arms had a puffy, protein shake swell to them.

'That's okay,' I told him, 'I can get it...'

'Don't be daft,' he said, and grabbed the suitcase by the handle.

I don't know who taught him to lift, but he absolutely spazzed it. No sooner had he hoisted it from the ground than his hands were reaching for his tweaked lumbar region.

'Bloody hell,' he cried. 'What have you got in that thing, bricks?'

'I told you I could get it,' I said, effortlessly scooping the suitcase up and transferring it to the boot.

The driver stared at me incredulously, nostrils flared.

'I've been working on my guns,' I joshed, flexing one of my spaghetti arms.

He was about to say something when Neil squirmed inside the suitcase and let out a muffled yelp.

'What was that?' asked the driver.

I considered running the dog lie again, but decided I couldn't be bothered and slammed the boot shut. 'Nothing to worry about,' I told him.

His eyes searched my face, then he looked me up and down, taking in my all-black outfit and trying to assess whether he had a Myra Hindley situation on his hands.

'No worries,' he said. 'Let's get going.'

I don't know if it was the prang to his masculinity, or whether he just didn't want to mess up his Uber rating, but he was done asking questions.

I got into the back seat and checked the estimated fare to my destination. Thirty bloody quid. One of these days I was going to have to lay my hands on a driver's license. It was ridiculous; I'd been conscripted by the forces of righteousness and tasked with vanquishing the vampire menace, yet I couldn't even execute a poxy three-point turn.

3

After a speedy drive to the outskirts of Bethnal Green, the cab driver pulled up to the edge of a derelict industrial park. I climbed out quickly and plucked the suitcase from the boot without bothering to say goodbye. I had the distinct feeling that we weren't going to end up friends, so why waste time with pleasantries?

Having waited for the cab to peel off, I turned sideways to manoeuvre through a gap in the rusted chain link fence that surrounded the park, and made my way inside. The suitcase's wheels rattled noisily over patchy tarmac as I dragged it past the remains of a haunted circuit boards factory. The jostling woke Neil up, causing him to throw another tantrum inside his pint-sized prison.

'Kill you! Drink your blood!' came his tiny cries.

I ignored him and marched onwards, hanging a right at the burned-out husk of a forklift that sat on the puddled remains of its tyres. Almost there. Up ahead, I saw what I'd come for, a decommissioned gas tower; a squat, corroded cylinder that served as the angels' base of operations.

'I need some help here,' I shouted as I pulled aside the metal sheet concealing the tower's entrance.

I heard the scrape of metal on concrete and saw Vizael hobbling towards me on his ivory-handed walking stick. 'Abbey, what are you doing here? You're supposed to be at home resting.' The old man was clean-shaven and dressed in a presentable, if crumpled, white linen suit. His lively eyes darted to the suitcase. 'What's this?'

As if in answer to his question, one of Neil's hands sprang through a hole in the zipper and began to claw frantically at the air. It reminded me of one of those novelty money boxes you used to see, with the skeletal hand that reaches out to grab a penny and drag it inside its tomb.

'It's Neil,' I explained over the sound of my boyfriend's frenzied shrieking. I felt the first salty sting of tears in my eyes. 'He's one of them, Viz. You've got to help me, I don't know what to do.'

Vizael placed a comforting hand on my shoulder. 'It's all right,' he said in his soothing radio voice. 'Everything will be all right.'

Just then, Gendith appeared on the scene, descending the tower's circular staircase, hips sashaying. 'Is that a vampire?' she asked as she strode over on her celebrity legs, casting a perfect catwalk silhouette. 'You brought a vampire into our home?'

'I brought *Neil* into your home,' I told her, squaring up to her frustratingly symmetrical features and flawless black skin.

Viz interjected. 'Help Abbey get him out of there before he hurts himself.'

Gen rolled her husky blue eyes, but did as ordered. 'We'll need to tie him down,' she said. 'I'll fetch some chains.'

I didn't much like the sound of that. I'd only just rescued Neil from the Clan's antiseptic dungeon, now there I was, being asked to strap him down again. Still, what could I do? Left to his own devices, he'd have taken a nice hot shower in my arterial blood.

Working together, Gen and I hauled Neil out of the suitcase, transferred him to a chair, and secured his extremities. I make that sound easy, but it was like wrestling an alligator. An alligator hopped up on PCP. Neil gnashed his fangs and threw his head back and forth like he was in the front row of a Mastodon concert. 'Drink your blood!' he cried. 'Drink your blood!'

Gen caught her breath and took a couple of steps back. 'This must have been their contingency plan,' she said.

'What do you mean?' asked Viz.

'Isn't it obvious?' she replied. 'If the Nightstalker foiled the Clan's scheme and saved this one, they'd make sure she died another way.'

I turned the idea over in my head. 'Are you telling me they turned my boyfriend into a Munchausen Candidate?'

'I think you'll find it's *Manchurian* Candidate.'

'I don't care what kind of fucking candidate they made him into, how do I change him back?'

Just then, Neil's eyes rolled into the back of his head and he went still.

'What happened?' I cried.

Viz approached the chair.

'Careful,' said Gen, 'he could be faking.'

Viz took her guidance under advisement, keeping Neil at arm's length. The old man placed a hand on his jugular. 'He's alive,' he reported, 'but it looks as though he's going to be out for a little while. The sun has taken a toll on him.'

'Of course it has,' Gen replied, 'he's a vampire.'

'Can you stop calling him that?'

'He's a vampire, Abbey. That's what he is now.'

'I don't care! Just... just...' My body felt heavy suddenly, like I'd been draped in a jacket with concrete in its pockets. I was so tired, so sick of this. I'd been on top of the world only a few hours ago, and now it seemed like the Clan had won after all. A sick joke at my expense. 'Can we get some time alone, please? Just me and Neil.'

'So he can wake up and sweet-talk you into fang-range?' said Gen.

'No, so we can talk. I know I can get through to him, we've been together too long for him to forget who I am. He just needs reminding, that's all.'

Gen shook her head. 'That's not how this works. Your boyfriend has been turned. He's your enemy now. You can't tame them, you can only kill them.'

'Gendith!' Viz scolded.

Gen backed down. She looked at me coolly, her blue eyes a

pair of frozen ponds. 'The boy you know is gone, Abbey. If you want to say anything to him right now, say your goodbyes.'

And she left, both of them did, but not before making double sure that Neil's bonds were good and tight.

It wasn't long before Neil came around – fifteen minutes at most.

When he woke up this time he wasn't screaming, nor was he threatening to drink my blood. He was just regular old Neil.

'What's happening?' he croaked, his voice rusty from sleep. 'How did I get here?'

He sounded completely normal, or about as normal as it's possible to be when you've opened your eyes to find yourself chained semi-naked to a chair, then opened them wider and found your girlfriend pointing the sharp end of a dagger at you.

'You know who I am?' I asked him.

'What? Are you joking?'

'Just tell me.'

'All right. You're Abbey. Can I please get out of this chair now?'

Okay, so he knew who I was, but he'd said my name once already, right before he'd tried to sink his teeth in me.

'I can't do that,' I said, wanting nothing more than to unchain him and give him a hug. 'The vampires… they did something to you.'

Those evil fuckers. It wasn't enough that they'd kidnapped my boyfriend and used him as bait, they had to infect him with their disease too? I felt anger boiling in the pit of my stomach, but despite the righteous indignation I felt, I knew I'd played a part in this mess too. I'd allowed this to happen. The life I'd chosen—the life Neil had never agreed to, never even been consulted on—had blown back on me and put him in peril.

'What did they do to me?' he asked, and as he said it, his tongue landed on his new teeth. He swept the tip over the points of his elongated incisors and winced. 'Well, I suppose that answers that question.'

I felt the brand grow hot and reflexively found my hand white-knuckling the grip of my vampire-killing dagger.

Kill the bloodsucker. Chop off his head. Burn his body to ash.

The brand, mainlining thoughts to my brain. I pushed them out.

'I'm going to fix this,' I said, as much for my sake as his.

Neil nodded unconvincingly, then tightened up as if he'd been punched in the stomach, his face lined with pain. 'I'm so hungry, Abbey. God, I'm hungry.' His belly let out a long, sour rumble.

'I'll get you something to eat,' I said, bouncing to my feet.

'No,' he said. 'I'm not hungry for food. I need…' He paused and looked up at me, eyes wet and wide, 'God, this is gross but... I need blood.'

'Jesus, Neil, I'm so sorry. This is all my fault.' I broke down and told him how guilt-ridden I felt about getting him sucked into the disaster zone of my life.

'Why didn't you just tell me?' he asked, and why hadn't I?

Because the angels had warned me not to, that's why. They'd drummed it into me that the war against the vampires was a secret one, and that no one besides us was to know about it. But I shouldn't have listened to them. Neil deserved to know what was lurking out there. Now, instead of being told about the threat I was facing, he'd become the threat.

He stared down at his hands; at the claws on his fingers. 'It's funny really, all that time I spent writing books about monsters and that… I thought I was writing science fiction, not science fact.'

I wanted to say sorry again, but the word had lost all meaning. Instead, I just cried.

'It's okay,' said Neil, face pained but doing his best to sketch out a smile. 'You've done me a favour, really. From now on I won't have to make up stories, I'll just crib them from you.'

Even after all this, he still knew how to make me laugh.

Another belly rumble and Neil doubled over. 'Christ, that really hurt,' he gasped.

'Neil, I don't know what to do.'

'Can you untie me at least? My wrists really hurt.'

I instinctively went to help him, then stopped. Was Gendith right? Was he trying to sweet-talk me so he could lure me into killing range? 'I don't know…' I said. 'Maybe that's not such a good idea. Not yet.'

'I'm so sick of being strapped down, Abbey. Please let me go.'

I felt sorry for him—of course I did—but I couldn't risk untying him. I'd seen too many vampires in action already, and I knew two things about them for sure: they were sneaky and they were strong. The moment I loosened one of those chains, there was every chance Neil would go snapping at my neck again.

'I have to keep you tied up,' I told him.

'Why?'

'Why do you think? It was only a few minutes ago you were trying to kill me.'

'What are you talking about?' He seemed sincere.

'Back at the flat? All the way here? Are you telling me you don't remember trying to open up my throat?'

'What? Shit, no! One minute I was in bed with you, the next I was waking up here tied to a chair.'

Could he be telling the truth? Was he just temporarily possessed back there? Maybe he was okay now. Maybe it had just been a funny spell. Except, he still had those fangs and that milk-white complexion. He sounded like Neil though. He sounded so much like Neil.

'Why are you looking at me like that?' he asked. 'It's me, Abbey. Come on, we've been together since college, I know everything about you.'

'Like what?'

'I know… I know you once ate twenty-seven slices of economy cheese in one go. I know your favourite film according to Facebook is *The Cabinet of Doctor Caligari*, and I know that your *actual* favourite film is that Steve Martin one, *The Man With Two Brains*. Oh, and I know that you like it when I use my tongue to trace the letters of the alphabet on your—'

'Okay, Romeo, that's enough of that. What else do you know?'

His voice dropped. 'I know that I love you.'

'I love you too, Neil.'

But was he Neil, or was he just some creature dipping his fingers into Neil's memories?

His belly snarled again and he folded so hard this time I thought he might snap in half. 'My stomach… it's turning itself inside out. I have to feed, Abbey. If I don't get some blood in me I'm going to die...'

Sick again. Always sick. Always suffering.

I'd already seen Neil go through so much, I couldn't stand to see him undergo anymore. And yet I couldn't help him either. Couldn't give him what he wanted, not without getting into trouble with the angels. Christ, Gen would kick my teeth into the back of my skull if she caught me aiding and abetting the enemy, or at least have a bloody good go at it. That's how focused she was on the mission. The mission to end the Judas Clan, once and for all, and at any cost.

Gen had every right to hate them too. I know I did. Ever since they'd started rising en masse a decade or so back, the Clan had been using their vampiric powers to infiltrate the upper echelons of high society. You see, the Clan weren't characters from a penny dreadful, they were a completely different breed of monster: bankers and stock traders and hedge fund managers, profiting wildly from mankind's misery, siphoning money from the poor and needy before they drained their bodies dry.

Still, just because Neil had been bitten by one of them, that didn't mean he had to behave like them. Did it? I just couldn't see it. Neil never cared about money, and he didn't have an evil bone in his body. He was a good guy. When the waiter delivered the wrong dish at a restaurant, he ate it. I knew him. I knew everything about him. I knew he liked to cook, I knew his favourite writer was Neil Gaiman, and I knew his eyes went crossed at the point of… well, you know.

I cast a glance over my shoulder. The angels were next door behind one of the tower's partition walls. Neil and I were alone. The coast was clear. So long as I was quick, I could get away with this. I had to at least give him the benefit of the doubt, right?

'Okay,' I whispered, 'I'm going to help you, but you have to keep the noise down.'

'What are you saying?'

'I've heard you eat soup, Neil.'

He chuckled. 'Thank you,' he said. 'Thank you so much.'

'Just a taste, okay? Enough to stop the pangs, no more.'

Like a jolted bobblehead he went.

I pushed up the sleeve of my jacket and saw his blood-shot eyes land hungrily on the white flesh of my wrist. For a moment I considered pulling my sleeve back down again, but then he looked up at me with his puppy dog face and that was that.

'I can't believe I'm doing this,' said Neil, even as he licked his lips in anticipation. 'This is just… mental.'

I put my arm to his mouth, ready to jerk it back again if he went at it too hungrily, but Neil kept his animal in check and dined with the utmost etiquette. Craning his neck slowly, he opened his mouth and bit down on my wrist. The tips of his fangs slid into my flesh—two quick pin pricks—and his mouth formed a tight seal around the wound. He sucked at the emerging blood like a babe at the teat, hungry, forceful, but not enough that it caused me any discomfort. As a matter of fact, I found the process surprisingly painless, so much so that I began to wonder if vampires had some kind of special numbing agent in their saliva.

It wasn't my first time feeding a vampire, which is a weird thing to say, I know. I'd already donated blood to an undead snitch in exchange for the information that got Neil off that altar, so I had some idea what to expect from the experience. With that vamp though, I felt nothing. Giving him blood was just a one-way exchange of bodily fluids, a business transaction. With Neil, I felt something. Some kind of charge, an intoxication, a heady trance that made me feel warm and snug and close and—

I felt woozy. Lightheaded. My balance left me and I had to throw out my free hand to grab Neil's chair for support. Neil fed hungrily, slurping loudly, his lips thawing out and growing hot. I looked down to see muscles springing up beneath his skin; muscles I didn't even know he had. The blood was making him strong again… too strong. I couldn't allow that.

'That's enough, Neil,' I whispered, trying to pull away from him.

He gripped me tight though, the O of lips clinging to my

wrist like a suction cup. Ropey veins stood to attention on his forearms, making him look like a bodybuilder after a serious pump sesh. I felt weak, powerless to stop him, but I knew if I let him carry on feeding from me he'd grow strong enough to break his bonds, and then what?

'That's enough!' I said, and this time I succeeded in pulling my wrist from his mouth.

As Neil withdrew, I saw blood on his teeth and got a flash of the monster inside, then he swilled out his mouth and returned to his former self.

I heard Viz's cane tapping on the concrete floor. 'Is everything okay in here?' he asked, appearing from next door.

I tugged down my sleeve to cover the bite marks Neil had given me. 'Fine,' I said, 'we were just talking.'

He eyed me warily for a moment, then said, 'Can you join us next door, Abbey? We need to talk.'

'Sure,' I replied, fearing the worst. 'I'll be through in a minute.'

Viz hobbled off, casting a quick glance over his shoulder before he went.

'Do you think he saw anything?' Neil asked.

'I hope not,' I replied. 'For both our sakes.'

4

I left Neil chained to the chair and went next door to find Viz and Gen waiting for me in the dojo.

'How is he?' Viz asked.

'He's okay,' I said, cautiously. 'He's stopped ranting and he knows who he is.'

'It's not *who* he is, it's *what* he is,' said Gen. 'That creature back there is a vampire, and the sooner you get that into your head, the sooner we can move past this.'

'Will you stop telling me how I'm supposed to feel?'

'Someone has to take charge around here.'

'Not you though. I don't work for you, Gen. We're a team. Viz does the nerdy academic stuff, you take care of the cloak-and-dagger business, and I... um...'

'And you are our shining sword against the vampire army,' said Viz, helpfully.

'Right. Except I'm not just some weapon to be used at your disposal. I have a say in what goes on around here too.'

'Of course you do,' said Viz. 'So tell us, what do you propose we do next?'

'We find a cure.'

'A cure for what?' asked Gen.

'What do you think?' I asked, throwing my arms in the air. 'A cure for Neil.'

Gen scoffed. 'The blood in his veins is wicked and black. There is only one way to cure that boy, and that's to put him out of his misery.'

'That's your prescription, is it, Doctor? "Take two shotgun shells and call me in the morning"?'

'It needn't be that drastic,' said Viz, stroking his chin, 'there is another way to cure Neil.'

'How?'

'We would need to slay the one who turned him,' he replied, 'and within a short enough space of time.'

'Great,' I said. 'Let's do that then.'

'It's not as simple as he makes out,' said Gen, sticking a pin in the balloon. 'There's no telling who sired the boy. The vampires who took him are all dead, which means it could be any surviving member of the Clan. Judas Iscariot himself could have turned him for all we know.'

'Fine,' I said. 'Then we find another way.'

Gen sunk her hands into her afro as though the skull beneath it might explode. 'There is no other way, girl. If we had the means to cure vampirism, do you really think we'd have allowed Judas to raise an undead army?'

We'd only recently discovered that the J-man was still alive and kicking when I stumbled across a secret tomb and found him hooked up to a blood pipeline; an underground viaduct that the Clan had built to restore him to full strength.

'Judas is the real threat right now,' said Gen. 'Wasting all this time on one doomed mortal could cost us everything.'

She was talking about the vampires' grand plan. Once Judas was back on his feet, him and his lot were preparing to bring about an Earthly apocalypse before they kicked in the gates of heaven and laid waste to the Holy Land. A real dick move from a gold-plated arsehole, but I guess you don't become an evil overlord just because someone forgot to baptise you.

'Listen to me,' said Gen, bringing me back to the present, 'there is no curing your boy. He's one of them already, he just doesn't know it yet.'

'Will you keep your voice down?' I hissed. 'He's right next door.'

I turned to Viz for some support, but instead of weighing in on the discussion, he hobbled across the room to one of his bookcases. He plucked an old tome from a shelf and blew off a swirl of grey dust.

'Interesting,' he said, adjusting his bifocals to read a page of spidery scrawl. 'Apparently, Neil's situation may not be as black and white as we first thought.'

'What are you saying?' I asked.

'I thought I remembered something about a cure in here, and it turns out I was right. According to my notes, there may be a way to reverse his condition yet.'

'Are you kidding me? A minute ago the only choice I had was to put a bullet in his brain, now you're telling me there's a way to make him better?'

'Yes. I apologise. My advanced years have left me rather forgetful. I'm afraid it happens when you've been around long enough to remember the Great Fire of London.'

Gen made a face at him. 'What are you blathering about, old man? For the last time, there is no cure. Now, let's finish this and get the vampire out of our house.' She looked to me. 'If you're too squeamish to do the deed, I'm happy to take care of it for you.'

'Yeah, thanks for the offer, but given the choice of murdering my boyfriend in cold blood or hearing Viz out, I think I'm going to go with the second option.'

Viz nodded sagely. 'According to my notes, there is a single recorded instance of someone curing themselves of vampirism. Apparently, in the early Fifteenth Century, a Jesuit priest was turned by a vampire and went on a holy quest to restore his humanity. Yes, yes, I remember this now. Quite the talk in Heaven, it was.'

'So?' I said.

'So what?'

'So how did he cure himself?' I cried.

'Oh,' Viz replied, slapping his forehead. 'Of that I have no idea.'

'Great. Super helpful. So where does that leave us then?'

Gen answered. 'It leaves us with a very limited amount of time before that creature next door turns completely.'

'How long?' I asked, sweeping my head back and forth between the angels. 'What are we talking? A week? A month?'

Viz grimaced. 'Until sundown.'

I checked my phone. It had just gone 2 p.m.

At this time of year, that gave us less than two hours to save Neil.

Less than two hours to find a cure that probably didn't exist.

Awesome.

5

'Carlo,' I said. 'We'll talk to Carlo.'

Since the angels weren't being any help, I figured we should consult a vampire expert, and who better to give advice on vampires than an actual vampire?

Carlo was the vampire I mentioned earlier, the one I'd given blood to. He was a deserter from the Judas Clan who traded gossip for a taste of the red stuff. Like I say, he was the one who passed along the information that helped me get Neil off the Clan's sacrificial altar, so I knew he could be trusted.

Gen glowered at me. 'Don't you think if Carlo knew a cure he'd have used it? Having vampire blood in his veins is a curse to him. He hates the Clan more than anyone.'

Somehow I doubted he hated them as much as I did.

I knew I was clutching at straws but I didn't care. 'I need to talk with him, Gen. I have to.'

'Fine,' she replied, in a tone that suggested it very much wasn't, 'I'll arrange a parley.'

'A parley? What are you talking about? By the time you've set up a meeting, Neil will be too far gone. I need you to take me to Carlo right now.'

And to her credit, she did, at least once she was done tutting.

We fired off in a cab; a cab that I footed the bill for. I wouldn't be seeing that money again, not in my lifetime. No expenses, no overtime, no hazard pay; I'm telling you, being a vampire-killing super-gal ain't all it's cracked up to be.

The cab pulled up at a shit apartment block in a shit part of Mile End. Litter was strewn all around the place, blowing freely, caught in the weeds, stuffed into every conceivable crevice. I saw an urban fox digging around the sprawling rot for food, gnawing through a bin bag and escaping with a half-eaten chicken carcass in its muzzle.

Carlo was holed up in an abandoned fifteenth-floor apartment in a run-down tower block, not unlike the one I inhabited in Thamesmead. Just like my block, Carlo's lift was out of order, but unlike my building, his at least had the excuse of being scheduled for demolition. Jesus, we lived some grim lives, and when you factored in the angels' living situation—squatting in a decommissioned gas tower on a derelict industrial estate—it seemed none of us was exactly living it up in this town. They say crime doesn't pay, but I'm telling you, being the good guy will send you straight to the poor house.

Gen and I made our way up fifteen flights of piss-reeking stairs until we found Carlo's floor and were finally able to unpinch our noses. The first thing I saw was graffiti. Sprayed in red paint across an apartment door that looked as though it had seen the business end of a police battering ram more than once, were the words JUNKIE SCUM.

'This is it,' said Gen, stating the obvious. Because a junkie is exactly what Carlo was. A junkie for blood.

I pulled out my dagger and used its pommel to rap on the door. 'Open up,' I demanded.

'Easy,' said Gen. 'He's on our side, remember?'

I supposed knocking on someone's door with the butt end of a bloody great knife could be viewed as a tad unfriendly, so I sheathed it and hammered on the door with my fist instead.

'Who is it?' croaked a voice from the other side. 'If it's the police, I know the law and I have every right to be here.'

'It's Gendith,' said my companion, 'and the other one.'

I heard a number of bolts slide open, then finally the door opened a crack, latched still by a heavy-duty chain. Through the crack I saw a pair of pinprick eyes drowned in the pool of a pale, stubbly face.

'What do you want?' Carlo sighed, obviously in no mood.

He looked bad. Actually, he looked like he was coming down from a four day meth binge. His greasy black hair was stuck to his head like he'd just gotten up, his dyed skunk stripe plastered to his scalp in a flattened S shape. On his feet he wore a pair of threadbare slippers that looked as though they'd been rescued from a charity bin. His upper half was only semi-concealed in a dressing gown that might just have lost a fight with a wheat thresher.

'We need to talk,' I told him.

He brightened, shoulders straightening, head popping up like a meerkat. 'You paying?'

'Yes,' I said, 'so long as I get what I need, and quick.'

Wasting no time, he swiftly unlatched the door chain, turned around, and jogged inside. I took this as a cue to follow him, despite the lack of any formal invitation.

'Sorry the place is a mess,' he said. 'I meant to tidy up last night, but that last batch you gave me really knocked me on my arse.'

He wasn't lying about the mess. The flat was an absolute pigsty – or at least what I could see of it was. The only light in Carlo's living room came from a dim glow that oozed through a narrow gap in the room's ratty curtains. Unlike other vampires, bloodsuckers from the Judas Clan were able to stand sunlight. Still, they took the dark where they could get it.

My eyes adjusted to the gloom and I saw junk strewn around everywhere; dirty laundry, empty cigarette packets, a stained mattress with no box-spring. The detritus of a broken life. It reminded me of the street outside, only instead of a fox picking through the litter, a cat slithered through stacks of heavy metal records. I found myself wondering if vampires could feed from animals, and if they could, whether Carlo had partaken.

'Take a seat, ladies,' he said, but we politely declined. Well, I did. Gen turned her nose up so high it's a wonder she didn't tip over backwards. 'Suit yourselves then,' he said, obviously hurt.

I actually found myself feeling sorry for the little runt. No one deserved to live in a place that smelled like R. Kelly's bed sheets. Carlo didn't want to be what he was any more than Neil did. For him, this really was a curse. Damn it, that was two vampires I had a soft spot for now. I was doing my Nightstalker credentials no favours.

Carlo sniffed the air and turned to me. 'That's weird... you smell of blood. Blood on the outside.'

'I do?'

'Yeah. Got that coppery tang in my nostrils.' His eyes twinkled. 'You've been fed on already, haven't you? You dirty girl.'

I felt colour mount my cheeks. 'Of course I have,' I stammered, 'I gave you some last night, remember?'

'Nah, this is a fresh feed. This is *today*.'

Gen grabbed me by the sleeve of my jacket. 'You gave blood to that boy of yours, didn't you?'

I didn't see any sense in lying. Gen's got this way of reading auras that makes her pretty good at rooting out fibs. It's an angel thing. 'So what if I did?'

'You foolish girl,' she cried. 'Why would you do such a thing?'

'I dunno, because I'm a nice person?'

'Nice people don't feed monsters.'

'Oh, what do you know?' I retaliated.

'With all due respect—by which I mean none whatsoever—a great deal more than you do.'

Carlo gave us a little wave to remind us he was still present. 'Can we get back on track, ladies? I've got a real hankering here.'

He was itching to get to it, literally in fact, scratching at his skin like he had bugs on him. Bugs *in him* even.

'First of all, we need something from you,' I explained.

'What's mine is yours,' he replied, throwing his arms wide. 'So tell me, what can I do for you lovely people?'

'It's my boyfriend, Neil. The Clan turned him into one of them.'

'Shit. Sorry to hear it, I know how that goes.' He shook his head sympathetically. 'So what do you need from me exactly? You want me to do away with him? No problem, I'm sure I've got a bit of wood I can sharpen around here somewhere.' He began rooting through his junk, sweeping aside some unpaid bills and a pile of outdated Kerrang magazines.

'Don't bother,' said Gen, 'I already tried.'

'I don't want you to kill Neil. I don't want *either* of you to kill him.'

'Oh,' Carlo said, straightening up. 'Then what do you want?'

'I want your advice. You're one of them—one of the Clan—except you're not really.'

'Quite right I'm not, can't stand the bastards.'

'But why? How come you didn't end up like the rest of them?'

He shrugged. 'Guess it just didn't take for some reason. Why that is, I do not know. I've got the fangs and I've got the hunger, but that's about where the vampire ends.'

'So there aren't any other Clan members like you?'

'Nope, I'm one of a kind, me. Now, if that's everything, I'd like my blood now.'

'Not until we get what we came for.' This visit was starting to look like a waste of time, but I couldn't shake the feeling that Carlo was holding out on me.

'All right then, cut to the chase. What are you after?'

I looked to Gen, then back to Carlo. 'We need a cure for vampirism.'

He laughed; a proper window-rattling, hand over-the-mouth guffaw. 'Bloody hell, girl, is that all? Yeah, I've got about six of them in the back room, let me go grab one.'

'I'm serious,' I told him.

He stopped laughing and looked to Gen. 'She's pulling my plonker, right? She actually thinks I know how to cure vampirism? Christ Almighty, don't you think if I knew a way to get this Clan blood out of me that I'd do something about my situation? Do something about all of this?' He kicked up a pile of rubbish and the prowling cat darted off with a screech.

Gendith looked at me as if to say, *I told you so.*

'So I take it that's a no then?' I asked Carlo.

'Yeah, that's a really big and bloody obvious no. I'm a lowlife bloodsucker who takes in stray cats, I'm not a magician.'

'Okay then,' I said, turning on my heel. 'In that case you've been no use whatsoever.'

I headed for the door with Gen in tow.

Carlo quickly changed his tune. 'Wait, don't go,' he begged, scratching his arm again. 'Maybe… I don't know, maybe there's a way to turn your boyfriend back after all.'

I was bluffing before when I made to leave. I sensed that he was keeping something to himself, and I knew a thing or two about stringing a man along.

Gen's eyes widened. 'What are you talking about?' she said, giving Carlo evils. 'You said there was no such thing as a cure. You've always said that.'

Carlo tried to throw some sunshine in his voice but only came off sounding more desperate. 'Your man's in the early stages, right? Like, not fully turned?'

'Right,' I replied, eager, a little hope getting its hooks into me.

'Okay, that means there's still a chance. Maybe. Possibly.'

'Bullshit,' Gen spat back. 'He doesn't know anything. He's only saying that so he can get his taste.'

But it didn't seem to me like Carlo was lying. He'd held something back before, and he'd only given it up when I threatened to leave and take the contents of my veins with me. 'Go on,' I said. 'Fess up.'

'I know a guy, okay? My blood guy.'

'Your blood guy?'

'Yeah. A Harley Street haematologist. Hooks me up with the red stuff… at least when I can afford to pay him.'

'Why are you telling us this?' I asked.

'Because he knows his shit, okay? If there's anyone out there who can do something for your fella, it's this bloke.'

'Do what exactly?' asked Gen.

'I don't know... give his blood a rinse I suppose. Get all that Clan taint out before it beds in proper. Christ, I'm not the expert.'

It all sounded a bit pie in the sky to me, but it was the best we had. 'Give us the address then,' I said.

'Sure, sure,' he said, hunting for a pen but returning with an eyeliner pencil. He blathered away as he scribbled on the back of a flyer. 'Look, I'm not promising anything, it's probably a load of hopeless bullshit, but this is your best bet, all right? You should know though, my blood guy won't talk to you willingly.'

'Why not?' I asked.

'Because he's with the JC.'

'He's Clanned up?' Gen replied. 'So what's he doing dealing with a traitor like you?'

'He deals with me because he thinks I'm on the up and up. You reckon I go to him looking like this? No chance. It's a suit and tie all the way, my girl. Same outfit I was buried in as a matter of fact. Should've seen me in my coffin, I looked positively spiffy.'

I snatched the flyer off him and turned to Gen. 'We've got everything we need. Let's go.'

'Oi,' said Carlo. 'What about me? Where's my taste?'

'I'll have to sort you out later,' I replied. 'Sorry, Carlo, but we're on the clock.'

And we were; it was gone half two now, meaning we had less than an hour and a half before sundown.

Carlo made a pathetic mewling noise. 'Please,' he said, begging like a dog, 'I need it…'

But we were already out the door.

6

We had to work fast.

The drive to Marylebone would usually have taken about half an hour, but I paid the cabbie a twenty to put his foot down and we were there in half that. I was dreading my next bank statement. If I survived the next few weeks, I was gonna have to find a way to earn some cash.

We rounded a corner onto Harley Street and I scanned the buildings for the address Carlo had written down in his junkie scrawl. Georgian townhouses with cast iron balconies and arched doorways passed either side of us; private surgeries and medical specialists for the rich and wealthy. I knew all about Harley Street of course; this was where balding footballers went to for hair plugs, and their wives for lip jobs and extra cup sizes. What I didn't know then was that Harley Street was also a hotbed of vampire activity, but the more I learned about the Uncanny, the more I came to realise that wherever there was money, the smell of the grave was never far behind.

'There it is,' I told the driver, pointing out of the cab window. '112 Harley Street.'

We pulled up, then Gendith and I waved the cabbie a cursory goodbye and jogged to the entrance of the building. Having bounded up a short flight of steps, we were presented with a stout black door and an intercom listing no less than half a dozen businesses. I double-checked Carlo's note, but there was no mention of any of them.

'Which one?' I asked Gen.

Gen carefully studied the list of clinics then stabbed a finger at a symbol next to a perfectly nondescript-sounding organisation called BIOLAB LABORATORIES. The symbol was similarly unremarkable: a small, round shape tapering to a point at its top end.

'What's that meant to be?' I asked. 'A teardrop?'

'A blood drop,' Gen corrected, tapping at the telltale clue. 'This is the place. Third floor.'

I went to try the front door but Gen barred the way.

'You should take a look inside first. Surveil the situation.'

The door was solid. No window, not even a keyhole.

'How am I meant to do that?' I asked. 'X-ray specs?'

'With your eyes,' Gen replied, and when I failed to respond to that, she begrudgingly enlightened me. 'You do realise you're able to see through walls, right?'

That took a silent second or two to sink in, I can tell you. 'You're shitting me?'

'No.'

'Right, so is there anything else I can do that you haven't told me about? Can I fly? Shoot laser beams? Ooh, can I turn into a car?'

Gen wiped a palm down her face, top to bottom. 'Learn your powers, girl. For God's sake, you're supposed to be the Nightstalker, the scourge of the vampire horde.' The words, "*Supposed to be*", came out dripping with venom. The way Gendith saw it, she was the one who should have been awarded the Nightstalker mantle, along with the dagger I wore under my jacket. She shook her head at me. 'What's the matter with you? Did you get that symbol on your hand from a henna kit?'

Believe me, if I could have pressed my palm to hers and passed on the brand like a transfer tattoo, I'd have done it, no question. Did she think I wanted to be in this situation? Running around town on a ticking clock, trying to cure my boyfriend of a disease with no known cure? Before that stupid knife found its way across my desk I was happy. Well, not happy exactly, but a fuck of a lot happier than I am since I learned vampires live in the city and have their own private blood banks.

'Well, Gen,' I sighed, 'at least you're consistent.'

'What's that supposed to mean?'

'It means you've been on my case from the moment I got this N on my palm, which—by the way—I never asked for. I mean, come on, what do you want from me? I've been buzzing around like a blue-arsed fly ever since I got yanked into this mess, so pardon me for not knowing I have frigging Superman vision.'

'It isn't my job to teach you, Abbey. I am not your mentor. Vizael is the only one misguided enough to have taken on that responsibility.'

'For Christ's sake, Gen, can you just pretend to be a friend and help me out here? Neil's life is on the line.' I was starting to hyperventilate. Starting to feel like I was seconds away from a complete mental breakdown.

Gen eyed me coolly. 'Very well. Since you haven't been taught how to use all of your abilities yet, we shall consider this an opportunity for some on-the-job training.'

I focussed up and caught my breath. 'Great. Just tell me what I have to do.'

Gen nodded. It can't have been easy, teaching a foolish mortal to use the powers that rightfully belonged to her—at least in her mind—but she swallowed her pride and did it anyway. 'Close your eyes,' she said.

'Don't I need those to, you know, see?'

'Close them, you prattling turd.'

I did as asked. 'Fine. Rude. Eyes shut. What now?'

'Now concentrate.'

'On what?'

'Concentrate on the impossible.'

That one left me a bit stumped. 'I don't get it,' I told her. 'How can I concentrate on something that isn't real?'

'Have you learned nothing since you were Sanctified?' she asked, wearing, I felt sure, her trademarked glower. 'Just think of what you've borne witness to already: vampires and ghosts and sorcery...'

'But I know those aren't impossible.'

'You do *now*. Before the brand opened your eyes, the undead belonged in horror films, and magic was just men in top hats pulling silk scarves out of fancy canes and scrubbing rabbit shit from top hats. Now you know better. Now you know that anything is possible.'

I felt Gen's words rolling around my brain, soothing me, placing me in a kind of trance. 'Okay, I hear you, so now what?'

'Now you *really* open your eyes.'

I followed along and took a peek, expecting nothing to have changed, but discovering a world gone topsy-turvy.

The door in front of me was no longer there, and neither were the walls beyond it. All that was left of 112 Harley Street were faint outlines, as though the entire building were made of freshly-polished glass. Even the ground beneath my feet was gone, leaving me hovering above a bottomless void. A wave of vertigo struck me and I felt my stomach make a valiant escape bid through my throat. I tried closing my eyes again, but saw right through my eyelids.

'Ugh,' I groaned, knees threatening to unhinge and send me collapsing into the void. 'How do I turn it off?'

'Stick with it,' Gen insisted. 'We're not done yet.'

I carried on looking, more out of a lack of choice than anything else. 'Sticking with it,' I assured her.

'Good. Now focus on the third floor and tell me what you see.'

The simple act of tilting my head back was like riding the loop of a roller coaster, but I just about managed to angle my eyeline to the building's third storey without throwing up.

'Can you make out any movement?' Gen asked.

I could; the outline of a solitary figure, milling about in one of the upstairs rooms. As I focused on the outline, the figure glowed blue and became more distinct. It was a man. A man in a lab coat.

'There's a guy up there,' I told Gen. 'Looks like a scientist.'

'Just the one?'

'Far as I can tell.' As I looked to Gen, my vision snapped back to normal, filling my world with solid objects. The rush of reality hit me like oncoming traffic and sent me rolling back on my heels.

'Easy there,' said Gen, catching me before I fell down.

I regained my footing and brushed myself off, embarrassed to have been captured mid-swoon. 'Why would there only be one vamp up there?' I asked.

'The hour of the day,' Gen replied. 'This is siesta time for most Clan members. It's no wonder the lab is operating on a skeleton crew.'

'Okay,' I said, gathering my wits after taking that disorientating roller coaster ride. 'Then let's get up there and question the guy.'

I tried the front door but it was locked. No surprise there. I tried it again, more forcefully this time, but it still wouldn't give. Gen put a shoulder to the door too, but it was rock solid.

'How do we get in?' I asked, but no sooner had I said it than an idea had formed.

I cast my mind back to when this whole merry-go-round had started, before I was the Nightstalker, back when I worked at the Lost Property Office and received my own doorstep visitor. The man who rang the bell that day—the one who turned out to be a vampire—had charmed his way inside using nothing more than the right words and a dollop of sexual magnetism. What if we could do the same to the guy on the other end of this intercom?

I explained my plan to Gen.

'I suppose it's as good a strategy as any,' she said, not exactly bolstering my confidence. 'So, who's going to do the talking?'

'You should, you're the looker. Just flutter your eyelashes and get him to open this door.'

I wasn't just flattering her. Gen was, regardless of her less than perfect attitude, physically stunning. She had the kind of flawless features that belonged on a billboard advertising an expensive perfume, and despite only ever dressing in clothes built for function, her presentation was always impeccable, her appearance never less than pristine. Even after a fight to the death—when I'd look ugly as homemade sin—she'd still manage to look as though she'd just stepped off a Milan catwalk, not a smudge on her skin, not a hair out of place.

Gen's lip curled slightly, and for a split-second she lost her perfect symmetry. 'I know little of seducing men,' she said, 'but I agree, I am by far the better looking of us.'

And so modest with it.

She elbowed me aside so I was out of view of the intercom's camera, and jabbed the button for Biolab Laboratories.

There was a long silence then, 'What do you want?' asked a gruff voice on the other end.

Gen gave the camera her best bedroom eyes. 'Hello, Sir, can I spare a moment of your time to talk about the work we do at Red Cross?'

'Not interested,' said the voice.

'Are you sure I can't tempt you?' asked Gen, unzipping her hoodie to show some cleavage. 'We're only asking for a small donation.'

Lord knows how, but she actually managed to make the word "donation" sound sexy.

Still the man in the lab coat wasn't biting. 'Please go,' he insisted, 'and kindly remove this address from your route.'

How he managed to dismiss her so easily was beyond me. Honestly, even I was a little bit turned on. Gen turned to me, out of ideas.

'If you don't leave now, I'm going to have to call the police,' said the man in the lab coat, drawing a line in the sand.

The time had come to employ Plan B: the nuclear option. Without warning, I stepped in front of the camera and slapped my hand against the lens, showing the man upstairs the big letter N on my palm. 'Do you know what this is?' I asked.

There was a brief silence, then, 'Yes,' he quavered.

'Then you know who I am and what I can do,' I told him.

'Wh-what do you want?' he asked.

'Just a chat.'

'Okay then. Um, then let's talk.'

'No can do,' I replied, 'it's got to be face-to-face.

'I can't do th—'

'Shut up and listen to me. Right now you have two options. Buzz me in and I promise all that's going to happen between us is a conversation. That's Option One. Option Two: you don't open this door, or call your friends, or do anything I don't like, and I'll bust in there and murder you seven ways to Sunday.' I was bluffing of course. Even though I had super strength and who knew how many other superpowers I hadn't been told about, I wasn't taking down that door any time soon. 'So what's it going to be, Doc? Open sesame?'

There was another interminable pause, then the door to the building gasped open, slowly, regrettably, like a mouth trying to keep a secret and breaking its promise.

I turned to Gen. 'After you.'

Gen grimaced and stepped inside.

'So, you never said I *couldn't* turn into a car…'

7

We were in. Now it was time to get what we came for.

The third floor was cold and quiet except for the soft whisper of background machinery.

'Hello,' I said, calling out for the scientist, but getting nothing back.

I drew my dagger from its sheath and it sparked with blue electricity. Beside me, Gendith pulled out her morning star and gave it a couple of preparatory whirls.

We moved along a corridor quietly, passing by a laboratory that was visible through a pane of thick glass (actual glass this time, not just in my head). We were in a large research facility, the kind you might see in an apocalyptic outbreak scenario; all gleaming white walls and great swathes of stainless steel.

I pushed open a door and Gen and I stepped into the lab proper. Everything inside was clean, organised, and smelled of bleach. A complicated machine whirred away, sorting dozens of blood-filled test tubes, rotating them, labelling them, and delivering them into neat metal racks. Through the glass door of a six-foot-tall cooler I saw dozens of IV bags, all of them pregnant with blood.

'Hello?' I tried again. Still no reply.

Then I saw a sudden flash of movement in the corner of my eye. At the far end of the lab, something was nudged, causing a beaker to topple over the edge of a desk and shatter on the tile floor.

We spun in the direction of the disturbance, weapons at the ready. Someone was hiding behind that desk, and doing a pretty terrible job of it.

Gen looked at me and made some complicated signals with her hands, the way they do in soldier movies. Obviously, I had no idea what any of them meant, though I certainly understood the look on her face as I stared back at her in bewilderment. It was a look that said—in no uncertain terms—*'Why have I been saddled with this absolute cretin?'*

In the end, Gen managed to communicate her message through a short game of charades. It was pretty simple stuff —*"You go left, I'll go right"*—hardly worth all the voguing, really.

Anyway, I followed Gen's order, tiptoeing over to the desk while she cut around the other side, the pair of us coming up on our target in a pincer movement. We stopped right before we made the final move. A couple of curt nods to make sure we were on the same page, then we swooped—

Except what we found hiding behind the laboratory desk wasn't a man in a lab coat. It wasn't a man at all. It was a chimpanzee.

It was only the size of a small boy but had strong, sinewy muscle under its downy black fur. Parts of the animal were shaved, and I could make out scars and puncture marks decorating its exposed pink flesh. The chimp's flattened face turned towards my own and peered back at me with soulful, human eyes. The poor creature made a frightened chattering noise as it quaked in our shadows.

'Hey, little fella,' I cooed, 'it's okay, no one's going to hurt you.'

Gen pointed to a cage, its door wide open. 'Your scientist must have let him out. Why would he do that?'

'I don't know,' I said, 'maybe he developed a conscience?'

No such luck.

The chimpanzee opened its mouth wide, and as its lips peeled back, I saw two giant fangs.

'You've got to be kidding me…'

Chimps had fangs—I knew that from the Attenborough shows—but these were the size of paring knives and were accompanied by the sudden appearance of black talons and blood-red eyes.

I managed to dodge the animal's first swipe, but then the second one came at me, too fast to avoid. I felt claws rake through my leather jacket and bite into the skin around my midriff. As I howled in pain, Gen came to my assistance, winding up her morning star and whipping the spiked ball at the back of the chimp's skull. The animal was too fast for her though, spinning about and fetching her a stinging blow to the side of the head.

Pow.

The punch landed with such force that it knocked Gen's head out of her hood, releasing a springy mass of woolly black hair. At the same time, bloody spit went flying out of the left side of her mouth and patterned the floor. As she staggered backwards, the vampire chimp returned its attention to me, flinging itself my way like it was jet-propelled, both fists raised high. A couple of anvils landed on my head, knocking me to the ground, turning my skull into a piñata of bees.

I heard a clattering sound and realised my dagger had left my hand and gone skidding across the lab floor, out of reach. I felt powerless. With the dagger in my hand I was a warrior, but without it, fighting a 'roided-up jungle beast, I felt naked.

I tried to recall the dagger to my hand, but couldn't focus beneath the rain of fists the chimp was bringing down on me. Instead, I did the only thing I could to defend myself, tucking my knees into my chest and crossing my arms in front of my face, shielding myself from the battering.

Gen came to the rescue, pouncing up from behind the chimp and wrapping the chain of her morning star around its neck. With a tennis champion's scream, she pulled the noose tight and the animal's eyes bugged from its head. Gen hadn't counted on the creature's animal agility though, and before she knew it, the chimp had thrown itself backwards and somersaulted over her head, releasing itself from the chain and almost dislocating her shoulders in the process.

Unexpectedly, the vampire chimp then bounded on to the desk and sprang for the ceiling. Grabbing hold of the track lighting, off it went, racing to the other end of the lab like it was swinging through jungle treetops. For a moment it looked as though the chimp was making an exit, then it came about and started back our way, picking up momentum as it went. The next thing I saw were the soles of the chimp's oversized feet as they came at my face like a pair of pistons.

The force of the kick sent me reeling and left me seeing through a red fog. I was hurting, but nowhere near as much as I ought to be. The brand on my palm turned blue and hot, burying the pain under an avalanche of adrenaline. I'd had enough. No more monkeying around (sorry).

With a sudden surge, I leapt at the chimp, screaming. It must have sensed a change in me—some animal instinct telling the creature that it had slipped down the hierarchy from alpha to omega—because as I landed, I caught a flash of fear in its all-too-human eyes.

Two years of RSPCA donations went out the window as I cracked the chimp in the face with my fist. Almost immediately, a bruise rose under its eye, swelling up like puffed bread dough. Now it was my turn to bring the pain. I threw in a left, then another right, pummeling the beast into submission. Rage consumed me, transformed me into a bar room brawler, turned my fists into two busted bottles of lager. The chimp's face was mashed potato. It's limbs went slack. Only the faintest gasp of air left its muzzle now. I looked down at my hands, slick with blood.

'What are you doing?' I heard Gen say over the thunder of my heartbeat. 'Finish it off.'

'No,' I said, coming to my senses.

'What do you mean, "No"?' she asked.

'I'm not going to kill it. It didn't ask to be turned into a vampire, just like Neil didn't.'

'None of them asked,' said Gen. 'That's not how this works. That doesn't mean we should just let them run amok.'

I couldn't do it though. Couldn't kill a lab experiment. Couldn't kill an innocent animal, no matter how dangerous.

'Help me get it back behind bars,' I said, hooking my hands under the sleeping chimp's arms.

Gen sighed. 'You think you're doing that animal a kindness, but the most charitable thing you could do would be to put it out of its misery.'

'Just get on with it, will you?'

Shaking her head, Gen grabbed the chimp by the ankles and assisted me in hoisting it back into its cage. 'Happy now?'

I snatched my dagger from the floor and gripped it tight. 'I will be when I find the fucker who did this.'

Him I'd put down gladly.

8

We left the main lab and crept deeper into the facility.

After a short while, we found ourselves in an area that looked like some sort of decontamination suite. A row of showers lined one side of the room, and on the opposite wall, hooded plastic suits hung from metal hooks. Still no sign of the scientist though.

I was fed up of playing hide and seek so I decided—even though I knew it would make me sick as a pig to do it—to use my x-ray vision to root him out. To my surprise, it didn't make me half as ill this time. The power came to me much easier, and with far less disorientation than before. And, as an added bonus, I found the scientist, hiding in a locker in the far corner of the suite, his glowing outline tattling on him no matter how hard he stifled his breath.

Shutting off my super-sight, I strolled over to the locker and rapped on its metal door with the blunt end of my dagger. 'Open up, dickless.'

After a few moment's hesitation the locker swung open and a man in a white lab coat stepped out, hands raised in surrender. 'Please don't hurt me,' he begged, his body cramped from confinement.

'Like you didn't hurt that chimp?' I said, grabbing him by the throat.

Something wasn't right. At this point I'd expect to see a glowing letter J stamped on the forehead of the person I was manhandling. Not this guy though. He was clean.

I pushed him away from me and he hit the lockers hard enough to leave a dent. He looked normal enough. Just a balding, middle-aged bloke in a lab coat as far as I could tell.

'What are you?' I asked him.

'I'm a person,' he stammered, 'just like you.'

'You're nothing like me. I don't pal around with vampires.'

Gen seized him by the wrist and pulled up the sleeve of his white coat.

'What are you looking for?' I asked.

'A marking.'

She turned his wrist over, but the flesh on both sides of his arms was bare and unadorned. I figured Gen would let him go after that, but instead she reached into her pocket and produced a slim, keychain torch. With a flick of her thumb, she switched it on and shone a blue light on his arm. There it was: a discreet tattoo of a letter J, revealed under UV light.

'He's a familiar,' Gen explained.

'Familiar with what?'

Gen rolled her eyes so far back she probably caught a glimpse of her own brain. 'A familiar is a human who works in the service of another, in this one's case, a vampire.'

'Why would anyone do that?'

'They're given gifts for their loyalty,' Gen explained, 'and a promise that they'll be turned one day.'

'Wait, I thought you said no one asked to be a vampire.'

Gen instinctively went to argue, but sputtered to a halt when she realised I had her beat. 'There are exceptions to every rule,' was the best she could manage.

'I still don't get it,' I said. 'Why would anyone want to be a vampire? Well, except for the immortality and the super strength and the pure coolness of it? Actually, I think I might have answered my own question there.'

The scientist used the lull in the conversation to try and make a break for it, but Gen's grip was too tight, and he bounced back like a yo-yo.

'Woah there, buddy, where do you think you're going?' I asked, stepping in his way.

'I'm sorry,' he said, sweating bullets. 'I didn't know what else to do. I'm scared, okay?'

'Scared? Scared like that animal next door that you used as an attack dog? Experimenting on animals? You should be ashamed of yourself.'

'What about the makeup you're wearing?' he said, referring to the warpaint that had been caked on my face so long I must have looked like a Batman villain. 'That stuff's not cruelty-free, you know? They just outsource it to China now.'

Now it was my turn to run from a losing argument. 'I didn't come here to discuss ethics with a man who works for murderers,' I said, taking the high ground. 'I saw the blood bags next door. How many people gave up their lives for that little lot?'

'You've got it all wrong,' he said. 'The blood we have here is synthetic.'

What was he telling me? *No animals were harmed in the making of this vampire food*?

'Keep going,' said Gen.

He obliged, talking a mile-a-minute, tripping over his own words. 'We manufacture our own blood here. Once we've perfected the compound and learned how to mass produce it, no one needs to die. Don't you get it? We're doing this in service of humankind.'

Was he on the level? A baby formula for vampires? An ethically-sourced blood substitute? It didn't really matter, at least not right then. The only thing that counted in that moment was Neil.

'I don't care what kind of Doctor Frankenstein shit you're up to here. The only thing I need from you is a cure.'

He looked at me, head cocked to one side like a dog learning a card trick. 'A cure for what?'

'A cure for vampires.'

The request didn't elicit quite the same response it had from Carlo, but the result was pretty much the same.

'I'm an expert in vampire biology, specialising in haematology, and I can tell you unequivocally that there is no such thing as a "cure" for vampirism.' He sounded the quotation marks out with his fingers, intimating that the idea of reversing the condition he pined after so badly would be like trying to cure a fish by sewing up its gills.

I didn't like the tone of his voice, so I grabbed him by his scrawny neck and the smug look slid right off his face. 'Try again,' I suggested, lifting him off the ground.

His eyes bulged. 'Who's... the patient?' he squeaked, suddenly cooperative.

'My boyfriend,' I snarled back.

That's when the scientist grasped the true gravity of his situation. 'When... when was he turned?' he asked.

'Last night.'

'Okay,' he replied, 'so he's new.' Even dangling by his neck, he couldn't disguise his jealousy. 'Then there might... be something... I can do.'

I dropped him to the floor. 'Talk, and fast.'

He rubbed his throat and spoke a couple of octaves lower than before. 'I don't know how to cure your boyfriend, but I can buy you some time. He hasn't turned yet, not completely. With the right combination of treatments, I can stall the process and put off the transformation.'

It wasn't the solution I was after, but it was obviously the best I was getting from this guy. I could tell just from looking at him that he was giving me everything he had.

'Show me,' I said, and he dutifully complied, opening the locker he'd been hiding in and producing a small Moleskine book.

'My research notes,' he said, thumbing to a double-page spread covered in tightly-packed handwriting and arcane-looking formulas. 'Everything you need to know about slowing the metamorphosis.'

Gen snatched the book off him and scanned the pages warily. 'Looks legit,' she said eventually.

'It better had be,' I said, grabbing the scientist by the lapels of his coat and shaking a couple of pens loose from his pocket.

He cringed, pulling his face away from me as though I were about to headbutt him. 'Whatever equipment you need you can take from next door,' he said, trembling from head to toe. 'Now please, you promised not to hurt me if I let you in here.'

It's true, I had. I loosened my grip, and the tight bundle of white cotton I was holding dropped from my fist. 'You can go,' I said.

Gen shook the scientist by the hand. 'Thank you for your help,' she said, quite unexpectedly, then, even more unexpectedly, pulled a hidden knife from her belt and thrust it into the man's heart.

It happened so fast I almost didn't see it. One moment I was thinking about our next move, the next I saw the handle of a knife sticking out of a lab coat.

'What the hell?' I screamed, as the stunned doctor slid from Gen's blade and slumped to the floor, blood flowing freely from a gaping hole in his sternum.

I crouched down to staunch the wound, but it was too late for that. The scientist looked right past me, gazing at the ceiling, the life gone from his eyes.

I bounded to my feet and shoved Gen in the chest. 'You just killed a man! Not a monster, a man!'

She fixed me with her cold blue eyes. 'You said yourself that he needed to die.'

'That was before!'

'Let me explain how this works. A vampire familiar only does what he does to become one of them. To become another member of the Clan.'

'I get that, but... but you can't just go around murdering people.'

'Why can't I? I was stopping a monster from being born, that's all. Consider it an abortion. Unless... you're not against that too, are you?'

'Well... no.'

'Good,' she said, wiping her knife on the dead man's body and leaving a thick red stripe across his white coat. 'Then how about we get out of here and save your boyfriend?'

She headed for the door, leaving the corpse of the scientist in her wake. On the way out, she executed the chimp too, despite my hollow protests.

I was beginning to see why not all angels had wings.

9

It was getting perilously close to sundown, which left me zero time to worry about the moral consequences of our visit to Harley Street. Instead, I hailed a passing taxi and bunged the driver another twenty to put some lead in his shoe.

Getting back to base was a mad scramble, but we beat the rush hour traffic and scraped our way to Bethnal Green with a little time to spare. Gendith and I burst into the gas tower, surprising Vizael, who was busy watching over Neil in our absence.

'Help us put this together,' I told the old man, dumping down an armful of medical equipment we'd lifted from the lab—bits and pieces drawn from the dead scientist's shopping list—IV bags, rubber tubes, hypodermic needles, a drip stand, plus some other key ingredients.

'What is all this stuff?' asked Neil, still chained semi-naked to a chair and at his wit's end.

I didn't have time to answer him.

Together, me and Viz assembled the apparatus, then Gen read from the notebook while I followed her instructions. She called out the names of various chemicals and their quantities, and I injected them into the drip bag as quickly as I could, fingers shaking, heart hammering. While I raced to keep up, I could see the light dimming through the crack in the tower's door as the sun dipped into the horizon. Neil's time was almost up. If this didn't work, he'd be lost for good.

'Are you sure about this?' he asked.

'You're going to be okay.'

'How do you know?'

'Look, we don't have time for what ifs, okay? Do you want me to do this, or would you rather turn completely? Well?'

Neil bowed his head, frowning.

While I worked, Viz's eyes stayed fixed on Neil, monitoring him, looking for any suspicious changes, making sure he wasn't about to break character and lunge for my neck.

As Neil sat in his chair, patient but terrified, I finished adding the last of the chemicals to the concoction. 'Is that it?' I asked Gen.

'That's what it says,' she replied, snapping the Moleskine shut.

The method we were following was simple enough, at least on paper. The idea was to dampen Neil's burgeoning vampirism by injecting him with a gradually increased infusion of substances known to be the bane of bloodsuckers. Inside the intravenous bag were garlic juice, colloidal silver, and holy water, among other things. According to the scientist's notes, the compound would delay the vampiric mutation and suppress the associated endowments, such as super strength and heightened agility. More importantly, it would also curb the blood hunger and general bad attitude that came with being an undead freak-beast.

'Do you trust me?' I asked Neil.

'I trust you.'

I looked into his eyes and ran a hand through his unruly mop. 'I love you,' I said, and kissed him on the mouth.

Enough of the sweet, now for the sour. I drew the cap off a cannula and plugged the needle into a juicy vein on the crook of Neil's elbow.

'Ow!' he said, but I was too busy hooking the needle up to the IV to give him any sympathy.

Time to let her rip. I turned on the tap and let the drip do its work. The formula snaked down the rubber tube and Neil shivered as it entered his system. I watched his face carefully, we all did, looking to see how he handled the infusion.

At first, it seemed to do nothing much. Once the initial shock had passed, Neil just sat there serenely as the solution continued to course through his veins. The sun was down now though, so I took serene for good. Serene trumped big fangs tearing my throat out any day of the week.

'How do you feel?' I asked.

'About the same I think. Not sure whether that's a good or ba—'

The sentence pinched off as Neil's throat went tight. His back arched as his body stiffened suddenly, turning his spine into a question mark.

'Neil?'

He didn't answer. The best response he could manage was a high-pitched gurgle, as though his voice were trapped behind a wet plug of mucus. I'd seen this before. When Neil's condition was at its worst—his cystic fibrosis—he was susceptible to respiratory attacks. They were scary and they were awful, but they could be dealt with, at least so long as he had the right medicine to clear his airways. His inhaler was at home though, and without that, there was little I could do but watch him suffer.

His eyes looked back at me pleadingly, bulging from their sockets. For a second, his voice broke through the plug, thin and distant. 'Help me,' he wheezed.

Neil told me once what it felt like to suffer these attacks. He'd said it was like having someone pour concrete into his lungs, then clamp an invisible hand over his mouth. He tried telling me more, but I had to ask him to stop. It made me sick just to hear it.

'He's not breathing,' I said, stating the obvious. 'What do we do?' My eyes flashed to the angels, desperate for an answer, for any answer.

They had none.

Then a thought occurred. 'Wait, he's a vampire, right? Does he even need to breathe?'

'Yes,' Gen replied, matter-of-factly. 'Vampires of the Judas Clan breathe air just like us.'

A last, fragile gasp rattled in Neil's throat, then he began to convulse, his limbs straining violently against their bonds. The force of the seizure tore the needle free of the cannula in his arm, and the contents of the drip spattered on the floor. The chair shook beneath his body, its wooden legs tap dancing on the ground, *clackety clack clack.* Neil was dying, spiralling downwards, faster and faster, tighter and tighter, into a helix, into a pinhole.

I had to do something. Working fast, I went to undo his chains so I could lay him on the floor and clear his air passage, but before I could get there, Gen intervened.

'It could be a trick,' she said, placing a hand on my wrist. 'So he can break free.'

I shook her off. 'I don't care!'

I barged past her and tore Neil's chains away like they were made of wet toilet paper. Head bowed, he slid from his chair, and I helped him gently to the ground.

'Neil?'

He'd stopped fitting and gone limp now. His jaw was slack, his limbs soft and rubbery. I looked into his eyes but they were vacant; lifeless as the glass marbles in the head of a Victorian doll. I placed a hand on Neil's face, which was already turning cold. His complexion had lost its natural hue and taken on a pale bluish colour. His palms, which had been slick with sweat a moment ago, were bone dry now.

I put the back of my hand to his mouth and felt nothing, not even a tickle. 'Neil?' I begged.

I checked for a pulse but his arteries were quiet, wrist and neck. He was catatonic. I felt tears spill from my eyes, but this was no time to give in to dread. Every second I wasted was another second Neil's brain was starved of oxygen. I remembered my First Aid training; the course I did with St John Ambulance. I needed to clear Neil's airway quickly, and doing that required an emergency procedure. Something drastic. Something I really didn't want to do.

I drew the hallowed dagger from its sheath.

'That's right,' said Gen. 'Put him out of his misery.'

'I'm not killing him, I'm making a hole in his throat. It's the only way to get him breathing again.'

I'd never performed a tracheotomy, nor had I ever wished too, but if I didn't act soon, Neil was a goner.

'You can't use the dagger on him,' Viz cautioned. 'It's made to kill vampires. One nick and he'll never stop bleeding.'

'What choice do I have?'

Either Neil died of suffocation or I gave him something to breathe through. Bleeding I could deal with—at least I hoped I could—but sitting by and doing nothing, that I couldn't do.

I moved the dagger to Neil's neck. For a moment I considered the idea of sterilising the dagger, but there was no time for that. My hand was trembling. I had to get a hold of myself. I knew from experience that the metal would break his skin with only the slightest contact, so I couldn't afford any slip-ups. Get this wrong and I might as well be sticking the knife in Neil's heart.

I swallowed and readied myself to apply pressure to the blade.

'He's already gone,' said Gen. 'Don't do this to yourself.'

'Just shut up and get me some bandages, okay? And a tube. Something I can put down his throat to help him breathe.'

I gripped the hilt of the dagger tightly and steeled myself. This was it. The moment of truth. I put the tip of the blade to the spot just below Neil's Adam's apple and prepared to make the incision—

When he sat bolt upright like a jug of ice water had been flung into his face.

I managed to pull the dagger back just in time to stop him from beheading himself. The rest of us lurched backwards in surprise as Neil let out a great hacking wheeze and coughed a blob of mucus halfway across the room. His fingers gripped me, digging into my shoulders like talons, then he went limp again and slipped back into unconsciousness.

'What happened?' I asked, clutching at him like a drowning woman to a passing log.

Viz smiled. 'Whatever you did, it looks as though it worked.'

'Are you sure?'

'The mutation's been stalled,' said Gen. 'I can tell from his aura. He hasn't turned. Not fully.'

I cast my eyes to Neil and saw that his fangs and claws had

retracted. The colour was returning to his waxy skin, and the Judas mark on his forehead—while still there—had become dim and indistinct. I put a couple of fingers to his neck and found a pulse this time. His chest rose and fell, shallow but steady. He was out for the count, but on the mend.

'He's stabilised,' said Gen. 'Just like the man in the lab coat told us he would.'

Yeah, the man she'd murdered.

'So what's the upshot?' I asked. 'Is he okay now?'

Gen shook her head. 'No, he's still affected. The complete transformation has only been postponed.'

'For how long?' I asked, searching her face.

'According to the notes we were given, instead of twenty-four hours, he now has a week left in this state. Give or take.'

Was that all? Seven measly days? I raked a scraggle of hair from Neil's brow and placed a hand on his chest, feeling the soft heartbeat beneath his ribs.

'Okay then,' I said, trying to remain positive. 'In that case we'd better come up with a full, lasting cure, and fast. Viz, anything new?'

Viz slumped his shoulders. 'While you were away I took the time to double-check my library. I searched high and low for anything even remotely connected to a cure for vampirism, but found nothing. I'm sorry to say this, Abbey, but its seems you've only succeeded in delaying the inevitable.' He placed a hand on top of mine. 'If I were you, my love, I'd use the time you've bought to accept what's coming and say goodbye.'

I snatched my hand from his. 'No,' I said. 'No way. Neil isn't becoming one of them, not while I have anything to say about it.'

'Abbey...'

'I said no! If there's nothing about a cure in those books of yours, then you'd better do something about it.' I pointed to the sky. 'You'd better call upon the author to explain.'

'What does that mean?'

'It's from a Nick Cave song. It means you need to get your God on the phone.'

Viz's eyes slid off me. 'You know I can't do that, Abbey.

Neither of us can. We haven't spoken to Him since He cast us out of Heaven.'

'Vizael is right,' said Gen. 'The Big Man's been screening our calls ever since He stranded us on this rock.'

I felt my lower lip begin to quiver, first with sadness, then with rage. I stuck out a finger, thrusting it at the angels like the point of a weapon. 'Maybe you've forgotten what you are, but I haven't. I can see the halos hovering over your heads. Whatever it is He marooned you for, you're still angels, and that means you're still part of God's flock.'

'So what?' asked Gen.

'So you'd better figure out a way to get the shepherd's attention, or my Nightstalking days are done.'

10

I reattached Neil to his drip and put him to bed. The angels had insisted he be kept restrained, which meant lashing him to the bed frame like the star of a BDSM video, just on the off-chance that he woke up and turned feral. It didn't look to me like he was attacking anyone though. That boy was out for the count.

I pulled a fold-out cot beside him and prepared to snatch some rest of my own. There was no going home now, not since our flat had been invaded by the Clan. The gas tower was the safest place we could be given the circumstances. Besides, I wasn't about to head out anywhere, I'd been on my feet for the better part of three days, and was bleary-eyed to the point of collapse.

My head had still been on its way to the pillow when I fell asleep, that's how tired I was. I didn't stay down for long though. When I came around, the sun had yet to crest the horizon, forcing me to scrabble around in the dark to check for the time. I squinted at the glowing digits on my phone to discover that it had only just gone three in the morning. Despite the time, I felt fully rested. I was never going to get used to that. Being forced to stay awake all night was an item from the Nightstalker superpowers list that I could really have done without. I mean, it's not like I could do anything worthwhile with the extra time it gave me, or at least not in that moment. Viz and Gen were asleep, and even though I'd have done anything to lay my hands on Neil's cure, without the angels' help, I had nowhere to go.

I splashed some cold water on my face. The base had no plumbing, so I had to make do with a wash bowl full of old rain-water collected from buckets on the tower roof. I checked my reflection in a shard of broken mirror balanced on a sideboard and grimaced at the sight of my eye luggage. I had to get out of that place. Had to kill some time until the sun came up and I could get back to work.

With the state Neil was in I didn't want to stray too far though, so I decided to take a short walk along the canal that ran around the back of the industrial park. Something told me I probably shouldn't have been out there on my own, but if I was ever going to learn to do my job without Gen chaperoning me, I figured I might as well act accordingly. I squeezed through the peeled-back panel that acted as the tower's front door and headed out into the night.

My breath formed in visible puffs as I walked alongside the canal, trailing behind me in wisps of dragon smoke. It was cold out – absolutely Baltic. Tangled thickets of lifeless thorn lined the outer edge of the towpath, interrupted by the occasional willow tree, which loomed overhead, leaning towards the moon-dappled water like respectful mourners. The canal was eerily quiet, save for the occasional sound of something fluttering over-head. A bird? A bat maybe? Did we even get bats in London?

My mind soon returned to more pressing matters, specifically, to Neil. What was I going to do about him? No, what were *we* going to do? It was high time the angels started pulling their weight. We had a serious knowledge gap that needed filling, and I couldn't plug that thing on my own. The way I saw it, me being the Nightstalker was a two-way deal: I did the brawling, and the angels worked my corner. I'd fight my hardest for them, but I needed to know they were there to look after me between bouts. Right now I was bleeding—bleeding like hell—and the only way they were going to patch me up was by figuring out how to make Neil better.

Frustrated, I kicked at a stone in my path, punting it into the murky canal. I watched the stone arc through the air then plop into the water, creating ever-widening ripples upon its surface.

Then I saw something else.

Something was moving beneath the water, causing bubbles to sprout to the surface. A fish? No, too big for that. I tried to make out what it was, but all I could see was the reflection of the night sky. The bubbles began to move, forming a path, heading in my direction. I took a step back and drew my dagger, lighting the water cobalt blue. The bubbles stopped, disappearing under the blanket of duckweed that clung to the bank of the canal.

Feet planted, I readied myself for whatever it was lurking in the depths of that fetid estuary. Nothing came though. Nothing showed. Of course it didn't. What had I been expecting exactly? Some inner-city Nessie? The Bethnal Green mermaid? I chuckled. I was meant to be the Nightstalker, but I'd managed to spook myself out at the sight of a few water bubbles. What an absolute twat. What would I do for my next trick? Run from my own shadow? Jump on to a stool as a mouse ran by? Shit a brick at the sound of a creaky door? My chuckle turned into a laugh; a great shrieking guffaw that left me clutching my sides.

Which was unfortunate, because it left me completely unprepared for what came next.

Two hands sprang from the duckweed, quick as snakes, grabbing me around the ankles. My arse hit the ground with a thump as my legs were pulled out from beneath me and my body dragged towards the canal. Freezing water stung my feet and filled my Doc Martens. I kicked out and my heel made contact with something. Something altogether hideous.

A head had appeared above the surface of the water, stalks twitching in the bony hollows of its eye sockets. The lurker in the canal was a thing of nightmares. A woman with bilious green skin, long lank hair, and razor-sharp teeth. A horror, empty of heart and brimming with spite. A creature as foul on the outside as it was within. I tried to recoil from her, but the lurker left me with nowhere to go. Claws like black iron dug into me as she clung on, dragging me into the foul-smelling water.

I tried to think of my next move, but the pain absorbed my full attention. Before I knew it, I was in the canal fully, submerged up to my neck in icy black water. I thrashed around and tried to free myself of the lurker's grip, but she held on to me like a vice. With a fierce tug, I was hauled beneath the surface, my cries of protest silenced as frigid water flooded into my lungs and turned my screams into mute bubbles.

I was drowning—suffocating—just like Neil had been, only hours before. While I was busy panicking, the creature shifted her grip, climbing on top of me, hands around my throat and driving me to the depths with powerful kicks of her webbed feet. I arrived at the bed of the canal and the lurker pinned me there, plunging me into the sediment. I was utterly blind, buried in blackness, enveloped by the void.

My heartbeat rang like thunder in my ears as I fought the creature, quickly at first, then slowing as panic turned into acceptance. This was not my domain. The canal belonged to the lurker, and I would die in it as surely as the sun was about to rise on a new day. Call me a pessimist, but if there's one good thing about pessimism, it's that you're never disappointed.

And often surprised.

The hands around my throat went slack as the creature pinning me to the canal bed unexpectedly released her grip. For a moment, I just lay there in disbelief, then my survival instincts kicked in and I boosted myself out of the mire and went rocketing up for dry land. The moment my head broke the surface I ejected about a gallon of putrid water. It was only when I stopped coughing that I realised why the lurker had let go of me.

Bobbing before me was the creature's green head, torn from the rest of her body and set adrift. Pitch black blood seeped from the ragged wound of her neck, settling on the surface of the water like an Exxon special. I tried to swim away from the spill, but I'd used up the last of my energy escaping the bottom of the canal, and my limbs had turned into silly string.

I felt myself begin to sink, but before I could return to the depths, something snagged hold of me. Not the lurker this time —she wouldn't be grabbing anybody any time soon—it was a new pair of hands that seized me now, not grasping, not swiping at me like some frenzied animal, but lifting me from the water and out of harm's way.

I felt ground beneath me and realised I'd been deposited back on to the soft earth of the riverbank. Rolling over to my side to cough up the last of the water I'd swallowed, I got a first look of my saviour. Sitting beside me, sopping wet from his dip in the drink, was a man of around thirty. Moonlight flecked his hair and gilded his perfect features. He was handsome. The kind of handsome you feel in your ovaries.

'What happened?' I asked between heaves.

'You were attacked,' he said, his voice warm and buttery.

'No,' I started, had a small coughing fit, then continued, 'shit.'

I heard a bubbling noise and turned to see the lurker's head swallowed by the ink black water.

'You killed that thing?' I asked, returning to my rescuer.

He nodded humbly, as though tearing a monster's head off with his bare hands was all in a day's work. What was he? Was he like me? A protector, a guardian, an instrument forged to combat the forces of evil?

Before I got to ask any of those questions, he started talking. 'It's dangerous being out here on your own,' he said. 'There are Uncanny creatures all across this city that are hell-bent on killing the Nightstalker, and they're going to come at you like iron filings to a magnet. You'll need to grow eyes in the back of your head if you're going to survive the life you've chosen.'

"Chosen", wasn't exactly the word I'd have used, but I let him have it.

'That... thing,' I said, shivering in the cold, 'what was it?'

'That was a river hag,' he explained. 'They drag their victims into the water so they can drown them and eat their bodies. Not exactly pleasant.'

'River hag? But this is a canal.'

He laughed. 'I don't think you should get too caught up in the semantics,' he said, 'the hags don't.' He turned to me fully, flicking his hair to one side.

And that's when I saw it.

A mark on his forehead.

The mark of Judas.

11

Whipping the dagger from under the folds of my leather jacket, I rounded on the vampire and brought the edge of its blade to his throat.

'Give me one good reason why I shouldn't ventilate you,' I demanded.

'Well, for one thing, I just saved your life,' he replied, 'which would make killing me a bit of a dick move.'

What the hell was happening? The man on the end of my knife belonged to the Judas Clan, that made me his mortal enemy, yet he'd gone out of his way to dive into a dirty canal and save me from being turned into hag food.

'What is this, a trap?' I asked, scanning the area and expecting the worst. 'Are there others out there?'

Had he rescued me from the depths just so the Clan could have the pleasure of killing me themselves?

'I came alone. Actually, I came to see you, and I didn't come to fight.' He pointed across the canal to the industrial park, his finger aimed at our base. 'If I wanted to harm you, I would have left you to the hag, or snuck into that gas tower and killed you while you slept.'

'I'd like to have seen you try,' I snorted.

In a flash, he seized the hand I was using to hold the dagger and whipped me around. By the time I stopped spinning, the weapon was in his hand and pressed against my throat.

'Okay, that's a pretty good try,' I admitted.

I clenched my eyes shut, ready for the end, but the end never came. Unexpectedly, the vampire removed the knife from my jugular, flipped it over so he was holding it by the blade, and presented me with the handle.

'I told you I didn't want to fight.'

He really was stunning. His skin was flawless and paler than the moon, and I could tell from the way his wet clothes clung to his frame that he had the kind of body that appeared in men's health magazines alongside pictures of protein shakes.

I rubbed my neck and snatched the dagger from him. 'Okay, so what do you want?'

'Just to talk. My name is Lauden. Lauden Crowe. I came to you because I wanted to try and make things right between the Nightstalker and the Clan. Or at least to open a dialogue between us.'

'Let me get this right; you turned my boyfriend into a monster and now you want to kiss and make up?'

He looked to the ground. 'No, that wasn't me, or my Clan. We share no affiliation with the people who did that. But that's what pushed me to put myself in danger and talk to you, face-to-face, before things twisted further out of control. Before there's no way back.'

'Nice try, mate, but I'd be more inclined to believe you if you didn't have the exact same forehead decoration as the blokes who kidnapped my boyfriend.'

I aimed the tip of my dagger at the glowing J on his brow.

'The vampires who did that were Wild Bloods,' said Lauden. 'Outcasts from the Clan who just want to cause pain. To kill. They're animals.'

'And you're what? Mother Teresa?'

'Compared to the Wild Bloods, yes I am.'

I wanted to argue, but maybe there was some truth to what he was saying. What if the "Wild Bloods" he was talking about were as representative of his people as the Alt-Right were of mine?

I looked Lauden up and down and tried to get a read on him.

He didn't dress like the rest of the Clan, done up like city boys, creases in their suits sharp enough to carve mutton. No, the vampire who pulled me from the canal wore jeans, white Converse trainers and a chunky-knit cardigan. Did people who wore cardigans murder people? It was hard to picture. Still, I called bullshit.

'Pull the other one. I've run into my fair share of vamps since I picked up this knife, and all of them have been bloodthirsty fuckers. Don't act like you're any different.' As I said it I thought of Carlo, pacing about in his squat and begging for blood like a junkie. Now there was a vampire who wasn't a monster, but then like Gen said, there's an exception to every rule.

'And what about Neil?' I said. 'He's the nicest guy I ever met, but he spends one night with your lot and now he's a psycho.'

'Not a psycho,' said Lauden, 'just hungry.'

'That right?' I sniffed.

'When a vampire is born, they wake with an insatiable appetite. They need blood, have to have it, like a babe needs a teat. It's why we prefer to be around when someone turns, to make sure they feed immediately, so that fervour, that rage, is snuffed out as quickly as possible. That way no one is hurt, and they become manageable.'

'And then what?'

'Then he's as human as you are. And don't kid yourself into thinking that my kind are inhuman. Blood pumps through our veins and oxygen flows through our lungs, just as they do yours.'

'That doesn't make you human. You're not like me. You're undead.'

'My kind are *undying*, meaning immortal. "Undead" is just a corruption, a slur, a word that's used by your kind to denigrate mine. It's just fear.'

I laughed until I had to wave my hand in the air as a flag of apology. 'So you're an oppressed people now? What is this shit, *Vampire Lives Matter*?'

Lauden kept his composure. 'We're not the bogeyman, Abbey. Most of us, at least. The real Clan—not the Wild Bloods you've tangled with, but people like me—only want to live in peace with the rest of you. To not have to hide away all of our lives, like we should be ashamed to exist. Nothing more, nothing less. Do we not have the right to live?'

'Listen, you did me a favour when you tore that hag thing's nut off, and you're easy enough on the eye, but what you're saying goes against everything I know.'

'Everything you've known since, what, Wednesday?' He looked down at me with a pair of hazel brown eyes that melted softly into a glorious milky green. 'All I'm asking is that you don't tar us all with the same brush. The likes of the Wild Bloods are a noisy, violent minority making us all look bad.'

I folded my arms. 'Oh yeah? And what about murdering people? Is that fake news too?'

'We don't need to murder to feed, but you already know that, don't you?'

I rubbed at my wrist, at the bite marks Neil had left me with.

'In any case, we're doing our best to synthesise a substitute blood. Once we have that, there'll be no reason for anyone to ever fear us again. Just imagine that.'

The bloke had an answer for everything, but I was determined to catch him out. 'If drinking blood is such a hassle, why haven't you tried to cure yourselves?'

His face creased. He looked hurt. 'Of what? Vampirism? Abbey, what we have isn't a disease.'

'Oh no, it's a real gift.'

'You're being sarcastic, but yes, it's a gift in many ways. And with that gift we can make some real changes. We can actually fix some things. Make life a little better.'

I felt my lips thin. 'Ta, but we've been getting by okay without the fangs, thank you very much.'

'Have you? War, famine, overpopulation, a ludicrous horror-toddler running the free world?'

'Whatever,' I said. 'If you really want to make some changes around here, you can start by helping me.'

'I think I just did, with the whole river hag thing a few minutes ago.'

'How do I reverse what your "Wild Bloods" did to my boyfriend?'

'You don't,' he said, letting out a long exhale. 'You don't because there is no way to do so.'

'I know that's not true. I already heard about a priest geezer in the olden days who went on a quest to make himself better.'

'Yes, I've heard that story too, we all have,' Lauden replied. 'Do you know what that quest involved?'

'Let's pretend I don't.'

'It involved him submerging himself in a bath of holy water for half an hour.'

'And that cured him?'

'Yes, it cured him of vampirism. And of life in general. He drowned himself.'

I remembered Gen's comment about putting Neil out of his misery, and considered that the vampire might be telling the truth. 'I'm going to figure it out. I'm going to fix him.'

'Fix him? He *is* fixed.'

'He's a fucking vampire!'

'I've been one for a long, long time, and look at me. Do I seem sick to you? Do I strike you as being in pain?'

He didn't, quite the opposite in fact. He seemed so *alive*. I thought about Neil, how his life had been. Struggling with illness. Struggling towards a death that would always come far too early.

'So what's the story?' I asked. 'How long have you been on my tail?'

'I've been keeping an eye on you because I think you're important. You could be the key to bringing an end to all this. To bringing peace at last. And, well, I want, for purely selfish reasons, to make sure you don't come to any harm.'

'From river hags?'

'In part. And from angels.'

This just kept getting better and better. 'Let me get this straight... you've been spying on me to make sure I don't fall foul of God's holy angels?'

'Look, I realise that my kind haven't exactly made the best of first impressions, but think about what you've seen. All of it. They call themselves angels, but do they really always act like angels?'

I thought back to Harley Street. Back to the slaughtered chimp. Back to the knife sticking out of that scientist's chest. Back to Gen, wiping a stripe of blood on his white lab coat.

'Angels are on the side of God,' I told Lauden, more for my sake than his. 'So don't go telling me they're baddies.'

'No one is saying that, but you should know that there are unlawful people among their ranks, just as there are among mine. And ask yourself this: why is it that I'm here? Why is it that my kind are the only ones trying to bring this war to an end with words instead of death?'

While I was busy trying to think up a comeback, I saw Lauden looking me over. Looking at the girl beneath the mish-mash of goth threads, the girl decorated with chipped black fingernails and a pentagram necklace she picked up on Carnaby Street. And going by the look in his eye, he rather liked what he saw.

Sensing that he'd held his gaze for long enough, Lauden coughed and looked away. I held back a smile. There was something sweet about the coyness of him, something human.

'You must be freezing,' he said, and he was not wrong, my knees were almost audibly knocking. 'Here, have my coat, I took it off before I dived in the water.'

He scooped a navy-coloured pea coat from the ground and handed it to me. I thought about turning him down, but the offer was so inviting I couldn't say no. Lauden might have been a cold-blooded creature of the night, but he seemed so warm. So personable. I wondered for a moment if he was using some special powers to manipulate me, but the brand made me immune to all that. No, what Lauden had was good old-fashioned charm. By contrast, Gen—one of my so-called teammates—was a pure void of charisma. She was so stiff, so inhuman, so robotic in her ways, that I'd come to wonder if she'd even pass the Turing test.

Lauden shook me from my daydream. 'The angels didn't come here to further the cause of humankind, their only mission is to hunt my people to extinction and get back in God's good graces. There's a word for that: Genocide.'

'You can talk. What happens when you get your way and

there's vampires running around everywhere? What happens to the rest of us then, eh? We'd be cattle.'

'The only people treating you like cattle are the ones who gave you this scar.' He took my hand in his and turned it over to show me the N seared into my palm. 'Just because they did this to you, doesn't mean they own you.' He looked at me with those dreamy eyes of his. 'They turned you into their weapon without even asking your permission. That's not right. You're more than that.'

'You don't know. You don't know anything about me.'

'Maybe, maybe not, but I know some things about the people you've decided to call friends.'

I didn't want to give him the satisfaction, but I had to. 'Like what?'

'The angels didn't come here by choice, they were banished here. Let go by God.'

'I already knew that.'

'Yes, but have you considered what that really means? It means they're fallen angels, and you know who else was a fallen angel?'

I thought back to Sunday school. 'Lucifer.'

He let go of my hand. I hadn't realised he was still holding it until that moment, but the moment it was gone, I missed it.

'You don't have to trust me,' he said.

'Handy, because I really, really don't.'

'Why would you? But just keep an eye out, and your mind open. Maybe you'll see things aren't so black and white. And maybe you'll start to see there's a way to end this where we can all live in peace. Where one side doesn't have to snuff the other out. Take care of yourself, Abbey,' he said, heading off down the towpath. 'You can keep the coat.'

Then he was gone, leaving me standing alone by the canal with plenty to think about.

I pulled the vampire's coat tight around my neck and breathed in his scent. I didn't smell death there. All I smelled was a man.

12

'He answered, Abbey! He answered my call!'

If you're confused reading that line, you can only imagine how I felt hearing it out loud.

It was only moments ago that I'd snuck back into the gas tower, stripped off my wet clothes and crawled into bed – now I was being shouted at and shaken awake.

My hand shot out and the dagger was in my fist, blasting from its sheath like a pistol from a gun and firing across the room to reunite with the brand.

The figure that had been shaking me let go and recoiled. 'Abbey, it's me.'

I knuckled some sleep from my eyes and saw Vizael standing at the foot of my cot. Sunlight streamed in through rusty holes in the tower wall, casting a heavenly corona around him. It was daybreak already. Apparently, more than a few moments had passed since I'd climbed under the covers.

'What is it?' I grouched, setting the dagger on the bed and letting out a yawn.

Viz beamed down at me cheerfully. 'I took your advice and prayed for guidance.'

I sat bolt upright. 'And what? The Big Man picked up the phone?'

'Yes!' he said, talking fast, his wizened hands flying like panicked birds. 'After all this time, He listened to my pleas!'

I was gobsmacked. God had finally stepped up. 'So what did He say?'

'Words of salvation, Abbey. The roadmap to a cure.'

All of Lauden's warnings about the angels went out of my head in an instant. I wrapped the bed sheet around me, scrambled to my feet, and placed my hands on Viz's shoulders. 'What is it? What do we need to do?'

'We need to perform a ritual. Science might not be able to cure Neil, but magic can.'

'Okay, okay, a ritual. We can do that. A five-pointed star, some candles, a bit of chanting. No worries.'

'I'm afraid there's a bit more to it than that. First of all, we'll need outside help to perform the ceremony. Help from a powerful magician.'

'Not a problem. This city's got magic out the arsehole, right? We can always talk someone into lending a hand. What else?'

'We'll need certain ingredients too. Common things for the most part: blessed chalk, a censer of sanctified incense, a dais of dogwood. And then... then there's the other thing...'

I felt a knot form in my stomach. 'What? What is it?'

Viz sucked some air between his teeth, the way car mechanics do, right before they slap you with an absolutely eye-watering quote. 'We need Pope blood.'

'Are you fucking serious?' I cried. 'Are you telling me I have to assassinate the Pope?'

'Of course not!' Viz shot back, wounded at the thought. 'Any Pope blood will do.'

'Oh, so just any old Pope blood, eh?' I mimed turning out my pockets. 'Let me have a quick look... no, nope, no Pope blood here!'

Viz pumped his palms at me, urging me to calm down. 'It's all right, Abbey. Fortunately for us, there is a sample of Pope Leo XIII's blood right here in London. All you need to do is convince the man who owns the blood to part ways with it.'

'Okay, that doesn't sound so bad. So who is this guy?'

Viz placed his hands together in an unconscious prayer. 'The man you need to speak to is Giles L'Merrier, the most dangerous magician in all of London.'

'I see,' I said. 'Well, in that case, oh deary bollocks.'

13

Convincing a grand wizard to give me a sample of Pope Leo XIII's blood; now there was an errand I never saw coming.

L'Merrier's Antiques was located on a side street off Portobello Road, not far from the market. Outside, a wooden sign bearing the shop's name in hand-painted cursive squeaked in the wind.

'So what's the plan?' I asked. 'We just walk in there and say, "Please can we have some of your Pope blood"?'

Gendith shrugged. 'Unless you have a better idea.'

I didn't, which made "smile and ask nicely" the best plan we had.

I took a deep breath and pushed open the shop door. The boutique was musty and cloaked in gloom. Antiques crowded the surprisingly roomy space; an imposing collection of rare and precious oddments drawn from centuries gone by. Though many of the artefacts had lost their lustre, they stood upon bowed shelves with their pride intact, varnished with a patina of age and wisdom. I breathed in the mellow aromas of oak and mahogany and old clays; ancient smells that had yet to evaporate, that had refused to be claimed by the passage of time.

Looking closer, I saw other things among the hotch-potch of relics. Unsettling things. Shrunken heads, an abacus adorned with glass eyes, a pair of bellows claiming to contain a dying man's curse, a tapestry decorated with an eerily lifelike depiction of an ancient battle; a battle whose combatants seemed to shift and squirm the moment they were looked away from, as though locked in some eternal skirmish. I saw wands too, spell books, figurines, the kind of stuff I might have found on Neil's writing desk, only this stuff wasn't purchased at the Harry Potter Shop or Forbidden Planet. This was the real deal.

I stepped up to the dusty shop counter hoping to be greeted by the owner. There was no one behind it though, not unless you included the life-size terracotta warrior stood there, arms folded and staring out at us blankly. The only sign of any human presence besides our own was an antique till covered in clunky keys that looked more like an aging typewriter than a modern day cash register.

'Hello,' I called. 'Anyone there?'

No reply.

'Looks like the place is deserted,' Gen whispered, perusing L'Merrier's wares.

Given that there seemed to be no one around, I decided to look the place over too. The question was, where in all of this junk was I going to find Pope blood?

Then I saw it.

Right there, a phial sitting on a red velvet cushion lining a small wooden casket. A phial labelled POPE BLOOD: LEO XIII (1897)

The casket was wide open and on display next to the till, sitting there like something you'd impulse buy. Like a last-second knick-knack you'd snatch up and pay for without a second thought.

Um, I'll take a dragon skull, a couple of mystical scrolls, and... oh, go ahead and bung some of that Pope blood on the tab, would you?

I looked over my shoulder to see that Gen had spotted the phial too. 'Are you thinking what I'm thinking?' she asked.

Stealing pope blood? Surely there had to be a special place in Hell for people who did that? Still, whatever got me out of that creepy little shack the quickest.

I checked for security cameras but found nothing, which was

hardly surprising given that nothing in L'Merrier's shop looked younger than Jack the Ripper.

Much as I didn't like the idea of pinching something that didn't belong to me, I didn't fancy haggling over it with the shop's proprietor either, particularly since I'd been warned about what a piece of work he was. The way Viz told it, before L'Merrier set up shop here, he was an ancient and extremely powerful wizard who strode across the world, destroying anything he took a disliking too. Would he do the same to me if I helped myself to his phial? Pissing a person like that off was bound to have consequences, but then Neil's life was hanging in the balance...

I went for the phial, but no sooner had I reached across the counter for it than a hand had shot out and gripped me by the wrist.

The terracotta warrior glowered at me, as animated as one of Ray Harryhausen's stop-motion skeletons.

Busted.

Gen came to my assistance, but was stopped by a new interloper: a rusty suit of medieval armour that sprang from the shadows and grabbed her from behind in a metal bear hug.

We struggled to break free of our captors but they were too strong. The suit of armour held on to Gen like a vice, while the terracotta warrior managed to get his other hand to the back of my head and force my face into the shop counter, pinning me there.

'Well well,' said a full-bodied voice from the back of the shop. 'What do we have here?'

I managed to turn my head just enough to get a look at the sideways image of a pair of eyes gleaming from the darkness. From out of the gloom stepped a solid-built man with caterpillar-thick eyebrows and and a head that was bald as an egg. He walked in confident strides, dressed in a tent-like smock that covered him from his neck to his knees. He should have looked ridiculous, but the effect only succeeded in exaggerating his powerful frame and making him all the more imposing.

This was Giles L'Merrier.

He came around the counter and cocked his head to one side so he could get a better look at me. 'Another foolish youngster seeks to covet my treasures,' he said, shaking his head pityingly. 'What is it with you Millennials, thinking you can help yourself to whatever you please? Millennials, I ask you! As though this Millennium of yours is any more significant than the one that preceded it.' He pounded his fist on the counter, right next to my face, so hard that he left a divot in the wood. 'Well, my young friend, I assure you, there is no "safe space" for you here.'

'Please,' I said. 'We're not thieves. Honest.'

'Oh no? I suppose you were going to pay me back at a later time, were you? Post an envelope under the door containing my remuneration? Is that it?' His jowls quivered as he worked himself into a fury. 'You will pay for this crime. Both of you will, I'll soon see to that.'

Just then, Gen managed to slip free of her captor and land the suit of armour with an elbow that sent its helmet toppling from its non-existent head. Wasting no time, she leapt at L'Merrier's back and drew a knife in one fluid motion, point aimed between the wizard's shoulder blades.

Attacking an unarmed man from behind? Lauden had a point; maybe Gen's halo could do with a spot of polish.

L'Merrier whirled around and dispatched his attacker with a weary flick of his wrist. Snatched mid-air by the wizard's magic, Gen went rocketing skywards, bounced off the ceiling, and crashed to the ground in an ungainly heap. She wasn't done yet though. Much to my surprise, she succeeded in springing to her feet almost instantly, and, undaunted, made a second run at L'Merrier.

She should have learned from the first time.

A couple of steps into her charge, Gen came to a stop like she'd collided with a brick wall.

Crunch.

If the mighty L'Merrier took any pleasure in turning the tables on his wannabe assassin, he didn't show it. Instead, he simply raised a hand and Gen was plucked into the air like a marionette tugged up on its strings. 'You dare?' he seethed.

He made a ball of his hand and I felt a change of pressure in the room that made my ears pop. Instantly, Gen reacted like she'd been taken in the fist of a giant; crunched into a ball, tight as a walnut. She screamed in pain.

'I could kill you a million different ways,' L'Merrier boomed, as Gen hovered before him like a foetus. 'I could make a rope trick out of your guts and strangle you to death with your own intestines. I could compress your brain into a marble. Transmute the contents of your stomach into hydrochloric acid.'

I heard a wince-making popping sound as one of Gen's bones came free of its socket. L'Merrier was going to kill her.

'Stop!' I pleaded.

'Why? Tell me why I should show this filthy cur mercy,' he said, tightening his meaty ham of a fist and causing Gen to shriek even louder. 'Tell me why I shouldn't crush her like a grape.'

'She only pulled a knife on you to protect me.'

'And who exactly *are* you?' he asked.

I thought about trying to break free of the statue's grip, about rushing the wizard and sticking him with my own knife. But instead of putting up a fight, I thought I'd take a shot at something else.

I'd tell him the truth.

A bit of a novelty, I know, but I figured I was meant to be on the side of the angels, so why not act accordingly?

'I'm the Nightstalker,' I replied. 'I guard the frontier between civilisation and a vampire—'

'Yes, yes,' he cut in, 'I know very well what the Nightstalker is.'

L'Merrier unfurled his fist and Gen collapsed to the floor, a panting, groaning mess. Addressing the statue pressing my face into the shop counter, the wizard instructed his earthenware enforcer to turn over my hands then, perching a pair of pince-nez on his nose, leant over and inspected the brand on my right palm.

'You really are the Nightstalker,' he said, incredulous.

'That's right. Why, what were you expecting, Kate Beckinsale in a skin-tight leather catsuit?'

L'Merrier shook his head, amazed. 'A female Nightstalker? Extraordinary. Then again, they did manage to put a monkey in space...'

Clearly, the only rational response to that comment was to kick the old bastard in the balls so hard he tasted them, but in the end, calmer thoughts prevailed.

'I didn't come here to steal from you, Mr L'Merrier. I'm on an important mission.'

He narrowed his eyes at me, then gave the terracotta warrior a nod. The statue took the pressure from my head, allowing me to stand up straight.

'Proceed,' said the wizard. 'Respectfully.'

I angled my head to one side and stretched the crick from my neck. 'I need your help,' I explained, as humbly as I could. 'My boyfriend was turned into a vampire, and I'm looking for the cure.'

The shopkeeper offered a stiff smile. 'You are telling me that you allowed your beau to become one of the enemy? Just what kind of a Nightstalker are you? How could you possibly have let that happen?'

'I don't know,' I said, throwing up my hands. 'Maybe it was… maybe it was just meant to happen. Maybe Neil being turned into a vampire is kind of a test. I mean, everything happens for a reason, right?'

'I believe it does,' said L'Merrier, 'and in this case, I believe the reason is that you are very bad at your job.'

The brand glowed hot in my hand. Once again, I felt the urge to propel the bloke's genitals into his throat. Once again, I stopped myself.

'I'm new to the job, okay? I'm trying my best out there, but it's me against about a million Draculas. Give me a chance, it's not like they taught this shit in school.'

L'Merrier harrumphed. 'Spoken like a true hero.'

I struggled against the statue pinning my wrists. 'Listen, I've had about as much of this as I can take...'

From the floor, Gen croaked a warning. 'Abbey, be careful…'

'No,' I said, feeling my cheeks flame. I turned to L'Merrier and looked him square in the eye. 'All I'm asking for is for a drop of Pope blood and a bit of friendly advice. That's all. Now, are you going to help me, or are you going to stand there like a fucking plum?'

Having overstepped my bounds somewhat, the statue spun me around and cuffed me hard across the side of the head.

L'Merrier snarled and held up a hand—I assumed to do away with me—but in a surprise turn of events, it was the statue who felt his wrath.

BADOOF!

As the wizard balled his hand into a fist, the terracotta warrior exploded, sending a cloud of fine sand every which way.

I looked to the ground to see Gen covered in the statue's remains, eyes wide under a blanket of orange powder.

L'Merrier sighed. 'Such a shame. A priceless antiquity, destroyed. Still, I will not abide violence in my premises.'

'Really?' wheezed Gen, still recovering from the spell that had threatened to crush her into a ball of meat and bone.

A thought occurred. L'Merrier had shown us a taste of his power, but when he blew up that statue, he'd shown us compassion too. His sense of what was good and right. So long as he had that in him—a heart under that fusty, belligerent exterior—maybe I could get through to him.

'Look, it's pretty obvious we've gotten off on the wrong foot, Mr L'Merrier, but I promise you, we are on the same side. All I want is to cure my boyfriend and get one more vampire off the face of this planet. Is there anything you can do to help me out? Anything at all?'

He looked to Gen lying on the floor, then back to me. 'The vampire who turned this… boyfriend of yours, to which clan did he belong?'

'The Judas Clan,' I replied.

L'Merrier seemed to tense for moment, then he tucked his hands into the sleeves of his smock and folded his arms. 'Many centuries ago, before I became the man I am today, I had my own brush with that particular tribe.' He regarded me like a monk; composed, serene. 'Judas and his kin were far fewer back then, numbering no more than a dozen. They were less powerful too, less… evolved. As a matter of fact, at that point in time, they were still affected by sunlight. Lethally so. At night though, they would move among the living with impunity, snatching victims from their beds and dragging them away to their den to be feasted upon. We were nothing but food to the Judas Clan, livestock to be slaughtered as they pleased... or so they thought.'

'You kicked back?'

The wizard squared his broad shoulders and stood tall. 'None of my fellow villagers was brave enough to face Judas and his vampires, not even during the daytime while they slumbered. Any man foolish enough to venture into their cave with a stake and mallet might succeed in destroying one of the creatures—perhaps even two—but after that, they'd be set upon by the rest and torn to ribbons. No, it would take more than brute force to rid the village of its oppressors. It would take a man of great courage and boundless ingenuity. A man named Giles L'Merrier.'

I tried not to roll my eyes as he went on (and on and on).

'I ventured into the cave alone; one man against a dozen. I didn't come bearing a sharpened rod of ash though, I came equipped with platters of polished metal. Why, you ask? I shall tell you. As I crept into the Clan's burrow, I strategically placed each of these platters upon a pole, and through a mathematical process of careful angulation, I was able to bring the outside of the cave into its very heart, and cleanse it of the disease that had taken root there.'

'You used mirrors to reflect the sunlight into the den.'

L'Merrier smiled. 'Very good. Perhaps you're more than a space monkey after all.'

'Cheers. Quick question though: if you wiped the Clan out, how come I'm still at war with them?'

L'Merrier's expression soured. 'Somehow Judas sensed my arrival and burrowed deeper into the cave, escaping the purifying light. By the time I'd summoned the rest of the villagers to help me root him out, the Clan master had fled his den and moved on.'

'Okay then. So help me finish what you started. Help me finish Judas off for good.'

The wizard waved a hand at me dismissively. 'Times have changed, girl. I no longer hunt vampires.'

'Why not?'

'Because I have far more pressing matters to attend to than

mere bloodsuckers. Judas and his Clan are but fleas to the mighty Giles L'Merrier.'

By this point, Gen had succeeded in peeling herself off the floor and clambering to her feet. Her right arm hung unevenly from its shoulder joint, limp and straight. 'Give it up, Abbey, he's not going to help us.'

I turned to L'Merrier. 'Is that right? Are you really going to stand there and do nothing?'

He stared back at me, his expression unchanged, unmoved by my plea.

'Fine, I said, anger boiling, doing what I could to keep the tears from my eyes. 'Thanks for nothing.'

I headed for the exit with Gen at my heels, stomping my feet as I went.

The wizard stopped me mid-march. 'Aren't you forgetting something, Nightstalker?' When I turned back, I saw he was holding the phial of Pope blood between a meaty forefinger and thumb. 'You're going to need this if you want to cure your boyfriend.'

I couldn't tell whether he was toying with me. 'Seriously?'

'Consider it yours.'

I took the phial from L'Merrier, half-convinced that he was going to snatch it away at the last second and do to me what he'd done to his statue. 'Thank you,' I said, meaning it.

'It is but a keepsake to one such as I. Do with the blood as you wish, but leave my shop knowing that this is the last favour I will ever grant you.'

'Okay,' I said, nodding like a dashboard toy. 'Fair enough then.'

I made to leave, but once again, L'Merrier called me back. 'There is of course one last matter to attend to.'

'What's that?'

He rung up a sale on the cash register. 'That will be £14.99. Would you like your receipt in the bag?'

14

I left L'Merrier's Antiques fifteen quid lighter but riding high.

'Well, that was easy enough,' I said, humming a jaunty tune and twirling the phial in my fingertips.

Walking beside me, Gendith winced as she popped her shoulder back into its socket. 'Oh yes. Easy peasy.'

'All we need now is a wizard to perform the ceremony who's more willing than baldy back there, and bingo-bango, we're off to the races.'

I'm not sure why I'd started talking like that exactly. I put it down the leftover adrenaline. The same adrenaline making me toss the phial around like I was cockily bouncing a set of Porsche keys on my palm. Of course it was a mistake. A big one. I was barely a hundred yards from the shop, strolling along without a care in the world, when the phial left my hand and failed to touch down again.

A black glove flashed into my periphery, accompanied by the *ning ning ning* of a two stroke engine. Before I could wrap my head around what was happening, the phial was being borne away by a leather-jacketed thief sat astride a sleek Japanese motorcycle.

Christ.

I'd succeeded in convincing the mighty Giles L'Merrier to

part with his Pope blood without killing me, only to lose it in a drive-by snatch-and-grab.

'Did he just…?' Gen started.

'Yes he bloody did,' I reported.

At which point I was already legging it after the thief, feet pounding the pavement as his bike weaved dangerously in and out of traffic.

Gen called to me. 'I'll take the back roads and see if I can cut him off,' she shouted, but I hardly heard her over the sound of my own raging heartbeat.

As I ran, the brand kicked in like a speedball of raw power, sending me exploding forwards. Every cell in my body was an atom bomb, all of them detonating at once. I felt incredible, indomitable, indestructible, like people in tampon commercials feel.

The bike was fast but I was moving at an impressive speed now, closing the distance, tearing up the tarmac in hot pursuit. The bike mounted a curb to swerve a jam of parked traffic, and picked up speed, leaving me chasing a smudged red tail light. If I didn't find a way to keep up, I was going to lose the thief for good.

I saw a bicycle courier coming up alongside me, grabbed him by the scruff of his reflective jacket, and hauled him off the saddle.

'Sorry, I need this,' I said, jumping on board, stabbing my feet into the pedals, and racing off after the thief.

The motorbike jumped a red light, rounded a corner and escaped down a narrow side street. I gave chase, slipping between pedestrians as they dived left and right of me. Thankfully, they were too busy dodging out of the way to take out their phones and frame a decent shot of the girl cycling a push-bike at forty-plus miles per hour, so they'd have no proof that any of this was happening. Which was a good thing. Like I said before, the war I was waging was a secret one, which meant I had to limit the amount of supernatural nonsense I got up to in public. Besides, I couldn't be getting arrested by the police, least of all now, with Neil strapped to a bed and about to turn into a full-blown vampire. I knew all too well what Gen would do if that happened: the same thing she'd done to the chimp back at that lab, the same thing she'd done to the scientist.

I made it to the corner the thief had taken and leant hard into the turn, only just managing to level the bike and get it upright again. I caught the burn of rubber in my nostrils as the back tyre skidded out and painted the road with a black stripe before gaining traction and propelling me forwards. Sweat stung my eyes as I pedalled frantically after the disappearing motorbike, which was already turning and pulling into another street. I wasn't having some vampire grab the pie from my windowsill and get away with it though. No effing way.

'Come on, come on!' I screamed, urging myself to pick up the pace.

The side street opened up on to Portobello Market. Among the buzzing throng of shoppers trawling stalls for bric-a-brac and vintage fashions I saw the motorbike, cutting through the crowd, caring for the safety of no one.

Refusing to let up, I weaved between the market-goers, ringing my bell and sending them scattering. Up ahead, I saw the motorbike blast through a greengrocer's stall, dispersing fresh fruit and veg all over the road. A watermelon exploded under the tread of my front tyre as I chased the bike to the other end of the market; the end selling second-hand goods and cheap socks, where the shoppers tapered out.

I was giving it my all, leaving nothing on the field. The thief saw how little distance separated us and revved his engine. He took a hard left in an attempt to cut down another side alley and shake me properly this time, but when he reached the other end of it, he found himself at an impasse.

Standing there, plugging the exit wall-to-wall, was a dam of shimmering light threaded with flecks of bright gold. On the opposite side of that dam was Gen, who had caught up to us on foot and summoned the magical barrier.

'You're not going anywhere,' she assured the thief.

She stood with her legs planted wide and her arms raised high; a human bulwark, cutting off the motorcyclist's only exit.

Well, the only exit bar one...

The bike pulled a doughnut and pointed its front wheel in my direction. As its engine idled, the rider flipped up the visor of his helmet and I saw two blood-red eyes fixing me with a burning stare.

The thief was a vampire, but then I'd known that from the start. The only question I had in that moment was whether he was one of Lauden's lot, or whether he was one of the so-called "Wild Bloods" I'd been told about. Was there really such a thing as a Clan offshoot that had been making my life miserable while the rest of Lauden's people kept themselves to themselves, or was the vampire who pulled me out of the drink running some scam? The only thing I knew for sure was that the guy staring me down looked like he wanted to smear my remains all over that back alley, and that made him enemy enough for me.

'What's the matter?' he growled, revving the engine of his bike. 'Scared?'

I felt a gulp travel up and down my throat. He had me outgunned.

'You are scared,' he said, face cut with a devil's smirk. 'Good. Scared blood is the best blood. The adrenalin gives it a nice kick. You're going to taste like the first coffee of the day.'

Laughing maniacally, he twisted the throttle and the back wheel spun out before it gripped tarmac and fired the bike my way at breakneck speed.

The vamp hugged the handlebars, reducing the drag and turning himself into a perfect, streamlined a bullet.

I briefly considered whirling my bicycle around and heading the other way, but I'd never outrun him. In any case, the brand wouldn't hear of it. The Nightstalker didn't run from vampires. The Nightstalker turned vampires into itty bitty pieces of ash. So instead of running, I pedalled right for him, playing a game of chicken, my spindly push-bike versus his souped-up crotch rocket.

Unsurprisingly, the vamp didn't deviate one inch. Instead, he kept his trajectory straight as a pin, coming right at me, nose aimed square in my direction, engine screaming. I went at him full-pelt too, pedalling like a nutter. I flicked my thumb and felt the bicycle click up a gear, its sprockets spinning smoothly beneath me as I mashed the pedals triple-time. My hair whipped back as I rode faster still, tearing down the alley so fast I felt like I was elongating. I had to reach maximum acceleration. Had to. If I didn't get up enough speed, I'd never make it to the downpipe on the alley wall in time. If the black streak heading my way got there first, I'd lose my chance to wrench the pipe from its fittings, turn it horizontal, and use it as a jousting lance.

Wallop.

The vamp took the makeshift lance in the chest and shot from his saddle like he was attached to a recoiling bungee cord. Meanwhile, his bike went skidding off in the other direction and crashed into a wheelie bin, tyres spinning madly.

I screeched to a halt next to the impaled vampire and kicked away the push-bike. The vamp lay on his back, holding the lance vertically, a desperate grimace etched into his pale white face. The spear had missed his heart by inches, but the slightest movement to or fro would turn him to ash.

I placed the tread of a Doc Marten on his belly and grabbed hold of the downpipe. 'Where's the phial?'

Hand shaking, the vamp reached into the top pocket of his leather jacket and produced the bottle of Pope blood.

'Give it to me,' I demanded.

He coughed and gave me a big, red smile. 'You'll never cure him, Nightstalker. There is no remedy for what we are. Soon enough he'll be one of us, another soldier in our army.'

With the last of his strength, he pulled back his arm and hurled the phial, whipping it at the alley wall.

'No!' I cried, leaping for the departing bottle like a goalkeeper going after a World Cup penalty.

There was no catching the thing though. The slim red phial slipped through my fingers and struck the brickwork with a cringe-making *chink*—

And yet somehow—whether it was the phial's sturdy construction, striking the wall at just the right angle, or plain good luck—the glass stayed intact.

I breathed a sigh of relief, but the roller coaster hadn't pulled into the station just yet.

The phial hit the ground and started to roll, picking up speed, heading for a sewer grate.

I scrambled after it, but there was no way I could cover the distance in time.

The phial raced along the gutter, soon to enter London's sewage system, where it would be swept away by a current of effluence, or claimed by some dirty sewer Fraggle. Or at least it would have if Gen hadn't jumped in and snatched it up right before it disappeared through the grille.

'Looking for this?' she asked, waggling the phial at me like a scolding finger.

'Nice catch,' I said, for once happy to be subjected to the angel's thin, know-it-all smile.

I heard a gurgling noise over my shoulder and saw the vampire lying where I'd left him, weaker now and struggling to keep the pipe in his chest standing upright.

I helped myself to my feet and went over to him. 'Sorry, chuckles,' I said. 'Looks like you're shit out of luck.'

I twisted the lance, found the vampire's heart, and turned him into a pile of soot.

15

'How did it go?' asked Vizael, greeting us at the door of the gas tower with a hopeful look in his eye.

'Smashed it,' I replied, brandishing the phial and giving its contents a victory swirl.

'Congratulations!' He gave me a fatherly hug. 'And what of L'Merrier? Did you manage to secure his assistance?'

'We tried, but he's staying Switzerland.'

'That is unfortunate, but perhaps for the best. Did he give you any trouble?'

'Nah, he was all right. He's a big softie so long as you don't mind bowing and scraping a bit. If you ask me, there's a decent man hiding under that big old muumuu.'

Gendith disagreed. 'Giles L'Merrier isn't a *decent man*. I can see his aura, and I can tell you this: he's barely a man, let alone a decent one.'

Whether Gen could see auras or not, I was starting to have serious doubts about how good a judge of character she was. This was a woman whose idea of a cure was a bullet in the brain-pan. A woman who ended conversations with a knife to the heart.

'Ignore her,' I told Viz, 'she's just bent out of shape because, well, L'Merrier bent her out of shape.' I flashed a big grin at Gen.

It was not reciprocated. 'Anyway, he gave us the red stuff, didn't he?'

'You think he parted with it out of the goodness of his heart?' Gen scoffed. 'He gave it to us because he had to.'

'Had to? Why?'

There was that know-it-all smile again. 'Because he isn't brave enough to risk using it himself. The truth is, the greatest magician in the Uncanny Kingdom is scared to go up against the Judas Clan, and that is not good.'

I waved her off. At that point it didn't matter what L'Merrier's deal was, we already had what we needed from him. So what if Gen was right and the almighty wizard was just some weird old guy hiding behind a curtain? Forget him.

'Whatever,' I said, clapping my hands together. 'Let's get back to the shopping list, shall we?'

Viz scratched his chin. 'If L'Merrier won't play ball, we'll have to petition London's next most powerful magician.'

'Great. So what's his name?

'Actually, it's a *her*,' Gen corrected.

I was a bit ashamed of myself for that, but ultimately, as always, I blame the patriarchy.

Viz pulled a pocket watch from his waistcoat and checked the time. 'The woman you need to speak to is likely to be found in The Beehive at this time of evening.'

The Beehive was a pub hidden down an impossible backstreet in Ealing that catered to London's many misfits and broken toys. I'd been there a few nights ago, celebrating a rare win, and rubbed shoulders with a werewolf and an ogre, to mention just a couple of the weird and wonderful creatures that called the pub their local.

'And this magician I'm looking for,' I said, 'what is she, like a witch?'

'Not exactly,' Viz replied, 'though she did once belong to a coven. Her name is Stella. Stella Familiar.'

Before I left for The Beehive, I decided to check in on Neil. I found him where I left him: in his cot, strapped down and unconscious still, but breathing normally.

I spent a while at his bedside, stroking his hair as he slept. If the peaceful look on his face was to be believed, I was in more pain than he was, and rightly so. I was the one who'd dragged him into this whole mess. Before I picked up the dagger and got the brand, the only vampires in Neil's life were the ones he wrote about in his novels. Vampires who lived in the shadows, not in the bright light of day. Vampires who swished their cloaks to show off their fancy red silk lining: comic book monsters with diabolical master plans, not corporate scumbags in tailored suits who forced me to act like a weapon.

A weapon.

That's what Lauden had called me, after saving me from that river hag. A weapon forged against my will. He was right. The angels had turned me into something lethal, but then so had his kind when they sank their fangs into Neil. When it came down to it, were either side really any better than the other?

'Abbey?'

My eyes darted to the cot and found Neil, awake and confused.

'Oh my God, Neil!'

I leapt on top of him and held on like a limpet. I wasn't thinking. All thoughts for my own safety flew out of the window the moment I heard him say my name.

'Are you okay? How do you feel?'

'Pretty good,' he replied, a little groggy maybe, but sounding like himself.

'Are you sure? Can I get you something?'

'A drink would be nice.'

I leapt off him. 'Sure, sure, let me just get you some water—'

He shook his head. 'Not that kind of drink.'

Of course. Stupid Abbey. 'I can give you something, okay. Just a little. To keep your strength up.'

'That's all I need,' he said. 'Honest.'

I offered Neil my wrist and he leaned towards me; as much as he could with his body strapped to the bed and his arms pinned by his sides. He bit down on my flesh like he had before, carefully, gently, like a teething kitten. He supped on me for a few seconds, then he pulled back, turning away to wipe his mouth on his shoulder.

'Is that all?' I asked, surprised at the speed he withdrew. 'Don't you want more?'

He chuckled. 'You're giving out free refills now?'

'No, it's just... is something wrong?'

'Nothing's wrong. I feel great.'

I'll confess to feeling a little rejected. 'You're sure you don't want any more?' I waggled my wrist at him temptingly. 'It's from my own special reserve...'

He laughed again. 'No, I'm full.' He put on a daft Cookie Monster voice. 'The Nightstalker's blood is full of goodness!'

'Keep it down,' I whispered, putting a finger over his lips and holding back a laugh of my own. 'I can't have the angels knowing I'm feeding you.'

'I'm sorry,' he said, matching my volume. 'It's just... I feel *really* good.' He sucked in a breath of air. 'I reckon I could run those nine flights of steps to our flat and my heart wouldn't skip a beat. I don't know what those vampires did to me, but I can tell you this much, it definitely doesn't feel like a curse.'

He certainly looked much better. The strongest I'd seen him in a long while, really. His oxygen tank was sat at home collecting dust, but despite that he appeared healthy, shiny and new, like he'd been buffed inside a rock polisher. Before he got bitten, back when he needed that tank, the doctors had said Neil's life expectancy was likely to be forty at best. Could being a vampire have changed that? Was this a blessing in disguise?

I remembered my encounter with Lauden. What if he was telling the truth? What if the Clan weren't monsters after all? What if all they really wanted was to let us live forever? To give us eternal life. Had I been playing for the wrong side ever since I got the N on my hand? Was I looking for a cure, or was I doing all this fighting, shedding all this blood, just to find a cure for something that wasn't even a sickness? As a vampire, Neil could be his own man—not a man with a debilitating medical condition, not some damsel I had to keep rescuing—a man with a clean bill of health and a life-expectancy that cleared his forties.

Then again, maybe Neil wasn't cured of anything. Maybe he was just high, the way Carlo got when I plugged some Nightstalker blood in his veins. I peered into Neil's eyes. His pupils were pretty big. Matter of fact, I hadn't seen them that size since he bought a cookie from a guy at Glasto. A guy with flowers in his hair who stank of patchouli.

I put a hand on Neil's chest. 'How do you feel? Are you okay?'

He smiled. 'Remember when we went to Comic-Con a couple of years ago?'

I did. One of his books had won a writing contest and the prize was two tickets to San Diego. 'Yeah, I remember. What about it?'

'I made it to the front of the queue for Hall H, Abbey. Fought my way past six-thousand screaming nerds to get a front row seat to that panel. Trust me, I can handle a bit of vampirism.'

I kissed him on the lips and pressed my forehead to his.

'Thank you,' I said.

'For what?'

'For being you.'

But was he really who I thought he was? Was he really Neil —*my Neil*—the boyfriend I'd had since college, or was he a vampire assassin who'd rip out my throat the moment my back was turned? There was no way of knowing, and that's why I had no choice. I had to find that cure. I had to find Stella Familiar and convince her to perform the ritual that would rinse the vampire blood from his veins and turn him back into the man I knew.

'I've gotta go,' I said, climbing to my feet and grabbing my jacket.

'Okay,' he said, 'but can I ask a quick favour first?'

'I can't let you out of that bed, Neil.'

'I know, I know, big scary vampire, grrrr.'

He always did know how to make me laugh. 'What do you want?'

'Can you give my nose a scratch? I've got an itch that's driving me absolutely mental.'

I smiled.

Now that I could do.

16

You'd be amazed by some of the stuff that goes on in this city without you knowing about it. Terrified, really. There's a whole other world lurking behind the one you see, a world of crazy, hiding at the heels of the mundane. The realm of the Uncanny is a message scrawled on the leaf of a notepad, an indentation pressed almost invisibly into the page below it, but it's there all the same; a psychopath's death threat embedded in an ordinary shopping list. The world you think so drab and boring is actually a madhouse. An open-air asylum.

Take The Beehive: a pub full of monsters, hiding in plain sight in one of the busiest parts of London. A clandestine drinking hole tucked away where only Insiders can find it, closed off to the likes of you and me. The only reason I'm on the invite list nowadays is because I have the brand, which works like a nightclub hand stamp that won't wash off.

How to describe the place? The Beehive had a sort of Tudor feel to it—dark wooden beams, leaded windows, hand-painted sign—but if someone told me it had been standing in its spot since the dawn of forever, I'd have probably believed them. It had an ancient feel to it. Timeless.

I pushed open the tavern's stout oak door and watched as curls of cigarette smoke crept through the gap like Cthulhu's tentacles. While the rest of London's drinking establishments smelled like stale beer and body odour these days, The Beehive's landlord, Lenny, somehow missed the memo on the smoking ban, and continued to let his patrons brown the pub's ceiling with tobacco.

But something else curled out of the door besides the smoke that day, something besides the usual jangle of voices and the clinking of glasses. Jazz music bled into the blind alley, saxophone notes, jumping and dancing, swinging along to the rhythm of an upright bass. I squinted inside the hazy tavern and saw a three-piece band performing in the far corner. They were fronted by a smoky-voiced chanteuse dressed in a figure-hugging sequined red dress, the kind you see draped over grand pianos in old detective films. The patrons who were paying attention to the band were rapt, but then they would be. The singer was a siren, and when I say siren, I mean a *real* siren, the kind ye olde sailors dashed their ships on the rocks to get a look at.

It's funny, before I got Sanctified, the closest I'd come to the supernatural was meeting a guy at a nightclub who told me he was a clairvoyant. When I asked him what my future looked like, he told me that I'd be rich one day. Oh, and that he could see me getting laid that night. Given the way that evening turned out—not to mention my three-figure bank balance—I seriously question that man's supernatural credentials.

These days, things were different. These days I was surrounded by bona fide weirdos: angels, vampires, ghosts, fairies, canal hags (sorry, *river* hags). And now here I was, stepping into an invisible pub, trying to hunt down a woman who belonged to a cabal of witches. Or used to at least. According to Vizaël, the founding members of the London Coven had been wiped out years ago, leaving Stella Familiar on her Todd. Viz didn't say how the Coven had met their end, just that there were a lot more monsters on the loose since the witches were taken out of the picture. Maybe that's why I was being set on from all sides by vampires. Maybe that's why my boyfriend was tied up to a bed and sporting a mouthful of fangs.

I had to wonder why the angels were so keen for me to hook up with someone who belonged in a coven. Weren't Christians and pagans meant to be at odds with each other? Witches consulted the dead, and there was stuff in the bible that strictly prohibited contacting the spirit world (Leviticus, if I remember right – all the nutty stuff is in Leviticus). Just another example of the angels playing fast and loose with God's law, I supposed. No wonder the big fella was so tight-lipped with the two of them.

I took a look around the bar but didn't see anyone who looked like she'd be comfortable stirring a cauldron. How was I meant to find this woman exactly? Look for the pointy hat? Follow the trail of tarot cards? Wait outside in the car park and see who left on a broomstick?

The pub landlord, Lenny, eyed me warily. 'Help you?'

Lenny was a giant. A grizzled man-mountain who towered over his bar, standing a clear three heads higher than what I'd consider tall. He was a brusque man, known for his no-nonsense attitude and hair-trigger temper. With his enormous size and his surly demeanour, I sometimes wondered if Lenny would be happier menacing Tokyo than being cramped behind a row of beer taps.

I took a seat on a nearby bar stool. 'Hi, Lenny. I'm after a woman called Stella. Know her?'

'She ain't here,' he said, wiping the counter with a rag that looked dirtier than the thing he was trying to clean.

In old detective films—the type that featured smoky-voiced women in red dresses sprawled across pianos—barmen were typically rich sources of information. Not so with Lenny. You'd find looser lips on a clam.

'Don't suppose you have a number, do you?' I asked him.

Nothing.

I shouldn't have expected to find any hospitality at The Beehive, much less help. The only reason anyone went to that place at all was to get away from the normals and kill themselves one beer at a time.

I felt my hand get hot and looked down to see the brand glowing blue.

I scanned the bar for any signs of danger, eyes flicking from patron to patron until something brought my eyeballs to a screeching halt.

Lauden Crowe sat at the other end of the bar with his back to me.

What the hell was he doing here? How could I be bumping into him again, twice in as many days? He had to be following me, right?

My hand instinctively went inside my jacket for the hilt of my dagger.

I saw Lenny's features curdle. Fighting wasn't permitted in his establishment. The Beehive was a safe zone, where blood enemies sat side-by-side.

I let the dagger stay where it was. Lenny wasn't to be messed with.

Shuffling along the bar, I approached Lauden and gave him a tap on the shoulder.

He swivelled around on his bar stool. 'Abbey? What are you doing here?'

'I was about to ask you the same.'

'Me? I'm having a beer.' He showed me his half-drained pint glass.

'I thought you lot only drank the blood of virgins.'

His eyes crinkled as he smiled. 'Is that an offer I hear?'

I snorted. 'Sorry, mate, that boat sailed a while ago.'

Lauden chuckled and shook his head. '*Virgin blood*. You know, that Bram Stoker fellow has a lot to answer for with his cobwebbed castles and his vampire bats fluttering out of garret windows. It's thanks to him that my kind are severely misrepresented in the media.'

'What about those sparkly Abercrombie models from the *Twilight* movies?'

'Oh, God,' he replied, 'those are the worst. I'll take Vlad the Impaler over those empty-headed miserabalists any day.'

I sat down on the stool next to him.

'Can I get you a drink?' he asked.

'What are you really doing here, Lauden?'

'Abbey, if you're trying to insinuate that I'm stalking you, let me stop you right there. I come to this place regularly, anyone here will tell you that. Now, can we please dispense with all this suspicion and move on?'

Hmm. I suppose I had been the one to happen across him, and The Beehive was the City's number one Uncanny hotspot. 'Okay then,' I said. 'Truce.'

He held up his hands in surrender. 'So, how are things? Are you continuing your mission to "cure" your friend?'

I was about to correct him and say "boyfriend", but didn't bother. Not sure why. 'You seem really invested in Neil keeping the fangs. What do you care so much about one vampire?'

'I don't. Not in the grand scheme of things. What I care about is you.'

Huh?

'That's nice and everything, but I'm doing fine.'

'Are you? I heard you were attacked by another Wild Blood, and that you put yourself in danger by consorting with Giles L'Merrier. If you're not careful, you're going to get yourself hurt, and that would be a real shame.'

'Oh yeah. Why's that?'

'Because I'm starting to grow rather fond you, Abbey, even if you have fallen in with a bad crowd.'

That I found genuinely funny. A bloodsucking creature of the night telling me that my angel friends were up to no good. What could I do but laugh at that?

'I'll take that drink,' I said.

I mean, fuck it, right? Even Jack Bauer took an hour off once in a while.

A moment later, Lenny was pushing two tall glasses of beer across the bar and taking Lauden's money. I watched the vampire take a sip of his beer and wondered, was he really enjoying it, or was drinking just something his kind did to pass for human?

'What did you get from L'Merrier's shop then?' Lauden asked. 'What's this magical cure-all of his?'

'What's it to you?'

'Nothing, I suppose, just making conversation. Or would you rather we sit here and talk about the weather?'

I thought about keeping the details a secret, but what did it matter? The phial was in safe hands with the angels. Besides, Lauden already knew where we were bunked up, so if he really wanted to mess with our shit, he'd have a thousand opportunities to do it.

'Pope blood,' I told him. 'L'Merrier sold us Pope blood.'

'Are you serious?' He punctuated the sentence by pounding a fist on his thigh. 'That's what the angels sent you there for? Wow. Did they get you to pick up some tartan paint and a bucket of steam while you were at it?'

I felt the corners of my mouth turn down. 'What are you saying?'

'It's all mumbo jumbo. I already told you about the priest who wanted to revert to "one of the living" and ended up experiencing rather the opposite effect. I'm sorry, but Pope blood isn't going to change what Neil's become. Whatever it is you're planning on doing, it's only going to hurt him.'

I narrowed my eyes at the vampire. 'Why would L'Merrier give me the blood if he didn't think it was going to help? You weren't there. He told me this whole big story about how he got into a fight with the Clan back in the olden days and—'

'Don't tell me, the one with the mirrors?' He rolled his eyes. 'If I were you, I'd take anything Giles L'Merrier says with a pinch of salt. The man is a well known fabulist. Did he tell you the one about the giant menacing a village too? Or the kraken ravaging the beaches of Blackpool? He slayed them all you know... with a mere flick of his wrist of course.' He took a swig of his beer. 'Complete bunkum.'

'*Bunkum*? *Fabulist*? What did you do, swallow a thesaurus?'

He threw back his head and laughed. 'I'm sorry. I've been around a long time and I forget that some words have fallen out of fashion.' He sighed. 'I'm just an old fuddy duddy, really.'

Hardly, I thought, the guy was sex on a stick. Why was that? As a vampire, he could use his powers of mesmerism to get pretty much anything he wanted, so why did he need to be a pretty boy too? From an evolutionary point of view, it would make more sense if he was plain-looking. The kind of person who slipped through the cracks, another face in the crowd. Handsomeness seemed like an unnecessary extra. A hat on a hat.

'You're wrong about the Pope blood,' I said. 'We got our information from a very reliable source.'

'Oh yes? From whom?'

'From God.'

'Okay, well I suppose that would trump what I have to say. Well, for your sake, I hope He's right.' Lauden pointed to my empty pint glass. 'Top up?'

I waited a couple of seconds. 'Go on then.'

I was starting to think Lauden might not be such a baddie after all. Evil people didn't get a round in, that's a fact. You think Hitler ever plonked a twenty on the bar and said, "This one's on me, lads"? Of course he didn't. He'd have made a sudden trip to the loo and hidden there until Goebbels picked up the tab.

Lenny set down another couple of beers and Lauden clinked my glass.

'Cheers,' he said, looking me in the eye, his lashes so thick and lustrous that I wondered for a moment if he was wearing eyeliner. 'To frenemies.'

'Cheers,' I replied, and clinked him back. I wet my top lip with foam. 'This is going to have to be the last one though. I've got shit-loads of work to do.'

I realised I was corkscrewing my hair with my finger and set my hand on the bar like a naughty girl who'd earned herself a rap over the knuckles. Why was Lauden having this effect on me? I mean, aside from the fact that he was charming, witty, and devastatingly handsome, what was the attraction? None of it stopped him being a vampire. Through a cleaner lens, Lauden was nothing more than a horror book villain in a nice cardie.

'Tell me about this Judas Clan of yours,' I said. It was a tactical request. I figured the more I learned about him, the less I'd like what I saw, and the weaker his allure would become.

He smiled like sunshine, which was ironic, given what he was. 'Are you asking me to willingly provide the Nightstalker with information that could lead to the extinction of my race?'

'I just want you to tell me something about your home life. Like, what do you get out of being in a Clan?'

He considered my question carefully. 'In the Clan I get to be part of something. Part of a family. That's a strong word to me, Abbey. A big deal. To know that I have people who I can count on. People who accept me, no matter what. I'm talking about *blood*. Do you know what I mean?'

I didn't. Not really. My parents had gone their own ways when I was a teenager. "Marriage is like a magic trick", Dad used to say. "It makes a man disappear before your very eyes." He was talking about his sapped masculinity at the time, but he put his credo into a practice more literally when he fucked off to the Costa Del Sol with his mistress. Mum… well, Mum didn't stick around for long after that. She stopped taking her meds and hanged herself in the garden shed. So no, I didn't know much about blood, at least not the way Lauden meant it.

'Family,' I muttered. 'People you can count on. Must be nice.'

'Did I say something wrong?'

'No, not at all.'

Aside from feeling a bit sorry for myself, I felt worryingly at ease in Lauden's company.

In fact, the more I prodded and pried, the lower my defences seemed to get. I tried to stay on point, tried to remind myself that he was the enemy, but it was getting harder and harder to see the monster in the man. The longer we talked, the more I began to wonder if he was telling the truth about his kind. I mean, what if some vampires weren't evil? What if they just got a bad press because of all the rest? Was it possible that the Clan were less like the coffin-dwelling monsters from a Hammer Horror than the glittery glampires of a Stephenie Meyer novel?

Glampires?

Okay, now I was punning, which meant I was definitely starting to feel the effect of those beers. How many had I necked now? Two? Three? Whatever the number was, it was either too many or too few. Or was I not as drunk as I thought I was? Was Lauden hypnotising me, worming his way into my brain and places more southern? Of course not, the brand made me immune to mesmerism. Christ, I was a mess. Stupid sexy Lauden.

It was only when I looked back to him that I realised he was still talking, and had been the whole time I'd been wrapped up in my thoughts.

'Are you okay?' he asked, sensing my mind had wandered elsewhere. 'You looked like you were miles away.'

'I'm fine,' I insisted, forcing a smile. 'What were you saying?'

He picked up where he left off—something about his early life and how he came to be in London—leaving me to return to my contemplations.

I had to get my shit together. I had a sick boyfriend counting on me. A sick boyfriend I'd been with for a long time. A very long time. God, we were young when we met. Too young, really. Falling in love at seventeen is easy, but it's a hard thing to hang on to. Would me and Neil really last? How many people who fell for each other as teenagers ever went the whole hog? Marriage, kids, growing old and wearing matching slippers; I just couldn't see it, and even if I could, would I have wanted it?

The brand throbbed in my hand as though it were reminding me of what I was meant to be doing; curing Neil of his vampirism, not knocking back beers with a vampire… with this drop-dead hunk of man meat with his swimmer's abs and his chiselled—

I felt a pang of disgust as I stepped back from myself. God help me, but Lauden had an edge to him that Neil just didn't have. Christ, he had more edges than one of those silly-shaped dice Neil used for his funny board games with the little plastic men. He was such a nice guy though. My boyfriend, I mean. *Such* a nice guy. Okay, so he wasn't exactly man candy in the Tom Hiddleston sense, but he was good for me. Great for me. Neil was my man broccoli: maybe not as tasty as candy, maybe not as desirable, but wholesome, and chock-full of goodness.

'...don't you think?' asked Lauden, rounding off a line of dialogue that I hadn't heard a word of.

'Oh yeah,' I said, taking a punt. 'Totally.'

He nodded, leading me to believe that I'd guessed correctly. 'One for the road?' he asked, polishing off his beer.

No chance. I was already getting close to the *staggering around the place with the back of my skirt tucked into my knickers* phase. One more drink and I was going to get super sloppy. And handsy. Handsy as a drunk uncle.

A druncle.

Oh shit, I was punning again. Definitely time to go.

'I've gotta shoot,' I said, pushing away the last of my pint.

'Already?'

'Yeah. Got some Nightstalking to do, you know how it is.' I tottered from my stool.

'Oh, okay then,' he replied, hangdog. 'When will I see you again?'

'I dunno. Around. Here and there. Thanks for the beers anyway.'

'Any time,' he said, helping me into my coat like the kind of gentleman they don't make anymore.

Before I could get off, Lauden produced something from his wallet. 'Take this. It has my home address on it.'

'A calling card? Jesus, you really do belong to another century.'

He gave me a smile. 'If you ever need to talk, now you know where I am. Just call me, Abbey, night or day.'

I took the card off him, nodded, and left before I did anything I regretted. Before I threw caution to the wind and let that handsome bastard ride me with his boots on.

17

The air outside was raw and lacerating.

I pulled up the collar of my jacket and headed for home. Not that the gas tower felt much like home. No matter how long I spent there, I was never going to get used to sharing a toothbrush holder with a couple of angels, especially since I was becoming increasingly wary of them. Why *had* they been excommunicated? Was it like Vizael said: that they'd been marooned on Earth as a punishment for failing to kill Judas back in the middle ages? Or was there more to it than that? The more I got to know Viz and Gen, the more flaws I detected, the more cracks I saw in their polished facades. And I'd only known them a few days. What would I know about them a week from now? In the short time I'd been running their errands I'd been left with a permanent scar, watched a baby die, seen a man murdered in front of my eyes, had my boyfriend turned into a vampire, and been almost killed more times than I could count. If these were angels, I sure as shit didn't want to meet any demons.

The orchestra of urban life played its eerie song as I trudged on through the streets of Ealing: the wail of a police siren, an argument bleeding from an open window, the distant, thrumming bass of a car stereo. The booze had given the evening a fuzzy, slippery filter, making me melancholic, making me think of Neil, making me think of Lauden.

I cut down a railway siding and headed up a foot bridge to cross the train tracks. I weaved as I climbed, my mind elsewhere, ignorant of the dangers I'd be warned about, forgetting the role I'd been lumbered with. Overhead, a row of lamps lit the way across the bridge, casting sallow pools of yellow so weak as to be pointless. I wouldn't even have noticed them if they hadn't begun to flicker.

Then sputter out.

When the lights came back on I saw a figure at the other end of the bridge, barring my way. An ivory-skinned woman with plank-straight raven hair was standing there, dressed in jeans and a leather jacket, not unlike mine. Her vibe was a bit more conventional though. A bit more proper.

I stopped where I was and got a better look at her, sizing her up. She was athletic-looking, dynamic and trim. The kind of flat-bellied bitch you see leading a spin class, or laughing at a salad in an advert for a thirty-day cleanse. How was it that vampires always looked so damned healthy? From the very first bloodsucker I'd laid eyes on to the one blocking my path right now, pretty much every bastard one of them could have been an underwear model. Lauden's claim that vampires weren't really dead had never seemed so true.

'Are you going to let me by?' I asked.

'That depends,' said the woman, lips pursed. 'Where are you going?'

'None of your business.'

'How about I make it my business?'

'Fucking hell, who writes your dialogue, Dan Brown?'

The woman raised a fist and it exploded, strobing with orange light, spitting sparks like something from an Eighties hair metal video. I caught an overpowering smell of ozone and realised that my hairdo had gone frizzy with static. Well, frizzier.

The woman took a step towards me, hand still burning, firing off molten arcs. Vampire magic. I'd seen it before. Not this kind exactly, but other impossible powers. Par for the course with these arseholes.

'I'm afraid I don't have time for banter,' said the woman, taking another step in my direction.

'Me neither,' I replied, pulling my dagger from its sheath.

She laughed. 'You're going to fight me, is that it? What are you, ninety pounds under that pile of cobwebs you call an outfit?'

Yeah, we were definitely done with the banter.

The brand spiked my system, turning my blood into hot lava. I charged at her, my blade swinging back and forth as I ran, a reaper's scythe.

I didn't make it very far.

The woman threw out her fist and unleashed a surge of I-don't-know-what that smacked into me, swept me sideways, and almost deposited me on the train tracks thirty feet below. Thankfully, I was able to dart out a hand and grab a guardrail just in time, saving me from the fall. I hauled myself back on to the bridge.

'Right, now I'm proper pissed off.'

I gave the dagger a flick and the blade extended to the side of a sword. The woman gave a little nod of appreciation then said some words I didn't understand that made the ball of angry surrounding her fist double in size. The blue glow of my brand was all but washed out by her dazzling light. I suddenly realised what it must feel like to be a guy stood at a urinal next to Jon Hamm.

Regardless, I rushed the woman again, one arm shielding my eyes from her epilepsy-inducing light show, the other swinging my blade in a big, cleaving arc. The woman's fist came to the boil and discharged a bolt of yellow fury, but I dodged this one and slashed her across the torso with my sword. She pulled back just in time to stop me doing any real damage, but I could tell from the look on her face that I'd taken her by surprise.

The woman looked down at the slash in her leather jacket, then back up to me, lip curled. 'You'd better be my size, girl, because I'm having that coat of yours.'

She threw her arms out to her sides and a thick, crackling band of energy wrapped around each of her fists, as though she'd slipped on a pair of magical knuckle dusters. This bitch meant business.

I swung my sword back like I was clearing brush with a

machete, then struck out at her. She deflected the blow with her fist, her knuckles meeting my blade with a shuddering clang that fired off another sizzling rain of sparks. I fought back, the brand fuelling me, making me strong, making me electric. The two of us went toe-to-toe, weapons clashing, fighting back and forth across the bridge like a couple of fencers, gaining ground, losing ground, tearing up the piste.

I saw sweat beading on the woman's forehead and poured on blow after blow, sapping her strength, wearing her down. I carried on applying pressure, forcing her to the furthest reach of the bridge, keeping her on the back foot. Another step and she'd trip up and go tumbling down the stairs on the other side. Just one more step.

'Enough!' she cried, and clapped her hands together.

A deafening shockwave knocked me off my feet and sent me skidding along the footbridge, right back to where I started. My ears rang from the blast and multi-coloured splotches danced before my eyes. I tried to get up but it felt like someone had snuck into my gut and moved my centre of gravity two feet to the right.

'Stay down,' the woman ordered, as I staggered about like a drunk at her ex-boyfriend's wedding.

Sensing that I wasn't going to give up, the woman decided to take the option away from me. Hooking a hand on to each of the bridge's handrails, she directed a charge of magical electricity through the overpass that travelled through my feet, locked my knees rigid, and sent me keeling over backwards.

This woman had zero chill.

I lay on the floor, groaning, feeling as though I'd been dragged down ten miles of dirt track.

The woman loomed over me. 'You know, you fight well for a young one.'

I forced a reply through a mouth that felt stuffed full of cotton. 'You're not exactly Betty White yourself, mate.'

'I'm older than I look.'

'You vampires always are.'

The woman tilted her head to one side. 'You think I'm a vampire?'

'Of course I bloody do.'

'Oh. I thought you were a vampire.'

'What are you telling me? If you're not a vamp, what the hell are you?'

'A familiar.'

I thought back to the scientist with the UV tattoo who Gen stabbed. 'You mean one of those Renfields who lap-dog for the Clan?'

'No. I'm Stella Familiar of the London Coven. Now, what is it you want with me?'

18

Okay, so chances are you sussed that one out before I did, but I'm willing to bet you weren't half-drunk and fighting for your life when you did. At least I hope you weren't.

Stella led me to her home in Hammersmith so we could have a proper sit down and chat.

'It's through there,' she said.

She steered me down a side street that terminated in a dead end, then pointed to a patch of brick wall decorated by a couple of old fly posters advertising a Russian Circus that had long since rolled out of town. Another blind alley, I bet. A solid wall, impenetrable to anyone who didn't know it was there, just like the one that screened off The Beehive. Another reminder that reality was just a thin skim of ice over a deep lake of dark water.

I took a step towards it.

'Careful,' warned Stella.

'It's okay,' I assured her, head held high, 'this isn't my first blind alley.'

My nose went squish as I walked it into a solid brick wall.

Stella made a noise like she'd just watched someone come off a skateboard in the most painful and humiliating way. 'A little to the side,' she suggested.

'Yeah I sort of worked that out.'

I rubbed my nose and took a crab-step to the right. Following her guidance I walked at the wall again, and this time I passed right through.

On the other side of the fissure was a black wooden door. Stella performed some hocus pocus to open it up, and after that, we were in.

The coven was different to how I imagined it. It didn't stink of joss sticks. There was no black cat weaving about the place. To me, it looked like a fairly ordinary home, at least until we arrived in the building's main room and I saw the rows of dusty tomes and a chalk pentagram scrawled on to a big grey slate on the floor.

'Nice place you've got here,' I said, trying to put a positive spin on the decor. 'Roomy.'

The coven was a long way from cozy. In many ways, it reminded me of my own place, only with even less cheer. My flat might have been basic and a bit tatty around the edges—okay, very tatty—but it was a home at least. There was love there. Creature comforts. Evidence of a life shared.

Stella ceded the room's single armchair and took a seat opposite me upon a three-legged stool. 'How did you hear about me?'

'A couple of angels told me to seek you out.'

'A couple? Ah, you must mean Vizael and Gendith.'

'You know them then?'

'I know a lot of weird and wonderful people: angels, mystics, trolls, a ghost detective—'

'You didn't know me.'

'No, but then you're a normal.'

I bristled at that. 'A normal? I'm the bloody Nightstalker.'

'Then you're a normal with a backstage pass.'

I was fed up to the back teeth with people making me feel like I'd won this gig in a competition. 'You think what I do is easy?' I snapped, feeling my face turn red. 'I sleep two hours a night if I'm lucky, I get attacked by monsters all day long, and now I have to take shit from you? I never asked for this life. You think I want to be a bitch in a kennel that only gets let off her chain when someone needs chewing on? Do you have any idea what that's like? To be made into someone else's weapon?'

A flicker of recognition crossed Stella's face and her expression softened. 'Yes, I do.'

I sat back in the armchair and folded my arms. 'Yeah, right.'

'Abbey, I know exactly what you mean. I was created by my witches for the express intention of acting as their enforcer.'

'So the Coven just… made you?'

'From dirt, rags and spit.'

'Then you're not even human. Not really.'

'No, I'm not.'

I suddenly felt very sad for this peculiar woman, alone in her draughty old house, living with the knowledge that she was different to everyone around her. Who did she speak to? Who could she call a friend? Viz had told me that the witches of the London Coven were dead now, leaving their familiar to fend for herself. Stella was on her lonesome here, an alien, abandoned on our planet with no place to call home. No wonder she sucked at hospitality (where the hell was my cup of tea?). I mean, I'd had a rough ride since I was given the brand, but at least I got to have a life before I picked up that dagger. Stella had been saddled with her job from day one.

I changed the subject. 'How did you end up running into me on that bridge?'

'I got a call from Lenny saying someone had been asking after me at The Beehive. Of course, he didn't mention that you were the Nightstalker, but then Lenny's not much for words.'

I nodded. No, he was not.

'So then, what do you want from me?' Stella asked, getting to the point.

I sat forward in my chair. 'I need a magician to perform a ritual that will stop my boyfriend from turning into a vampire.'

'Stop?'

'Yeah. Thing is, he's sort of halfway there.'

I could tell she was about to make some smart comment about the Nightstalker letting her boyfriend get turned into a vampire, but the look in my eye told her to keep it to herself. 'I take it you've considered killing his sire? The vampire who turned him?'

'Believe me, I'd love nothing more than to stick a stake

through that guy, but it's a needle in a haystack situation out there.'

Stella pinched the bridge of her nose. 'I don't know. You mentioned a ritual before, but reversing vampirism… I've never heard of such a spell.'

'Trust me, it's a thing. God said so.'

'I see. And which God was that exactly?'

'You know, the normal one. Crosses, Christmas, Communion. Loves an ark.'

Stella bobbed her head, unimpressed. I guess it shouldn't have come as much of a surprise that she wasn't big into Christ, what with being a pagan and everything.

'I'm perfectly happy to help you, Abbey, but if I'm going to bake the cake, I'll need the recipe book.'

'Anything. Just tell me what you need.'

'All reversal spells require a scroll of undoing.'

'Right. And where do I get one of those then? Another curio shop?' I pointed to her book shelves. 'Sure you haven't got any scrolls in that musty old pile over there?'

'I'm sure. And in any case, most magic scrolls aren't really scrolls anymore.'

'They're not?'

'Papyrus doesn't have much of a shelf life, but that's okay, it's the writing that's important, not the paper.'

'But if there's no paper, where do the words go?'

She cocked an eyebrow at me. 'Surely you've heard of computers, Abbey? I'm sixty years old, and even I have some idea how digitising works.'

'So you're telling me that the spell I need is on a machine? Do I just need to Google this thing?' I reached for my phone but Stella stopped me.

'Don't waste your time. If there is such a thing as a ritual to reverse vampirism—and it's a very big *if*—the spell won't be anywhere online.'

'Then where?'

'Somewhere hidden. Somewhere secure. Somewhere guarded by the people who most want to keep it from being made public.'

The Clan.

If I was going to get that cure, I was going to have to go right to the source.

19

I didn't need the angels to tell me where to head next.

'What do you want?' asked Carlo, his scarecrow frame blocking the doorway to his flat.

'Just a tiny, teensy little favour,' I said, pinching a millimetre of air.

'Forget it. You're not getting anything, not after you stiffed me last time you were here.'

'But I come bearing gifts,' I chirped, holding up a cup with a straw sticking from its lid.

'You brought me a McDonald's strawberry milkshake?'

'Oh no, I drank that.'

'So... you brought me an *empty* McDonald's strawberry milkshake?'

'Not exactly.' I smiled and popped the lid.

Carlo's eyes widened. 'Is that what I think it is?'

'Yup.'

Carlo snatched the cup from me and scurried back into his grungy little squat like Gollum with the One Ring.

I followed him inside. 'Sorry, that was the best blood container I could find. There might be a bit of milkshake mixed in with it, but don't worry, you can have that for free.'

He sucked on the straw in a way that was almost pornographic, slurping up the last of the concoction and looking back at me with shiny, doped up eyes. 'Man, I needed that. I'm telling you, it is not easy making do with regular blood.'

'Really?' I asked, oddly proud. 'My blood's that good, is it?'

'Like flying First Class to Hawaii. Trouble is, now the regular stuff's like boarding the plane home and having the stewardess point you to Economy.' He slumped into a ruptured bean bag, making it burp up some more of its insides.

'Well, I'm glad you like it anyway,' I said, too afraid of catching something to sit down. God, it really was an awful shit-hole of a place. 'I know it's none of my business, Carlo, but you really shouldn't be living like this.'

'What's the matter? Worried I won't get my security deposit back?'

I laughed, but it was bittersweet. This man of rags and bones, this human dog-end, sat amongst his rubbish and his old records, waiting on a fix. And who was I but his scheming dealer, exploiting his addiction for my personal gain?

'Where's Gendith?' he asked, sparking up a cigarette.

'Busy.'

'Hmm.' He ran a hand through the ratty tangles of his hair. 'Not sure I'm happy dealing with the Nightstalker one-on-one. Doesn't feel safe exactly. No offence.'

'Safe from me? Come on, there's nothing to worry about. Not if you tell me what I need to know.'

'See, that right there sounds a lot like a threat.'

'It isn't, I promise. So long as you talk.'

Carlo sighed and sunk deeper into his bean bag, too high to give a shit. 'Go on then, what are you after?'

'Information. Where do the Clan keep it?'

'Depends. What kind of info d'you need?'

'The Top Secret kind. The kind you keep on a secure server, somewhere very, very safe.'

'Ah, gotcha. That would be The Crypt.'

I wasn't expecting him to be quite so forthcoming, but I wasn't looking a gift horse in the mouth either. 'I see. What's that then?'

'An underground facility where the Clan keep their most classified data. If what you're looking for is anywhere, that'll be the place.'

I considered what he was telling me. 'So you're saying there's a giant database on the Judas Clan just lying around in some old bunker? Does Gen know about this?'

'Nope.'

'Why not?'

'Because she never asked this nicely.'

He craned his head to the flat's artex ceiling and stared up at a water stain with the look of a man witnessing the birth of the universe. The Nightstalker blood was kicking in hard. It wouldn't be long before euphoria gave way to oblivion. I had to act fast.

I snapped my fingers, realised I didn't know how to snap my fingers, and nudged him with my foot. 'Hey! Stay with me.'

'What?' he mumbled, reluctantly dragged back to reality.

'Tell me more about this Crypt. What are we talking; some musty old cavern full of cobwebs and reel-to-reel computers?'

'Nah,' he slurred. 'Hi-tech compound. Hack-proof and proper fancy. All the bells and whistles. Blah blah blah...'

Before he could crash out, I pushed my phone into his hands. 'Tell me where.'

He begrudgingly pecked out the details I needed, cursing periodically when autocorrect got too heavy-handed with his typing, then nodding off each time the spike of anger wore off, prompting me to jab him awake again.

'What are you looking for down there anyway?' he asked, lazily sliding my phone across the floor to me.

'Same as before. A way to reverse vampirism.'

'Right, right, yeah. Your boyfriend. I remember…' he grinned idiotically, his eyes staring off in separate directions. Time for me to take off, I reckoned, but before I went, I had one last question.

'Are the Judas Clan really evil, Carlo? All of them, I mean.'

'Yup. 'cept for me.'

'What makes you so different?'

'Dunno. Freak of nature? Runt of the litter? Why d'you ask?'

'No reason.'

Of course there was. Regardless of how he got to be who he

was, Carlo was proof that the fight between good and evil—the war between the angels and the Clan—wasn't as black and white as it may have seemed. If Carlo wasn't a bad guy, that meant there could be other shades of grey between. Other vampires who weren't trying to break the world in half. Other vampires like Lauden.

A trickle of drool seeped from between Carlo's lips, which I took as my cue to leave. I headed for the door, leaving him to vegetate, but I'd only half-turned the knob before he murmured some parting words.

'If there really is a cure, Abs... please… please let me know.' His voice was plaintive, pleading, an addict experiencing a brief sliver of clarity before returning to a fog of narcotic bliss.

I nodded to him and he smiled back before his eyelids dropped like a pair of iron portcullises.

20

'No!' said Gendith, banging a fist on the table top. Her voice echoed off the gas tower's curved wall like a bullet. 'Absolutely not.'

'What is your problem now?' I asked, fed up with her constant shitty attitude.

'I'll tell you what my problem is. We know absolutely nothing about what's inside this so-called Crypt of yours. We have no blueprints, no run-down of the facility's security measures, no idea of how many people crew the place. With that many unknowns, a break-in simply is too risky.'

'Calm down, Gendith,' said Vizael, giving her a look over his glasses from across the table.

'Calm down? *Calm down*? You seriously expect me to risk my life infiltrating a high-security bunker because she won't relinquish a simple attachment?'

Now it was my turn to thump the table. 'Is that what you think a boyfriend is, Gen? An attachment? Christ Almighty, no wonder you don't have one.'

She spat back like a cobra. 'In case you forgot, you were Sanctified by God. That means the mission comes first, and the mission is to destroy vampires.'

'We're going to destroy vampires! Lots of vampires. But

before we do that, we're going to stop my boyfriend becoming one.' It felt strange talking about Neil that way while he was only upstairs, but it needed to be said. 'It's our fault he's in this pile of shit, so if there's a way to get him out of it, it's on us to throw down a rope.'

Gen settled her features into an expression that I think was meant to look sympathetic but only served to make her look all the more haughty. 'Just because he looks like your boyfriend, doesn't mean there's anything left of the person you knew. Make peace with his fate and move on, Abbey. Don't jump in the casket with him.'

'Breaking into The Crypt is about more than just fixing Neil. Don't you get it? If this cure works, we can use it on *all* the vampires. That's how we destroy them, not by sticking a dagger in them one-by-one, but by turning them back into us.'

Gen's voice was like a knife. 'And how is that going to work exactly? Do you have an infinite supply of Pope blood we don't know about? Why don't you just admit the truth: the only reason you want into this bunker is to save your doomed boyfriend.'

'That's not true.'

'Don't lie to me, girl, I can read your aura.'

'Fuck your aura.'

Viz rapped the floor with his walking cane, exhausted by our behaviour. 'Listen to yourselves, the two of you, going in circles like dogs chasing their tails, round and around in maddening circles and getting nowhere. Enough. Stop this madness.' Gen and I took a moment to compose ourselves then, when it seemed as though we'd passed the point of tearing strips off of one another, Viz continued. 'This is what we know about the bunker: it was built as an air-raid shelter during the war, then turned into a deep-level telephone exchange in the Fifties before being purchased privately around ten years ago. What it is now, no one knows.'

'But we do know,' I cut in. 'The Clan bought the place and called it The Crypt.'

'...Says a junkie who'd tell us just about anything for a fix of your blood,' Gen interjected.

'Oh, so he's a junkie when the dirt he gives us doesn't suit you?'

Gen snorted. 'You don't know what you're talking about. What is this "Crypt" of yours even supposed to be?'

'What it is,' I shot back, 'is a giant, underground server farm containing masses of valuable data on the Clan.'

Gen did a double take. 'Server farm?' she said, her interest piqued. The cogs started whirring. 'If we had access to a resource like that we could get the names of any number of high-ranking Clan members. With that kind of knowledge we could put a major dent in their operation.'

She and Viz shared a look.

'What?' I asked.

'Nothing,' said Gen.

Viz leaned back in his chair, arms folded as he chewed on his lip and weighed the merits of the mission. Finally, he spoke. 'If raiding this Crypt is what the Nightstalker decrees, then that is what shall be done. Abbey, you have done so much for us already. It's time we did something in return and cured Neil of this terrible disease.'

I liked the sentiment of that very much, but the bit that really caught my ear was hearing one of the angels refer to Neil by his name. It felt good to get some recognition that he was an actual human being, not just some liability, a damsel in distress.

'Thank you,' I said.

'Very well then,' Viz replied, smiling. 'Let us discuss how we are to burgle this fortification.'

'There's only one way to pull this off,' Gen replied, all business, 'and that's using stealth. We'll need to break in undetected, secure the payload, and be out in the smallest window of time possible.'

I raised a hand. 'Not to be a pain in the arse, but do we really need to plan this thing out like it's a heist? I'm the Nightstalker, you know, not Danny Ocean. Can't we just march in there and twat the tits off anyone who gets in our way?'

I didn't really fancy myself as a cat burglar. I'd never stolen anything outside of a bit of makeup from Boots, and I couldn't even pull that off without getting busted.

Gen shook her head. 'This is the only way. Barging in there guns blazing will only get us killed. The Crypt is the Clan's home ground. If we trip an alarm, we'll be stuck in a rat hole with who knows how many bloodsuckers. It's stealth or nothing.'

'She's right,' Viz agreed. 'You'll need to be invisible. A pane of polished glass. A stealth bomber—'

'The office temp at a staff Christmas party. I get it, I get it.'

Fine then. We'd go in sneaky. I kept saying I wanted to be more than just a weapon, now it was time to act like it. 'Stealth it is,' I said.

We talked for a little while longer, then decided we best part ways and get some much-needed rest. Gendith was the first to leave the table, heading up the spiral staircase to bed, a curt nod her goodnight. I was about to do the same (only a bit more politely) when Viz stopped me.

'Before you go, one last thing.'

'What's that?'

'Vampires have night-vision, so there's every chance it will be pitch black in the depths of that bunker. Tell me Abbey, can you see in the dark?'

'Um, not since I last checked.'

'Of course not.' He slapped his forehead forgetfully. 'Give me a moment...' he hobbled over to an old steamer chest, opened it up, and rummaged around inside. 'Here, take this.'

He handed me a green plastic case about the size of a lunchbox.

'What's this?' I asked.

'Night-vision goggles. Army surplus that we recently... recovered.'

I decided not to bother asking him where exactly he'd acquired it from, and opened up the box to get a look at my gift. Inside, sat on a bed of foam padding, was a tuna sandwich.

'What the hell is this?'

Viz's eyebrows shot off his forehead. 'Oh, I'm terribly sorry, that's my lunch. I was wondering where that had got to.' He took the sandwich and had himself a bite. 'Don't worry, I'll find those goggles in the morning.'

'What if I hadn't checked and went into battle with the forces of darkness carrying a bloody fish sarnie?'

The old man shrugged. 'I'm sure you'd have acquitted yourself somehow. Goodnight, Abbey.'

And off he tottered to bed.

I did not sleep easy that night.

21

'I'd like to state for the record that I still think this is a terrible idea,' said Gen.

'Yeah, I sort of worked that out the fiftieth time you said it.'

The two of us were making our way across a plot of vacant scrubland not far from the North Circular. We were dressed in head-to-toe black, which wasn't much of a stretch for me, considering the somewhat limited palette of my wardrobe. Not that I usually wore a balaclava. That was new.

While I felt sure that the dark apparel would serve us well once we made it inside The Crypt, up above it, the camouflage wasn't doing us any favours. The sun was at its highest point in the sky, making us stand out like a couple of poos in a punch bowl. If it seems weird that we'd plan a heist for the middle of the day, remember that solar noon is when the Clan are at their absolute weakest. Yup. Not just a hat-rack, my friend.

'This must be our entry point,' said Gen, crouching down by a rusted grille overgrown with weeds and brambles.

'What is that, an air duct?'

'Looks like it.'

Another reminder that vampires of the Judas Clan needed to breathe. If they didn't need oxygen, they'd doubtless have sealed the shaft up a long time ago, but no, they weren't walking corpses, and they needed air just as much as we did. Could it be that Lauden was dealing me straight, and his kind were more like us than I cared to admit?

Get your head in the game, Abbey. Now is not the time.

I crouched down beside Gen and used my dagger to hack away at the vegetation covering the opening until I found us a cranny we could get a lever into. Working together, Gen and I made short work of the corroded metal, prying the grille open and rolling it off to one side.

A vertical shaft fell away beneath us, so deep that I couldn't see the bottom.

'Give me some recon,' Gen ordered.

'Huh?'

She sighed. 'Take a look and tell me what's down there.'

I gave it a gander but the shaft was dark as squid ink. 'Buggered if I know,' I said.

'Use your eyes, girl.'

This time I gathered what she meant: my Go Go Gadget Nightstalker vision. I hadn't had cause to use it since we were at the lab on Harley Street, and that already felt life a lifetime ago. I only hoped I could remember what Gen had taught me, and that I'd be able to turn the ground beneath us into glass. I pressed my fingertips to my temples and concentrated hard, pouring my focus into the pit, forcing my senses to explore spaces beyond their limited range. I stood there for ages, sweat pouring off me, but try as I might, I just couldn't do it. No matter how many layers I peeled back, no matter how hard I pushed, the shaft was too deep, too dark.

'It's no good,' I said, giving up and letting my eyesight return to normal.

'I see,' said Gen, giving me a thin little fuck-you smile. 'In that case, I'd like to state my record fifty-one times.'

I huffed and peered back into the shaft. 'How do we even get down that thing?' I asked.

'With this.' She unhooked a backpack from her shoulder and emptied its contents at my feet. On the ground, I saw an electric winch, a couple of climbing harnesses, and I don't know how many metres of nylon rope. In her hand, Gen held a remote of some kind.

'Battery-powered,' she said, squeezing the remote's trigger and causing the winch to unspool.

'First the night-vision goggles, now a fancy grapple rope? Very snazzy. You guys have really upped your game.'

'We're vampire hunters, of course we're equipped with the proper inventory. What did you expect, a wooden chest full of stakes and mallets?'

'Well, sort of, yeah. Anyway, this is some serious covert ops, behind enemy lines, Tom Clancy shit.'

'Tom who?'

'I don't know, but Neil's got a tonne of his Xbox games.' Gen ignored me and went about securing the winch in place. 'I'm just saying, this is some pretty high-tech stuff for a couple of golden oldies living in a grubby metal shack.'

Gen shot me a look. 'That "shack", as you call it, is that way for a reason. The tower is off the grid and out of sight, which means the Clan have yet to discover our base of operations, and should they ever succeed in tracing its location, they're in for a nasty surprise.'

I let the moment hang, assuming that Gen had put the pause there to build suspense, but apparently she'd finished talking. 'Well, go on then, you big tease' I said, 'what's the surprise?'

Gen smiled. 'Before it was bombed during the Blitz there used to be a cathedral where that industrial park now stands. The whole site is built on hallowed ground.'

'And that works against vamps?'

'Of course it does.'

'Then why isn't Neil affected?'

'Because he's yet to fully turn.'

'Ugh. Someone really needs to write all these rules down.'

But wait… the Clan *did* know where our base of operations was, or at least, Lauden did. When I ran into him the first time, he pointed to the gas tower and told me that if he'd wanted to kill me, he'd have done me in while I slept. Admittedly, not the greatest way to make a first impression, but another point in his favour considering that the park wasn't currently surrounded by an angry mob of bloodsuckers.

'Time to go,' said Gen, slipping on a climbing harness and

clipping herself to the grapple rope. Before I could raise any further questions, she stepped backwards over the lip of the shaft and glided away like a spider descending on a length of silk. Ten seconds later she touched down at the bottom with such grace that I barely heard her feet hit the ground.

I keyed my head mic (of course we had head mics). 'Are you okay?' I asked.

'Affirmative,' came her voice in my earpiece. 'Now you go.'

I really wished Gen had stuck around to explain how rappelling worked before she back-flipped into the void, but that's how she was; strong, capable, and determined that everyone keep up with her breakneck pace. In a way, it was flattering that she had enough confidence in my abilities to let me ride without training wheels. In another way, it was extremely annoying.

I stepped into my harness and buckled it up as best as I knew how. Meanwhile, Gen returned the rope, along with the trigger that activated it, which was tied to the rope's end and sent up on automatic.

Secure in my harness—or as secure as I was going to get—I hooked the rope to one of its many clasps and prayed that I'd chosen the right one. I took the remote in my hand and wrapped my finger around its trigger. Was I really going to do this? Sure I was. I'd never been great with heights, but the brand didn't care. I felt its power coursing through me, tuning out my surroundings, drowning my fears with a nice big dose of adrenaline.

'Here we go,' I told myself as I took the leap of faith and stepped backwards into oblivion.

I squeezed the trigger on the remote, the winch came to life, and off I went. The first few feet were pretty terrifying, even with the brand numbing my anxiety, but once I'd made peace with being horizontal, I began to get the knack of it.

Look at me go!

As I descended, I came to realise that the harder I pressed the trigger, the quicker the rope unspooled, and so the more confidence I gained, the more pressure I applied.

The temperature dropped as I abseiled deeper into the shaft, sending a chill down my spine. Down below I could just about make out Gen, waiting for me at the bottom of the well. Wanting to impress her with my newfound climbing skills, I kicked out hard and bounced off the wall like a ninja. Big mistake.

My cockiness caused the rope to shift position and find a rusty fragment of metal on the lip of the shaft. As the cord ground against the sharp edge I heard a horrific fraying noise and felt particles of hot nylon shower my face.

Fuck fuck fuck.

I was going to come a cropper, I just knew it, and I still had a good fifty feet between me and the landing. I considered kicking out again and freeing the rope from the abrasive part of the opening, but worried that the act might further strain the cord and make my situation even worse. The best thing I could do, I decided, was get to the bottom of that shaft as fast as humanly possible. I squeezed the trigger tight and the winch hit top speed, unravelling like a kicked toilet roll.

Whoosh.

I was free-falling, picking up speed, racing to the base of the shaft at maximum velocity, then—

Crunch.

I hit the ground and my legs gave way like dry kindling. I cried out in pain, but Gen clapped a hand over my mouth, silencing me.

'Keep your voice down,' she hissed.

My ankles were in bits. It hurt. Holy shit, it hurt. A high-pitched squeal escaped from between Gen's fingers like the whistle of a boiled kettle. Then, over the noise of my own tortured cry, I heard a new sound, the scraping and popping of busted bones as the brand did its job and repaired my injuries. Within moments, my ankles had knitted themselves back together and the pain had vanished.

'Ahh, that's better,' I sighed, giving my feet a couple of rotations.

'What the hell were you playing at up there?' Gen insisted.

'I didn't have a choice, I had to get the rope down in one piece.'

She scowled at me. 'We'd better hope it's strong enough to carry us back up again, or we're stuck down here, fool.'

I climbed to my feet, happy to discover that my legs were fit enough to support me. 'Let's just get what we came for, shall we?'

I slipped on my night-vision goggles and took a look around. Carlo was right. The Crypt wasn't some squalid, cobwebbed dungeon, it was a modern installation, a concrete fallout shelter with breeze block walls, fire-proof doors, and aluminium walkways. More like the inside of the Death Star than a place you'd stick dead bodies in. Of course it was. The Clan were a sophisticated operation, not crazed bloodsuckers from a Universal Horror.

Okay, so we were in, but where was the server farm? We'd set down in a corridor heading off in either direction. Either side of us was a door, the portholes of which revealed another corridor running crosswise. We were at a literal crossroads.

'Which way?' asked Gen.

Of course I didn't want to admit that I had no idea, so I turned away and tried my best to look thoughtful while I waited on something to pop into my head. As I searched for inspiration, my eyes landed on a thick bundle of fibre optic cables running along the ceiling and heading through a hole in the wall above one of the doors.

'Thataway,' I said snapping my fingers and once again failing to do so.

I went to press the button that released the door but Gen shot out an arm and stopped me. 'First of all, we put these on.' She reached inside her pack and produced what looked like a couple of tightly-folded outfits.

'What are they?' I asked.

'Cool suits.'

'Like… Vivienne Westwoods?'

She gave me another of her patented black looks. 'No, you imbecile, *cool suits*, as in suits that lower your body temperature.'

I was starting to get a little ticked off with her attitude. 'Hey, don't forget who you're talking to here. *I'm* the Nightstalker, okay? You're just the sidekick in this little dynamic duo.'

'*Sidekick*?'

'Yeah. So be thankful I don't do what Batman does to Robin and dress you up like a big shiny target.'

Choosing not to address that comment, she slapped one of the outfits against my chest, knocking the wind out of me. 'Put it on.'

I unfolded the outfit; a lumpy, one-piece boiler suit. 'Why would I wear this?'

'To avoid setting off a temperature-activated alarm.' She drew my attention to a steel panel bolted to the door, stencilled on which was a symbol of a man standing next to an oversized thermometer. 'I've seen this before. Beyond that door, the facility is set up so an alarm trips if a hot-blooded person enters. The suits are lined with a refrigerant gel that will lower our body temperatures and trick The Crypt's security system into thinking we're cold-blooded vamps.'

'And you just happened to bring these along?'

'I believe in being prepared.'

Of course she did, Girl Scout that she was. It's a wonder she wasn't wearing a sash covered in activity badges, the absolute boffin.

I shook out the suit I'd been given and stepped into its leggings. The fabric was wadded with ice packs, the kind you'd use to reduce a swelling, or stick in the bottom of a picnic basket to keep your sarnies chilled. I pulled the suit up to my waist, fed my arms into the sleeves, and zipped up. I felt as though I'd stepped inside an igloo.

'Brrrr,' I shivered. 'How long do we have to keep these on? My nips are like pygmies' dicks in here.'

'Not long. The suits will only do their job for a short while, so we'll have to operate quickly. Set your stopwatch for fifteen minutes.'

I rolled up a sleeve and went for my timepiece.

'Synchronise... now.'

We stabbed our start buttons and set our timers running.

'I can't believe how badass this is,' I said, unable to hide my excitement. 'Neil's going to shit a brick when I tell him we broke into a top secret bunker wearing night-vision goggles and balaclavas.'

'Will you please stop doting on your boyfriend and concentrate on the job at hand?'

With less than fifteen minutes on the clock, I didn't have time to get into a big argument with her, much less strangle her to death with her own halo, so I left it at this: 'Neil *is* the job, Gen. He's why we're down here. Don't forget that.'

I drew my dagger and pushed open the door, determined to get what we came for.

22

We pushed on into the vault, following the snake of overhead cables to what I really, really hoped would be the server room.

The Crypt was big; a vast network of tunnels and chambers riddling the earth like a badger's burrow. I hadn't counted on the place being quite so large, but then I suppose I shouldn't have been surprised. The Clan's pockets were plenty deep.

We crept along a corridor, chasing the cables, moving in long strides but doing our best to keep our noise to a minimum. We'd been tracking the breadcrumb trail for maybe five minutes when a thought occurred… why hadn't we encountered any vampires? Yes, we were doing a decent job of staying under the radar—not counting my sloppy, smashed-ankles landing—but surely we should have run into someone by now, even if by chance. Unless the place was unmanned, and why would that be, considering the value of The Crypt's contents?

'Why don't I use my x-rays?' I asked.

'Because we don't have time,' Gen replied. 'We have to keep moving.'

She was right. The clock was ticking, and switching to Nightstalker vision was still pretty time-consuming. Until I'd mastered that power, we were better off pushing on and dealing with things as we found them than bumming about like sitting ducks.

'I don't like this,' Gen whispered as we carried on down the corridor. 'Too quiet.'

'Don't worry,' I said, 'I'm sure we'll find someone for you to kill soon enough. Chill out.'

Ha. *"Chill out"*, I said, with the pair of us dressed in cool suits. I really was a card.

We rounded a corner and I caught sight of another unexpected security measure.

Up ahead, a web of red lasers crisscrossed the corridor, forming a fine weave of electronic tripwires. Jesus. Our assignment had gone full-on Mission Impossible. How in the name of sweet Siouxsie Sioux was I meant to make it through that mess? I was the Nightstalker—a blunt instrument, a human battering ram—not a frigging cat burglar. All things considered, I'd rather we *had* run into some guards. At least I could have twatted my way through those. Getting past this tangle was a precision job, and precision was not my watchword.

'Bollocks,' I huffed.

While I was busy cursing and wondering how in the hell we were going to bypass this cutting edge cat's cradle, Gen got to work. Off she went like a ballet dancer, no mucking about, dancing into the complex jungle of lasers, supple as a fish. Her lithe body fell into impossible poses as she slipped into the web, her movements nimble, the lines of her frame long and clean as she cut through the spaces between the red beams with ease. When she emerged on the other side moments later I could see she hadn't so much as broken a sweat.

'You're up,' she announced. 'Use your eyes, tread carefully, and remember to watch out for those mum hips of yours.'

If I could have reached out and slapped her I would have, but she was safe on the other side of the lasers; a guard taunting a prisoner through the bars of her cell.

I checked my stopwatch. The seconds were counting down. No time to waste.

Without any further hesitation I cartwheeled into the web of lasers, perfectly balanced, free as water, a thing of absolute grace and beauty—

Just kidding, my arse broke a laser beam and set the bells ringing in two seconds flat.

AROOOOGA!

Klaxons blared loud enough to wake the dead. Lights strobed and searched, burning out the images on the inside of my night-vision goggles. In a heartbeat, the facility had transformed from a static, lifeless place into a buzzing, angry hornet's nest.

I tore off my goggles and blinked until my eyesight returned. Red bulbs painted the bunker the colour of blood as the alarm continued to blare. I saw a flash of movement and whipped around to see a wall-mounted security monitor. The screen was divided into quadrants showing various sectors of the bunker, all of which had come alive and were bristling with burly soldiers, goose-stepping in our direction. The soldiers were huge—as big as any men I'd ever seen—and dressed kind of like Gestapo officers in black military outfits and knee-length boots. Nazi hulks? This I did not need.

Gen looked at the monitor and checked her watch. 'We were only in that spot five minutes ago,' she shouted over the screaming alarm.

'Let 'em come,' I called back, drawing my blade and feeling the brand flare hot in my palm.

'No. Too many to fight.'

'Too many? We've faced down more vamps than that.'

Gen gritted her teeth, forming a hard white line. 'Not like these we haven't.'

I looked closer at the monitor. She was right, these were different to the vamps I'd seen before, more muscular, more animal, less like city bankers than something you'd find in a late-night creature feature.

'We have to pull out,' said Gen. 'Right now.'

'No. We still have time. We stick to the mission and we find that server room.'

Gen scowled. She obviously disagreed with me, but she'd been instructed by Viz to follow my orders to the tee. She was a stubborn, hot-headed cow, but she knew where to draw the line. Why she let the old man call the shots I didn't know, but I was glad the pecking order was what it was. 'Okay then,' she seethed. 'Lead the way, Batman.'

We took off down the corridor, feet pounding the metal walkway as we ran. It wasn't long before we reached the end of the cables and arrived at our destination; an air-conditioned data centre full of whirring, flashing machinery configured into aisles of rack-mounted towers. The only problem? It was sealed off by a row of steel bars, five inches thick.

'Help me get through this thing,' I said, wrapping my hands around a couple of bars and wrenching them as hard as I could.

I strained until my eyes bugged from my skull, until my teeth hurt, but even with Gen's help, the gate wouldn't budge. I flicked the dagger, turning it into a sword, and hacked away at the steel bars. Try as I might, the blows I dealt only glanced off, showering the floor with electric blue sparks.

Bugger, bugger, bugger.

'It's no good,' said Gen. 'The whole thing is sealed with maglocks.'

I didn't know what that meant exactly, but it definitely didn't sound good. 'You got anything left in that bag?' I asked. 'A magic lockpick? Some hi-tech cutting tool?'

Gen was at a loss. Even she hadn't accounted for this degree of security. No Girl Scout badge for her, not this time.

'We have to abort,' she said, but I all but tuned her out.

I hadn't come this far to throw in the towel now. There had to be some way of opening that gate. Some release. A switch. There was always a switch, I'd watched Neil play his Xbox enough to know that much.

Then I saw it. Through the bars, a control panel on the far wall of the server room.

'That's it,' I cried. 'That must open the gate; an emergency release in case someone gets locked inside.'

'You don't know that, and even if you're right, how are you going to get to it?'

I touched the tip of my sword to the ground and pressed down until it magically telescoped back into a dagger. 'Like this.'

I took a step back, pulled the knife alongside my ear, and lined up a shot between the bars. It was going to be a tough throw. I'd need pinpoint accuracy to slice the almost impossible angle required to get the blade between two walls of servers and across thirty feet of ground. Still, the clock was ticking, so I took a steadying breath, held it, and let the dagger fly—

The blade went wide, ricocheted off a server stack, and embedded itself in a patch of wall to the left of the panel. The dagger's pommel quivered with spent energy, taunting my futile effort like a tiny waggling butt.

'Balls,' I muttered.

In any other scenario that would have been the end of that, but the dagger shared a bond with my brand that pisses in the shoe of physics.

I willed the weapon to return to me and it obeyed my command, exploding from the wall and boomeranging back to my hand. Flakes of masonry trailed after the blade as it spun, turning over and over, singing a low, swift tune as the metal razored through the air. I snatched hold of the dagger as it returned through the bars, fingers closing instinctively around its leather hilt, gripping it tight.

'You're wasting your time,' said Gen. 'Even if you could hit it, what are the chances of you activating a release button?'

Not to be deterred, I lined up another shot and let the dagger loose for the second time. This throw went even further askew, burying the dagger up to its hilt in one of the servers and making it spit up a spray of sparks like it was dying of robot consumption. Christ, I really hoped that wasn't the machine carrying the data I'd come for.

'They're almost on us,' said Gen. 'Come on, Abbey, it's time to go!'

'One more! Just give me one more try!'

I pulled back the dagger, found my target, and gave it everything I had.

The blade took off, threading the needle like it was borne aloft by the hand of God.

Prang.

The metal pierced the control panel and the gate swung open.

'Yes!'

Gen stood there for a moment, aghast, then turned to me. 'Maybe you're not just a face after all.'

'I think the expression is meant to be "pretty face".'

She raised an eyebrow. 'Have you looked in a mirror lately?'

'Tell you what, how about you give your tongue a rest and get to work, eh?'

Putting the sass on ice, Gen strode into the server room and went searching for the command console. Having located it, she plugged in a flash drive and furiously tapped away at the keyboard, trawling the system for the words to the scroll of undoing.

My eyes flicked to the corridor behind us, then back to Gen, then back to the corridor, searching the semi-darkness for the first sign of our pursuers. My heart thundered beneath my rib cage. My nerves were wound tight as springs.

'Got it,' Gen yelled triumphantly.

'Seriously? You found the cure? Are you sure?'

'Yes, I'm sure.'

I snatched the stick off her and stuffed it into my pocket. 'Then let's get out of here while we still can.'

We ran, doubling back to the shaft, praying that we didn't collide with any of those lumbering hulks along the way.

No one gets that lucky.

We were hurtling down a corridor, maybe halfway to our destination, when an arm the size of a tree trunk shot out from around a corner and clotheslined Gen flat.

Pow!

I saw the glow of two amber eyes hovering eight feet off the ground. A two-tonne slab of muscle in a black military uniform and jackboots loomed over Gen's prone body. The creature's face was monstrous and strangely underdeveloped, foetal almost. It opened its huge mouth, revealing a pair of fangs the size of garden shears. I had no idea what I was looking at. I'd never seen anything like this thing, but whatever it was, it looked as though it could suck a ham through a drinking straw.

Turning its attention back to Gen, the vampire hulk made a death metal growl and clasped its hands together, fingers interlocked to form a single fist the size of a wrecking ball. The beast raised the meaty mitt above its head, making ready to smash the angel flat. I had to act fast. The whole of my life dilated into a single thought.

Take him down.

With no time to lose, I unleashed the dagger, sending it winging for the hulk's ugly baby head. The target practice back at the server room must have honed my shot, because a fraction of a second after I loosed the blade I saw one of the amber lights wink out.

Bam, right in the peeper.

The hulk stumbled, rocking back on its heels, ready to keel over—

Then changed its mind and went back to work. The hulk bunched its hands together and made another wrecking ball fist, seemingly unperturbed by the knife sticking out of its ruined orbit. I tried to recall the dagger so I could have another shot at it, but the blade was stuck. No matter how hard I strained, I couldn't dislodge the weapon from the monster's thick skull.

I had no choice, I was going to have to get hands-on with this thing.

The hulk raised its bunched hands over its head, muscles tensed, ready to pummel Gen into a pancake. As it wound up for the death blow, the brand kicked in, juicing my system, sharpening my senses, making time slow down. The hulk threw its fists at Gen's skull like a dropped anvil, but I was already in motion, charging the beast with raw, animal hatred.

My feet left the ground and I felt myself leaping high into the air, my body doing the work, my brain on autopilot. I landed on the hulk's shoulders and my legs instinctively wrapped around the beast's bull neck, scissoring it tight. The monster thrashed and bucked, trying to shake me loose, but I held on, thighs taut, refusing to let go. I rained a blistering hail of fists on the hulk's skull, but it absorbed them like slaps from a little girl. Like we were playing a game of pat-a-cake.

It didn't matter how hard the brand worked for me, I wasn't going to make a dent in this thing, not with my bare hands. I needed a weapon. My weapon. Clinging on for dear life, I reached around to the front of the hulk's head and seized the dagger's hilt in my fist. Digging deep, I pulled as hard as I could, wrenched the weapon free, and went at the creature like I was chipping a block of ice. Bits of meat and bone flew from the creature's head as I stabbed and jabbed. Just the noise of it was sickening, let alone the sight. Finally, the dagger sank into the jelly of its remaining eye and the creature's arms fell limp by its sides.

The muscles of the hulk's neck went slack between my thighs and it spilled forward, carrying me to the ground.

Boom.

A mini-earthquake as the knuckle-dragging monster slammed into the deck with the power of a demolished skyscraper. Gen came around with a start as the beast struck the ground by her side. Rolling over, she saw the hacked-up monster lying next to her with a knife sticking out of its eye socket.

She let out a panicked yelp. 'Good God.'

I sat on the hulk's back, legs crossed, mock-buffing my nails. 'Morning sleepyhead.'

'What happened?' Gen groaned.

'Oh, nothing much, I just took out hefty here single-handedly and saved your life. No biggie.' I stroked my chin. 'Wait a second, aren't *you* supposed to be the guardian angel?'

I stood up and held out a hand to help her off the floor. I half-expected her to bat it away, but she took it, pulled herself up, and wrapped her arms around my shoulders.

'Thank you,' she said, clinching me hard, her breath hot in my ear.

Well, that certainly came out of nowhere. The "thank you" was surprise enough, but physical contact to go with it? My world was *shook.*

Now, you could argue that standing around cuddling while the klaxons wailed and death closed in was a bit of a daft thing to be doing in that moment, but I needed that hug. That simple little gesture was the most affection Gendith had ever shown me. The most affection *anyone* had shown me since Neil got bitten by a vampire. I hugged Gen back, good and tight.

'Are you smelling my hair?' she asked.

'No,' I replied, trying to make out that I hadn't been inhaling her scent, which, if you must know, smelled like a little slice of Heaven.

Gen pushed me away, disengaging from my embrace.

I coughed awkwardly, decided I'd better get back to work, and went about the grisly task of retrieving my dagger. Reaching down, I plucked the knife from the vampire hulk's skull and it came free with a sickening *squish*.

'That's weird,' I said crouching low and inspecting the vampire closer, 'hefty doesn't have a J on his forehead.'

'That's because he's not Clan. Not really. He's more like a pet, an attack dog, grown from Clan DNA. We call them tanks. They're strong and tough, but they're brainless and don't have the tolerance to sunlight that their masters have, so they can only serve them in darkness.'

Just then I felt the walkway vibrate under my feet and heard jackbooted heels ringing off metal. More of them were coming. Lots more.

Gen grabbed me by the wrist. 'Come on, we have to get out of here.'

I slammed the sticky blade of my knife back into its sheath and got going. Concrete flashed past us as we doubled back to the shaft, running like hell to keep our distance from the incoming tanks. Heavy footfalls rattled the ground as we ran, spurring us on, driving us like cattle in a thunderstorm. Lungs on fire, I hurtled after Gen, desperate to make it back to the surface, thighs burning as I raced the final leg.

'There,' Gen shouted.

I don't know how we did it, but somehow we managed to make it back to the entrance shaft without running into any more Nazi monster babies.

'Get going,' said Gen, handing me the rope.

'No, you go,' I replied, handing it back.

'Don't argue with me,' she insisted, thrusting the cord into my hand.

This little dance was getting us nowhere. Whether Gen was trying to get me out of harm's way due to some renewed sense of duty I didn't know. Maybe she felt like she owed me one after I saved her life back there. Or maybe she just wanted to use me as a guinea pig in case the frayed rope snapped on us. All I knew for sure was that there were a bunch of jumbo jackboots marching our way, so rather than continue the argument, I decided to take matters into my own hands.

'Ladies first,' I said, clipping the rope to Gen's harness and squeezing the trigger that activated the winch.

Whoosh.

Off she went, legs pedalling air as she went whizzing to the surface. I heard a few unsavoury words crackle in my earpiece as she rocketed up the shaft, then she reached the summit, clambered topside, and unhooked herself from the winch.

'Send it down,' she cried.

I set the winch in reverse and unspooled the rope, lowering it back into the bunker, thankful that Gen's weight hadn't snapped it (of course it hadn't, the narrow-hipped bitch).

Crashing noises rumbled through the corridors and ductwork. I checked behind me to see a tank heading in my direction, coming my way with long, loping gaits and murder in its eyes. The rope snaked down out of the darkness and I snatched the metal clasp at its end as fast as I could. With just a few metres of ground left between me and the charging tank, I slapped the clasp on my harness and activated the trigger.

I'd only made it a few feet into the air when I felt something grab hold of my ankle. The tank had latched on to me, its grip heavier than a trailer hitch. Looking down, I saw the beast's hideous face leering up at me, another overgrown hulk baby, identical to the one I'd planted a knife in earlier.

The winch strained under the excess weight, but continued to carry me up the shaft with the tank in tow.

I heard Gen's voice in my ear. 'You have to shake that thing, the rope won't take it.'

Sure enough, I heard a sickening creak as the frayed cord unravelled some more, wearing thinner, about to snap.

'Kick him. Stab him. Just do something!' Gen screamed.

'Just a little further,' I called back.

The winch screamed and whined. The rope was down to a thread. I was fifty feet up and hanging on by a prayer.

Gen barked in my ear. 'It's going to give.'

'A little more…'

And then it happened.

Brilliant, scalding light, flooding in from the surface.

The first ray of sunshine lanced into the shaft and struck my passenger like a bolt of lightning. I felt a tremendous flash of heat as flames ripped through the tank's body and turned it BBQ black. As I rode higher up the shaft and further into the light of day, a horrible scream flew from the beast's mouth, far too high-pitched for its frame. It was a nightmare sound. The sound of a baby pulling a hot kettle on to itself. I was about to press my hands to my ears to blot it out when the noise stopped abruptly. Looking down, I saw the tank's jaw unhinge from the crumbling bones of its skull, then the remains of its charred skeleton came apart and went tumbling into the void.

The whole thing happened in two seconds flat.

The second after that, the rope gave way.

I felt my heart rear into my throat.

I was falling.

Falling to the bottom of the shaft, where I'd either be killed by the impact, or murdered by the things waiting for me there.

(I really hoped it was the first one).

I closed my eyes and readied myself for the end as gravity's quicksand sucked me down—

Then I felt something snag me and realised I was dangling mid-air.

I looked up and saw Gendith hovering above me, her hand hooked into a strap on the back of my harness.

'Now who's the guardian angel?' she asked.

23

The sun was on its way down by the time we ping-ponged back to base.

I rocked into the tower with the flash drive pinched between my forefinger and thumb, holding it aloft like something holy. Like something divine. 'We did it, Viz!' I screamed as I raced up the tower's spiral staircase. 'We found the cure!' I barged into my bedchamber to find Viz sat by Neil's cot. 'Didn't you hear me?' I gushed, waggling the drive. 'We got the words for the scroll of undoing.'

The old man turned from Neil's cot, his face ashen. 'Sit down, Abbey.'

'Why? What's wrong?'

Then I saw Neil. He looked awful. Even from across the other side of the room, he looked awful. I stumbled over to his bedside and pushed Viz aside, my stomach clenching, fear taking hold of me. He was unconscious, his breaths coming in shallow, unsteady gasps. A cold sweat glistened on his gaunt features. He looked thin, wrung out, like a set of bagpipes that had been squeezed until the tune ran out.

'What happened?' I asked, my head whipping to Viz.

'I'm at a loss,' he replied. 'He was fine and then…'

'You told me I had a week to find the cure. It's only been a couple of days and he looks like he's at death's door.'

'It doesn't make sense,' said Viz, his face even more lined than usual. 'He's on the drip still… the transfusion is being administered exactly as instructed…'

'Does he need blood? I can give him blood—'

'You don't cure a man of vampirism by giving him blood,' said Gen, sticking her oar in as always. 'Besides, look at him, he's in no state to feed.'

What was going on? Neil had been so vital the last time I'd seen him. Why this sudden turn for the worse?

Neil coughed, surprising us all. Bile dribbled from his quivering lips as he turned to face me. 'Abbey,' he wheezed, then his eyes rolled back into his skull and he was gone again, lungs rattling as tiny breaths quivered inside of them, small and bird-like. I clamped on to his skeletal hand, afraid to squeeze it too tightly in case it shattered in my grip.

'Well?' I cried, desperate for the angels to help me, to offer some sort of solution, any sort of solution. 'What do we do?'

They looked to one another then back to me, but neither answered.

'Get out of my way,' I said, knocking the angels aside, heading for the door.

'Where are you going?' asked Gen.

'To see Stella Familiar,' I shot back. 'Before it's too late.'

'I'll come with you,' she said, giving chase.

'No,' I said, holding up a hand. 'I'm tired of being chaperoned.'

'Then leave the flash drive here at least.'

'Why would I do that?'

'You've met Stella. Does she seem like the kind of person who has a computer lying around? Leave the drive here and let me extract the information.'

Something about the way Gen was acting made me want to cling on to that drive tighter than ever.

'Just sit there with Viz and make sure my boyfriend stays alive. Do you hear me? I'm counting on the two of you.'

A beat, then she nodded, Viz too.

I pushed through the door and pounded down the metal

stairs, feet ringing against the steps like the peals of an executioner's bell.

I managed to navigate the Bermuda Triangle to the London Coven without Stella's help this time.

Having slipped through the magical fissure in the blind alley's brick wall, I arrived at the hideaway's polished black door and pounded on it with the butt of my dagger.

'Stella? Stella!' I hollered, feeling like Stanley Kowalski in *Streetcar*.

Eventually, the door cracked open and Stella appeared on the other side, dressed in nightclothes. 'Abbey? What is it?'

'I need your help.'

'Can it wait until the morning? I just got done with a mummy that woke up in the British Museum and threatened to snuff out the sun.'

By way of an answer I barged past her into the coven.

'Fine,' she said, 'I'm sure your business is far more important than mine.'

I thrust the flash drive at her. 'I need you to transcribe what's on this. Right now.'

'Abbey, I need to sleep. I have a whole city to protect, and not just against vampires.'

The way she said it, it's like she was a doctor, and I was just a dentist. Sure, you might come to me if you needed a filling done, but if you wanted something doing outside of the mouth, forget about it.

'It's about Neil,' I said.

'I appreciate that, but—and I mean this in the nicest way possible—Neil's only one person. He's just not my top priority right now.'

'Of course not,' I seethed. 'No one ever wants to make Neil a priority.'

Stella placed a friendly hand on my arm. 'Let me make you a cup of tea, Abbey. You look shattered.'

'There isn't time!' I was crying. Crying with violence. 'Neil's on his last legs. I need you to perform the ritual right now.'

'What do you mean?' Her face knotted with concern. 'We should have days before that's necessary.'

'I don't know what's happening, okay? All I know is he won't see sunrise if you don't help me.' I stabbed the flash drive at her like a weapon.

'Okay then, forget the tea.' She took the stick from my hand. 'Come along.'

She led me to a small study that contained a simple desk and —much to my surprise, and no doubt, Gen's—a brand new laptop computer. It didn't look right, a modern slab of tech in that fossilised, lonely little place.

Stella caught me eyeballing her computer. 'Nice, isn't it? A policeman friend of mine insisted I get one. Something to bring me into the twentieth century, he said.'

'Twenty-first.'

'Of course, yes. I always forget about that one.'

She flipped the laptop open and it powered up. I expected her to slide the drive into the USB port and get to work, but instead she turned the whole machine on its side and started stabbing at the holes like a horny teenage boy.

'What are you doing?'

'Give me a second,' she said, one eye closed as she did her best to force the stick into the laptop's power socket.

It was horrible to watch. No way was I standing around watching while she pecked away at the keyboard with a single finger. 'Give it here,' I huffed as I planted one arse cheek on her chair and yanked the laptop in my direction.

I pulled up the files. Spreadsheets. Nothing but spreadsheets. I scanned the documents for anything that looked like the words to a ritual, but all I saw were rows of names and addresses.

'What is this?' I asked. 'It looks like contact info. That's not what we went in for.' I continued to rifle through the documents until there were none left. 'Where's the spell?' My voice was rising with panic. 'Is it hidden somewhere? Is it encrypted?'

Stella turned to me. 'There is no spell on here, Abbey.'

'No. It has to be here somewhere. Gen said it was. She promised me.'

'Well it's not on there. Maybe she was mistaken.'

'Mistaken?' I screamed. I stabbed the laptop's screen with my index finger. 'What is this? What is this stuff?'

Stella spoke calmly, like a parent dealing with a toddler about to go from a hissy fit to a full-on wobbler. 'As far as I can see, what you have there is a long-list of vampire Captains and Generals.'

I felt an eyelid twitch.

Captains. Generals. High-ranking Clan members. The kind Gendith said we should be seeking out instead of wasting our time looking for Neil's cure.

Anger boiled up inside me. A bait and switch. I'd fallen for a fucking bait and switch. Gen had betrayed me. Both of the angels had. Viz had never spoken with God. There was never a cure. The whole thing was just a smokescreen, a means to keep me distracted from what the angels were really doing: pushing on with their mission to wipe out the Clan. All of the running around I'd done, all of the hope I'd felt… all for nothing, all of it false. They didn't care about Neil, and they sure as hell didn't care about me.

I could see everything so clearly now. When I went to Viz and Gen about The Crypt, they'd sensed an opportunity. An opportunity to funnel my rage, my focus, and twist it for their own selfish ends. They sent me into that bunker thinking I was saving my boyfriend's soul, when all I was really doing was furthering their vampire genocide.

'I thought they were helping me get Neil back on his feet,' I stammered, 'but they were just using me. No wonder Gen didn't want me taking this stick off her.' I threw it to the ground and crushed it under my heel. 'Lauden was right.'

'Who's Lauden?'

'I'll kill them,' I said, ignoring her question as the brand grew hot in my fist. 'I'll kill them both.'

'Abbey, listen to yourself, you're talking about killing angels.'

She went to put her hand on my arm again but I shoved her back. 'Get away from me, bitch.'

Was she with them too? Was she in on this?

Stella stepped away from me, hands held up in surrender.

'You're making a big mistake. Don't do this. This isn't what you do.'

'You don't know me.'

'Yes, I do. I know the angels made you into a weapon, just like the Coven did to me.'

I didn't care to hear her little spit and rags story again. I went to push by her, but she snagged hold of my sleeve. 'Abbey, listen to me – just because they turned you into a weapon, doesn't mean you have to act like one.'

I shouldered her aside and headed for the door. My fists were two red murder balls. Stella was right, the angels had made me into a weapon... and this weapon was about to backfire.

24

I burst into the gas tower like a bullet from a gun.

I saw no sign of the angels on the ground floor, so I pounded my way upstairs, knuckles white, jaw set. When I kicked open the door to my sleeping chamber I found Gen, sat by Neil's bedside.

'Abbey, I'm so sorry.'

'You're about to be,' I told her.

But she wasn't apologising. Not like that anyway. She was sorry for Neil.

'We did everything we could,' she said, folding her hands in her lap and hanging her head, 'but he didn't make it.'

'What are you talking about?' I cried, rushing to Neil's side, refusing to face the truth.

But the truth didn't care.

Neil's head laid sideways on the pillow, facing away from me. I took him in my hands and turned his face to mine. His eyes were closed, his lips blue. 'Neil?' He wasn't breathing.

I clawed back his sheets and put my hand to his heart. It had stopped beating.

I heard Gen's voice behind me. 'One minute he was with me, the next he was just… gone. If it helps, I don't think he was in any pain.' She sounded far away, as though she were at the end of an impossibly long tunnel.

Somehow, amongst all of the thoughts boiling inside my head, I remembered my First Aid training. 'Did you try CPR?' I screamed, loud the first time, louder the second.

When the question returned a blank-eyed stare I went to work, placing the heel of my hand on Neil's breastbone and pumping down with all of my weight. I kept going, sweat pricking my face, tears streaming from my eyes as I delivered one compression after another, desperate for him to recover, for his eyes to open, for a breath to slide out from between those pale blue lips.

'It's not working,' said Gen.

'I can see that,' I shouted back.

I lifted Neil's eyelids and saw two glass marbles. He was going to need more than just oxygen. I drew the dagger from its sheath and Gen pulled away from me. But it wasn't for her. Not yet anyway.

I drew a red line across the palm of my left hand and made a fist over Neil's face, squeezing a trickle of blood into his open mouth. The blood ran into his throat until it welled up over his lips and streamed down his hollow cheeks onto the pillow beneath. I massaged his throat in a bid to get him to swallow, but his body stayed still and cold. I drew back from him, the room quiet now save for the sound of my teeth grinding and the pitter patter of blood on the room's wooden floor.

I swept a hand down Neil's face, closing his eyes, then turned to Gen with so much hate radiating from me it's a wonder I wasn't giving off steam. 'You did this,' I hissed.

'What are you talking about?'

'You killed Neil.'

She backed away, hands out in defence. 'Abbey, you don't know what you're saying—'

'Oh, I know. I know you sent me on a fucking wild goose chase while you killed my boyfriend.'

'I already told you what happened—'

'Yeah, you did. You told me dry-eyed and cold as a fish.'

'That's just who I am, Abbey. It doesn't mean I don't care.'

'Don't lie to me! You wanted Neil out of the picture right from the start. Right from the moment he was bitten.'

Gen threw up her arms. 'So what if I did?' She stopped backing away and squared her shoulders. 'Yes, I believe our mission is bigger than a single person, I've made no secret of that. It doesn't mean I killed your boyfriend.'

As she stood there, thin-lipped and furious, I remembered the hug she'd given me back in The Crypt after I put down that tank. That Judas kiss. I'd saved her life, and in return, she'd taken Neil's.

'He was getting better,' I said. 'The vampire blood was making him strong. He would have lived forever, but you poisoned him.'

I pulled the dagger from its sheath.

'What are you planning on doing with that?' Gen asked.

'What do you think?'

'Listen, you're upset, you're not thinking straight. If I'd wanted to kill Neil, why would I have done it now? I could have executed him any time you left this tower.'

'No, you couldn't. You needed his death to look natural so I'd carry on doing your dirty work. You needed me to hate vampires more than anything. Except now I know better. Now I know who the real enemy is.'

'You need to calm down and think for a minute.'

'Oh yeah? You know what I'm thinking? I'm thinking it's pretty fucking suss that you wanted to hang on to that flash drive so badly.'

'To keep it safe. Why else would I care?'

'Stop playing innocent with me, Gen, I saw what was on the drive. Not the cure, just a shopping list of Clan Captains.'

Gen faltered. 'That's not right… I… I did my job...'

'Liar. You're lying. And you know what the worst part is? You did it for nothing.' I pointed to Neil's body with the tip of my knife. 'Neil's dead and the drive's destroyed. Now no one gets what they want. No one gets anything.'

'Abbey, do you really think I'd kill an innocent man? I'm an angel.'

'Yeah, you're an angel. The angel of death.' I started towards her.

'Put the dagger down,' she demanded, dropping into a fighting stance, legs bent, arms up. 'Right now.'

I swung the knife at the ground and planted it in a floorboard beside my foot with a decisive *thwang*. 'You think I need this to fight you? I'm going to murder you with my bare hands.'

The rage came out of me faster than a spout of magma and twice as destructive.

Gen whipped out her morning star to defend herself, but I took it from her, snapped it over my knee, and tossed the broken halves east and west.

Suddenly my fist was slamming into her face.

She stumbled away from me, rubbing her jaw, eyes narrowed. 'I don't want to hurt you,' she said.

'Don't worry,' I spat back, 'you won't.'

The brand flared bright and my blood hummed in my veins. There was a frozen moment of stand-off, then we dived back at each other.

I came down on her knee and her leg buckled, sending her crashing to the ground. Before she could right herself, I stepped in and gave her a taste of shoe leather, stamping on her hard with the heel of a Doc Marten.

Gen looked up at me, her bottom lip split in two. She gobbed a blotch of blue angel blood on the ground, along with half a molar. 'So, that's how it's going to be, is it?'

It was. Not a ballet. Not a polite exchange of ideas. This was going to be messy: a grindhouse rampage of shattered bones and broken teeth and popped eyeballs. I was going to make Gen suffer. For what she'd done to me. For what she'd done to Neil.

I felt another swell of anger and went at her again. She looked unsteady on her feet as I charged at her, but she was only baiting me. The moment I arrived within attack range, she came to life, sweeping me in the side of the head with a lightning-fast roundhouse kick.

I reeled backwards, my ear throbbing from the blow, flash bulbs popping behind my eyes. While I was busy regaining my balance, Gen pressed the attack, launching off her back foot and firing a knee into my gut. The blow sunk in, knocking the wind out of me, then the floor came up and kicked me in the face.

'Stay down,' Gen insisted, circling me like a boxer as I laid on the ground.

But I wasn't done yet. Not by a long shot.

I bounced to my feet, lashed out, and drove my fist into Gen's face with a blunt crack.

She staggered backwards, nose bent out of shape, twin streams of blue blood pouring from her nostrils. Scowling, she pinched the bridge of her nose and set the cartilage back in place. 'Enough,' she growled.

Instead of coming at me with a kick this time, she came dirty.

Using the scant daylight in the room—which amounted to little more than a few mote-laden sunbeams lancing through the cracks in the tower wall— she used her powers to make the rays solid. Four flaming javelins hovered before her. That was a new trick. I'd seen her create walls out of light before, but never weapons.

The spears came at me. I dived to avoid them, but one caught me in the shoulder, threw me to the other side of the room, and pinned me to the tower's curved metal wall.

The spear burned as it held me there, making my flesh sizzle, making me scream.

'Are you finished?' she asked, panting from exertion.

Red-hot pain throbbed in synch with the jackrabbit beat of my heart. I screamed until my breath whined in my throat, but I wouldn't give in, wouldn't relent.

'I'm going to kill you,' I promised, eyes watering.

Gen held the flaming spear in place, nailing me to the wall like a framed picture as she summoned another javelin. 'Please, Abbey. Don't make me do this...'

I barely heard her. Instead, I channelled the pain she was feeding me, channelled the fury, turned it into fuel, turned it into power.

The gas tower began to shake. Dust drifted down from the roof. The walls began to bow outwards, causing rivets to fall loose and cracks to appear between the metal panels. The whole structure groaned like a sinking battleship.

Gen pedalled backwards, eyes darting all around, her spare spear winking out of existence. 'What's happening? What are you doing?'

I smiled with bloody teeth and showed her the brand on my palm, which shone bright as a cluster of stars. 'I'm ending this.'

Blinding blue fire erupted from my palm, making Gen recoil even further. I didn't know what I was doing exactly—much less how I was doing it—all I knew was that it felt right. Felt good. I reached for the javelin piercing my shoulder, wrapped my hand around its shaft, and felt fury's dial turn up to eleven.

The blue fire enveloped the yellow flames of Gen's spear, then consumed it, swallowing it whole, drinking it down until there was nothing left.

Before Gen could make sense of what I'd done, I cannonballed at her, dived for her waist and took her down. She sat up, trying to lever herself off the ground, but I bounced her skull off the floor with a head butt. I straddled her torso, pinning her arms to her side, then pounded her in the face with a hammerblow fist. More angel blood slicked her chin, but I felt no mercy.

I punched her again.

And again.

I punched her until I felt parts of her skull sliding around under her skin.

I raised a shaking fist over my head, ready to punch a hole through her head and into the floorboards beneath—

'Abbey!' cried a voice over my shoulder.

I turned to see Viz framing the doorway, propped on his ivory-handled walking stick, a look of pure horror on his face. 'What are you doing?' His eyes flicked to Gen, then to Neil.

Inexplicably, I felt guilty. Like I'd been caught doing something awful rather than avenging my boyfriend's murder and giving his killer the justice she so rightly deserved.

One of his killers.

I clambered to my feet and recalled the dagger. In a flash, it dislodged from the floor and delivered itself to my hand.

'You were supposed to be the Nightstalker,' the old man quavered. 'How could I have been so wrong?'

I flicked the dagger, turning it into a sword, and went to finish the job I'd started.

Viz threw out his hands and sunlight flooded into the chamber, drawn by his power, streaming in through the extra rips I'd torn in the tower's wall. The rays came together as one, coalescing into a single, solid column of light that came at me like a battering ram.

Crunch.

The ram punched me through the wall of the tower and left me in the dirt a floor below. I felt like I'd been run into by a lorry. My ribs were in pieces. I felt something warm running down my front and realised it was my own blood. My head rolled to one side and I saw a shard of glass embedded in the earth beside me; the mirror from my sideboard, the one that had sat by my wash bowl. I saw my reflection in the glass, my face freckled with blue blood. Angel blood. No, not an angel. The Patron Saint of Bullshit.

Groggily propping myself up on my elbows, I looked back to the tower to see Viz watching me through the hole in its punctured wall. He drew a slim blade from his walking cane and leapt twenty feet to the ground, landing like a cat.

'Leave this place and do not come back,' he boomed.

I was in no state to fight. I'd have to give the brand time to heal my injuries if I was going to stand any chance of defeating him, so I forced myself up on trembling legs, turned the sword back into a dagger, and sheathed its blade.

'This isn't over! This is really fucking far from being over,' I said as I hobbled away, picking my way through the wreckage and stomping on the embers of a partnership burned.

25

In an upside-down world where angels are evil, the creature of the night is your friend.

The afternoon had already bled into evening by the time I arrived at the address on the card. The card Lauden had given me back at The Beehive. He was right. I'd been playing for the wrong side from the very start. The fact that the angels were on the side of God didn't make them righteous. God caused floods, slaughtered children, burned down cities. God was no friend of mine. Since when had I been devout anyway? Since when had I had faith in The Lord Almighty? My arse hadn't warmed a church pew since Sunday school.

The address Lauden had given me was a Hyde Park mansion with an immaculately landscaped front garden the size of a football pitch. It looked like a bucolic country estate that had been picked up by a UFO's tractor beam and inexplicably set down in the inner city. A set of wrought iron gates protected the mansion's entrance, eight feet tall and made of twisted black rods. The gates opened electronically from inside the big house, but I was in no mood to announce myself.

I grabbed an iron bar in each hand and wrenched them apart with ease. I had my strength back. My ribs were good, and except for a pain in one knee that had left me with a slight limp, my wounds were pretty much mended. It wouldn't be long before I returned to the gas tower.

I stepped between the warped gate and crunched down the long gravel path to the mansion's front door. Immediately, two lunks appeared from a guard house that was so comically small they looked like clowns evacuating a prop car. The guards were thirteen-feet tall stacked end-to-end, with necks so thick you could chop meat on them. They drew batons from side holsters as they beelined for me, looking like two hams with eyes.

'That won't be necessary,' said a voice from the mansion's stately porch. It was Lauden, lit by an antique gas lamp. He shooed the guards away, and I joined him on the front steps. 'It's good to see you,' he said.

'You were right,' I told him. 'About the angels.'

His expression turned suddenly grave. 'Come in,' he said, leading me into his home.

The mansion was the size of the Vatican and just as opulent; all rich, polished woods, ornate ceiling roses, and hand-woven rugs. It absolutely *oozed* class. This was the residence of a Crown Prince. The kind of place that would take a small army of servants to keep clean, despite most of its rooms never being used.

'Don't let the henchmen fool you,' said Lauden, guiding me to the drawing room, 'I'm not a Bond villain.'

He turned to me, smiling, and saw that I was in no mood for jokes. 'Sorry. Please, take a seat. Can I get you a drink?'

I shook my head. Regardless, Lauden nodded to a butler hovering next to a grand piano, and moments later, a tray of tea was set down next to me. I sat down in a leather armchair facing Lauden.

He waited until we were alone. 'What did they do?' he asked.

I could hardly bear to say it but somehow I formed the words. 'They killed Neil.'

'But… I thought you were trying to cure him? I thought *they* were?'

'So did I. But they never wanted to, not really.' Tears stung my eyes.

'I'm so sorry, Abbey. I am so, so sorry.'

He leaned forward in his chair and took my hands in his. Without hesitation, I pulled him towards me and wrapped my arms around his neck, burrowing into his body. Tears sprang forth like water from a dam, spilling down my face, soaking the collar of his cardigan. Sensing my need to be held, he enveloped me, hugging me tight, one hand on my upper back, the other around my waist. This wasn't the hug of someone performing a perfunctory gesture. This wasn't the rigid, robotic clinch of a casual acquaintance fulfilling some mandated social etiquette. Lauden's touch made the room warmer somehow. Made my future seem a little less bleak. This was no vampire. No cold-blooded monster. This was a friend. This was everything the angels weren't, and if I'd only listened to him when I had the chance, Neil might still be alive.

'I have to go back,' I said.

'What for?'

'To get Neil. They still have his—'

Lauden wouldn't let me say it. 'Will they give him back so easily?' He could see the state of me. See that I'd had to fight my way out of there.

'I don't care, I'm getting him back.'

I still couldn't believe Neil was really gone. After everything we'd been through together, after all the ups and downs of our relationship, this is how it had ended. I knew we wouldn't last forever—the deteriorating medical condition he suffered made sure of that—but to have him taken away from me so young… it made me angry beyond words.

Lauden backed away as the brand glowed, leaking blue light between my fingers. 'What are you doing?'

'They want an attack dog? They're going to get an attack dog.'

I was going to make them pay for what they did, worse than I had any vampire.

'You shouldn't do anything rash,' said Lauden. 'Angels aren't to be trifled with. Celestials are very powerful. They could kill you.'

'Tell that to Gendith, I just kicked the toffee out of her. Next time I see her I'm sending that bitch to heaven where she belongs.'

Is that what happened to dead angels? It seemed like cheating to me; to be banished from a place, only to be rewarded with free re-entry upon dying. Maybe they just ceased to be when they died, like I assumed I would until I found out God existed and paradise was a real place.

'You're grieving,' said Lauden. 'Stay here and spend the night in my spare room. I won't lie to you and tell you that everything will be better in the morning, but you'll be able to think more clearly then. What do you say?'

I wanted to argue, but I had nothing left in me to argue with. I was dead on my feet and emotionally wrung out. Paper thin. I sighed and nodded.

'I'll show you the way,' said Lauden, as he led me out of the drawing room and up an impressive wooden staircase, the kind that forked off in two directions at the top.

He guided me into a spare room that was bigger than the footprint of my entire flat. All I saw as I stumbled into the dimly-lit chamber was a bed like a drift of snow; feathery, white, and irresistibly soft.

'Lauden?' I said, and he paused, turning back to me in the doorway.

'Yes?'

'Thanks. Thank you.'

He smiled and nodded. 'See, not so bad for a scary monster, eh? Get some rest.'

I tipped my weary head towards the bed's pillows and was out before my head made contact.

When I woke up I didn't know where I was. Not right away. All I knew was that I wasn't at the gas tower anymore, not by a long shot. The place I was in now screamed luxury, or at least whispered it softly across a cool, crisp pillow. The silken bed sheet I was lying beneath clung to me, smooth and light as a billowing cloud. Where was I? Where was this room with its polished oak furniture and its curtains like a wedding dress; expensive ivory cloth with lace at its edges. Was this paradise? Had I died and gone to heaven?

Heaven… angels… betrayal... Neil.

The events of yesterday lined up in my head like some twisted word association game, and all at once I knew where I was and how I'd come to be there. I sat up and propped my back against the bed's hand-carved headboard. Scanning the room, I saw my phone on a bedside table. How did it get there? I checked my surroundings some more, saw my coat hung over the back of a chair, my dagger dangling from its harness, my shoes tucked underneath, and realised that someone had undressed me and put me to bed. Not in an ungentlemanly way —I wasn't showing any major skin—just enough to make me comfortable.

I reached for my phone to check the time. Turning it on brought up an image of Neil on my home screen. In the photo he was sat in a wheelchair, wearing a grey suit and a bald cap. It was the summer we'd gone to San Diego together, when his book had won us tickets to Comic Con. He was dressed as Professor X, a costume he'd chosen because it allowed him to get about without using too much lung-power, and also because the chair provided a handy hiding place for his oxygen tank. That was Neil, goofy, but practical. I enlarged the image to get a better look at him, and saw his smile. *I have my whole life ahead of me*, that smile said.

There was a knock on the door.

'Who is it?' I asked. I was already on my feet and pulling on my shoes.

Lauden stepped in just as I was strapping into my harness. He looked bright-eyed and bushy-tailed, which surprised me given that he wasn't meant to be a daytime creature. 'What are you doing?' he asked.

I punched my dagger into its holster and fastened the clasp. 'What am I doing?' I said. 'Painting this thing blue with angel blood, that's what I'm doing.'

'I think that's a bad idea.'

'Don't tell me what to do. Nobody does that, not anymore.'

I pulled on my jacket and started for the bedroom door, but Lauden stopped me.

'Okay, if you can't be talked out of it, at least let me come with you,' he said.

'To do what?'

'Someone should be watching your back. And if an angel won't do it, maybe a vampire can.'

'Do what you like,' I replied. 'Just don't get in my way.'

I watched the gas tower from across the canal, flat on my stomach, spying through a pair of long-range binoculars. The binoculars were Lauden's, as was the insistence that we keep our distance. We were lying together on the roof of a bird-shit-covered, soon-to-be-demolished council block, the best vantage point we could find to snoop on the industrial park without being seen.

'Looks like you had quite the fight,' he said, noting the gaping hole in the tower's side.

'Next time I won't piss around,' I said, eyes on the prize.

'I understand you want revenge—of course you do—but you won't beat them, not on home ground, and least of all at this time of day when they can turn every ray of sunshine into a weapon.'

I handed him back his binoculars. 'For a bloke who dresses like a J Crew model, you seem to know an awful lot about war.'

'How else do you think I survived this long when my kind are under constant attack? You've got to be on your toes, every day, every minute. The moment your guard drops, a witches' familiar shoves a stake through your heart.'

'Or a Nightstalker.'

Lauden smiled, just a little. 'Right.' He put the field glasses to his eyes and peered through the lenses. I watched him as he surveilled the tower with hawk-like intensity.

He jerked his head to the right suddenly. 'There,' he said. 'Movement.'

'Is it them?'

I didn't bother waiting for an answer – instead, I snatched the binoculars from him and pressed them to my face. Two figures had emerged from behind one of the park's dilapidated buildings and were heading in the direction of the gas tower. It was Viz and

Gen. They were dragging along an old hand truck, the kind warehouse workers used to move stock pallets around. The truck rattled as it bounced over cracked tarmac, empty.

'I don't get it. What were they unloading?'

I tried to get a read of the angels' expressions but they were too far away to make sense of their features. I continued to watch as they reached the tower and dumped the hand truck, parking it next to an old Workmate bench. Propped up against the side of the bench were planks of wood, cut to various lengths. On top of it I saw a hammer, a box of nails and a cutting saw. Someone had been doing some carpentry, but what were they building?

Then it dawned on me. A coffin. They'd built a coffin.

'Neil's dead because of them, and now they've buried the evidence.'

They'd disposed of my boyfriend's body without ceremony, and all while I was half a mile away, an uninvited guest, forced to watch through a set of binoculars.

I tossed the glasses from the roof and heard them smash on the ground below. I turned to Lauden, and through my tears, I saw something unexpected. I saw that I wasn't the only one crying. Lauden was crying too. 'What's wrong with you?' I asked, digging my fists into my hips.

'We shared a bond. Neil had Clan blood in him when he was taken from us. That made him family.' There was real pain in his voice. 'Should I not cry when family dies?'

We? Us? Family?

As someone who'd never really had anyone looking out for them, it was hard to comprehend the basic concept of family, let alone the idea of caring for someone you didn't even know. In any other circumstances I'd have found Lauden's display of grief gross—the crocodile tears of someone on Facebook mourning a celebrity they only knew from the telly—but I actually found it comforting. In all the time I'd spent with the angels I was never once made to feel like kin. We weren't bonded by blood, we were soldiers, thrown together by chance and bound by lies. The angels never cared about me, not like Lauden did. Lauden who cared so deeply about family that he could grieve for someone he'd never even met.

'Please don't attack them,' Lauden insisted. 'Not now, not like this. It's too dangerous. The angels have been waging war for centuries, they're God's own holy avengers.'

'No they're not. God cast them out, remember? Do you understand what that means? A guy who kills first born children just to make a point decided that those two were bad news. You see why I can't let them live?'

'They'll kill you, Abbey. With or without that brand, they'll burn you alive.'

'I can take them.'

'Abbey, if you go down there, there's nothing I can do to help you. The tower is built on hallowed ground. Once you cross that line, you're on your own.'

'So what? You think I should just let them get away with Neil's murder?'

Lauden stepped towards me, gently placing his hands on my arms. 'No, I just… I don't want to see you end up the same way Neil did.'

I gazed up into his eyes, and for a moment, for a single, solitary second, all the anger melted away. All the fury and the urge to kill disappeared as I felt his touch.

But just for that moment.

'Okay,' I said finally, sliding the dagger back into its sheath and pulling away from him. 'Okay, you win.'

Lauden's shoulders sagged and he let out a long sigh. 'Thank you.'

I stayed locked on the gas tower, eyes boring into it like a pair of deep sea drills. Lauden might have thought he'd averted a crisis, but all he'd really done was delay the inevitable. I was going back to that tower after sunset, when there was no light left for them to turn into weapons, and I was killing everyone inside.

26

Lauden was busy fetching me a glass of wine when I cut and run.

An hour later I'd navigated the smelly game of Twister that is the London Underground at pub chucking-out time, and found my way back to Bethnal Green. To the other side of the canal. To the gas tower.

I was considering a plan of attack when it occurred to me that I should do a proper recce of the tower before I went charging in there, sword swinging. Using my Nightstalker x-rays I concentrated on the structure until its walls melted away and revealed the building's insides.

Its empty insides.

As far as I could tell, the base had been vacated. The angels had done a runner, and who did that but the guilty?

Where had they gone to? Were they laying low, keeping their heads down, knowing I was coming for them? Or had they already moved on? Were they pushing ahead with their mission, slaying vampires, maybe even trying to draft a new Nightstalker, some other chump to rope into their twisted little scheme?

Or maybe I was wrong. Maybe my powers were playing up and the angels were hunkered up in the tower after all. I had to know. No way I was missing a chance to make them pay for their sins.

Treading softly, I approached the gas tower and took a peek through the peeled-back panel that acted as its entrance. From the looks of things, the place was empty, but not evacuated, as I'd first assumed. The most telling sign that the angels had yet to clear out was Vizael's book collection, which sat on bowed shelves, untouched. The old man wouldn't have left that behind; those dusty tomes were far too valuable to him. So, the angels were undeterred. Despite my promise to end them, they hadn't budged an inch. This did not make me a sunny bunny.

I exited the tower and decided to go looking for Neil's burial place, but I didn't know where to start. The hand truck the angels had used to move his homemade coffin hadn't left any visible tracks, and there was too much ground to cover, thousands of square feet dotted with dark, vacant buildings. I spent a while going over the area but didn't find anything. No freshly dug-up ground, no cross to mark his grave, no nothing. That's assuming there was even a grave and they hadn't just dumped his body and set it on fire.

I turned back to the tower and felt my fist close tighter than an eagle's talon. *Make a fire of your own*, my mind screamed. *Burn it. Burn it all.* I felt the brand glow hot in my hand, spurring me on, demanding justice. The angels weren't God's avengers, I was. I was the Nightstalker: His holy sword, the scourge of the wicked.

I marched across the lot and back into the gas tower, stomping the ground, fist glowing blue. I knew what I had to do. I was going to use the power God gave me, use it to punish the ones who betrayed Him, use it to raze their operation to the ground.

I reached the centre of the tower and planted my feet. Fury boiled inside of me, hotter than any I'd ever known. I thought back to my fight with Gen, back to when I'd snuffed out her spear with blue fire, and tapped into that same anger. Immediately, my body began to tremble, vibrating at first, then shaking violently like I was riding an old roller coaster, a real bone-shaker. As the anger inside me rose, a spark ignited in my hand, and the brand spewed fire. I had become pure wrath. I pointed my palm ahead of me, aiming it at Viz's library, blasting it with a jet of scorching blue flames, painting it with perfect hatred.

At first the fire lapped at the bottom of the bookshelves like a thirsty kitten with a saucer of milk, then the flames caught with a great *whoof* and burned bright. The blaze quickly became an inferno, igniting the ancient texts, blistering furniture, racing up the walls to the rafters above. The heat coming off the fire should have melted my skin like candle wax, but I remained impervious to its warmth. Instead of running for cover I stood there watching as the tower burned down around me, the flames I'd projected gutting its insides, reducing it to a charred skeleton.

I stepped from the burning remains of the tower like a phoenix, clothes blackened but body intact. The fire continued to blaze hot and blue, like a bonfire doused in some alien petrol. A column of smoke rose from the pyre, yanked sideways by the wind, carrying dirty grey ash across the canal and off into the city beyond.

I'd lit a beacon. This was my message to the angels: I was coming for them, and there was nowhere left for them to hide. Not any more. Wherever they ran, I'd find them, and I'd see to it that they burned in the fires of Hell.

I heard the wail of sirens and took off before the fire brigade showed up.

'I suppose I don't need to ask where you've been?' said Lauden as I crunched up his pea gravel path and barged past his two henchmen.

'You and me need to talk,' I replied. 'Right now.'

He nodded and dismissed the heavies, who sloped off to their ludicrously small guard house. I stomped up the steps of the mansion's porch and met Lauden in the threshold.

'What is it?' he asked, his face lined with concern.

'I saw those things in The Crypt,' I told him. 'The giant monster babies dressed like Nazis.'

I examined his face for any trace of guilt, but all I saw was confusion. 'I'm sorry,' he replied, thrown for a loop, 'but I have no idea what you're talking about. Monster babies?'

'Don't lie to me, Lauden. You keep saying the Clan aren't the bad guys, but how the hell am I supposed to square that with all the crazy shit I saw in that bunker? Genetically engineered monsters? That's pure Bond villain stuff.'

'Listen, I don't know what this Crypt place is, but it sounds like Wild Blood business to me.'

'Oh, isn't that convenient? Every time a vamp comes at me with his fangs out, he's a "Wild Blood".' I'd been pushing all of this stuff to the back of my mind since our first conversation, but I couldn't kid myself any longer. Just because Lauden looked respectable, didn't mean he wasn't a monster. If the angels had taught me anything, it was that. 'I met Judas you know,' I said. 'Saw him with my own two eyes. I don't care how much non-threatening knitwear you drape yourself with, if that's the man you serve, if that's who you call family, then you're no fucking hero.'

'Judas isn't who you think he is.'

'Get real, will you? A withered old mummy with tubes full of blood sticking out of him? He's a wrong 'un and you know it.'

'So you're going to judge an old man based on his looks? Bit ageist.'

I couldn't help but laugh at that. 'Look, there's no way Judas isn't a villain. I mean, come on, the clue's in the name.' Maybe Lauden wasn't a bad guy. Maybe he was just brainwashed; a good man with some wonky ideas. Whatever he was, he was co-signing with the Devil, and he needed to know that.

'Judas isn't the man the bible makes him out to be. Consider his so-called betrayal of Christ—'

'Ugh, what is this, Sunday school? Because the only reason I ever went there was so my parents could get some free babysitting.'

'Please, forget what you think you know about those old stories and really consider what I'm about to say.'

I nodded. 'Fine, go on then.'

Lauden spoke slow and steady. 'Jesus was destined to be crucified. He'd already turned himself into the Romans before Judas got involved, so his death was never in question. The only question was, how would he be judged by the Almighty? Judas knew the answer to that. Only he saw what Jesus was doing: he was committing suicide. Judas realised that by doing that, the son of God was denying himself a place at his Father's side. So he stepped in. He turned on Jesus so he could die for his friend's sins. For Mankind's sins. He bore the hatred of humanity so humanity could be saved.'

I scratched my chin. 'That's some tricky thinking. I mean, whichever way you slice it, the man's still a betrayer.'

'Not a betrayer, a martyr.'

Bullshit. I told him about my encounter with Judas: how I'd found my way into his inner sanctum, how I'd tried to kill him before he invaded my head and set his dogs on me. 'Go on then,' I dared him. 'Talk your way out of that one.'

Lauden cocked his head to the side. 'Let me get this straight… you invaded an old man's home and waved a knife in his face, and you wonder why he didn't invite you in for tea and biscuits?'

More tricky thinking. 'Look, you can twist my words as much as you like, but the bloke basically said he was going to start a vampire apocalypse.'

'Not an apocalypse, a utopia. An end to hunger and disease. Imagine it: people with the wisdom of centuries passing on the gift of eternal life. No more suffering. A world united. We don't want to bring death, Abbey. We don't want to hurt anyone. We want everyone to live. To *really* live.'

I searched his eyes for any trace of deceit but found none. If he was lying I'd hate to play him at poker. Still…

'Your master said he was going to drain my boyfriend's blood out of a big hose. Maybe that flies where you come from, but as far as I'm concerned, that is not cool.'

I felt a pang of heartache. Neil had survived all that just to be murdered in his sleep by a couple of angels. There's irony, then there's *irony*.

Lauden saw the sadness etched into my face. 'Look, I don't know what Judas said to you, but wouldn't you say just about anything to intimidate someone who was threatening to kill you?' He placed a palm on my cheek. 'The old man doesn't know you, that's all. Not like I do. To me, you're family.'

I pushed his hand away. 'I never got on with the family I was born with, so why would I want another one?'

'Look, I've been as open as I know how to be, Abbey, what else do you want from me?'

'Nothing, I don't want anything.'

With a gentle finger he reoriented my face, holding the gaze I didn't want to give. 'Then why can I hear your heart pumping inside of your chest like a snare drum?'

He could sense the blood pulsing through my body, the blood of the Nightstalker, which I knew from experience was nigh on irresistible to his kind. And yet he'd never once tried to take it from me. I'd given him every opportunity to drain me to a husk, but he'd always kept himself in check. That had to mean something.

'I torched the tower,' I blurted. 'The angels, I burned their base to the ground.'

Lauden's eyes widened. 'You did?'

'Yeah. And it felt good. But I'm not done. I'm not even nearly done.'

'What do you need?'

'I need you to help me finish the job. Will you do that? Will you help me?'

Lauden nodded slowly. 'Of course, Abbey. I'd do anything for you.'

Something powerful stirred inside of me as I stood staring up at him; an electricity, a hot spike of delirium.

But it wasn't the brand.

Not this time.

I grabbed Lauden by the lapels of his cardigan and thrust him up against the wall of the hallway, knocking an oil painting off its hook. I pressed myself close to him, close enough that I could feel his body through my clothes. Without asking for permission, I seized him by the back of the neck, pressed my lips to his, and poured my tongue into his mouth. He responded instantly, kissing me back with raw intensity, circling his hands around my hips and pulling me tight against his torso.

I spun him around and dragged him down to the ground, the hallway rug bunching up beneath us as we squirmed around on the waxed wooden floor, our bodies a mess of grasping limbs. Lauden flipped me on to my back and I kicked out with my heel to slam the front door shut. As I unbuttoned my top he pulled up my skirt and I felt his fingers migrate lower, exploring the skin beneath. There was something about Lauden's touch that lit me up from the inside, making my flesh tingle in a frenzy of static. He was so confident. So capable. Having him on top of me was nothing like having Neil there, all raspy and struggling to catch his breath. Lauden was strong and warm and alive, healthy and as human as I was, nothing like the living corpses the angels had sold me. The ones I'd been told were my enemy.

'Is something wrong?' Lauden asked, sensing that I'd become caught up in my own thoughts. 'Do you want me to stop?'

There was an intensity to his gaze that poured kerosene on my flame.

'God, no,' I said, as I arched my back and reached for his zipper.

27

That night I slept well, at least for a little while.

I woke up in the mansion's master suite, draped across the mattress of Lauden's four poster bed. Turning over, I gazed up at the canopy, all fine silk drapery and breezy white swags, and wondered what it must be like to be him. To be rich and timeless and powerful. When I thought of my sorry lot in life—my broken family, my piss-reeking tower block, the job I didn't have—well, it didn't compare too favourably. Who cared if Lauden's wealth wasn't totally legit? What did it really matter where it came from? So what if he rigged the stock market or failed to pay some taxes, everyone was scamming the system somehow. Why shouldn't I be part of it? I'd played it straight my whole life and look where it had gotten me.

I rolled over and turned to face Lauden's pillow, only to find his side of the bed empty. I ran my hand over the dent in the mattress. Without him there the room suddenly seemed chilly and foreboding. I checked my phone. It was four in the morning. I sat up and wrapped the kingsize bed sheet tight around my shoulders, wondering where Lauden had wandered off to. After a moment of internal debate I decided I needed to know, so I turned the bed sheet into a toga and headed for the door.

As I padded barefoot down the runner of the mansion's impressive wooden staircase I saw a crack of light coming from under a door on the ground floor. Someone was awake still. The butler maybe? Or is this where Lauden had got to? I knocked lightly on the door and pushed it open to find myself in a kitchen. The appliances were top-of-the-line stainless steel, the counters, real marble. Sat at a rustic wooden breakfast bar was Lauden, dressed in a nightgown and reading a newspaper.

'What are you doing up in the middle of the night?' I asked, then, 'oh right, yeah, you're a vampire.'

Lauden folded his newspaper as I sat down beside him. 'And what are you doing awake at this hour?' He slapped his forehead playfully. 'Oh yes, of course, you're the Nightstalker.'

How had we arrived here? A vampire and the Nightstalker, huddled around a kitchen island, making cute jokes at four in the morning?

I stretched and realised that the crick in my neck I'd been carrying around since my fight with Gendith was gone. 'That's quite the bed you have there,' I told Lauden. 'It's like something Mister Gray might own.'

'What were you expecting? Did you think I slept hanging upside-down?' he said, smiling.

I laughed at the image he'd conjured, and as I did, I felt a pang of shame. There I was, yukking it up with another man while Neil's body had barely turned cold. I realised then that I hadn't really grieved for him yet. Not in any real way. I'd raged, I'd taken out my anger on Gen, I'd thrown myself into the arms of another, but I'd yet to mourn his passing. It would be a while before I felt that true sense of loss, and when it came—when the wave finally hit me—I knew it would be devastating. Until that happened, I'd do what I always did in this kind of situation – stuff my guilt-hole with as much food as I could lay my hands on.

'I'm starving,' I said, realising that I hadn't eaten for the better part of two days.

'Not a problem,' Lauden replied, putting a hand on my shoulder. 'Let's retire to the dining room, shall we? I'll have the help rustle you up some breakfast...'

He began to steer me to the door.

'Don't go waking Jeeves on my account,' I said. I noticed a

stout wooden door in the corner of the room. 'Got anything in that larder? Some cheap cheese will do; Dairylea Slices, or one of those little string bags of Mini Baby Bells...'

I went to the door, and as I did, I saw Lauden flinch.

'What's the matter?' I asked. 'Something in there you don't want me to see?' I was joking, or at least I was until I noticed the giant padlock on the door. I took it in my hand and felt its weight. What the hell was he keeping in there that called for that kind of security? I looked back to Lauden. Had I read him all wrong? Was he a monster after all? Had I found his secret stash; a locker full of corpses hanging by their ankles, suspended from the ceiling by meat hooks? Was I the Devil's fucking concubine?

'What's in there?' I asked.

'Are you ever going to trust me?'

I tore the padlock off with one sharp tug, which pretty much answered that question.

It wasn't a larder. Beyond the door I found a staircase leading down to a basement.

Lauden sketched out a smile. 'I promise you, that's not where I keep the cheese.'

I narrowed my eyes at him. 'What are you keeping down there?'

'Listen, I don't know what you're looking for, but you won't find it in my cellar.'

'We'll see about that.'

I marched down the creaking steps, one hand on the wall to steady myself. The air was cool and musty and dark. At the bottom of the steps my arm brushed against something: a cord dangling from the ceiling. I gave it a yank and a row of dim bulbs flickered to life.

The cellar had been dug deep and offered plenty of headroom, its timber beams looming a good four feet above me despite the bed hair I was wearing. The walls were rough-cut stone, and the floor dusted with fine gravel. It reminded me of a dungeon, the kind goblins lurked in, hoarding chests of gold coins, protecting their riches from the clutches of foolhardy adventurers. All that was missing from the tableau were flaming torches fixed to the flagstone walls.

I took a look over my shoulder and saw Lauden's silhouette in the doorway up above. 'Go ahead if you must,' he said, his voice betraying a burr of disappointment.

Was I rooting around in his cellar for nothing, or was he playing with me, acting hurt in a bid to convince me that I was wasting my time? That the knot in my stomach was of my own making?

I turned back and continued into the cellar, moving along a lengthy corridor, racks of wine bottles either side of me, their necks pointing out like the gun barrels of two firing squads looking to catch me in a crossfire. The corridor continued until it opened out into a spacious chamber. Inside the chamber, from a distance, I saw wood, lots of it, and for a moment I convinced myself that the room was lined with coffins. Caskets containing sleeping vampires, or worse, chilled human bodies, ready for consumption.

But no.

The chamber was full of barrels. Wooden casks, the kind used to store alcohol.

I felt a hand on my shoulder and almost bounced off the ceiling, despite the cellar's generous headroom.

'You see?' said Lauden. 'This is where I keep the wine, not the cheese.'

I felt my shoulders sag as relief washed over me. Wine. Just wine. 'I'm so sorry, Lauden.'

'It's fine. Really.'

'It's just... I thought you were a beer man.'

The corners of his mouth crept into a grin. 'I have a broad palate.'

I shivered as the adrenaline wore off and the chill of the cellar struck me. 'I need to get some sleep. I swear I'm going head mental.'

'Totally understandable,' he replied. 'You've been through a lot.' His eyes twinkled. 'Now let's get you out of the cold and back into bed. Vampire's orders.'

I laughed. 'Okay, but if it's all right with you, I'm going to have a splash of wine to help me nod off.' I found a dusty wine glass, gave it a wipe with my bed sheet toga, and went to turn a casket's tap.

Lauden grabbed me by the wrist. 'Forgive me, but the contents of that cask are extremely valuable. So long as all you're looking for is a tranquilliser, let me steer you towards a more fitting bouquet…'

I felt that knot in my stomach again. The one telling me I'd read my host all wrong. 'What's in that wine barrel, Lauden?'

'What do you think?' he replied, daring me to state the obvious.

I felt my heartbeat begin to slow. What was I thinking? What else would be in a wine barrel but fancy plonk? I was being overly cautious. Scratch that; I was being an idiot. I'd jumped into bed with a guy too soon and the guilt of it was making me paranoid. Painting pictures that weren't really there. There was nothing wrong with Lauden. The only monster in that room was my own sense of remorse. This was my issue, not his, and I wasn't about to go my whole life being suspicious of a man who'd laid down his life for me.

Then again, fuck it.

I tore the lid off the barrel and peered inside to find—

Wine. Ruby red wine.

Or at least I thought so.

Something floated to the surface of the liquid, something pale that appeared for a moment then disappeared out of view before bobbing up again. I saw a mouth, wide open as if gasping for air, only this was a mouth that had long since drawn its final breath. Buoyed on the wine, staring up at me with pruned, lifeless eyes, was a human head.

It wasn't wine, it was blood. Barrels and barrels of human blood.

28

Lauden let out a long sigh. 'After all the hours I put it, after all that work, you had to be nosey, didn't you?'

I backed away from him, clutching on to the bed sheet, the only thing covering my naked body. 'What is this…?'

He ignored me. 'You didn't question the angels when they groomed you—when they turned you into a killing machine against your will—oh no, you fell in line just like that. But I put *one* padlock on a door and suddenly you're Miss bloody Marple.'

I was reeling. 'But the flash drive... they betrayed me.... they killed Neil…'

'Did you really think we'd let you into The Crypt unless we wanted you there? Did you think we'd make it that easy? You tripped a silent alarm the moment you set foot in the place. It was child's play for us to hack your download and make it so your drive returned a dummy file.'

'So… Gen did what she was supposed to do?'

'Of course, she's an angel. But it didn't matter what she did, because her work was compromised before the two of you had even left the bunker. You never had the cure. You never had anything.'

His words washed over me like a bucket of cold sick. What had I done? I'd beat the hell out of Gendith, almost killed her, burned down the gas tower and torched the angels' home. All because of Lauden. I understood now. Understood it all. He couldn't set foot on the holy ground the base was built on, so he'd tricked me into razing the tower instead. He'd been hoodwinking me right from the start. Using reverse psychology to bend me to his will. Winding around me like a snake.

Neil wasn't the only one who'd been turned, I had too. Turned this way and that. Turned like a tornado.

I'd been so stupid. I'd let him poison my mind, let him tempt me to his side of the street and set me against my only real friends. I'd let anger get the better of me, let it cloud my judgment. The angels didn't kill Neil, it was my own stupidity that put him in the ground. The brand made me immune to mesmerism, but a vampire had fooled me anyway. That snide fuck.

I unfurled my fist, and within moments, the dagger had sped from the master suite, flown down two flights of stairs, and snapped back into my hand.

'What are you doing?' asked Lauden, retreating a step.

'Something you should have done, dickhead: killed the enemy when you had the chance.'

'You're not my enemy, Abbey.'

'Oh no?' I took a step toward him, dagger gripped tight, teeth clenched.

Lauden smiled. 'We're way past fighting, Abbey, don't you see? We've come too far for that. Now is the time for us to work together.'

I managed a laugh. 'You think because you tricked me into sleeping with you there's a "we" here? And I thought I was the mug.'

'Don't dismiss the idea out of hand.' He used his palm to paint an arc in the sky. 'Imagine it: the Nightstalker and the Judas Clan, allied, committed to the same purpose.'

'Why would I ever let that happen?'

'Because together we'd be unstoppable! Look at the world we're living in and tell me it doesn't need to change. The Clan have tried steering humanity in the right direction, but there's a limit to what we can achieve so long as you're working against us. Stop fighting and work with us! Together we can build a world free from old age, free from pestilence, free from war. A world where people can live life to its fullest; a life of music and poetry and love. I wasn't lying to you about any of that. About what we want. About what *I* want.'

I gave him a look that could have melted steel beams. What was he banging on about? He'd lied to me, manipulated me, turned me against my friends, and now he wanted me to believe he was trying to create a better world: a hippy dippy utopia powered by good vibes and yoga and wheatgrass enemas?

'So, that's the plan, is it?' I scoffed. 'You, me, and the Clan – one big happy family?'

'Exactly!' he replied, failing to detect the sarcasm in my voice, or just plain ignoring it. 'This is your chance to be part of something that really matters, Abbey. To finally belong. To make a positive, lasting difference.'

'And I'm supposed to just forget about all of the people you've murdered, am I? About the giant monster babies? About the head floating in that barrel?' I stabbed a finger at the gruesome artefact.

'The man that belonged to was a priest,' Lauden replied. 'A sexual abuser. The church wouldn't do anything about him, so I did. Okay, did I need to chop him into pieces and put him in a wine barrel? Technically, no, I'll give you that, but I promise you, the man deserved no less.'

'You're a real gent, you know that?'

His brow knitted. 'The point is, we don't kill for sport or satisfaction, we only kill to survive, and when we do, we're choosy about the life we take.'

'This is ridiculous,' I said. 'You're not going to convince me you're a good guy just because you're a faddy eater.'

'Unlike your kind, we don't take the lives of our prey en masse. We don't keep our food locked up in cages so we can murder them on conveyor belts. We hunt as we need to. As we *have* to.'

I tightened my grip on the dagger and continued my advance.

'It's not too late, Abbey,' he said, backing off. 'This doesn't need to end in violence. You don't have to be the unthinking weapon they made you.'

What if he was right? I could stick him with my knife, but then who would I have left? My family were long gone, Neil was dead, the angels were my enemies. Like it or not, Lauden was all I had now. A man who'd saved my life. Who was rich and powerful. Who seemed—in his own nutty way—to actually want to make the world a better place. Yes, he'd killed, but then so had I. Maybe he had the right idea. Maybe we were better off together. God knows I dressed like something from a horror movie, perhaps it was time to finally act the part.

But no, I wasn't one of them. I wasn't some creature of the night. I just dressed a bit moody.

The brand flared blue and hot and I felt a slice of adrenaline. I flipped the dagger into the air and snatched it so the point of the blade was facing down. 'Nice pitch, Lauden, but I'm giving you a hard pass.'

His charming grin hardened into a death's-head rictus that all the cuddly cardigans in the world couldn't disguise. The nice white smile had vanished, revealing the howling maniac inside. 'Typical,' he spat. 'You humans are so squeamish - one little severed head and it's tears before bedtime.'

'Yeah, sorry to disappoint.'

'It's a bit late for that, girl. Do you have any idea how much effort I put into this whole scheme?'

'The scheme to turn my boyfriend into a vampire and have him rip my throat out?'

Lauden smiled, showing off that rictus grin again. 'You've got it all wrong, Abbey. That's not why we turned him. Not at all. We turned him to show you that you could learn to be with one of us. To share a bed with a vampire.'

'If that's true, why did you kill him?' I asked, feeling my eyes turn wet.

'Oh, we didn't kill him, Abbey, but that's a story I don't have time for. Not now. The only thing left to do at this juncture is kill you.' He shook his head, disappointed. 'And all because you had to have some cheap fucking cheese.'

He snarled and his facial features turned sharp and feral. The letter J flared on his forehead and fangs ejected from his gums, long and sharp. How had I mistaken Lauden for anything but a monster? He was a bloodsucking hellspawn with ice water in his veins and screaming bats in his skull, and no amount of charm or sophistication was going to change that.

In a way, it was refreshing to find out that the Judas Clan were evil after all. In this world of political double-dealing and fake news, when you could never be sure who's on your side, when even Nazis dressed in polo shirts, it was heartening to learn that there were some old-fashioned villains out there who just wanted to watch the world burn.

'I don't know how I ever saw humanity in you, Lauden, because you're not human. You're a different species.'

'A superior one,' he hissed. 'I was here first. You're just a trespasser on my world. And now you're going to die.'

'Suits me,' I replied. 'This was getting a bit talky for my liking anyway.'

I went for him in two fluid strides, dagger raised, ready to strike—

But he was faster.

It happened in a flash. No warning. No cue. No dramatic swell of music. One second I was going for him, the next his fist was sinking into my gut, knocking the air out of my lungs. As I unfolded myself I saw his other hand eject a set of claws, then the talons were raking across my face, scoring my cheek with four deep red lines.

He licked his fingertips, tasting my blood. 'Rhesus negative. A rare vintage.'

I swung the dagger at him but he evaded it easily, twisting his body to one side and leaving me swinging at air. The speed that he shifted out of my way made me feel like I was moving in slow motion. Like I was fighting underwater.

He struck my throat with a deft knife-hand strike, crushing my jugular. I gasped and coughed, clawing at my windpipe, suffocated until the brand kicked in and healed the damage. Before it could do that though, Lauden delivered a punch to my face that knocked me flying. A jolt of pain thundered through my skull and I stumbled back, gagging as blood pooled in my mouth.

'Is that all you've got?' he crowed, smirking infuriatingly at me.

I went at him again, all martial, no art, running at him like a train, dagger extended in front of me. Again, he clobbered me, but this time I went down, arms flailing, legs flopping, a squid in a washing machine.

I hit the ground. White hot pain, cold hard stone. My head was thumping a real club banger. My brain was in screensaver mode.

Lauden was ridiculously strong - far more powerful than any vampire I'd encountered so far. I could run at him as many times as I liked but I was never going to beat him. I couldn't afford to keep making the same mistake. To be a fly banging against a window pane until it dropped dead on the sill.

'You know,' I croaked. 'You're pretty spry for a dead guy.'

He grinned, showing his fangs, then landed me with a back-hand that sent me crashing into a wall of wine barrels. The impact cracked open a cask, spilling its contents, soaking me in gallons of blood and offal. I was covered in the stuff, head to toe and hip to hip, one tiara away from looking like Carrie on prom night.

'Well, don't you look tasty?' Lauden trilled.

He beat on me some more, punching me, kicking me, carving me up with his razor-sharp claws. I staggered about under the onslaught, ankle-deep in blood, human organs squashing under my feet like grapes. I was groggy, weaving erratically, punch drunk.

A smirk decorated Lauden's lips. 'So you're the chosen one, are you? Who chose you, Stevie Wonder?'

This guy could seriously choke on a vertical mile of dick. 'I'm… the Nightstalker,' I wheezed. 'And I am going to fuck you up.'

'You're no Nightstalker,' he shot back, staring at the dagger I was only just about managing to keep a hold of. 'All you are is a gullible little girl with a piece of oversized cutlery and bad table manners.'

He kicked the dagger out of my hand and it disappeared to the bottom of the blood pool.

This guy.

Anger bloomed in my belly and heat travelled up my gullet like acid, cloying in my throat. I looked down at my hand and saw the lines on my palm light up, turning into a glowing blue delta. The brand kicked in like pharmaceutical cocaine, energising me, revitalising me, filling me up with rocket fuel.

I roared and lashed out with a super-charged fist. This time I was fast enough. This time Lauden was the one moving in slow motion. My fist collided with his cheekbone, making his head snap back like a streamer caught in a hundred-mile-an-hour wind. While he was reeling from the whiplash, I punched him again, and again, each blow slamming home with the force of a sledgehammer, battering him, pummelling him, beating him to within an inch of his life. I recalled the dagger to my weapon hand and grabbed him by the balls with the other, squeezing his nads until the pips squeaked.

I was about to deliver the death stroke when a shadow fell on me from behind. Lauden's two henchmen were there, toting a hooded prisoner.

'We found this one lurking outside,' said one of them.

He whipped off the hood, but I knew who was under there before his hand even touched the cloth.

They had Gendith.

29

'Drop the knife,' ordered one of the henchman (doesn't really matter which one).

I did as asked, placing it on the lid of one of the few intact wine barrels. I kept hold of Lauden's nuts though.

'Jesus, you look terrible,' I told Gendith, and she really did.

'I just got the shit kicked out of me. What did you expect, Helen of Troy?' She spat some blood on the ground, which hardly messed up the decor.

For the first time since I'd known her, Gen didn't look like she just stepped from the pages of a fashion mag. Not only was she banged up from the fight we'd had, she'd been knocked about by the two lugs either side of her too. Her skin was lumpy and patterned with all the colours of a rainbow. Actually, more like all the colours of a swamp.

'Why are you dressed in a bed sheet?' she asked, not unreasonably.

'Forget about that. What are you doing here?'

'Where else would I be? I'm your guardian angel, remember.'

'Shut up, both of you!' ordered one of the henchmen (again, it doesn't really matter which one).

'Just a minute!' I fired back, tightening my grip on Lauden and making him squirm.

I was bloody and battered, but far from beaten. Trapped in a stand-off, the henchmen could only watch from the sidelines as Gen and I continued our conversation.

Gen explained that while I'd been busy burning down the gas tower, she and Viz had been with an eaves, trying to figure out my location so they could reason with me. That's how she'd managed to track me to Lauden's mansion. She was lying in wait on his grounds, observing, when she heard a commotion in the basement and came to check it out. She didn't make it far before she was set on and captured though. Obviously.

'Even after everything I did, you were still looking out for me?'

'Of course,' she replied. 'We're a team. Whether you like it or not, we're a team.'

The mushy cow. Still, I felt myself weaken as she said it, and as I did, Lauden took the opportunity to free himself of my grip. One second I had him, the next he was six feet away and back on his feet.

'Well, this has all been very touching,' he said, mocking us, his voice a dainty little bell. 'You know, you two would make a charming couple.'

I glared at him. Gen did too.

'Ooh, daggers,' he said, feigning fright. 'Speaking of which…' He twitched his hand at me, gesturing for me to hand over my weapon.

'You've got to be joking,' I said, grabbing the dagger. 'Why the fuck would I go and do that?'

I felt a sharp tug then realised the dagger was no longer in my hand. Lauden had somehow eaten up the distance between us, snatched it from me, and retreated out of range again, all in the blink of an eye.

'Because if you don't, I'll just take it off you anyway,' he smarmed.

I'm telling you, when it came to motherfuckery, that guy took first prize.

I shot out a hand and willed the dagger to return to my fist, but Lauden tightened his grip, refusing to let go. I felt sweat prickle my forehead as we engaged in a heated tug o' war, wrestling over the blade, fighting for dominance. I poured all of my concentration into the task of retrieving what was mine – pictured the brand as an electromagnet, pulling on metal, dragging the dagger back to my hand. Finally, Lauden's grip broke and the dagger fired back into my grasp, making me scream in full-throated triumph.

A fleeting grimace appeared on the vampire's face before he dismissed it with a shrug. 'Dagger or not, this little display is over.' He ordered his henchmen to bring Gen closer; close enough that I could see the panic in her eyes. 'You don't stand a chance. The fight is three against two, and one of you is incapacitated.'

'I can work with those odds.'

He chuckled. 'I don't think you fully understand the situation you're in, Abbey.'

'Oh, I think I do.' My eyes flicked to Gen's. 'Duck!'

I swung the dagger in a wide arc, and as it cleaved the air, its blade transformed into a sword. A heartbeat later, a pair of very surprised-looking heads were splashing down on the cellar's bloodbath floor.

'I make that two-to-one in my favour,' I said. 'How do you like those odds?'

That shut him up, but not for long.

Lauden was quick as a viper's strike. Before I could even twitch, he'd snatched Gen by the wrist, whirled her about like a spinning top, and appeared behind her with a pistol pressed to her temple.

'Enough!' he cried.

I stared at the gun. 'You're telling me you had that thing stuffed down your dressing gown the whole time?'

'I like to be prepared,' he sneered.

Another bloody Girl Scout. Maybe I should have just left him and Gen to it, I thought, I'm sure they'd have got on like a house on fire.

I pressed the tip of the sword to the ground, making it dagger-sized.

'I know what you're thinking,' said Lauden. 'You're thinking you can hit me with that thing before I shoot this gun.'

'Very clever,' I said. 'You don't even need a knife with that super sharp mind of yours.'

I took aim and his lip curled. 'You should know that even if you score a bullseye, the resulting muscle contraction will ensure that I pull this trigger and your girlfriend dies.'

'I'm not her girlfriend,' said Gen, kind of missing the point if you ask me.

'Enough chatter,' said Lauden, 'either you toss that knife to the ground or I give this angel a new set of wings.'

I held the dagger beside my head, muscles tensed, feeling like a Jack-in-the-box, ready to spring.

Gendith's eyes were about as wide as a person could open them.

Lauden's finger stroked the pistol's trigger, daring me to make a move.

The room was so silent that when I blinked I heard the crackle of my own eyelashes scraping against each other.

I wrestled with what to do, wracking my brain for a solution, stumped by the impossible problem I faced—

Then I saw the loophole.

I hurled the dagger.

Not at Lauden.

Not even at the wall behind him, so I could kid him into thinking I'd missed, then get him with the boomerang as I recalled the blade.

No.

I hurled the dagger at the gun in his hand, shattering it to bits.

He stared at the pistol's trigger guard, which hung uselessly from his index finger like an oversized ring.

Checkmate.

'Sorry to shit on your picnic there, old boy,' I said, snatching the dagger from the air as it rubber-banded back to my hand. 'By the way, I totally faked it.'

'No you didn't,' he replied.

'Well, the third time I did.'

Gendith grimaced, then elbowed Lauden in the gut. He shrank from us like a whipped puppy. The tables had turned. He couldn't take us both on and he knew it.

'Don't do this,' he pleaded. 'Please don't do this.'

You'd have needed a mop and bucket to clear up all the flop sweat coming off him.

I stalked towards him, face emotionless, eyes unblinking.

'You're more than this, Abbey. You're more than just a weapon.'

'I am more than a weapon,' I replied, keeping the dagger level, 'but not today.'

I darted out a hand and grabbed him by the collar of his gown before driving his head through the lid of a wine cask.

Crack.

My muscles knotted as I held him down, pressing his face to the bottom of the red stuff. His legs kicked behind him like he was swimming the front crawl, but I refused to let go, performing an unholy baptism, absolving him of his sins. He arched his spine violently, forcing himself upright, and for a moment his head appeared above the surface of the blood, his skin full of splintered wood, needles in his cheeks, needles in his lips and eyes. He gasped, sucking down a breath of air, blubbering, begging for his life.

His life.

Lauden didn't have a life. Yes, his kind needed oxygen, just like we did, but I knew now that the similarity between us ended there. Lauden was a monster, and monsters didn't get to live.

The brand throbbed and I ducked him again, holding him down with the fury of God's own thunder, until finally, mercifully, Lauden's legs stopped kicking. I let go of his collar and he slid to the ground, dropping to his knees in a ghoulish parody of prayer.

I stood there, panting, feeling the effect of the brand wear off, feeling my limbs lose all tension. Gendith draped an arm around my shoulder and we stood there a while, looking down at Lauden's body as if he might pop back up on his heels like a cheap slasher villain. But he didn't. Lauden was dead and he wasn't coming back.

'That's strange,' said Gen, cocking her head. 'His aura, I've seen it before.'

'Where?'

Gen turned to look at me: 'I've seen it on Neil.'

'I don't get it.' And I did not. Like, not even close.

Gen turned me around so we were looking directly into each others' eyes. 'It means this is the vampire who sired Neil, and if you kill the sire, you cure the kin.'

'But... Neil's dead.'

She clenched my arms. 'Not necessarily…'

30

'You're telling me Neil was just sleeping?' I cried as we ploughed through the mansion's front gate in a stolen BMW.

I'd scrubbed the blood from my face and snatched my clothes as we hurried out of there, so I looked vaguely respectable in the passenger seat, or at least not like I'd done a naked slip-n-slide across a cattle house killing floor.

'Not sleeping exactly,' Gen replied, twisting the wheel and blasting the beamer through a set of red lights. 'More like a deep coma. A chrysalis stage before a human goes from being alive to undead.'

'I don't get it. Why did you tell me he was dead then?'

'Because we thought he was dead. Only the most powerful, pre-plague vampires can cause a state of hibernation like that, and as far as we knew, we'd driven those from the city years ago.'

So Lauden was old. Really, really old.

'Okay, Neil didn't die, he just slipped into a coma and now he's waking up? That's good, right?'

'Probably.'

'What do you mean, *probably*? What did you do with him?'

'We buried him.'

'Where?'

The car smashed through a rusty chain link fence and I realised we were back at the industrial park already. Gen hit the brakes and we screeched to a halt in front of a decrepit, half-collapsed warehouse. The front of the building was decorated with a large, weather-beaten sign that read HAPPY HARRY'S TOY FACTORY in once cheerful colours, now stripped away by time.

'Are you serious? You buried my boyfriend in a creepy doll factory?'

'We didn't want him to be disturbed.'

She stepped out of the car and headed into the warehouse with me in tow.

The roof of the building was rotted through and full of holes, as though God had taken exception to the place and hosed it down with machine gun fire. Inside, peering out at us from every angle of the large grey space, were lifeless glass eyes buried in dusty plastic faces. Dolls; hundreds of them. Little girls with long synthetic hair, cracked features and petticoats made of mouldy lace. Little boys with curls and button down shirts, dressed like tiny funeral directors. A fucking horror show. No wonder the place went out of business.

We weaved between water-damaged boxes full of assorted appendages, across scattered and disarticulated limbs, heads and torsos cracking under our feet like eggshells. Finally, we reached Neil's resting place, a giant hole in the factory floor. From the looks of things, a couple of decades of water damage had caused part of the warehouse to subside, cracking the building open, right down to its foundations. At the bottom of the chasm was a patch of exposed earth that had been recently turned over. Also at the bottom of the hole was Vizael, who had a shovel in his hands and was in the process of digging.

'I phoned ahead while you were getting dressed,' Gen explained.

I dropped into the hole beside Viz and wrapped my arms around his back. I was so happy to see the old man that the world turned blurry through my tears. 'I'm sorry, Viz,' I blubbed. 'About the tower. About your books. About everything.'

He smiled back at me. 'It's okay, Abbey, you can make it up to me by getting Neil out of there.'

He didn't need to ask me twice. I grabbed the shovel off him, sunk it into the ground, and wrenched a clod over my shoulder. The tool became a blur as I went at the task like a madwoman, sending great arcs of soil in every direction. Then—

Snap.

The shaft of the shovel broke in two, shearing right at the part that the metal met the wood, rendering it utterly useless.

'No!' I cried, but all was not lost.

Gen leapt into the hole, dropped to her haunches, and started digging at the earth with her bare hands. 'Are you going to help me or what?' she asked.

Snapped out of my momentary stupor, I fell to my knees and joined her, using my hands as shovels, tearing up frenzied fistfuls of earth. Viz did likewise, and the three of us worked together, clawing at the ground until the soil turned to clay, clawing until our muscles stung and our hands bled.

My fingernails scraped against something solid and I swiped away a patch of earth to see wood hiding beneath. 'This is it.' I made a fist, cracked open the lid of the casket, and hauled a muslin-wrapped body from within. I set Neil down and tore the shroud from his face.

The first thing I noticed was that the J had gone from his forehead. The second was that he wasn't breathing. 'Neil? Neil?'

He lay there, inert, eyes fixed and vacant.

Were we too late? We'd raised Neil from the dead, only to let him die again in the most grisly manner imaginable, buried alive. I beat my fists on his chest, not to perform CPR this time, just out of rage. It took both of the angels to tear me away. 'I'm sorry, Neil,' I sniffed, tears streaming down my face. 'It's all my fault.' I tipped over backwards and fell on to my behind, sobbing like a baby.

Then I felt a warmth, landing on the back of my head like a sympathetic hand. Only it wasn't a person. Wasn't a human's comfort. I tilted my head to the sky and saw shafts of light pouring in through the holes in the warehouse roof. The sun had risen on a new day, hot and uncharacteristically bright. I turned to Viz and saw him beaming bright as the sun.

'Look,' he said, pointing to the floor.

A lozenge of orange light had fallen across Neil's face, bringing the colour back to his skin. As the morning light bathed him, a gasp escaped from his lips and I saw his chest begin to rise and fall.

I scrambled over to him in disbelief. 'Neil!' He didn't respond. I put my hands on his chest. 'He's breathing.' I checked for a pulse and found a steady throb. 'Neil?' I turned to Gen. 'Why isn't he answering me?'

She smiled. 'Give him a chance, he just came back from the dead.'

'You don't know. What if he's just in another coma?'

'He's fine, I can tell from his aura. Trust me, all he needs is some rest.'

I leapt to my feet like my legs were spring-loaded. 'It's a fucking miracle!' I screamed, grabbing Viz in a bear hug and lifting him off the floor.

Viz laughed. 'Yes it is,' he said. 'It's a fucking miracle. Now I don't suppose you'd mind letting me go before you shatter the rest of my ribs.'

Sorry,' I replied, setting him down. 'I just got excited.'

He patted me on the back, still smiling, then turned around and began to haul himself out of the hole, heading back to the factory floor.

'Where are you going?' I asked.

'I'm going to go outside and say a prayer to God,' he replied. 'Whether He's listening or not.'

He gave me a final nod then departed.

I grabbed Gen and the two of us clung to each other like a couple of drunks. 'We did it,' I said, planting a big wet smacker on her cheek. That close to her face, I noticed something. 'Are you… are you crying?'

'No,' she insisted. 'I have something in my eye.'

'Both of your eyes?'

She pushed me away playfully and wiped a sleeve across her face. 'Shut up.'

I took her by the hand. 'I'm sorry I stopped trusting you. God, I was such an arsehole.'

'It's okay, I'm an angel, and we're the queens of forgive and forget. But yes, you were an arsehole. You owe us a new base, too.'

'No worries, I'm sure I've got something lying around.'

She squeezed my hand and drew me close. 'It's good to have you back, Abbey.'

I heard a cough. 'Well, I don't mind telling you,' said a familiar voice, 'I feel rubbish.'

It was Neil. He was awake.

'Holy shit, Neil, you're alive!'

'Right,' he replied. 'So why am I wearing a funeral shroud again?'

I didn't bother to explain, I just dropped to my knees and hugged him for all I was worth.

'I can't believe it,' I gushed, peppering kisses all over his face. 'You're actually alive. How do you feel? Are you in any pain?'

'You know what, I actually feel pretty good considering… well, whatever happened to me.'

We'd get to that, but before we did, I was going to let Neil know just how much he meant to me. I dipped my face to his, moving in for a kiss to end all kisses, but just as our lips were about to meet, he recoiled.

'What's wrong?' I asked.

Did he know? Did he know about Lauden and me? Could he sense it? Christ, please no.

But no, that wasn't it.

Neil's hands went to his chest. For a moment I thought he was having a heart attack, then the muslin shroud he was wearing started blooming red spots.

'He's bleeding,' said Gen.

I looked to Neil, who was just as surprised as we were. 'What's happening?'

I tore open the fabric wrap and saw a red slash on his skin. A red slash that was quickly joined by a new one, which appeared magically, as if carved by some invisible claw. Another slash, then another, each of them just a few millimetres deep, but frightening in their purposefulness, terrible in their unstoppable design.

'What the fuck is happening?' Neil reiterated, terrified.

'I don't know,' I screeched back, not knowing what to do, scared out of my wits.

Together, the lines began to form a pattern, joining up like handwriting, and only once they'd stopped did I realise they formed a message.

Neil lay there panting, chin pressed to his chest, trying to read the words carved into his flesh. 'What does it say?' he asked, wounded and scared, but alive.

I read the message.

It said BLOOD FOR BLOOD.

I whirled around to Gen. 'Blood for blood? What does that mean?'

She enunciated her words carefully, dropping each of them like a rock. 'It means you killed someone with a very powerful friend.'

To Be Continued…

BLOODLINE

1

Job one was to figure out who carved the words *Blood for Blood* in my boyfriend's chest. Job two was to chisel my reply into their face.

I kicked the door so hard it turned into kindling. On the other side of the mess I'd made was a swanky boardroom overlooking London Bridge. By my hip was the archangel Gendith, swinging a morning star and belting out an ear-splitting war cry.

We were about ninety floors up the Shard and interrupting an emergency meeting of highly-ranked Clan members. I'm talking about vampires, and not the wounded souls of a paranormal romance; all sparkly skin, brooding loneliness, and private writing. No. The Judas Clan are bloodsucking monsters with a taste for the red stuff that's matched only by their hunger for riches. Hungry, corporate psychopaths who open necks with the same relish they open the great vein of commerce and leech society dry.

Today's meeting wasn't about siphoning our financial system though. The subject of today's little enclave was *How to Kill the Nightstalker,* London's heroic protector, and God's designated vampire-killing machine. That's me, Abbey Beckett, former office clerk, card-carrying goth, and lover of cheap cheese. So you can imagine how surprised the delegates of that conference were when *I* crashed the proceedings, not just because I definitely,

definitely wasn't on the invite list, but because the door my companion and I had just burst out of was meant to lead into a stock cupboard nowhere near big enough for two people.

I'll explain how I pulled off that little trick later. Getting into the hows and whys of it now will only create needless exposition, and we're starting *in media res* with this one. Neil, my boyfriend, taught me that phrase. He's a writer. "Into the middle of things", it means, or "opening in the midst of action". Yup, this is me, giving you exposition on why I won't be opening with exposition. See, this is why I prefer to let my fists do the talking... speaking of which...

An informant of ours, Carlo, tipped us off about this particular vampire hive. That's what we call Clan gatherings, by the way: hives. This one was set in a room with a long oval table surrounded by high-backed chairs, frosted windows to keep out the worst of the sunlight, and a Powerpoint slide projected on a large rectangular screen. It might not strike you as the most obvious forum for a room of bloodsucking monsters, but like I say, that's how the Clan operates. Believe me when I tell you that the evil that goes on in this city happens way more in its boardrooms than it does in its darkened alleyways.

A dozen heads turned our way as Gen and I made our entrance, all of them dressed in anonymous grey suits; the white man's burka. The guy at the head of the table—a guppy-mouthed Gordon Gecko wearing a good pound of styling wax—stood up and gave me a look like he was trying to calculate Pi in his head.

'What the—?'

I lopped off the top of his skull like it was nothing.

While I was busy using his Armani suit to clean the blood off the blade of my sword, I felt a dozen sets of peepers rubbing on me. As I looked up and returned the gaze of the wide-eyed, gore-spackled delegates, it seemed incumbent upon me to say something. But what? At first I was stuck for an opening line, then I spotted a brainstorming diagram projected on to the slideshow behind them and found my inspiration.

'How do you like that for a thought shower?' I asked.

I looked around the table. Not a titter. The vamps stayed in their seats, stock-still and death-gripping the armrests of their swivel chairs as they gawped at their colleague's skullcap, which had come to a rest in the middle of the table and sat there like Ed Gein's ashtray.

I gave the assembly a shrug. 'Tough crowd.'

Gendith made a snippy little cough. 'If you're done polishing your stand-up, can we please get on with purging this hive?'

That's Gen for you; brusque, no-nonsense, and always to the point. Basically, as annoying as she is fierce. She was right though. We were there on my insistence since I'd decided I was tired of reacting to threats and wanted to cause some of my own. *Let's bring the hurt to the vamps,* I'd said, *No more mucking about*. So this was no time for cracking quips, no matter how incredibly clever and devastatingly on point they were.

If you'll allow me to hold the freeze frame for a few seconds longer though...

Why this particular hive, you might be asking. Was the man whose head I'd just ventilated the one who carved up Neil? I doubted it. Too easy. Plus, he didn't really look like the magician type, and it would have taken some real black juju to score a guy's flesh from halfway across town, which is precisely what the mystery man had done to Neil. At first, I'd assumed the J Man himself was responsible—Judas Iscariot, my big bad—but I'd been assured that that couldn't be the case. Despite being the master of the Clan, Judas was in a weakened state still, and wouldn't have the strength to perform that kind of magic, at least not yet. No, whoever it was that cut up my boyfriend was an underling. Someone powerful, but not beyond my reach.

I had an aim. The problem was, I didn't have a target, so all I'd encountered to date were the kind of garden variety vampires arrayed before me in that boardroom: stuffed shirts with Js on their foreheads. Worker bees. Scrubs.

Okay, off with that pause button...

The brand that was burned into my palm kicked in, hot and bright, shooting my system with mongoose blood, lighting up my brain like a malfunctioning pinball machine. I lifted my sword over my head and the vamps ran, scattering like a pack of dogs from a wheelie bin full of fireworks. They needn't have bothered, Gen had already cut off the only door out of there, and was swinging her morning star menacingly.

I sighed and skewered one of the terrified vampires through the heart, turning him to ash.

'Another pack of nobodies,' I told Gen as she brained an attempted escapee. 'This isn't getting us anywhere.'

The vamp whose skull Gen had shattered slumped backwards over a laptop, setting the Powerpoint presentation in a tizz and painting the panicked faces of the trapped delegates with a variety of bleeding edge buzzwords.

'Have patience,' Gen replied. 'If we keep doing what we're doing, we're sure to work our way up the chain eventually.'

I murdered another bloodsucker without even doing him the honour of looking his way.

'Look, I like rolling out the hits as much as the next girl, but we've been at this for weeks.' I shoved my blade into a vampire's temple and pushed it through his cranium with a satisfying *shunk*.

'Trust me,' she replied, caving in another vampire's skull, 'sooner or later, a lead will present itself.'

I was starting to doubt that. We'd busted up a couple of dozen hives already, and so far no one of consequence had dared pop their head above the parapet. As far as I could tell, we were in exactly the same place as we were the day Neil got cut.

One of the bolder vampires scooped up a fountain pen from the boardroom table and tried sticking it in my neck. I gave him a kick in the pods for his trouble and kneed him in the head so hard he got a taste of his own brains.

'Do you mind?' I asked, as he sank to the ground, dead as a dildo. 'I'm trying to have a conversation here.'

I returned to my discussion with Gendith as I ploughed through another vampire, showering the room in an arterial gush. 'We're looking for a magician, right? Surely there must be some spell that can help us find one? You know, like a… like a tracking device?'

I made my sword fun-sized, lined up a shot, and tossed the dagger through the air, piercing the heads of two vamps in a row.

'A tracking device? You think there's some magical Grindr for spell-slingers?'

'How the hell do you know about Grindr?' I asked. 'I thought you were an angel.'

I recalled the dagger to my hand and planted it in the eye socket of an attacking vamp, scoring another effortless kill.

'I'm an angel, Abbey, not a saint.'

She wrapped the chain of her morning star around a vampire's neck and pulled on it so hard his head popped off like a champagne cork.

'What about a magic doodad to find the wizard then? You know, one of those enchanted artefacts? Maybe that L'Merrier bloke has something that could help us out.'

I hacked off a vamp's head and used it like a football, toe punting it into the surprised face of another.

'L'Merrier?' said Gen. 'Did you forget the part where he said he'd murder us if we ever set foot in his shop again?'

'Right, right. What about Stella Familiar then? Can she help?'

Gen raked a vamp down the face with the spiked ball of her weapon, leaving him looking like he'd lost a cage match with Freddy Krueger.

'I tried Stella already,' Gen explained, 'but she's backed up dealing with some unruly demigod or other.'

'It's always something with that girl.'

A shadow fell over me and I whirled around to see a vampire leaping from the edge of the boardroom table. In his hand he clutched a smashed water jug, now little more than a plastic handle attached to a wicked glass spike. Stupid, Abbey. Stupid. I'd taken the outcome of the fight for granted and let my guard down, and now I was going to get my throat opened.

There wasn't enough time to deflect his blow or move out of the way, so you can imagine my relief when a spiked ball swung into view and connected with the vampire's face so hard it sent his jaw to the other side of the room. His body hit the ground, twitched for a second or two, then went still. That was the end of them. The last vampire standing.

'Don't get cocky,' said Gen. 'This is no time for complacency.'

'Aw, Gen, I never knew you cared.'

'Your death means about as much to me as any other mortal's.'

I grinned and tickled her chin. 'You luuurve me.'

Her ebony skin did what it could to preserve her dignity, but she was blushing to the roots of her hair. 'If you don't shut up right now, I swear I'm going to throttle you to death.'

One of the bodies on the floor suddenly leapt to its feet. The vampire opened his mouth like a feeding python and lunged for Gen's vocal cords.

I launched my dagger, landed it, and sent him keeling over backwards.

'Honestly, Gen,' I said, parroting her words, 'this is no time for complacency.'

Gen shot me evils as I waggled my eyebrows at her. Just insufferable.

I stood and watched the impaled vampire scramble along the floor like he was swimming side stroke, a dagger buried in his chest. Before he could make it any further, I planted the tread of a Doc Marten in the square of his back and pinned him to the carpet.

'Who did it?' I asked.

'You might need to be a little more specific,' he replied.

'Which one of you pointy-toothed pricks carved up my boyfriend?'

'I don't know what you're talking about,' he complained.

'That's really too bad.' I paused for dramatic effect. 'For *you*.' Nailed it.

'Please don't kill me, I'm too young to die!'

'Too young? What are you, two, three-hundred years old?'

I caught a stink like a soiled nappy and looked down to see that he'd turned his trousers into a toilet.

'Jesus, man, have some self-respect.'

It was obvious that the miserable pooper under my boot wasn't going to lead me to my magician, so I executed the guy before he could embarrass himself any further.

'Well, I don't mind telling you, I got zero job satisfaction from that,' I told Gen, wafting my hand under my nose.

I signed up to this gig to be a monster hunter, but the assignments I'd been taking lately reminded me of the pointless busy work I used to do at the Lost Property Office, only with added stabbing. I was destroying cell after cell—cleaning out boardrooms, torching drug shipments, purging sacrifice sites—but I wasn't getting any closer to my goal. I was chasing a magician, but all I kept finding were empty suits. Cold leftovers from a turd buffet.

Then one day everything changed.

2

I was kicking back at home base when it happened. Not the gas tower; if you recall, I'd accidentally (very deliberately) burned that place down. No, this was our new base in the Square Mile, London's financial district.

The Vault, as we'd taken to calling it, used to be the basement of an old bank strongroom. The place was *hardcore*. Its walls, floor, and ceiling were fortified with high security steel panels, and the only door in was made of three-foot thick reinforced steel, and strong enough to keep out a fleet of Sherman tanks. In other words, The Vault was locked up tighter than a gnat's arse.

How could we afford to live in a place like that? Simple, we bought it. Outright. We'd come into a bit of a windfall recently, having looted a rather wealthy vampire. Bloodsuckers can be real magpies, particularly ones belonging to the Judas Clan, who knew better than anyone how fickle the financial market could be. Quite often they kept large portions of their riches unbanked, squirrelling their assets away where they're at their safest, close at hand. Lauden Crowe was one such vampire, as I discovered after I slayed him and turned over his mansion. Lauden wasn't some mid-tier Clansman either, he was a big player, the kind of guy who had an annual yacht polish budget. The kind of guy who got lost looking for his kitchen. In one safe alone I found gold bullion, precious gemstones, and enough hard cash to buy

The Vault in a single payment. We even got ourselves a ping pong table!

It was early evening and I was sat in the part of the basement we'd converted into our communal area; the War Room as we'd taken to calling it. Before we'd furnished the place with a Camelot-style round table and started using it for strategy meetings, the area used to be the bank's safe deposit room. We hadn't had a chance to completely redecorate yet, which meant the room still featured thousands of tiny boxes that opened up to even tinier drawers, all of them empty since the money men moved from the premises a few years back.

I wasn't doing anything much, just listening to some Southern Death Cult and whittling a piece of wood to pass the time. Whittling away the hours. In my hand I held a magic dagger crafted by The Almighty to prevail over the tyranny of a vampire army, and there I was, using it to carve myself a… I don't even know what I was carving...

'Making your own sex toys now?' asked Neil. 'Thrifty.'

Squeak squeak squeak. The sound of Neil's oxygen tank as he wheeled it over, took a seat beside me, and parked it by his leg. Since I'd stopped him becoming a vampire and he'd turned fully human again, his cystic fibrosis had returned with a vengeance. A couple of nights previous, he'd had a coughing fit so severe that I'd had to whack a mucus build-up off the walls of his lungs large enough to fill a teacup.

'You feeling okay?' I asked. 'Good nap?'

'Yeah, feeling just amazing as always, thanks,' he replied, rubbing his eyes with the heels of his hands.

He turned to me and the top of his dressing gown fell open, showing me his chest. Showing me his wounds. The cuts that he'd been given were deep—not deep enough to damage any organs, thank God—but deep enough to have left him permanently scarred.

I traced my finger along the crude slashes of the mystery magician's message.

Neil saw my face darken and pulled his gown shut. 'Nothing new under there,' he said, sketching out a smile.

I think part of him was actually happy that he'd been carved up, like he was proud of his war wounds. They were a sort of badge of honour, I supposed. Proof that he wasn't just a bystander in all of this.

Neil saw my brow knit and sensed my anger. 'Look, if trying to find this guy is driving you crackers, maybe you should pull back on it. For a while, at least.'

'What are you saying? You want me to give up? Some fucker sliced a death threat into your skin.'

'Yeah, I hadn't forgotten,' he replied, hand tightening on his gown. 'I just wonder if, I dunno, it might be best if we stayed off his radar. The guy's obviously got some skills, and the last thing I need is to wake up and find a big old dick carved into my face.'

Neil had never been one to hold a grudge, but that wasn't me. My old boss once spoiled the ending to *Breaking Bad* for me and I keyed his Audi from front to back. No, I wasn't going to rest until I rooted out the person who cut Neil, and fed them cock-first through a wood chipper.

I heard the clack-clacking of Vizael's ivory-handled walking stick on the concrete floor, and turned to see him hobbling our way. The old man was dressed in his regulation crumpled white linen suit, and holding a phone flat in his free hand like a waiter serving an entrée.

'What have you got there?' I asked, but before he could answer, a voice began squawking from the phone's speaker.

'I think I've got a live one,' said the woman on the other end. 'Well, technically a dead one.'

It was Gendith, who was out in the field, looking for leads on our phantom wordsmith.

Viz set the phone down in front of me and I craned my ear to it. 'What's going on, Gen?'

'I picked up some chatter and went to check it out. There's been a death in the neighborhood. You know that Crossrail development going on down the road?'

'The big tunnelling job?'

'Yes. They're saying a construction worker lost his life there just now.'

Viz leaned in to the phone. 'An industrial accident?' he asked.

'That's the obvious,' replied Gen, 'but I'm not so sure. I'm thinking they might have ruptured a plague pit.'

A plague pit—or a Dracula factory as I'd taken to calling them—was a mass grave of Plague victims, buried during the Middle Ages and disturbed by London's regeneration efforts. One of the first things I'd learned when I became the Nightstalker was that modern vampires were folks who'd died during the Plague, only to have their souls corrupted and rise up against the living. Matter of fact, the whole Bubonic Plague thing only started because Judas Iscariot took a dive into the Thames and poisoned London's drinking water, but let's not get bogged down in all of that now. You already know my feelings on exposition.

'Where exactly are you?' I asked Gen.

As she fed me the address, Vizael rifled through some documents on a nearby desk and fetched a couple of rolled up sheets of paper. Placing them down before me, he overlaid the two sheets and pinned down their corners with his cane and a couple of half-empty coffee mugs.

'There,' he said, pointing to the location Gendith had given us. 'It lines up perfectly.'

The bottom sheet was a modern day map of the local area, while on top of it, traced on a piece of see-through drafting paper, was a map of medieval burial grounds that Viz had lifted from a historical archive. Like Viz had said, Gen's location overlapped a plague site exactly.

'Okay then,' I said, 'more vampires, whoop-dee-bloody-doo. Is any of this going to help me find the magician?'

'Quite possibly not,' Viz replied, matter of factly, 'but then you are the Nightstalker, charged with destroying vampires, not just those that you bear a personal grudge against.'

I sighed. He was right. Besides, it beat lounging about in a windowless bunker doing bugger all. I'm telling you, that place was sucking the life out of me quicker than a horny succubus.

'Okay, fine. I'll be with you in a wee bit,' I told Gen, and stabbed the disconnect call button.

I threw on my harness, plugged the dagger into its sheath, and slipped my arms inside the sleeves of my leather jacket.

'Keep the home fires burning,' I told Neil, 'I won't be long.'

Like a kid in class trying to get teacher's attention, he held up a finger. 'Actually, I was thinking maybe I'd tag along on this one.'

I laughed, thinking he was joking, then caught his expression. 'Wait, you're serious?'

'Yeah. I mean, I might as well, right? I'm not doing anyone much good in this place.' He scratched his nose, causing his breathing tube to twitch beneath his nostrils like a mouse's whiskers.

'Right. It's just that, well, it's kind of a slaughterhouse out there. You must get that, right, what with the whole getting kidnapped, being put in a coma and having your chest carved up thing?'

'Yeah, but that was before,' he replied. 'I didn't know about any of this Uncanny stuff back then, but now I'm clued in. Now I'm ready for it.'

'I don't want to sound like a dick, Neil, but how exactly are you "ready"? What are you going to do when a fight kicks off, drag your oxygen tank into battle?' I rapped a knuckle on the side of the cannister. 'If someone so much as strikes a match near this thing you'll go up like a bomb.'

'So what are you saying?' he asked. 'I spend the rest of my life in a hole staring at these four walls?'

'Not your whole life, just until I've made ribbons out of the bloke who used you as a human Post-It note.'

'And how long till that happens?

'I don't know,' I replied, throwing up my hands.

'Exactly. None of us knows how long that's going to take. It could be weeks yet, months even, or maybe you'll never find them, what about then? So long as I'm part of all this, let me be part of the team.'

I turned to Viz, who stood by wearing the expression of a child whose parents were about to enter into a very messy divorce. 'Could you give us a second?'

'Gladly,' he replied, making himself scarce.

I returned to Neil, taking his hand in mine. 'You don't want this. Trust me. You don't need all this drama.'

'Are you serious? I'd kill for some drama, Abbey. Do you

know what I did last night while you were out putting vampires in body bags? I binge-watched a whole season of *RuPaul's Drag Race*, that's what I did.'

'I'm sorry.'

'So am I. I can't believe BenDeLaCreme walked off, she was a total shoo-in!'

'This isn't a joke, Neil. This is life and death.'

Neil tapped his oxygen tube, then opened his gown a little to show off his carved up chest. 'Yeah, I'm kind of used to life and death situations by this point.'

I gave his hand a squeeze. 'Look, I get it, okay? You're tired of being left out. You're tired of being the damsel in distress. I completely understand, but that doesn't mean I'm going to let you throw your life away just to show me what a big man you are. You *are* a man. *My* man.' I turned my hand over and showed him the N-shaped brand on my palm. 'If you were the one chosen to be the Nightstalker I've no doubt in my mind that you'd do a kick-ass job of it, but you weren't, and that means you have no business messing with vampires. I'm sorry, but that's the way it is.'

His mouth puckered into a tiny slot. 'I'm not saying I should be the tip of the spear or anything, I just want to be involved. Surely there must be something I can do to help out?'

'Okay, maybe there is, and when I get back we'll all have a sit down and figure out what that is, but right now, can you sit tight for a couple of hours while I kick the shit out of some blood-suckers?'

He sagged his head. 'Okay then, fine.'

I gave Neil a peck on the cheek, caught Viz's eye over his shoulder, and mouthed, 'Time to go.'

It broke me up to treat Neil like a stay-at-home mum, but what was I supposed to do? Being the Nightstalker means taking charge and making some unpopular decisions. They don't tell you this when you sign up to be a vampire-killing super-bitch, but disappointing your loved ones is all part of the package. That and some sky-high dry cleaning bills.

3

When I told Gen that we'd be with her in a wee bit, I wasn't lying. Getting to her was as easy as stepping through a door.

A magic door.

When I said there was only one way into the base before, I didn't mean there wasn't another way *out*. Technically, The Vault has two main doors, but my favourite one—the magic door—is strictly one-way.

Vizael had it installed after he got tired of me complaining about the transport situation. There's only so many times a man can listen to someone grousing about Uber fares and overpriced train tickets before they cough up for a reality-defying magic portal. If I've said that once, I've said it a thousand times.

We paid through the nose for the door—gave an eaves a gold nugget the size of a baby's fist to build the thing—more money from Lauden's stash. Still, you can't put a price on magic I say, and it really is a hell of thing. Just think about where you want to go, turn the handle, and there you are, bingo bango. That's how me and Gen bypassed ninety-something floors of security and sprang out of that stock cupboard in the Shard. Told you I'd explain that. You can always count on old Abs.

Naturally, even a magic door has its limits. It can't take you *absolutely* anywhere, otherwise I'd have used it to crash Judas' hideout and kick his arse purple. No, the door can only take you to places whose location you're already familiar with, so no using it to become a one-woman FedEx, or leapfrogging to alien planets (believe me, I tried).

We stepped into the door—me and Viz—and instantaneously bridged the distance between home base and a smelly back alley in Whitechapel. The exit we stepped out of was the back door of the Golden Lotus restaurant, and would continue to be so the moment we were done with it. Like I said, the door is a one-way deal. It doesn't completely solve the transportation problem, but it does cut out half of my emergency cab rides, and spares me a whole bunch of rush hour tube journeys, squeezing my way out of carriages packed so tight I feel like I've been given birth to.

We emerged from the alley and headed off to meet Gen. The sun had gone down on the day, and the moon lit the city like a monochrome photo, whites on blacks and little in between. After a short walk, we arrived at Gen's location, a huge building site walled in by hoardings twelve feet high.

'You sure you're up for this?' I asked Viz.

'Oh, don't worry about me, dear, it will do me good to give the old bones some exercise.'

All right then. Unlike Neil, I knew from experience that Viz could handle himself. I'd seen him in action, and even though he could be a bit scatterbrained—well, *a lot* scatterbrained— he was far from the old codger he appeared to be.

We made our way to the pin Gen dropped us and found her standing among a throng of people amassed around the site's entrance. I pushed my way towards her and shouted over the din.

'What's going on?'

'These vultures came to see if they could get a look at the body,' she replied, shaking her head.

There aren't many things that unite us in the so-called United Kingdom, but if I were to whittle it down to three, they would be as follows:

A deep appreciation for a morning cup of tea.

A mutual hatred of queue jumpers.

And a love of sticking our noses places they don't belong.

And the congregation would not go home disappointed today. The crowd parted as a gurney appeared, on top of which laid a black plastic body bag. Phone cameras flashed, a police cordon was lifted, and a couple of paramedics wheeled the cadaver to the back of a waiting ambulance.

'Have a look inside,' said Gen.

'Inside what?'

'What do you think? The bag.'

I turned to her and gave her the kind of look that angry librarians give over their glasses. 'Tell you what, Gen, how about you look inside the bag with the dead bloke in it?'

'If I was the woman with the x-ray vision, I would,' she retorted, 'but since you were the one God Almighty saw fit to give Nightstalker powers—not me—I don't really have that option.'

The rear doors of the ambulance were swung open and the body loaded inside.

'It's now or never,' said Viz, as we watched one of the paramedics head for the driver's door.

'Fine,' I said. 'One magic x-ray, coming right up.'

I closed my eyes, tuned out my remaining senses, and activated the part of my brain that could see through solid objects. Opening my eyes again, I concentrated on the back of the ambulance and poured my focus into it, peeling back metal, stripping away fibreglass, until I was through the wall of the vehicle, into the body bag, and looking at the body inside.

What I saw was a total mess. Seriously. The bloke looked like he'd been chewed up and spat out. I felt my lunch making an escape bid and clapped my hand to my mouth.

'That bad?' asked Gen.

'He looked like he's been turned inside out. What do you think did that?'

'That's what we're here to find out,' said Viz. 'Come with me.'

I followed him to the front of the throng until we were within earshot of two constables manning the cordon. Over their radio we heard dispatch relay a message that the officers were to keep the perimeter secured until the uniforms arrived, which gave us a limited amount of time to investigate the site before the suits showed up.

'What do we do?' I asked Viz.

He sagged his shoulders. 'I don't like doing this unless it's absolutely necessary, but needs must...'

He aimed himself at the police officers and used his hands to perform a complex series of gestures, moving them back and forth and in and out, looking for all the world like an old-timey switchboard operator using a telephone exchange, plugging and unplugging invisible jacks. After about a minute of this, he let his arms fall by his sides.

'I didn't know you could vogue,' I said.

'Go ahead, we can enter now.'

'You what? Just walk right by those two policemen?'

'Precisely,' Viz replied, tapping his noggin. 'Perception magic.'

He waltzed past the constables and ducked the DO NOT CROSS police tape. Neither of the officers batted an eyelid at this.

'Well,' said Gen, 'get a wriggle on then.'

I was hesitant obviously—who wouldn't be?—but she seemed so confident, and the clock was ticking. I sidled up to the constables, checking their eyes weren't following me, then limboed under the cordon. True to Viz's word, his Jedi Mind Trick worked, and I passed by unscathed.

We were in. The three of us made our way through the cleared-out construction site until we saw the mouth of a tunnel up ahead and entered it, heading underground in search of the scene of the "accident".

After a short descent, the tunnel opened out into a cavernous area full of portable floodlights, hanging yellow cables and more CAUTION signs than you could shake a stick at (so many in fact that there was a good chance one of them warned against doing exactly that). Up ahead was a mountain of excavated ground that had been cleared by a boring machine; a giant cylinder driven by huge hydraulic rams and mounted with a rotating cutterhead powerful enough to tunnel through solid rock. Beyond all that, on the far wall of the cavern, was the massive, perfectly round hole it had left in its wake.

I approached the boring machine and inspected the cutter-head. I turned back from the machine to Gen. 'You said it was a drilling accident, right?'

'That's what I picked up on the scanner.'

'Then how come I don't see any blood?'

A new voice broke the silence. 'Oi! What are you lot doing?' A foreman with a yellow hard hat, high-vis jacket, and a belly like a space hopper jogged on to the scene. 'You can't be down here!' he barked, sending spittle flying from his flapping gums.

Viz looked at him curiously, angling his head around the man's portly frame and getting a look at the giant helping of fat setting up shop in his backside. 'Excuse me, sir, but did you know you're displaying a generous portion of intergluteal flesh?'

'You what, mate?' spat the foreman.

'He means your arse is hanging out,' I clarified.

The foreman inserted his thumbs into his belt loops and hoiked up his jeans. 'Look, either you get going right now or I'll give the coppers a shout.'

'Something happened down here,' said Gen, 'did you witness it yourself?'

He regarded us suspiciously. 'Who are you lot then, the press?'

'Sure,' I told him. 'Why not?'

His eyes darted about, checking that there was no one around to overhear our conversation. 'To be honest, I don't give a monkey's who you are, but if you want the story, it's gonna cost you.'

'One of your team just died and you're on the take,' I said. 'You seem really swell.'

'We don't have time to negotiate with this idiot,' said Gen.

'Who are you calling an idiot, you bloody coo—'

Gen grabbed him by the throat and lifted him off the floor. 'I wouldn't if I was you,' she hissed. The fat man's face reddened and his eyes bulged from his skull like a couple of stress-relieving squeeze toys. She set him back down on the ground before he choked to death, and put on an eerie, smiling voice. 'Now, how about you be a good little boy and tell us about this "accident"?'

For a second I thought he was about to blow his stack, but when he spoke, it was in the tone of a bored politician at an all-day press junket, answering a question with the same heavily-rehearsed spin statement that he'd already trotted out a hundred times since breakfast. 'There was an accident,' he said. 'A drilling accident. That's what happened. A drilling accident.' His eyes were glazed over, his voice unnatural.

I looked to my companions. 'He's full of shit, right?'

'Not exactly,' Gen replied, reading his aura. 'He thinks he's telling the truth.'

The foreman stood there with a blank look on his face, jaw slack, mouth wet.

'Mesmerism,' Viz explained. 'A vampire must have got to this man and programmed him to recite a cover story.'

I know what you're thinking. Seems a bit convoluted, right? I mean, why go to all that trouble? Why the masquerade? Okay, so the reason the Clan employs dirty tricks like this is because staying incognito is the cornerstone of their survival strategy. Out in the open, they'd run the risk of the rest of us using our superior numbers to rise up against them. That's one theory. The other theory—our theory—is that if the inhabitants of London were to learn that vampires existed, and had infiltrated the highest echelons of society, they'd lose their collective shit and everything would go tits up on a city-wide scale. Given that neither faction knows which way things would actually go, we play it right down the middle and keep our war in the shadows. It's a Mutually Assured Destruction kind of thing.

'Right then,' I said, 'vampires it is. When isn't it vampires?'

I coshed the foreman over the head with the butt of my dagger and he hit the ground like a sack of hammers.

Gen glanced down at the man's unconscious body, then back up at me. 'Was that strictly necessary?' she asked. 'Or did you forget that the dagger you just clubbed him with can wipe minds?'

'I did not.'

The angels stared at me, shaking their heads.

'What? Oh, come on, the guy was a dick! Twats get smacks, right?'

A noise came seeping out of the mouth of the tunnel: sounds of scratching, moaning, shuffling. The three of us froze.

'So this is where the sausage is made?' I whispered. I'd never seen the Clan birthing process up close and personal before, which made this a rare treat.

I used my Nightstalker vision to scan the recesses of the tunnel and saw several stooping figures lurking in the darkness.

'What do you see?' asked Gen.

'Vamps,' I replied. 'Maybe a dozen, all huddled together. I don't get it, why are they just waiting there like that?'

'They've been asleep for centuries and have just gorged themselves on fresh blood,' Viz explained. 'They're recuperating.'

Gen chipped in. 'You'd be groggy too if you'd been asleep since the Middle Ages. We should act soon though. Once they're finished resting, they'll move on down the tunnel and surface elsewhere in the city.'

'What's the plan then?' I asked. 'Business as usual? Rock up in there and stab anyone with oversized eye teeth?'

'If I might,' suggested Viz, 'I'd like to propose a more profitable stratagem.'

'Such as?' I asked.

'The first order of business for this fresh batch of vampires will be to join with their brothers. I would suggest that instead of slaying them en masse, we allow one to survive and track him to his destination.'

'Right,' I said, cottoning on. 'Wait until he's joined with his boys, then fuck up the whole posse.'

'In a manner of speaking, yes,' Viz replied. 'It's a method I arrived at many years ago, back in my own fighting days.'

Given his frail body and the way he held himself—hunched over like his spine was a wilting flower—it was easy to forget that Viz was once a total badass. Don't get me wrong, you still wouldn't want to jog the bloke's pint, but he wasn't the threat he used to be. The guy who cut a swathe through a vampire army, took on Judas Iscariot himself, and left him lying at the bottom of the Thames. Of course, that was the thing that led to the second wave of vampires we were facing now—the ones who dredged Judas out of the drink and took over the financial sector—so the old man wasn't exactly in the black, success-wise.

'I have a question,' I said, 'how is it the vamps know where they're going after they wake up? What is it, like an evolutionary thing?'

'I have to confess, I don't exactly know,' Viz admitted. 'I have theories, but I can't say for certain how the fledgling vampires navigate. Something to ponder…' he trailed off, stroking the underside of his white beard with the back of his hand.

'All right then,' I said. 'Let's get this little production on its feet.' I used the pommel of my dagger to bang on the metal cutterhead of the boring machine. 'Grub's up, you bunch of gannets! Get it while it's hot, it ain't getting any hotter!'

Viz drew a slim silver blade from his walking cane. Gen began whirling her morning star in a figure-of-eight. I planted my feet and squared my shoulders as the moans from the tunnel grew louder. Soon enough, snuffling figures began to emerge from the gloom, hatching like chicks from an egg.

The figures were dressed in rags and had puckered, albino-white skin that made them look as though they'd fallen asleep in the bath and only recently clawed their way out. They looked nothing at all like the vampires I'd encountered so far. These were not the sexy aristocrats of the night I'd come to know and hate. These were shuffling corpses, diseased and hunched: extras from *The Walking Dead*, not men of taste and refinement. Only once they'd woken proper would they smarten up their acts, don sharp suits and develop the Clan's signature preppy polish.

The vampires came towards us, arms outstretched like sleep-walkers, faces slick with fresh blood. I flicked my dagger to the side, lengthening its blade like an extendable baton.

'Party time.'

The fight that followed was nothing to write home about. Seriously. You might think I'm being lazy with my description there, but trust me, it was a whole load of nothing. If the barney we'd had in that boardroom was a breeze, you can imagine how quickly the three of us dispatched a few sloppy old sleepyheads barely out of the cradle. Honestly, it was done and dusted in less than a minute. *Swoosh! Swoosh! Swoosh!* Slicing vampires from top to bottom and left to right, opening them up like boxes of flat-pack furniture, then—

'Stop!' Viz shouted.

I managed to pull back the swing of my blade just in time to avoid beheading the last of the vampires.

'We need one alive, remember?'

'Oh right, yeah. Sorry, got a bit kill happy there.' I turned the vampire around and gave him a swift boot up the arse. 'Go on then, get cracking,' I told him.

The vampire stared at me over his shoulder for a moment, then off he shuffled into the tunnel, back the way he came.

'We'll stay here and clean up the bodies before the police arrive,' said Viz. 'You get after that one.'

'Remember, you're not to engage,' said Gen. 'Track the target to the gathering point and radio us with the intel.'

'Roger that,' I said, firing off a sarcastic salute.

Then off I went, heading after the bloodsucker with a merry tune upon my lips.

We're Off to See the Wizard, if you must know.

4

The vampire quickly picked up speed. By the time he'd exited the tunnel and found his way on to the streets, I was having to use the full power of the brand to keep up with the nippy little swine.

Up ahead I saw the raggedy vampire spring into the air, trampoline off the awning of an off license, and skitter up the side of the building. Thank Christ it was late and there was no one around to see him, or our little "secret war" would have been all across YouTube faster than *Gangnam Style*.

I grabbed hold of a drainpipe and shimmied up to the roof just in time to see the vamp leaping to the next building down the street, moving like a ghost, his feet kissing the rooftop on the other side. I'm telling you, it was some real parkour shit. When those guys woke up they *really* woke up.

Off I went after him, the brand pumping me up, giving me what I needed to bridge the distance between the sloping rooftops. I took a leap but only just made it across, landing hard on the other side, dislodging a patch of slates and losing my footing so I ended up hanging off a gutter, feet pedalling thin air. I dangled there for a few seconds until I could gain purchase, then clambered up on to the roof with all the grace of a dog climbing out of a swimming pool.

The vamp was a good way ahead of me now. I was determined to stay on him though, so I kept going, eating up ground, the wind whistling in my ears. I lost sight of him for a moment as I bounded across to another rooftop, and paid dearly for my carelessness. An elbow appeared from around a chimney stack, connected with the bridge of my nose, and sent my eyes spinning like the wheels of a fruit machine. The force of the crack almost sent me skidding off the edge of the building, but I managed to crouch down and plunge the dagger into the roof beneath me, slowing my descent until I came to a last-second stop. Tiles tumbled away, dislodging a chunk of gutter and smashing down on the street below. I breathed a sigh of relief and pulled myself up. Close one.

The vampire was a dot now, no bigger than the *Contact Us* link on a local council's website. Still, I refused to give up. I ran and I ran until I felt like I was going to chuck up a lung. Until my heart was pumping broken glass. And eventually, after a chase that all but killed me, I was back on his rear end.

The vampire leapt to the balcony of an adjacent office block and pushed through a fire escape, barging inside and setting a security alarm ringing.

'Not a chance, mate,' I growled, vaulting to the balcony and tearing off after him.

I pursued him down a couple of flights of internal stairs, through another door, then deeper into the building. The vamp raced through an open plan office, toppling furniture, trying to slow my progress, but by now my pot was really boiling. I took three long strides, made it within striking range, then bulldozed him into an exterior window.

Crash!

The tackle carried us through the shattered glass and landed us in an alleyway two storeys down. I came out on top, using his body as a crash mat, cushioning the impact of the fall. We skidded across the deck, rolled a couple of times, and came to an abrupt halt against the alley's brick wall, right next to the back doors of a Poundland.

'Got you, you slippery little shit!' I screamed, dagger to his throat, temporarily forgetting that I was only meant to be chasing the guy, not killing him.

Oops.

He stared back at me with the mad, darting eyes of a cultist before I removed the knife from his windpipe and let go of the scruff of his neck. Unable to believe his luck, he took to his toes and went to peg it off down the alley. Let him run, I thought. Little did he know we were playing a game of catch and release. Or at least that was the plan…

I heard a *squeak squeak squeak,* followed by a hollow *Clang!*

Oh crap...

A large metal cylinder came crashing down, splitting the vampire's skull in two. He slumped to the ground leaking grey matter, limbs slack and lifeless.

'Neil!'

'You're welcome,' he replied, lowering his oxygen tank to the ground and setting it back on its wheels, a big, smug smile on his face.

I pushed the dead vampire off me and shot to my feet. 'What the hell was that?' I demanded.

'What?' he replied, confused. 'You were in trouble so I helped you out. Usually people say "thank you" when that happens.'

'I wasn't in trouble, you plum. Christ, look at this mess. That was my one lead.' I ran my palm down my face. 'How did you even find me out here?'

'I used the share location app,' he said, holding up his phone, 'then I took the magic door through there.' He thumbed the back exit of Poundland.

Ugh, of course he had. After he got kidnapped that time, I'd insisted I be able to track him through his phone—just in case it happened again—and it seemed only fair that deal go both ways. Apparently, my overprotectiveness had blown back on me, big style.

'I was supposed to crack the case,' I fumed, 'not that idiot's skull.'

'I'm sorry, okay, but maybe if I wasn't kept in the dark all the time, stuff like this wouldn't happen.' His puppy dog eyes slid off me and went to his feet.

'I'm sorry, okay, I don't mean to keep you in the dark. It's just safer.' The cystic fibrosis was enough to deal with, did he really need to shorten his lifespan even more?

'I'm so tired of puttering around in that basement, Abbey, tapping away at a keyboard all day long, just to pass the time.'

'I'm sorry, but really, what's new? You were stuck indoors before. How is this different except for the decor? At least now you have a ping pong table.'

'Yeah, but when there's only me playing it's a bit one-sided. Twenty-seven days I've been stuck down there. It's like prison. No, it's worse than prison, in prison you get to look forward to getting out one day.'

'You will get out, just as soon as I'm done with the magician who cut you up.'

'And when exactly is that going to be?'

'I don't know, Neil, but it could be a while if you keep on braining our leads!'

His voice dropped. 'You don't get it. I'm so tired of feeling like a supporting character in all of this.'

'Come on, you're so much more than that. Just because you're not some sword-swinging tough guy with muscles on his muscles, doesn't mean you don't bring your own talents to the table. Just not, you know, the war table.'

He pushed me away and gave me a sour look. 'Did you want to patronise me any more while you're at it? God, I feel like the bard in a *D&D* party.'

I wasn't one-hundred percent sure what that meant, but I think I got the gist of it. 'I'm sorry, I was trying to be nice.'

He pointed to the dead vampire splashed across the ground at our feet. 'You see that? I did that. Okay, so maybe I shouldn't have killed this *exact* vampire, but doesn't the fact that I took him down show you I'm not just some liability?'

I got what he was saying. He was saying what most blokes say when they're feeling emasculated: *show me the problem and I'll show it my fists.* Neil was overcompensating, throwing himself into danger just to prove to me that he was a man. And I understood his anger, I really did. If I'd been kidnapped by a pack of vampires and almost turned into one of their own, I'd want some payback too. Thank God he didn't know I'd slept with the one responsible for doing it to him in the first place, because that would have really poured some salt in the wound.

'No one's saying you're a liability, Neil. We'll find more stuff for you to do, I promise, just not on the front line.'

He scowled at me. 'You don't get to choose what I do, Abbey. If I want to kill vampires, I can kill vampires. I've earned that right.'

He turned away and headed off down the alley, dragging his blood-smeared oxygen tank.

Viz and Gen appeared behind me, puffing and panting.

'What happened?' asked Gen, pointing to the dead vampire leaking his brains on the cobbles.

'Boyfriend trouble,' I replied, ramming my dagger through the creature's breastbone and turning him into ash.

5

As I'm sure you can imagine, there was more than a whiff of tension in the air after that. When I made it back to home base—back to the room I shared with Neil—I found his bed pulled apart from mine and pushed to the far side of the room. Subtle. The light was dimmed and he was clenched up under his duvet, asleep, or at least doing a decent impression of it.

'Great,' I muttered, before turning off the light, shucking my clothes, and crawling into my lonely little cot.

He'd be okay in the morning, I told myself. Once the initial anger had worn off, he'd be okay. His masculinity had taken a prang, but that wasn't the end of the world. The male psyche was a fragile but easily repaired vessel. A bit of ego-stroking here, a bit of *actual* stroking elsewhere, and he'd be right as rain. I rolled over, pulled the bed sheets tight to my chin, and sleep swallowed me whole.

I wasn't sure how much time had passed when I came around. The lights were out, and down there in that windowless basement with nothing to see by, I was blind. So utterly blind that it was as if my eyes had been scooped out of my skull and dropped down a deep, dark well.

I went for my phone but it wasn't there. As a matter of fact, the whole bedside table had gone. Maybe Neil had moved the table when he relocated his cot to the other side of the room, and

I'd left my phone in the pocket of my jeans. No, that didn't make sense. Why would he go to the effort of dragging my table away? Unless he'd done it out of spite? I dangled my arm over the bed, fingers searching for the pile of jeans I'd left on the floor, only I couldn't find those either.

The dagger.

I'd use that to light my way. Draw it from its sheath and light the room up neon blue. Except that wasn't where I'd left it either. I'd dumped it on the floor with the rest of my clothes, hadn't I? What the hell was going on?

I heard a noise. Distant breathing, weak and wet sounding, as if the person making it was plugged with mucus. As if their own bile had pooled in their throat and they were drowning in the stuff.

'Neil?'

No response.

The breathing continued, feeble and shaky.

'Hey, Neil?'

Still nothing.

It gave me the shudders. I swung my legs over the edge of the mattress and set my bare feet on the vault's cold concrete floor. With my arms held in front of me, I took a couple of paces in the direction of Neil's bed, trying to find the wall so I could feel my way there.

The wall was gone.

Panic took hold of me.

Where was I? I had nothing to navigate by. Nothing except for my bed, and when I tried retreating to that, guess what I found...?

Nothing.

It was as though I were wandering around in a void. In a black hole. Where was I? What I wouldn't have given to have reached out and had my hand graze a light switch, to turn on a bulb and make the room bright and familiar, but there was nothing there. Nothing but the ground beneath my feet, and even that was beginning to feel uncertain.

'Neil, wake up.'

I said it again and again, getting louder each time, but he

wouldn't respond. Wouldn't so much as stir. I listened to his breathing, my only compass in the darkness, my North Star. I carried on walking towards the sound.

And walking.

And walking.

The dimensions of the room were all wrong. Even if I were crossing it from corner to corner and tripping over nothing on the way, I still shouldn't have covered that much ground. It was as though the room had grown. Grown to the size of a football pitch. And yet I could tell I was making progress. Could tell I was getting closer to the sound of Neil's laboured breathing.

Fingers fishing the air ahead of me, I drew closer still. Close enough that I could hear the hiss of Neil's respirator. My leg bumped into something. Neil's bed. I searched out with my hand and felt his body under the covers. There he was. There I was. The both of us, together, in the same space.

'Neil, wake up. It's me.'

I gave him a shake and felt his body shift and roll over. It was okay. Everything was okay. He was breathing, I was breathing, everything was all right. I must have been sleepwalking. All that scrambling around in the void, that must have been my mind playing tricks on me, sending me in circles, pinwheeling me about on the spot. Silly sod. I thought I was going out of my mind, but I was just disoriented. Groping around in the dark like a zombie, too tired to understand where I was.

And that's when the lights came on.

So bright that I couldn't see.

So bright that it felt like daggers in my eyes.

So bright that I thought I might never see again.

And yet when I did get my sight back, when I did see what was going on, I almost wished I had gone blind.

The person under the sheets wasn't Neil.

Lying there, in Neil's cot, was a naked old man with a body like a featherless turkey, wrinkled and pale.

I recoiled in horror, falling to the ground and sliding backwards on my behind before my body seized up completely. I was cold. Paralysed. It was like someone had taken an Abbey Beckett voodoo doll, plunged it into a bucket of ice water, and squeezed it so hard it split at the seams.

The old man threw off the bed sheets and turned to me. His face was like something from *Fangoria* Magazine, long and sharp, and covered in yellowed, waxy flesh stretched tighter than drum skin. A wisp of white hair clung to his withered scalp like a feather stuck to the top of a rotten egg.

'Hello, Abbey,' he said.

It was Judas, the vampire lord himself, and I wasn't in The Vault, I was within his innermost sanctum, a featureless, white-walled room so dazzling I could barely see through the cracks of my eyelids.

Judas came closer, moving with surprising grace, swaying to a music only he could hear. I tried to retreat, tried to scream, but my body was fixed in place, my mouth a locked cage.

He stepped closer, then moved away, then closer again, arms sweeping back and forth like a couple of lazy pendulums.

Finally, I forced out some words. 'Get the fuck away from me,' I hissed.

I tried recalling the dagger to my hand, but nothing came. I was unarmed.

Judas pushed his face close to mine, so close that I could make out the individual creases of his papery hide. So close that I could map the liver spot continents of his egg-bald head. I felt a hot spike of bile in my throat and gagged.

'What's wrong?' asked Judas. 'Aren't you pleased to see me?'

'What did you do with Neil?' I barked, still rooted to the spot.

'Oh, he's perfectly safe,' Judas replied. 'Back in the real world.'

Real world? I was just dreaming. But then why wasn't I waking up?

Judas smiled, his teeth as white as piano keys. 'You're trying to work out why you're still asleep, aren't you?' His amber eyes bored into me. 'I can see your thoughts, Abbey. See them plain as day. To me, you are an open door.'

Judas had been inside my mind before. Just as I'd invaded his inner sanctum, he'd infiltrated my consciousness, made me see things, tried convince me to take my own life. And now here he was again, violating me while I slept, raiding my dreams.

'What's the matter?' he asked, tilting his head to one side. 'Does my visage displease you?'

The look on my face must have told him everything he needed to know, because without the need of an answer, he began to change.

His waxy, yellowed skin split like tree bark, revealing a layer of new flesh beneath, pink as a newborn baby's. Thick hairs sprouted from his scalp until he was decorated with a lush head of raven-black hair. His amber eyes melted into a soft caramel colour, vibrant and piercing. In less than a minute, Judas had transformed from a withered, disgusting old man to the type of bloke who whispered inspirational quotes to himself at the gym. He clicked his fingers and suddenly he was wearing a tailored suit and designer shoes.

'There, is that better?' he asked. 'I can be anything I want here, Abbey, and I can come to you at my leisure. We are linked now, the two of us. Bound together like a knot.'

Anger rose within me, and my blood began to thaw. I found my voice. 'Who did it? Who carved up my boyfriend?'

Judas grinned at me wolfishly. 'Now, where would the fun be in telling you that?'

'What are you, scared? I thought you lot were meant to be tough, and you're worried about giving me one little name?'

A laugh rattled in his throat. 'You think us scared? Girl, we are darkness, we are beasts of prey, unbound by earthly rules, taking from you as we please. Scared? We are fear itself.'

'Bollocks, mate. Look at you, you're nothing to get in a twist about. You call yourself a predator, but you're a parasite. You act all rock star but you don't even have the guts to face me in person. I'm not scared of you, old man, I pity you. You're just a corpse that doesn't know any better.'

His features contorted, eyes caving in until they were completely black, jaw unhinging so wide I thought his face would split open like a seam of fabric, then from inside the void of his mouth came a scream so horrible, so utterly terrifying, that it left me feeling like I'd given birth to a block of ice.

'Your time is at an end!' he said. 'The Clan will rise up, the trumpets of Revelation will play, and The Reaping will begin. Soon we will own everything. Consume everything. And when we have drained this world dry and left it a husk, we will kick down the doors of Heaven and feast upon the flesh of the angels.'

'Not if I have anything to say about it,' I replied, though I didn't sound very convincing, even to myself.

'On the contrary,' he replied, 'you will be the one who makes all of this possible.' He placed his hands behind his back like he was about to present me with a gift, and when he brought them back again, his fingers were tipped with giant, glistening syringes. 'You are the key to it all, Abbey. I will kill everyone you love, I will burn this world to the ground, and will do it with your blood pumping in my veins.'

He lunged forward, sticking me with the needles, and drained my body to a hollow shell.

6

I was back in the room, back in my bed, head pounding, mouth as dry as cotton.

'Neil.'

I flipped over and there he was, in his cot across the other side of the room. He grunted, still asleep, and pulled his covers over his head. His respirator hissed, and his breathing came steady and strong.

I let out a long sigh. My phone laid on the bedside table, my jeans and dagger on the floor, right where I'd left them. You might think this would be a good moment for me to have taken a breath and let the tension leave my body, but I was way too fired up for that. Oh no, this camel's back was officially broken.

I whipped off the blankets, tugged on my clothes, and pushed through the bedroom door. Moments later, I was barging into The Vault's War Room like I was about to announce a fire.

Vizael sat at the round table fiddling at something with a pair of pliers, while nearby, Gendith played a game of Patience with naked lady cards.

'What the hell is this?' I demanded.

They turned to me as one.

'What's the matter?' Viz asked.

'We have vampires to kill and you're sitting around like it's peacetime, playing cards and pissing about with handicrafts.

We've got to up our game, people! Seriously, the paint in this place is watching *you* dry.'

Gen played another card without looking up from her game. 'What exactly is it you want us to do?'

'I want you to help me find Judas so I can kick his teeth in,' I replied, 'right now.'

'Really,' said Gen. 'Don't you at least want to take a shower first?'

Viz hobbled over and gestured for me to take a seat next to him on the sofa. His thick, white eyebrows were high with concern. 'What is it, Abbey? Why this sudden need to face off against Judas?'

'Isn't that the mission?' I replied, my voice like a knife. 'To kill the head of the Clan?'

'No,' said Viz, 'the mission right now is to terminate the magician who notched a death threat in Neil's flesh.'

'Forget about that, let's skip to the end and take out the big boss.'

Viz shook his snow-capped head. 'Even in his weakened state, Judas poses far too big of a threat.'

I threw up my arms. 'I met him once and walked away, didn't I? Just get me into that hidey hole of his and let me at him.'

Gen sashayed over and took an armchair opposite us. 'I've been by your side for weeks, watching you fight. Vizael is right. You don't have the goods; not yet.'

I bounded to my feet, spring-loaded. 'You wanna try me, tough stuff?'

'Oh, please,' she replied, wafting a hand in front of her face, 'you have a long way to go before you're ready for that battle. Good Lord, you haven't even learned all of your powers yet.'

'I've learned enough.'

'You have no idea. You are meant to have the gymnastic prowess of an Olympic athlete by now, but your movements are dull and flat-footed. Your sword skills should be second to none, but they're pedestrian at best.'

Viz chimed in. 'And you haven't even begun to learn the Lazarus hand.'

'The what now?' I asked.

'When you have really dedicated yourself to this job, when you have fully mastered your powers, you will be able to use the brand to revive the dead.'

I stared at the N on my palm. 'Seriously? Like, bring people back to life?'

'Provided they have only recently crossed over, and the damage they have sustained isn't too catastrophic, yes.'

Wow. I sunk into the sofa to contemplate what it would feel like to wield that kind of power. The power over life and death.

'The point of me telling you this,' Viz went on, 'is that you are still learning the ropes. Master your powers, then we will talk about confronting Judas.'

But his words only succeeded in spurring me on. That's the way I am – if you want me to do something, all you have to do is say no.

'Don't you get it?' I said. 'This is an arms race. The longer I wait, the more powerful Judas becomes. The time to strike is now, before he's up and running.'

Viz leaned forward, hands propped on his cane, his angel-blue eyes soft with concern. 'What is this really about, Abbey? Why the sudden urge to take on the Clan's master?'

'I saw him last night. Judas. He came to me in a sort of vision thing.'

'Are you sure it wasn't just a cheese dream?' asked Gen. 'I've seen the inside of our fridge, and it's mostly yellow.'

'It wasn't a dream,' I shot back. 'He was in my head, talking to me.'

She turned up her nose. 'Oh, yes? And what did he say?'

'Not a lot. Just trying to wind me up. Get under my skin.'

Viz's forehead folded like a concertina. 'I should examine you to make sure no harm can come of this.'

'If he wanted to hurt me, he would have,' I said. 'Anyway, you're right, Judas can wait. We should stick to the job at hand and find that magician.'

Venting some spleen had brought me a measure of lucidity. I wasn't ready to face Judas, I could see that now. One little visit in my sleep and he'd made a wreck of me. The magician though, that was another matter. All I needed was to get my hands on him.

Viz smiled. 'Very well, what do you propose?'

'I want to go back to the point we lost that lead. The runner. Maybe in the cold light of day I can pick up the trail.'

'Good idea,' Viz replied.

'I already combed that whole area,' said Gen. 'Trust me, the trail is cold.'

'Perhaps,' said Viz, 'or perhaps you weren't looking through the right lens.'

'Come again?' said Gen, balling her hands into fists and burying them in her hips.

'The whereabouts of Judas' sanctum is a mystery,' Viz replied, 'but the same needn't be true of our errant magician.'

He swept his arm to The Vault's back door; the magic one we'd had the eaves build us. 'Why don't you push that open and I'll show you what I mean?'

My eyes went to the door, then back to the old man. 'Okay, then,' I said, making for the portal.

'Are you sure you don't want to invite your boyfriend along?' Gen teased.

I turned my ear back to the bedroom and heard typing—angry typing—the kind Neil made when he was pissed off. He was obviously busy venting some spleen of his own. Best to leave him be, I reckoned.

'Grab your kit and let's go,' I said.

I ushered Gen and Viz through the portal, stepped through to the other side, and closed the door quietly behind me.

7

On the other side of the door, the rain beat down like we were something unpleasant God was trying to hose off of His decking.

Gendith squeezed her afro under her hood. 'There's no way we're finding anything in this mess.'

It certainly didn't look promising. The storm had erased any trace of the dead vampire, to the point that not even a speck of ash remained.

Viz tapped his walking stick on the cobbles. 'The reason we're not seeing a trail is because the trail is invisible.'

'Okay, so how are we supposed to follow something invisible?' I asked.

'Something you said before set a thought clanging in my head. You asked me how the vampires knew where to go after they'd broken free of a plague pit, and I told you I didn't know. Oh, I had my suspicions—a pheromone they were drawn to maybe, some in-built homing instinct—but nothing I'd ever put to the test. At least not until now.'

He reached into his white suit jacket and produced an antique pendant on a long, thin chain. He handed it to me and I studied it in my palm. The pendant was round, made of solid silver, and embedded with a small green gemstone.

Gen cocked an eyebrow. 'And that piece of costume jewellery is going to solve our problems how?'

Viz continued, unperturbed. 'Put it on,' he told me.

I draped the pendant around my neck and let it sit on my chest. It clashed a bit with my pewter bird skull necklace, but fashion was going to have to take a back bench on this one.

'Is it working?' I asked.

Everything seemed the same to me. It was only when I looked up from the pendant that I saw the world had changed.

Stretching off down the alley was a thick tendril of swirling grey smoke.

'What is that?' I asked.

'That,' said Viz, grinning with pride, 'is magic.'

The tendril hung in place like something from a cartoon; a nose-twitching aroma that picked a hobo off his feet and carried him to a tasty window ledge pie. 'Magic, eh?'

'Yes,' Viz replied, a twinkle in his eye. 'And where there is magic, there is apt to be a magician.'

Someone was laying those breadcrumb trails. Someone was making paths for the freshly-risen vamps to follow. Maybe someone with the kind of sorcery that could carve words into a man's chest.

'You've been busy,' I told Viz, impressed.

'Of course,' he replied. 'Why, what did you think I was doing? Handicraft?'

'No! Well, a bit,' I admitted. 'Okay then, what do we do now?'

'Now we terminate a magician,' Viz replied.

'Sounds like a tip-top plan to me,' I replied and set off, following the smoke tendril, out of the alleyway, off to wherever it might lead.

'Well, would you look at that?' I said, glancing over my shoulder at Gen. 'A Grindr for spell-slingers...'

By the time we arrived at our destination the rain had eased up, leaving behind a low grey sky that robbed all joy from our hearts. Just another day in London town.

The breadcrumb trail lead us to a Gothic two-storey building in Aldgate; an old mission hall according to some info I pulled up on my phone. The building's windows were boarded over.

'What is this place?' I asked.

Gen drew my attention to a cornerstone mounted by the front door. 'The Society of the Black Sun,' she said, reading out the inscription. 'An old boys' club.'

'Of course it is,' I sighed. 'Why are they always men; the vamps, I mean? You never see a lady vampire, do you?'

The question hung there, unanswered.

'Why don't you use your Nightstalker vision to give us a picture of what's inside?' Viz suggested.

I tried, but it didn't help. The walls were infused with an impenetrable blackness, as though they had been insulated with crude oil. 'I can't see anything,' I said. 'It's like looking into a black hole.'

'The walls must be masked with concealment magic,' said Viz, tutting with annoyance.

I shook my head and my eyesight returned to normal. 'Whatever. I don't need to know what's in there to beat the crap out of it.'

'Don't be so trigger happy,' said Gen. 'So long as we're entering into unknown territory, we need a plan of action. I suggest we make a precision infiltration and converge on the enemy using a staggered two-front manoeuvre.'

'Right,' I said. 'Or we could just walk in through the open door there…'

I pushed and it swung open with a lusty creak. The entrance was hanging off its wrought iron hinges, as though someone had taken to it with a battering ram.

Viz shrugged, Gen shrugged, and the three of us stepped inside.

It took my eyes a couple of seconds to adjust to the murkiness of the building's dingy foyer. The wood-panelled walls were decorated with animal trophies and oil paintings of old men in frilly tunics and ruffs. Hanging from the ceiling was an ornate chandelier, dripping with fine crystal.

Something smelled. Smelled *bad*. 'What is that?' I whispered, covering my nose with the sleeve of my jacket. It stank like rotting meat and emptied bowels. My stomach heaved. What kind of sick shit were the members of this club into?

'Anyone else wondering why the door wasn't locked?' asked Gen.

We drew our weapons and pushed on. Using the pendant to guide us, we followed the smoke tendril deeper into the building until we arrived in a large meeting room with a flagstone floor, a fireplace big enough to park a bus in, and wallpaper made of better stuff than most wedding dresses. The detail that really jumped out at me though, was the bodies.

A couple of dozen vampires lay strewn about the place, scattered in various contorted poses, all of them torn to shreds. Milky, dead eyes stared helplessly from slashed faces, lipless mouths hung unhinged. Flecks of doughy white maggots squirmed within mangled flesh, feverishly tunnelling into hunks of gore. The bodies were a couple of days old at least and had begun to turn into bad cheese.

'Jesus wept,' I gasped.

'Language,' Vizael replied.

I managed to overcome the shock pretty quickly. This wasn't my first massacre. Not by a long shot, unfortunately.

I picked my way through the carpet of torn-up bodies, following the smoke tendril to its point of origin. The floor was sticky with blood, the bodies so numerous and disjointed that avoiding them was like tiptoeing through a great, fleshy minefield.

There.

The tendril terminated at a single body lying face-down in gore. The end of a very grisly rainbow. The body was missing all of its limbs; a torso with a head was all that were left. From the looks of the bloody stumps that stuck out from the torn sleeves of the corpse's suit—a suit that cost more than your car—the appendages had been slashed away, clawed off with the raw strength of an angry bear.

I reached down, gathered a fistful of the vamp's jacket, and flipped the body over. An unfamiliar face stared up at me. His fangs were out and his eyes were blood red, meaning he'd died in full-on monster mode. The fella had obviously gone down swinging, not that it had done him much good. Besides having his limbs ripped off, his belly was split wide open and emptied of guts.

I stooped to examine him closer. So, this was it. This was the guy. This was my magician.

Or was it?

'How do we know this was the vamp who cut Neil?' I asked my companions. 'Are we sure these aren't just more worker bees?'

'These are no mere soldiers,' said Gen, probing the lingering auras of the dead. 'These were captains.' She stood up straight. 'This was a gathering of some of the Clan's best and brightest.'

Whoever made this mess was obviously a big player. 'Who did it then?' I asked. 'Who filleted all these Draculas? And why?'

Viz coughed. 'Perhaps this might be a clue,' he said, pointing to an unexplored corner of the room.

There, in a nook, written on the ground in great loops of human intestines, was a message:

Blood for blood.

I looked back at the magician's open belly and realised he'd been made to contribute bodily to the killer's grim cursive.

'Looks like he wasn't our man after all,' said Gen, stating the obvious.

For the briefest moment I actually felt a sense of relief. Of excitement even. Whoever carved up Neil was still out there, and that meant I still got to make them suffer.

Then I thought about it some more and felt sick. The person I was looking for had torn apart a whole room full of people just to send me a message. A room full of Clansman no less, emptying their bellies of their intestines like a magician pulling out silk scarves. What kind of a vampire kills fellow vampires just to make a point? Exactly how badly had I pissed this turd off that they'd be prepared to do this?

Whoever the culprit was, I'd well and truly wandered into their sniper scope. How did they know I'd come here? Was it because I'm the Nightstalker, and the Nightstalker and dead vampires go hand in hand? Or was I being watched? Were there eyes on me right now, spying from the shadows, waiting to pounce?

I'd wanted to take the fight to the person who harmed Neil, but now I was here, now I'd seen what they were capable of, I was beginning to wonder if I'd bitten off more than I could chew. It would take a total monster to have caused this much destruction, and now I could feel their breath, hot on my neck.

'I've found something,' said Gendith, dipping a hand into the cored belly of the corpse at the end of the smoke trail. 'Here.'

She showed me an object held between her forefinger and thumb: a false fingernail, long and talon-like, like a porn star's. Painted on it was an unfamiliar symbol, gold on black. Thanks to the pendant Viz had made me, I could see the glow of magic it gave off. Powerful magic, bright enough to make me wince. I took the fingernail from Gen and shoved it into my jacket pocket.

'Let's get out of here,' I said. Fear had found me, making my legs go weak and my stomach lurch. 'Let's get out of here right now.'

8

Out in the cool night air, away from the nauseating stench of blood and rot, the swell of panic subsided. Whoever was doing this—whoever it was leaving me death threats spelled out in flesh and guts—they were going to wind up on the wrong end of my dagger; that was a promise.

I turned to Gen. 'So, to summarise, we went into an old boys' club looking for the person who carved up Neil, only the person who *actually* did it wasn't the one we thought it was, and had already killed the person we had it pinned on?'

'Correct,' Gen replied.

'Wow. We're really failing upwards.'

'Yes. And now, with the fingernail, we have a clue to work with.'

About bloody time. Finally, we were making progress. Finally, we weren't chasing our tails anymore.

We decided the next best move would be to visit our vampire informant, Carlo, to find out what he knew about magical manicures. Given that we weren't too far from home base, it would have been quicker to get to him through our magic portal than it was taking the Underground, but I wasn't interested in taking the shortcut. Taking the shortcut would have meant dealing with Neil, and that was a headache I was happy to move down the schedule.

So, while Vizael returned to The Vault to make his own investigative inroads, Gendith and I did our Miss Marple shit with Carlo.

As we set off, a thought occurred. 'Do we even know where Carlo is? Didn't the council demolish the place he was squatting in a couple of weeks back?'

'Don't worry,' said Gen, fishing a piece of paper from her pocket, 'he left us a forwarding address.' She pulled out another piece of paper, then another. 'About fifty times in fact.'

After a long and boring journey we arrived in an urban scrubland on the wrong side of the London Orbital; all knee-high weeds, scattered concrete buildings, and skeletal electricity pylons. A giant, canary yellow shed made of corrugated metal stood in the middle of a crop of derelict warehouses, right next to a motorway flyover.

'A storage unit? Carlo's living in a storage unit?'

'You could almost feel sorry for him, couldn't you?' Gen replied.

'Almost.'

The big yellow storage shed stood ahead of us like a gleaming gold filling in a mouth full of rotten teeth. Gen led me into the building and down a series of low, breeze block corridors lined either side by metal shutters. She stopped by the entrance of one of the storage units and rapped on it with her knuckle.

'I'd cover your nose if I were you,' she said.

'Why?' I asked, and got my answer almost instantly.

The moment the shutter shot open, I was assaulted with a smell that could have stripped paint.

Carlo stood before me wearing an oily denim waistcoat decorated with a faded Motörhead patch. A skunk stripe fought a path through dark, matted hair that matched the colour of his eye bags. The man was so frail he was almost transparent. He looked doomed; a mangy, half-feathered pigeon with stumps for feet.

'What up, blood?' I asked, forcing a laugh. 'Get it? Because you're a vampire?'

Gen shook her head contemptuously. 'You're lucky you have your looks.'

Carlo stared at me with wild, blood-shot eyes. 'Abbey! I

thought I'd lost you!' He wrapped his arms around me and gathered me up in a bear hug. 'It's so good to see you.'

'And what am I?' asked Gen. 'Chopped liver?'

Carlo set me down. 'I don't know that you're as useful as all that,' he replied. 'At least livers have blood.' His tongue flashed across his lips.

He beckoned us inside his... I hesitate to call it a home... more like a lair; closer to an animal's den than a place a human being would lay their head. I scanned the unit's dingy interior, which was lit by a solitary lamp clipped to a car battery. Except for a half-deflated blow-up mattress, some dirty laundry, and a handful of Eighties vinyl scattered across the concrete floor, Carlo had nothing. It was hard to imagine, but somehow these new digs of his were even grimmer than the squat we'd found him lurking in last time.

'I went looking for you at the gas tower,' he blurted, a note of panic in his voice. 'Every day I went looking.'

'But that place burned down weeks ago,' I replied.

'I know,' he screeched, 'but I didn't know where else to go.' He shot Gendith an evil look. 'Why didn't you return any of my messages? I thought we were friends.'

Gen examined her cuticles. 'How about we have less bitching and more snitching?'

'Whatever,' Carlo replied, 'as long as I get my taste.'

As usual, the info I was after was going to cost me. To kill the owner of that fingernail, I'd need to pay for his whereabouts. *Blood for Blood.* Everything in my life seemed to revolve around the stuff.

'You'll get your taste,' I told Carlo, 'but first I need to know about the vamp who's rocking this look...' I showed him the black fingernail with its gold, runic inscription.

'You're telling me this belonged to a Clansman?' he said.

I nodded and he raised an eyebrow. 'Well then, if I were you, I'd start with crossdressers.'

'Why a crossdresser?' I asked. 'Why not a woman?'

He looked to Gendith, then back to me. 'Because there are no female Clansmen, Abbey. Didn't you know that? The clue's kind of in the name. Clans*men*.'

Gen nodded. 'He's right.'

No wonder I hadn't seen any lady vamps on the end of my dagger.

'I don't get it. Don't dead women crawl out of those plague pits too?'

'No, and we don't know why,' Gen replied. 'All we know is that the corruption transmitted in Judas' blood only affects those with an XY pair of chromosomes.'

'And you didn't think to mention any of this on the way here?'

Gen shrugged. 'I suppose I'm not as hung up on gender as you obviously are.'

I thought about it some more. 'What about once the vamps have risen? Can't they go on to make lady vamps?'

'Same deal,' Gen replied. 'It's in the blood. The Clan are men only.'

'Actually,' interjected Carlo, 'that's not strictly true...'

'Oh come on,' said Gen, waving him off with her hand. 'That was an age ago.'

'What?' I asked. 'What was?'

Gen sighed. 'Back at the turn of the first Millennium—after centuries of fruitless attempts—Judas did succeed in siring a female. A single vampire countess, born of his blood, bred and raised to be his bride. A vampire by the name of Savina.'

'So... a daughter slash wife? Ugh, that's nasty.' I turned to Carlo. 'You people are messed up, you know that?'

Carlo raised his hands. 'Preaching to the choir, love.'

I returned my attention to Gen. 'I don't get it though; how did Judas make a lady vamp in the first place? You just told me the Clan were one big sausage party.'

'Who can say how Savina came to be?' Gen replied. 'She was a freak birth. A one-of-a-kind aberration.'

'Again,' said Carlo, raising a hand, 'that's not one-hundred percent true—'

'I was just getting to that,' Gen huffed. She took a breath, then returned to her story. 'In time, Savina broke away from her sire and went on to create her own progeny. Over the centuries, she was responsible for creating a number of female vampires, and together they formed a breakaway faction, separate from the Clan.'

'I'm betting Judas wasn't too chuffed about that,' I said.

'No, he was not,' Gen replied. 'In fact, when he discovered Savina's treachery, he ordered the capture of her entire coterie. One by one, Savina and her people were rounded up, tied to stakes, and put to death. So you see, there are no female Clan members in the UK, which makes this history lesson little more than a pointless diversion.'

Now it was Carlo's turn to shrug. 'Says you. Me, I like the details. Brings the history alive.'

I propped against a wall and considered what I'd learned. Could some other creature have been responsible for tearing up that old boys' club? What about a werewolf? My understanding—at least going by what I'd gathered from Neil's books, which had proved freakishly accurate so far—was that werewolves and vampires were always going at it. What if one of those had wolfed out and torn up those vamps? Or could it have been someone like me? Some rogue slayer with a beef against blood-suckers? No, neither of those theories made any sense. The *Blood for Blood* message was meant for me specifically, and I was pretty sure I hadn't rubbed any werewolves the wrong way. As for the rogue slayer theory, that was just wishful thinking. I was on my own out there. Just me and my holy handlers, fighting the battle for Heaven and Earth.

Carlo snapped his fingers at me. 'You okay, Abs, you kind of tuned out on us there. You're not sick are you? Be a shame if that blood was spoiled.' He laughed nervously. 'Who am I kidding, I'd drink that stuff if it was dipped in dog shit.' He made unconscious chewing motions, like a dog waiting on his food bowl.

Gen hooked a hand on Carlo's scrawny shoulder. 'You won't be getting a drop of blood until you tell us who that fingernail belongs to.'

'How should I know?' he bleated. 'Do I look like I hang around with crossdressers?' He caught himself. 'Not that I'm making any judgments...'

A string of curses unraveled from my tongue. Another wasted

trip. 'Come on, Gen,' I said, heading for the door, 'we're wasting our time here.'

'Stop,' Carlo yowled.

'What?' I replied.

'The fingernail,' he said, scratching at himself, eyes wild and pleading, 'what if instead of trying to work out who it belonged to, we worked out where it came from?'

'Okay,' I said, 'so where's that then?'

'I don't know,' he replied, exasperated. 'I know the Clan, not manicurists.'

Gen harrumphed. 'Looking at the state of you, I'd say you could use a manicure, not to mention a haircut and about ten laps in a pool of Dettol.'

Carlo scowled at her. 'Is that any way to talk to your host? I know it doesn't look like much, but you are a guest in my home, Gen. Have some respect.'

I let them squabble while I held the fingernail to Carlo's solitary lamp, inspecting it up close. The detail of the rune was exquisite, its paintwork precise and beautifully rendered. 'I think he's on to something,' I said. 'This is a pro job. Surely there can't be too many people out there doing high-end magical manicures like this?'

Gen thought on it, then bobbed her head in agreement. 'We can work with that.'

The game was afoot. We had enough to get moving with now, and besides, our noses couldn't stand another minute trapped inside Carlo's sordid little grief hole.

'Here,' I said, tossing him a phial of Nightstalker blood. 'Don't use it all at once.'

But before I'd even finished my sentence, he'd necked the lot and sunk into his half-inflated mattress. 'Ah, that's the stuff,' he gasped, interlocking his fingers and placing his hands behind his head.

I turned to leave. 'See you around, Carlo.'

'Wait, don't go,' he cried, suddenly animated. 'Where's this new base of yours? How do I get in touch with you guys?'

'You don't,' said Gen, and turned away from him too.

Carlo sprang to his feet, scrambled for the unit's only way

out, and spread his arms wide, blocking our exit.

'Move aside, vampire,' Gen hissed.

Carlo held firm. 'It's not a big deal. I just need an address, that's all.'

I reached into my jacket for the hilt of my dagger. 'I like you, Carlo, but if you don't get out of my way right now, I'm going to go through you like a dodgy curry.'

Ridges sprang up on his face and the blacks of his eyes widened to the size of ten pence pieces. His lips peeled back, revealing an extended set of canines, slick with saliva—

Then all at once he was Carlo again. A swift wipe of a hand across his face and he'd returned to normal. In a flash, he'd changed from a rabid animal back to a bedraggled, pitiable man, as pathetic as he was harmless. 'Sorry about that, ladies,' he said, stepping aside. 'Got myself a bit hot under the collar there. All better now.'

He tried to pass off his behaviour with a wonky smile, but I wouldn't soon forget what I'd seen that day. I'd glimpsed a side of Carlo that I hadn't known before – an evil lurking beneath the surface, like a snake in tall grass. Carlo might not have been Clan, but one thing was for sure, he was all vampire.

Gen and I ducked under the shutter and I drew it closed it behind us.

'Come back soon,' we heard Carlo say, struggling to be heard over the rattle of the metal. 'Don't be strangers!'

I slammed the shutter to the ground and we made off down the breeze block corridor, back the way we came.

'Is he going to be okay?' I asked.

'He'll be fine,' Gen replied.

'That was a bit mean, wasn't it, what we did back there.'

'We only did what needed to be done.'

I chewed my bottom lip. 'I don't know. Do you think we should have just told him about the new base?'

Gen shook her head. 'I may not understand much of this new world, Abbey—your obsession with small dogs, your constant need for validation, why any adult would want to own a selfie stick—but I do know this for certain; you never *ever* give a junkie your home address.'

9

We headed back to base to see if Vizael had anything to contribute to The Case of the Magical Manicurist.

'You handled that well,' said Gendith, as we walked the final leg home.

'I'm sorry,' I replied, taken aback. 'Was that... a compliment?'

Delivered by anyone else, I would have taken those words for a bit of friendly reassurance, but coming out of Gen's mouth, they sounded gilt with gold. To the best of my recollection, Gen had complimented me on precisely two occasions since I'd known her, and one of those I'm pretty sure was sarcastic.

'It was hardly a compliment,' she scoffed. 'I just meant that it's good to see you taking your role as the Nightstalker a bit more seriously.'

More seriously than all the other times I'd thrown my bone marrow in the meat grinder in service of the job? Whatever. Gen was dishing out praise, and that's all I cared about. A compliment. *An actual compliment.* Whatever next?

'You were good too,' I said. 'I mean, not that you aren't always good. I don't know how you do it really, no matter what gets thrown our way, you're always so calm and focused.'

'Well,' she replied, 'to be fair, I have been around a lot longer than you.'

'How long exactly?'

'Since the Seventeenth Century,' she replied, then her voice dropped. 'But I think we've heard enough history for one day.'

One little morsel of backstory and she was already clamming up on me. I tried my luck to see if I could tease out any more titbits. 'You know, Gen, whether you like it or not, one of these days I'm going to figure you out.'

She looked back at me with an unknowable smile. 'What is it you wish to know exactly?'

'Oh, loads of stuff!' I said. 'Like, how did you wind up being an angel? Why were you kicked out of Heaven? And what's the deal with you and Viz?'

Gen measured her words carefully. 'I was made an angel after I was martyred. After that, God assigned me to Vizael to help him combat the Judas Clan.'

'You missed out the part about why you got the boot from Heaven.'

'Perhaps another time,' she replied, pointing her eyes to the ground as we walked down the steps into The Vault.

Seemed that was all I was getting for today, but at least it was something. Gen wasn't exactly an open book yet, but the spine was starting to crack.

'No worries,' I told her. 'I wouldn't want to interfere with the whole brooding amazon thing you've got going on there.'

She punched me playfully in the arm and I dug a knuckle into her shoulder.

'Well, well,' said Vizael as we entered The Vault's common room, palling around. 'Look at the two of you getting along. I'm not sure I like it. It's all quite unsettling, really.'

Gen collapsed on the sofa. 'What have you got there, old man?' she asked, pointing to the book sat in his lap.

He showed us its cover, which read BOOK OF RUNES. 'I've been doing some research on the fingernail we recovered, and I think I've identified the magical inscription painted upon it.' He flipped to a bookmarked page and showed us a sketch that was a dead match for the symbol on the nail. 'A rune of wounding,' he explained. 'An enchantment imbued with powerful magic designed to cause grievous physical damage to its victim.'

That explained how the nail's owner had been able to tear

apart all those vampires so efficiently. 'What are we talking?' I asked, flopping on the sofa next to Gen. 'Vampire magic?'

'No,' he replied. 'This is the work of a specialist enchanter.'

'Who?'

'I have no idea, and whoever they are, I can't imagine they're in the business of advertising themselves.'

'Why not?' I asked. 'If you could make magical fingernails that turned people into mincemeat, wouldn't you want to make some money from it? I know I would.'

'That's a good point,' he conceded, scratching his head and dislodging some dandruff. 'Why didn't I think of that?'

'Because you're a doddering, senile old man,' said Gen, somewhat unhelpfully.

Ironically, Viz didn't hear her, possibly because he wasn't wearing his ear trumpet. He hobbled over to one of his many bookshelves, made a selection, and returned with a thick tome the size of a phone book. 'So, you're looking for a merchant, correct? Someone who trades their services for money?'

'I suppose so, yeah.'

'Well, this is a listing of all of the supernatural vendors operating in the Greater London area. Just think of it as a sort of... Uncanny Yellow Pages.'

So, not just the size of a phone book, but an *actual* phone book.

Viz leafed through the pages until he arrived at the section listing Nail Salons. 'There,' he said triumphantly. 'Two establishments that cater exclusively to the Uncanny. If your theory about the enchanter being a merchant is correct, we have succeeded in narrowing the nail's provenance down to two possible sources.'

How about that? Off-the-map nail salons for London's weird and wonderful. There really was something for everyone in this city. A whole new world to explore. Maybe one day, when I wasn't too busy slaughtering vampires and fighting for my life, I'd take a little tour and check out the sights.

'Okay then,' I said, getting to my feet, 'let's go see some nail salons.'

'Not now,' Gendith replied, stifling a yawn. 'Look at the time, girl.'

I did. It was late. Gone midnight late.

Viz agreed with his fellow angel. 'Get some sleep, Abbey. You can continue the investigation in the morning.'

I supposed it did make sense to stage my visit during opening hours, while the person doing the enchanting was present (provided this merchant theory of mine held water, and that the person who painted the rune really was flogging their talents for cash). Besides, if I was being honest with myself, the main reason I was in such a hurry to get out of The Vault wasn't so much about what I was looking for, but who I was avoiding.

Neil.

We were well overdue an argument, and, sadly, there was no running from it.

'I know what you're going to say,' I told him as I stepped into the bedroom, hands held up in surrender. 'You're pissed off with me. I shouldn't have snuck off without you before. You're right, I'm a terrible girlfriend, you can say it.'

Neil was across the other side of the room, sat on his bed, propped up against the headboard and reading from his Kindle. He set the device down and looked up at me. 'I *am* pissed off with you, Abbey. You shouldn't have snuck off like that. But you're not a terrible girlfriend.' He patted the mattress, beckoning me over, and I plonked myself down on the bedspread beside him. He shifted his weight from one buttock to the other, searching for the right words. 'Look, I get it. All of this chasing, all of this fighting, I know you're only doing it for me. And you're right, I shouldn't have involved myself in the mission like that, not without you knowing. I'm sorry, that was stupid.'

'It wasn't stupid, Neil. You killed a vampire on your first try. In any other situation you'd have been given a medal for that, and all I did was shout at you for it.'

'It's okay,' he replied, placing a hand over mine. 'It's fine.'

'It's not fine. You've put up with so much already and I've treated you like shit.'

He squeezed my palm. 'You're sorry, I'm sorry... why don't we both do ourselves a favour and let it go?'

'I'd like that,' I said.

'Okay then,' he said, holding out his hand, 'truce?'

'Truce.' I knocked his hand aside, wrapped my arms around him, and gathered him up in a long, indefinite hug.

'Easy,' he wheezed, 'I might need these ribs.'

Remembering my strength, I loosened my grip. 'Sorry about that, you big Jessie.'

As we sat there, staring into each other's eyes, he traced a thumb along the N scorched into my palm. 'I just realised, we both have scars now.'

We did. Whether we liked it or not, we were in this thing together.

'Hey, Abbey?'

'What?'

'Wanna push the beds together tonight?'

'What kind of a girl do you take me for, mister?' I said, leaning towards his mouth.

And then I ate the face off him.

10

The sun came up reluctantly the next morning, barely illuminating a sky grey as a dead whale. Not that I minded. Since I'd made up with Neil, I had a song in my heart and a whistle on my lips. I also had a mission: crash those nail salons, find out who that manicure belonged to, and extract my pound of flesh.

Having reviewed Vizael's Uncanny Yellow Pages, it was decided that Gendith would scope out one nail salon, while I investigated the other. Gendith headed to the Kingsland Road to make enquiries at a Korean salon, and while she was busy doing that, I made my way to Hackney to try my luck at a Vietnamese place.

Kims Nails (along with its maddeningly errant apostrophe) was located at 23b Well Street, not far from Homerton Station. Or at least that was the idea. When I arrived at my destination—a grotty, East London street with a short parade of shops, half of which were abandoned and fly postered—I discovered that the address didn't even have the decency to exist. There was a 23a and a 23c, but no sign of a 23b.

'Bollocks,' I muttered, pacing back and forth. 'Big bollocks.'

I checked across the road, I checked either end of the parade, I all but checked under a manhole cover, but there was no sign of a nail salon anywhere.

I returned to the space the salon should be, a spot between a defunct dental surgery and a forsaken fancy dress shop, but there was nothing there but a bit of wall decorated with a faded yellow ADT alarm.

Then I had a thought.

Kims Nails was an Uncanny joint, not unlike the London Coven or The Beehive, both of which were concealed down blind alleys, hidden invisibly, away from prying eyes. Tucked away down secret streets, where Uncanny types could go about their business unseen.

I approached the parade and found a point equidistant from the two abandoned businesses, right about where you'd sandwich the entrance to an interdimensional nail salon. I peeled a glance over my shoulder, saw the coast was clear, and placed my right palm on the nondescript patch of wall.

'Do your thing, hand bling.'

True to form, the brand glowed hot and blue, and as it did, the wall rippled and became transparent, as though it had been transmuted into water. I checked over my shoulder again, saw I was alone, and stepped through the wall, into the space beyond.

I arrived in a gap between the buildings that shouldn't have existed; a short stretch of alleyway terminating in a door crested by a pink neon sign reading KIMS NAILS. God, that missing apostrophe was going to kill me. What I wouldn't have done for a long brush and a bucket of pink paint.

I pushed open the salon's glass door and was met by a pungent smell of coconut oil and insufficiently-masked body odour. Kims Nails wasn't a fancy, exposed-brick boudoir serving cocktails and fizz to rich society women. Kims Nails was a brightly-lit, poorly-ventilated pit, crammed elbow-to-elbow with bored-looking Vietnamese women in paper face masks.

Stacks of dog-eared beauty magazines from decades past littered the waiting area, sun-bleached photos of models fought to conceal cracks in the walls, and the linoleum floor was peeling away as if trying to extricate itself from the premises. In most respects—aside from the fact that it was hidden in an invisible alley—Kims Nails was like most cheap, inner city salons. The main thing that set it apart were the services it offered, which were written in pink marker pen upon a wonky whiteboard.

Underneath the generic in-fills, shellacs, and glitters, were some specials not seen in your typical manicurist. Big ticket items like nail jobs enchanted with runes of dexterity, glyphs of pick-pocketing, and syllabary of speed (the last of which—I naively assumed—was to help a person up their WPM, but turned out—as things often do—to be a sex thing). Kims Nails offered other services too, as indicated by the "Ask the manager for details" notice at the bottom of the white board. I was willing to bet that the rune of wounding painted on the nail we'd recovered in that vampire's belly was one such off-menu item.

The salon's proprietor sat at the counter next to an outdated computer, refreshing herself with a motorised hand-fan. The eponymous Kim was an elderly Asian lady in a silk kimono. She had a bowl haircut, a trim figure and a tiny slot of a mouth. 'Good morning,' she said, greeting me. 'How are you today?'

'Oh, you know,' I replied, 'south of okay, north of dead.'

I looked over Kim's shoulder and scanned the row of customers behind her. There were five of them, all human-looking, hands down, palms placed flat on tables like they were conducting solo séances. Nail technicians attended to each of them, nattering to one another in their native tongue, no doubt saying derogatory things about the customers whose talons they were shaping, painting, and buffing.

This was my first time setting foot in a nail salon. My personal manicure regimen consisted of a lick of self-applied black nail varnish every couple of weeks to hide the grit behind them, and that was about it. No, I was nothing at all like the women sat in those swivel chairs, their makeup pristine, their hair just so. I didn't belong in that place at all. I stuck out like a dick scrawled on the Mona Lisa

'Miss?' said Kim, growing increasingly concerned as I stared right through her.

The shop's customers turned to see what the fuss was about. I studied them, noticing a few details I hadn't before—scales on one, horns on another—but saw nothing to suggest they were connected to my case.

I returned to Kim. 'I'm looking for a man.'

'Aren't we all, my dear?' she chuckled, flashing me a devilish grin.

I scowled at her, not amused. Well, sort of amused, but not giving her the satisfaction. Not if she was in the business of equipping villains with deadly manicures anyway.

'I'm looking for a specific man. A vampire.'

At least that was the working theory. Honestly, I didn't know what I was looking for. A Clansman with a beef so bad he was prepared to hack up his own brothers just to send me a message? A renegade vampire like Carlo? Or was it something else entirely? A werewolf? A lady Van Helsing? A frickin' Pokémon?

I placed the false nail on the counter in front of Kim. 'What do you know about a crossdressing vampire who wears these?'

Kim folded her arms. 'I don't divulge the personal details of my clients. That's privileged information.'

I smiled. 'If you're waiting for me to tuck you a note, you are shit out of luck.' I drew my dagger and it fired up big and blue. 'Now, let's try that again, shall we?'

Kim panicked, dropping her hand-fan, which went skittering across the counter like a whirling dervish. The white-masked salon staff downed tools and bolted for the exit. Customers screamed, snatching up their Yves Saint Laurent clutch bags and fleeing the salon.

All except for one.

A woman with an impressive beehive hairdo stalked towards me wearing a hint of a smile, her eyes calm and emotionless. Her skin was alabaster white, her lips full but bloodless. I looked at her hands and saw ten, long black nails, each of them decorated with a gold rune that matched the one I'd placed on the shop counter. There she was. After all that treading water, I'd finally found my culprit.

I thought I was just chasing a lead. I hadn't gone to the salon expecting to find my target, but from the looks of things, she'd stopped by to get a replacement for the missing nail; the one she lost during the slaughter at the Society of the Black Sun. The same nail that she now had a full set of – talons that could tear flesh apart like it was soggy tissue paper.

The proprietor, Kim, took this as her cue to leave, stepping out from behind the counter and edging her way to the back wall. Meanwhile, the beehive-haired woman continued towards me, still wearing that half smile. The brand flared hot as she closed in, sending me a warning. Letting me know that I was in danger.

The woman came to a halt in front of me, flexing her fingers. I gripped the hilt of my dagger and it pulsed in my hand, purring at my touch like a stroked kitten. Kim gathered up her kimono and scurried for the back door, slamming it shut behind her and ramming home a half-dozen of deadbolts. Shit was about to go down. All that was missing was the serenade of a spaghetti western and the haunting rattle of spurs.

The woman with the beehive cocked her head to one side. 'So you're the Nightstalker?' she tutted. 'I always thought you'd be bigger.'

'I'm big enough, don't you worry.'

Beehive hissed and her gums sprouted a pair of white knives. A letter J glowed on her forehead: J for Judas. She was Clan after all. But that couldn't be right; there were no female vampires in the Clan, Gen had sworn by it.

'I thought you lot had all been done in,' I said.

'You thought wrong.'

It wasn't like Gen to give bad intel, but the evidence was plain to see. This sister was Clanned up, or at least she had been.

'Well, go on then.' I said. 'You cut up my man just to get my attention; you want to tell me why?'

Beehive's eyes glittered. 'Oh, that wasn't me, not even close. Compared to the one you seek, I am but a flea.'

And yet she'd still single-handedly ripped apart a room full of Clansmen on home turf. This did not bode well.

'Do you want to tell me who did do it then, because whoever they are, they forgot to sign their name.'

'I think not,' the vampire replied, a smile quirking her lips.

'So you just work for the person who did it, is that right?'

She nodded.

'Well, that's good enough for me.'

I didn't know who her boss was or why she was targetting

me, but I did know one thing for sure: the bitch standing in front of me was getting her frigging wig knocked off.

I aimed the dagger between her eyes and heaved the thing at her so fast it could have melted a tunnel through a snowdrift. Instead of trying to step aside or duck the thing, the vampire fanned her hands in front of her face and knocked the dagger clean out of the air, deflecting it into a nearby mirror. The glass shattered, its pieces tinkling off a ceramic sink as it showered to the ground.

Beehive tutted. 'That's seven years bad luck.'

'Better that than only having seven seconds to live,' I said, recalling my weapon and stomping her way.

I lashed out at her with the blade, but the metal glanced off her talons with a single, pure note. The shock of the impact travelled up my arm and stung my elbow with a sudden drill-bit of pain.

Beehive went on the attack, whirling about like the Tasmanian Devil, her claws ripping through the air. I backed away, deflecting her attacks as best I could, doing what I could to make sure my blade stayed between me and her diamond-edged talons. Occasionally she would swing wide, missing me and connecting with walls, furniture, solid metal; all of which tore apart under the unrelenting savagery of her onslaught.

The vampire rained down another flurry of attacks, wearing me down bit by bit. I failed to knock aside one of her swings fast enough, and earned a swipe across the shoulder for my trouble. Blood oozed from the wound in great scarlet gushes, and I felt my stomach lurch as I staggered back, dizzy, eyes blurring. The dagger tumbled from my grasp and landed on the peeling linoleum with a dull thud.

Beehive grabbed me by my decidedly less impressive hair, and shook her head condescendingly. 'How on Earth did you wind up being the Nightstalker? Did you lose a bet or something?'

I felt my legs starting to give way beneath me, but I was determined not to pass out. If I could just stay conscious for a little while longer, the brand would take care of my wounds and I'd be back on my feet. I focussed up and felt my vision begin to return, along with the rest of my senses. I straightened up, determined to see the fight through.

'Go back to Transylvania, you stone cold bitch.'

I leaned forward, pressed my face into Beehive's chest, and bit her on the tit.

She screamed and pushed me away, but before I let go, I lobbed a headbutt her way and smashed her nose flat.

She reeled backwards, blood streaming from her nostrils, her perfect ski slope nose bent at a right angle.

She looked at me, wild-eyed, furious. 'My orders are to not kill you, girl, but I am about ready to disobey.'

'Give it your best shot, pug-face.'

Her nose began to reform, straightening out, cartilage clicking back into place until her face was pristine again. She healed like me. How was I supposed to fight that?

I took a wary step towards her and she cocked an eyebrow, daring me to take another. 'Are you sure you want to do this?' she asked. 'I won't go easy on you this time.'

'Oh, I'm sure,' I replied, scooping the dagger off the floor, its blade sparking electric blue.

Beehive smiled, touched a finger to her fully-repaired nose, and used the leftover blood to paint her cheeks warpaint red. 'Then come and get it,' she snarled.

Both of my feet left the air as I leapt across the room, dagger raised high, determined to nail the vampire to the floor. She wasn't having it though, and managed to dodge the thrust and return a backhand that almost took out an eye. I felt a tickle snake down my chin and gingerly touched my face, hoping it was sweat. My hand came away red.

I swung the dagger at Beehive in a wide arc, but she was too fast. In the blink of an eye, she managed to duck the sweep of the blade and return a slash that sawed off the lapel of my leather jacket and scored four fresh cuts across my chest. I careened to one side, hand clutching the wound, pain burning deep. I was getting torn to ribbons. Another one of those and I'd be dead from blood loss before my healing powers had any chance to stitch me back up.

'Had enough, Nightstalker?' the vampire mocked.

'I dunno,' I replied, hunched over, doing my best to stem the blood leaking out of me. 'I reckon I might have a little left.'

'Is that right?' she said making her way over to me. 'Enough for one of these?'

She lifted a high-heel and kicked down hard.

Crunch.

My leg split in two and spat out some shinbone.

It was, without a doubt, the most painful thing I'd ever experienced.

But it didn't matter. It didn't matter because it put the enemy right where I wanted her.

I flicked the dagger, extending it to full-length.

Hiss.

The hot, blue blade entered Beehive's belly like a newly-forged sword plunged into a bucket of ice water.

I held it there, the metal piercing her torso and jutting two feet out the other side.

'I got you, you toothy slag.'

I was about to twist the sword at the hilt and finish her off when she turned suddenly weightless. Instead of sliding along the blade and bumping to a stop at the hilt, she began to break apart, her body disintegrating. At first I thought she was turning to ash, but that only happens when a vampire is stuck through the heart. No, this was different. This was something else.

The disintegrated particles hung in the air, swirling about in a roughly human form, red in colour. I could make out the vampire's body, her limbs, even her head, with its grinning set of vaporous fangs. This vampire wasn't dying, she was *changing*; turning from a solid to a gas. From a person to a mist.

That was a new one. Still, nice to have a bit of variety in one's vampires, I reckoned. I'd soon get bored battling bloodsuckers if they weren't all so unique.

I swung my blade at the vampire's midriff, but it sliced harmlessly through her gaseous body. I was fighting a ghost. A vampire ghost who was in a real hurry to get gone. By now, the red mist was dissipating into a formless cloud and beginning to drift away, snaking around me, its tendrils searching for the exit.

I took a second to marvel at what I was seeing. A person

turning into gas was completely implausible. It spat in the face of science, and yet there it was, a total impossibility, making a beeline for the front door. I didn't spend too long cogitating on the phenomenon though. I'd learned from experience that when you see something crazy like that, you don't consult a peer-reviewed journal on the matter, you go after it and you club it to death.

Except I wasn't going anywhere, not with my leg snapped in half like a Kit Kat.

The red smoke disappeared through a crack under the door, leaving me sat on the shop floor, hugging my busted leg, waiting for my powers to knit my shin bones back together and close up the last of my claw wounds. It was ten minutes at least before I was fixed enough to be able to stand up though, and by that point the vamp was long gone.

'Fuck,' I hissed.

I'd made a right pudding out of that, make no mistake.

Then again...

I looked to the ancient computer behind the counter and saw a tab on the screen marked Membership Records.

I hobbled over to the door leading into the back room, the one the salon's proprietor was cowering behind, safeguarded—or so she thought—by a half-dozen deadbolts.

'Hey, magic nails lady,' I said, rapping on the door with the pommel of my dagger. 'Sorry about your shop, but I'm going to need some info on the woman who just farted her way out of your front door.'

I didn't mind threatening her, even if she was old. The woman sold weapons to villains, and even if she didn't, the missing apostrophe on that shop sign was crime enough.

11

I fired into the War Room like a bullet from a gun, tossed my dagger on the ping pong table, and flopped down on the sofa, still drenched in blood.

Gendith peered up from her game of Patience. 'Tough day at the office?'

I let out a long sigh and threw back my head, defeated. 'Yeah, something like that.'

Neil appeared from around a corner, eyes wide. 'Oh my God, Abbey, what the hell happened?'

'Don't worry,' I said, 'it's not my blood. Actually, it is. All of it. But I'm better now.'

I had a few cuts left, but thanks to the brand, I'd soon be completely healed, not a single scar to show for my epic battle.

Neil squeaked his oxygen tank my way and sat down beside me. 'Are you sure you're okay?' His eyes searched my body, inspecting my wounds.

'I took a couple of lumps, but honestly, I'm fine. The frustration hurts worse than the rest.'

Gen played another card, still caught up in her game. 'So I take it you found the person you were looking for?'

'Not exactly,' I replied, 'but I found someone who works for them.'

'And you let him get away?'

'Not a "he", a she.'

Gen placed her cards down and peered at me with incongruously blue, narrowed eyes. '"She"? You mean the person we've been looking for isn't even connected to the Clan?'

'Oh, she was connected all right, unless the big J on her forehead stood for jerk-off, which actually wouldn't surprise me at all.'

Gen shook her head contemptuously. 'You seriously expect me to believe you encountered a female Clansman, despite the fact that they were systematically put to death around two centuries ago?'

'Yup.'

'Impossible.'

'Oh, my mistake,' I said pantomiming an apology, 'I guess I wasn't attacked at all. I must have just walked into a giant spinning propeller.'

The *clack clack* of a walking stick announced the arrival of Vizael. 'Perhaps the chronicle of events regarding the Clan's witch hunt is not as historically accurate as we have been led to believe.'

'You think?' said Neil, plucking a gobbet of congealed blood from my hair.

Gen stroked her chin, taking it all in. 'A sect of female renegades taking out Clan members... it almost sounds like they're on our side.'

'I've got a poison pen carved into my chest that says otherwise,' Neil argued.

Viz settled into his armchair. 'Fascinating,' he said, considering the new information that had come to light. 'But of course, all of this raises the question, what is it that the person leading this sect has against you, Abbey?'

In other words, who was that gassy bitch at the nail salon working for? I didn't know for sure, but if there's one thing I did know from hate-watching about twenty seasons of *The Bachelor*, it's that when two women come to blows, more often than not, it's over a man.

Blood for Blood.

Had I been looking at it all wrong? What if the message

carved into Neil wasn't a Clan reprisal; a threat for wiping out Judas' men? What if the threat had been written by a woman, and written in the name of love? What if this was personal?

'Lauden,' I said, without even realising my mouth was forming the word.

'Lauden?' replied Neil, wrinkling his nose. 'The vampire who tried to turn me? What's he got to do with anything?'

As far as Neil knew, Lauden Crowe was just the big bad in my last quest, and I'd been keen to make sure that's all he knew. The fact that I'd stupidly let Lauden take me to bed was information he didn't need, at least as far as I was concerned.

I cleared my throat. 'Lauden Crowe.' I made a big play out of slapping my forehead. 'What if the person who sent us that death threat was related to him somehow?'

'Related how?' asked Gen.

'I don't know. A mother, a sister… maybe even a lover?' I added the last part like an afterthought. Like I didn't already have it all figured out.

'An interesting theory,' said Viz, corkscrewing his cane absent-mindedly. 'Very interesting. If you will allow me some time, I will consult with my notes, cross-reference my findings with any relevant historical documents I can find—newspaper clippings, census records, library archives—and see if I can turn up any information on Mr. Crowe's known associates.'

'You could do that,' said Gen, holding up her iPad, 'or you could just read this…'

On screen was an old sepia photo of Lauden. Judging by the quality of the website's design, with its clashing colours, poor font choices and scrolling ticker, the site she'd arrived at either belonged to a small town church, or a swivel-eyed conspiracy theorist.

I took the tablet from Gen and started reading. 'Christ,' I muttered, scanning the lengthy story, which had been broken down into a convenient—if hard on the eyes—timeline.

'What is it?' asked Neil.

'It's a whole thing on Lauden. A calendar going all the way back to the 1600s.'

Gen moved around the back of the sofa to read over my shoulder. 'So he started out as a tinker, did he?'

'Until he married into money,' I replied, having read a little further. 'Says here he took the hand of a wealthy aristocrat. Heir to a fortune. Talk of the town apparently, a wealthy debutante marrying some grubby pleb.'

'There's more,' said Gen, skipping ahead some. 'He married three more times after that.'

She pointed to a selection of photos of women wearing fine silks and frilly ruffs. 'Each of them wealthier than the last.'

That must have caused quite a scandal at the time, I thought, no wonder it was a matter of public record. But Lauden being a gold digger wasn't the thing that piqued the interest of our amateur historian. The thing that really caught his interest was the man's longevity.

'Look, there he is again,' I said, pointing to an entry dated in the mid-1700s. An accompanying wedding photo showed him looking not a year older. 'Holy shit.'

Why hadn't I thought to look into the guy before I slept with him? I had a phone. I should have Googled the bollocks off him.

'The name keeps popping up,' said Neil. 'Again and again and again.' And it did. All over the UK, in one record after another, for more than two more centuries. 'How did he get away with this?'

'Records were spotty back then, and not widely circulated,' said Viz.

Besides, he explained, even if someone had seen Lauden's photos side-by-side, they'd have assumed they were looking at two different but extremely similar-looking men. No one lived that long. It was impossible. So without concrete evidence, without the internet, no one was joining the dots. Not until the person who built this website came along.

'Look,' said Gen, 'here he is again getting married in 1857. So many wives. He must have been quite the charmer.'

'Sounds about right,' I replied, forgetting myself.

'What's that supposed to mean?' asked Neil.

'Nothing.'

'Wait a second,' said Gen, inadvertently digging me out of my hole, 'no, it can't be... oh my God, look...'

She aimed a shaky finger at a wedding photo; not at the groom, not at the bride, but at a middle-aged woman sitting in the background.

'What?' I asked, eyeballing the picture, 'who is she?'

Viz took to his feet and hobbled over. 'Good Lord,' he said, setting his glasses on the bridge of his nose and studying the photo. 'It's her.'

I squinted but I was sure I didn't recognise the woman. She was sat in a church pew, hands folded in her lap, humble, but knockout gorgeous.

'That,' said Viz, barely able to catch his breath, 'is Savina Iscariot.'

'Savina Iscariot?' I said. 'As in *bride of Judas Iscariot*? As in the first female vampire?'

'The same,' Viz replied.

'Well, fuck.'

'Indeed.'

I studied her face. Savina Iscariot. 'Who was she to Lauden though? I was thinking she'd be married to the bloke, but there she is sat in the front row, all prim and proper, looking like someone's mum.'

'I believe you are right,' said Viz, 'and I'm willing to bet that is the groom's side of the aisle she's sat on.'

'So you're saying she's Lauden's mother?'

'Yes and no,' said Gen, who had carried on reading. 'Savina has been around since the turn of the First Millenium; she'd be far too old to be his birth mother.'

'So you're saying she's his *vampire* mum? The person who sired him?'

'That seems a fair assumption,' said Viz.

Something didn't add up. I turned to Gen. 'You told me Savina broke away from Judas and formed a ladies club behind his back. Why would a woman who did that want to buddy up with a crafty little sponge like Lauden?'

'For his money,' she replied, bluntly. 'The men had all of it back then. Most likely, Savina made him her slave so she could tap into his riches.'

So, Lauden had made a packet taking advantage of silly rich girls, only to have his fortune leeched off him by another woman. I got a little pang of satisfaction from hearing that, at least until I remembered that Lauden had died ridiculously wealthy. Then I remembered we bought the place we were sitting in with the exact same wealth, which squared that circle right up.

Scrolling down Gen's iPad, I read the blog piece all the way to the end, right up to the author's conclusion that Lauden Crowe was an immortal vampire, cursed to walk the Earth for all eternity. He was mostly right I supposed, except for the part about Lauden walking anywhere. Old Stabby Abbey had seen to it that he wouldn't be doing that again in a hurry.

In any case, the author had missed the point. Lauden wasn't the story, Savina was. The woman in that photo, lurking in the background, scheming in the shadows. That bitch had it all worked out: make a guy your willing servant, take his riches, then sit back while he makes even more money, all the while pretending to be his suspiciously young-looking mother.

I scrutinised Savina's picture, mentally transposing a crosshair over her face.

'Well then,' I said, 'looks like we've finally found our magician.'

12

I was woken the next morning by my alarm pawing angrily at my face. Groaning, I swiped the phone's off button, but the noise persisted.

Squeak squeak squeak.

Not the sound of my alarm. What was that noise? A mouse? A rat? I pushed away the blankets and immediately felt the cozy warmth of sleep slip away. Swinging my feet over the edge of the bed, I sat up and scooped the crust from my eyes. It was only then that I realised I'd woken up alone.

I heard a low murmuring noise and turned to see a figure standing in the corner of the room. It was Neil, dressed in his underpants and a faded Thundercats t-shirt. Sat by his side on its squeaky trolley was his oxygen tank, its breathing mask attached to his mouth still, as far as I could tell. He was facing away from me, muttering something to himself. Something incomprehensible. Something that didn't quite sound like English.

'Neil?' I said, setting my feet on the cold floor and taking a step in his direction. 'Are you okay?'

He continued murmuring, completely oblivious to me. His hands danced before him, gesticulating wildly, like he was engaged in a spirited debate.

'Neil, you're freaking me out,' I said, almost upon him now.

He stayed facing away from me, head pointed to the corner of the room like he'd been put on time-out, muttering still in that garbled tongue. The strange words tumbling from his mouth sounded angrier now. The debate had turned into an argument. An argument that I got the distinct impression Neil was losing.

Taking one step closer, I reached out to place a hand on his shoulder. Was he sleepwalking? Stuck in a nightmare? Or was I the one dreaming? Would I turn him around to find something awful: a grinning skull where his face ought to be, or something even worse than that? The face of Judas, withered and drawn, his amber eyes staring back at me from those deep black sockets...

'Neil?'

I hooked a hand on him and his muscles stiffened, causing him to stand ramrod straight. He whirled around, wild-eyed and white as snow.

'Abbey?' His voice steamed up the inside of his sleep respirator like something from *Blue Velvet*. Panicked, his eyes darted around the room, trying to place himself within it, trying to figure out how he'd come to be where he was. He unhooked the strap of his mask and lowered it. 'What's happening? What's going on?'

He sounded like himself again. Thank God.

'You were sleepwalking,' I said, giving him a hug. 'It's okay.'

'Really?' he said, shivering slightly as he collected his senses. 'I haven't done that in years.'

True. As far as I knew, he'd only done it once since I'd known him. We were on a rainy, disappointing holiday in Cornwall, staying in a cheap B&B, when I woke up to find him taking a piss in the wardrobe and saying, "Hopscotch, hopscotch, hopscotch" over and over again. We'd laughed about it at the time, even though it had been pretty unsettling to witness (not to mention gross). Neil's condition isn't exactly synonymous with midnight rambles, so I was glad when it turned out to be a one-off incident. They say unfamiliar surroundings and stress are a common trigger for sleepwalking, so we put it down to that and moved on. And now here we were, living a stress-heavy life in a concrete tomb, miles from home. No wonder Neil was pacing about in his sleep and having imaginary conversations. Honestly, it's a wonder he hadn't cracked completely by this point. It's a wonder both of us hadn't.

'Go back to sleep,' I told him, leading him half-conscious to the bed.

I tucked him under the covers. He yawned and his eyelids began to droop.

'Where are you going?' he mumbled, drifting back to sleep.

'Me? I'm going to get some WD40 for that frigging trolley of yours.'

Savina Iscariot.

I'd been searching high and low for the person who cut up Neil, and now I had a name. A face too. The only question now was, where exactly was Savina hiding? As far as anyone who knew her was concerned, Savina Iscariot was dead. Executed for betraying her sire; tied to a stake and torched. And yet somehow she'd survived her punishment and disappeared for centuries without the Clan ever finding her. What were the chances of our little outfit tracking down someone that good at laying low?

The best (and only) connection I had to Savina was the woman I'd tangled with back at the nail salon – the bitch with the Amy Winehouse haircut and the claws. She'd managed to give me the slip then, but thanks to some none-too-polite questions I'd asked of the salon's proprietor, I now knew that Beehive ran a boutique bathhouse in Mayfair, a well-to-do area in the West End of London. So, while Neil stayed home catching up on his sleep, the rest of us decided to treat ourselves to a little spa day.

'No splitting up this time,' said Vizael, keeping a wary eye on the building across the road, the polished front door of which was flanked by a couple of painstakingly-manicured potted cypress trees. 'Go in together, scout the place out, and report back to me with your findings.'

'Affirmative,' said Gendith. She turned to me. 'Did you hear that? Don't just go in there guns blazing. This is a recon mission, understood?'

I fired off a cheeky salute. 'Aye aye, Cap'n.

Gen scowled at me and shook her head. 'Idiot.'

'That's enough,' said Viz. 'I'll stay here and keep an eye on the exits while you two surveil the premises. Now go, quickly, while the sun is still high.'

It was almost solar noon, when the vampires of the Judas Clan were at their weakest, so we took heed and did as Viz ordered, heading across the road before the sun dipped any lower.

The bathhouse was a far cry from Kims Nails. The reception area was warm and inviting, decorated in natural textures; polished marble and raw wood and animal skins. Off to one side were shelves lined with orchids and expensive, take-home spa treatments, each of which cost more than most people paid for their weekly food shop. The air was rich with the smell of jasmine and the piped-in sound of falling water. Behind the reception desk stood a handsome young man with a sharp jawline and a soul patch.

'Good afternoon, ladies,' he said, showing more teeth than I realised a human had, 'do you have an appointment with us today?'

'No appointment,' Gen replied. 'Any chance you have an opening?'

While she kept the receptionist distracted, I used my Night-stalker vision to peer through the walls of the building and locate our prey. I found her right away. Her Marge Simpson haircut made her easy enough to pinpoint among the rest of the bath-house's inhabitants. There she was – sat in a large room with a vaulted ceiling at the opposite end of the bathhouse.

'You're in luck,' the receptionist told Gen as he scanned his computer screen, 'we've had a cancellation, so we can offer you an appointment in half an hour. If you'd like to take a brochure of our treatments, there's a seat for you right over there.' With one hand he gestured to a waiting area furnished with a sofa covered in hand-stitched leather upholstery, and a glass table bearing an impressive ornamental geode. With the other, he produced a brochure listing seaweed wraps and coconut rubs and hot stone therapy. As he slid it across the desk, I noticed something on the inside of his wrist, small and discreet, but there it was.

A letter S.

Savina's coterie bore the mark of Judas on their foreheads—an unavoidable product of their lineage—but the person standing before me had been marked in honour of his own master, Savina Iscariot. And this wasn't a mark that only I could see either, this mark was written in ink, which meant the receptionist was a familiar; a mortal who'd pledged themselves to a vampire in exchange for becoming part of the gang one day. Not an innocent turned against their will, not someone who died in the Plague days and got woken up by a big drill, just a regular fella who wanted to carry on fitting into his size 28s, and decided bleeding the world dry was a small price to pay.

Gen took the brochure from him and smiled politely. 'Come on,' she told me, noticing my fists ball tight, 'let's have a sit down and wait for our appointment, shall we?'

'I've got a better idea,' I said, grabbing the receptionist by the collar and heaving him into a wall. He hit it with a sound like a glacier cracking and slid to the floor.

Gen pinched the bridge of her nose. 'Very subtle.'

I pulled my dagger. 'Let's boogie.'

I led Gen further into the building, heading for the room I'd seen our target occupying. Other familiars came, but we went through them like a pair of wheat threshers, until eventually we came to our destination.

We arrived in the bathhouse's sauna, a huge steam room with imposing columns supporting a curved ceiling inlaid with gold. The walls were covered in navy blue tiles laid out in a neat diamond pattern. The decor was a mishmash of styles: Roman, Russian, Danish, Japanese, you name it. Birch brooms hung from the walls, a hot rock steamer sat in the room's centre, and a statue of Buddha sat cross-legged in an alcove. Also sat there, lounging on a pine bench and completely in the nip, was the vampire I'd taken to calling Beehive.

'Oh, hello,' she said, waving at us with the only thing she was wearing; her false nails. 'Don't you two make a cute couple?'

'First a manicure, now a sauna?' I said, fanning the steam aside. 'You really like to pamper yourself, don't you?'

I bet if I was to turn her upside down, I'd find an arsehole bleached whiter than a virgin bride.

I made my dagger sword-sized and took a step towards her.

'You ladies need to relax,' she said, her voice a throaty purr. 'Grab some towels, take a load off, get a massage.'

'Are you going to tell me where your boss is?' I asked. 'Or do I have to carve a message into *your* chest?'

'I should hope not,' she replied, kneading her breasts, 'I just had this whole area exfoliated.'

'Tell us where she is,' said Gen, trying to keep her eyes up so as not to be distracted by the woman's nudity, but doing a less than wonderful job of it. 'Tell us where we find Savina.'

Beehive smiled. 'You figured it out then, did you? Well done. Gold stars all round.'

Gen spoke through gritted teeth. 'Either you tell us what we need to know right now... or you die.'

'Ooh, listen to you,' Beehive replied, prancing on the tips of her toes, her words cruel and mocking. 'So tough. So fierce.'

The heat in the room was brutal. Sweat poured down my face, free-flowing like condensation on a window pane, invading my eyes. Even Gen had taken on a glossy sheen. It really was far too hot for catty banter.

'I've had enough of this,' growled Gen, losing her temper, 'let's end this bitch.'

'I thought you'd never ask,' I replied, then turned to Beehive. 'We're going to kill you now.'

'Darn it,' she said, snapping her fingers, 'and I was only a couple of tokens short of a free Subway.'

We rushed the vampire, weapons swinging, but before we could cover the distance to her, she broke apart and turned into a red mist again. Old gas bag, up to her same old tricks. The mist cut through the steam, looking to head past us and slip out the door.

'Not this time you don't,' I said, grabbing one of the birch brooms from the wall, cutting off the exit, and fanning furiously.

Caught up in the wind I was making, the red mist was

buffeted back into the sauna, where it hovered, uncertain, before turning solid again.

Beehive stood there, reconstituted, a wicked scowl on her face. 'You had to make things difficult, didn't you?' She reached a clawed hand into the sauna's rock steamer and fished out a red-hot boulder. 'Catch,' she said, firing the meteor my way.

I caught the rock all right, only with my head instead of my hands. It hurt like nothing else. I put a hand to my face and felt my singed skin, felt my jaw, hanging off its hinge. I clicked it back into place and shot the vampire eye lasers. 'I'm going to beat you upside down and inside out.'

I charged her with Gen at my side, sword swinging, morning star whirling. Beehive brushed us aside with her talons, deflecting our blows, throwing off angry sparks, returning attacks that ripped through our clothes and gouged at our flesh. We were fighting two against one, and Beehive was holding us off with ease. If this was what one of Savina's underlings was capable of, I could only imagine what the boss lady herself had going on.

Gen took a backhand that delivered her into a support column with so much force she cracked stone. Beehive lashed out at me with her other hand, but I managed to dive out of the way just in time. The vampire's enchanted claws tore five great furrows in the ground where I used to be, sending chunks of splintered tile spraying everywhere. I came up swinging, but Beehive knocked my sword aside again, hard enough that I lost my grip on it this time. The weapon went spinning across the tile floor, then came to a screaming stop as Beehive stamped down on it with her bare foot. I tried to recall the weapon to my hand, but the pampered cow held the flat of its blade pinned under her heel.

'Come and get it,' she goaded.

I willed the sword to return to me, and the brand glowed fierce and blue as it struggled to reunite with its partner. No matter how hard I tried though, the sword wouldn't budge. Beehive had it fixed in place.

What could I do?

I looked to Gen. She was down. I needed that sword. Even

when I had it I was no match for this vamp, but without it...? Without it I didn't stand a chance.

No.

I'd fought my way out of worse than this. I was the Nightstalker. The goalkeeper standing between the mortal world and a vampire apocalypse. I didn't need a weapon to do my job. Because the most dangerous weapon in this fight wasn't a magic sword, and it certainly wasn't a vampire's enchanted claws. The most dangerous weapon in this fight was *me*.

I stopped trying to reclaim my weapon and concentrated instead on putting an end to the monster stood on top of it. I felt the brand go nuclear in my hand, flooding me with power, firing me up like a napalm enema. Fully juiced now, I shot out a hand, grabbed the statue of Buddha from its alcove, and swung it at Beehive's head.

Crack.

A split appeared across her forehead and opened up into a big, red smile.

'You... you...' she burbled.

I grabbed her by the neck and swung the statue again, raining down blow after blow, colouring her in huge purple welts until I felt her skull give way and saw her body go limp. I let go of her and staggered back freckled with blood.

'Feel better?' asked Gen, lying at the foot of the column she'd been hurled into, rubbing her head.

'I feel like a whole new woman,' I replied.

Gen came over to inspect what remained of our suspect, and grimaced at the sight of her pulpy leftovers. 'So much for getting any answers out of her.'

'Hey, you're the one who threw a wobbler,' I replied, 'all I did was follow your lead.'

Gen pointed to the dead body. '*That* was our lead.'

I looked down at the statue in my hand, slick with blood. 'Beaten to death with a Buddha statue. How do you like that for irony?'

I felt a buzz in the pocket of my jacket and realised my phone was ringing. It was Vizael.

'What in the name of the twelve apostles is going on in there?' he asked.

'Oh, nothing much, just a bit of a snafu with the vampire lady. Why do you ask?'

'Because you have incoming.'

'What? Who?'

'Police. Lots of them.'

The receptionist, he must have woken up and dialled 999. I knew I should have thrown him harder. The man had a soul patch, for Christ's sake.

I picked up my sword, made it dagger-sized, and turned to Gen. 'We have to get out of here.'

'What about the body?'

I cast an eye to the battered corpse lying on the floor, which was more puddle than person. 'I reckon her days of crime are over, mate.'

'No, you cretin. If we let the police get an autopsy of the body, the normals will know vampires exist. That can't happen.'

'No problem,' I said, making stabbing motions with the dagger. 'I'll stick her through the heart with this and they'll have to hoover up what's left of her.'

But before I could get to work, the room was swarmed with a firearms unit dressed in ballistic vests and armed with big scary rifles. I put up my hands.

'Weapons on the ground!' yelled a female plainclothes officer with a severe bob haircut and an even more severe pistol, which she was pointing right at me.

'What do we do now?' I asked Gen out of the corner of my mouth.

'You're the Nightstalker, you tell me,' she hissed back.

The dagger. The one I was clutching still, despite the warning I'd been given. I could use it to mind-wipe the coppers; blank their brains like I did those commuters when I accidentally turned an angry ghost loose on the Underground (long story).

'Look away,' I told Gen.

In one smooth move, I flipped the dagger upside-down and used my thumb to press the hidden button that activated the pommel. The gem came to life and the room lit up, flooded with amnesia magic. When I opened my eyes again, I saw the firearms unit pointing their rifles to the ground, jaws slack and staring back at me like I was an algebra test. Unfortunately, the plain-clothes officer in charge of them didn't share in their confusion. Okay, she was a *bit* dumbstruck by her cohorts inexplicably becoming drooling vegetables, but it wasn't affecting her aim, which remained fixed squarely between my eyes.

'What the hell is going on here?' she asked, stroking the trigger of her gun.

It wasn't an unreasonable question, all things considered. A headless corpse in a beauty spa? I've had nightmares that made more sense.

'If I were you,' I told the officer, 'I'd turn around and toddle off like this never happened.'

She cocked the hammer of her pistol. 'Drop the weapon and get down on the ground. Both of you. Right now.'

I sighed and turned to Gen. 'It can never be easy, can it?'

While the officer was busy with me, Gen whipped out her morning star, wrapped its chain around the officer's pistol, and snatched it from her grip. Gen rushed her, shouldering the woman flat as she pegged it for the way out.

'Sorry about that,' I told the dazed officer. 'She's got a real temper on her for an angel. Um, not that she's a real angel, obviously… I just… I just mean she does a lot of work for charity and erm...'

'Come on, let's go!' Gen called after me.

'Gotta scoot,' I told the officer, before I dug myself in any deeper.

As I took off after my companion, the officer collected herself with remarkable speed, reclaiming her pistol from the other end of the sauna before giving chase. Gen and I burst out of the bath-house and on to the street.

'I'll lead her away,' said Gen. 'You take care of the body.'

I nodded and peeled off from her, legging it across the road and ducking into the side street where Viz was hiding. I watched from around a corner as the officer charged off after Gen, maintaining a breathless foot pursuit.

I slid down the alley wall, lungs burning, drenched in sweat.

Before I could collect my senses, I heard sirens and saw a couple of meat wagons screech up to the bathhouse and unload a fresh batch of cops. The new arrivals headed inside to join the firearm unit, who would just about be coming around from their stupor and wondering how they'd come to be standing in the middle of a bloody murder scene.

Nice one, Abbey.

Our lead was dead, the law were on our tail, and now I had a heavily-guarded dead body that I somehow had to make disappear. I bashed the back of my skull against the brick wall in frustration. How could I have botched this so royally? *Bathhouse Bloodbath,* that's what the headlines would say. I was so embarrassed. If only I could have gone back in time and done things differently, or at the very least, scrubbed the day's events from my memory so I didn't have to relive them.

I turned to Viz, holding up the pommel of the dagger. 'This brain wipe thingie... I don't suppose I can use it on myself, can I?'

13

Viz used some perception magic to make sure we stayed unseen as we kept watch on the outside of the bathhouse.

'Can't you do your Jedi Mind Trick thing again so we can sneak in there and drag out Beehive's body?

'Not on that many people,' he replied. 'It's taking everything I have to conceal us now.'

The plainclothes officer with the bob returned to the crime scene, empty-handed, I was glad to see. Gen had obviously succeeded in giving her the slip. That was something at least. Not so helpful were the crime scene photographers who showed up, then the paramedics, then the reporters. Pretty soon, the place was swarming with bodies.

'How the hell are we supposed to get in there?'

'We don't,' said Viz, pointing to a trolley being wheeled out of the front door of the building.

The vampire's body bag was loaded into the back of an idling ambulance, which then pulled away and took off down the road. The body was going to find its way to the authorities and the whole jig would be up, all thanks to me. I was sure to get my Nightstalker license revoked for that one.

'I have to follow it—' I said, about to fire out of the alley, but Viz barred my way with his walking stick.

'There's no need to give chase. The body is being delivered to

St Pancras Mortuary.' He showed me his phone screen. 'Look, I found it on the Google.'

Seemed the old man wasn't as technologically inept as Gen made him out to be.

I noted down the address, then ordered an Uber and hitched a ride.

The mortuary was parked on a featureless bit of land surrounded by railway bridges and dormant cranes. I was determined to keep a low profile this time, so I snuck into the building like a ninja with sore feet, sliding by a daydreaming receptionist and mind-zapping a bloke in a white coat who stepped out of a corridor between me and my prize. If you consider a headless corpse a prize, that is.

I arrived in a viewing gallery connected to the autopsy suite. Through an observation window, I could see a coroner; an Indian woman in a blue plastic apron and scrubs. She was attending to a body laid out on an aluminium table; a naked female with soup for a head. I ducked down and watched the doctor through the glass of the observation window as she began her examination of the body.

'Alrighty then, let's get this corpse talking.' She activated a microphone that hung from a cord above the body, then rattled off the date of the post mortem, the suspected time of death, and the location the deceased was discovered. Nearby, a camera on a tripod recorded the session.

The doctor circled the body, still talking. 'Unidentified caucasian, no jewellery, displays no identifying marks, residual scars, or tattoos. Fingers are decorated with false nails, black and gold, around three inches in length, markings unknown. The deceased has been subjected to massive head trauma, cranium reduced to fragments, brain heavily damaged. Injuries are consistent with a frenzied, blunt force attack.' The doctor leaned in closer. 'Contusions on right upper arm suggest the victim was held in place while the trauma occurred.'

As I looked on, the doctor went to a clipboard and made

some notes. I could make out a diagram of a body on the front page, the type used to indicate wound placement. She drew a short line across the diagram's right arm, then scratched a big, fat cross across the entire head area. Whistling to herself, the doctor stroked her chin for a moment, then snapped on a pair of latex gloves.

'Commencing internal examination,' she said, her hand travelling to a tray of medical tools and selecting a wicked-looking scalpel.

Okay, that's enough of that, I thought. Bashing Beehive's head in was one thing, but I wasn't sticking around to watch her autopsy. Yuck.

I aimed the pommel of the dagger through the observation window and gave the doc a flash of the old brain-eraser.

Or at least, I tried to.

I pressed the button again, but nothing happened. I pressed it once more, gave the dagger a shake, even rolled its hilt around in my palm like I was trying to wake up a dying battery in a remote control, but still nothing. The brain-eraser was all out of juice.

I muttered something unchristian under my breath. Hearing me, the doc spun around, and I only just managed to duck her beady eyes as she scanned the viewing gallery. I waited for a few seconds until she started narrating into the microphone again, then inched my head up to get another look.

'Proceeding to open up the chest and abdominal cavities,' she announced, pressing the tip of the scalpel blade into the corpse's sternum. I placed a hand over my mouth to keep hold of my breakfast as she made a Y-shaped incision, then began emptying the body of its innards. She placed organs into various bowls and balanced them on scales, noting down their weights, then slopped a big bundle of guts on a metal tray.

As fascinating/disgusting as it all was, I knew it was only a matter of time before the doc realised the body she was dealing with wasn't strictly human. I had to figure out a way of getting her out of that theatre so I could sneak in, slip my dagger into the corpse's chest and destroy the evidence.

The doctor picked up a heavy-looking device with a circular

blade. 'Opening rib cage.' She switched on the saw, which came to life with a tooth-jarring whirr.

That gave me an idea. I couldn't blank her brain, but I could use the sound that saw was making to cover my footsteps, get in close, and cold-cock her to the back of the head. My plan had careened wildly out of control, but I figured at this point, I might as well steer into the skid.

I made my way to the door that led between the viewing gallery and the autopsy suite, but when I tried the handle, it wouldn't give. The door was locked from the other side. Great, now what?

The bone saw cut out and slowed to a low burr before going silent again. Not knowing what else to do, I made my way back to the observation window to see what the doctor was up to. She placed the saw down and inserted a stainless steel crank into the exposed rib cage, prising the bones apart like the jaws of an animal trap.

A quizzical look crossed her face as she examined her findings. 'That's strange…' she said, 'that's very strange...'

She reached in to prod the cadaver's heart with the tip of a metal prong, but recoiled suddenly, clutching her hand and sending the polished implement ringing off the tile floor.

'Fuck,' she cried, not altogether professionally. 'To anyone reviewing this tape, that was the sound of me lacerating my hand on a bone splinter.' I saw a trickle of blood run off the heel of her palm and plop into the corpse's open chest cavity. The doctor whipped her hand away, cursing some more. 'Now I've gone and contaminated the body,' she sighed, looking to the camera. 'Well, it looks like this little movie is getting deleted.'

Bang.

The doctor sprang backwards at the sound. 'What the hell was that?'

Bang.

It came from the direction of the operating table. The body, did it… did it just twitch?

No. Not possible.

Bang.

The fist of the headless body hammered into the aluminium table, hard enough to leave a divot.

The doctor's face turned ashen.

The corpse's hands sprang open, its talons screeching on the metal as the body forced itself upright.

It was alive.

The blood had brought the vampire back. Woken her from the dead.

As the doctor's knees unhinged and her backside hit the floor, the corpse began to change. Blood flowed from its neck wound, thick as tar. The gunk climbed in thick folding waves, then began to congeal into something solid. A head.

The vampire was growing a new head.

I rushed to the door of the theatre and hammered on it. 'Open up!' I shouted, but the doc was too out of it to hear me. I grabbed the handle and tried to force it, but the door was sealed tight. 'You need to let me in!'

The vampire was fully-formed now, chest sealed tight and all back to normal, right down to the beehive.

'No, no, no!'

The brand glowed hot and blue, powering me up. I kicked the door flat and stomped over its ruins to find the vampire sinking her teeth into the doctor's neck.

'Let go of her,' I demanded.

Beehive threw back her head and hissed, teeth stained crimson, naked chest slick with blood. She released her meal, and the doctor slid to the ground, her eyelids fluttering closed.

I snatched the dagger from inside my jacket and went to work, but the blade hadn't even left its sheath before the vampire dissipated into a formless red mist.

'Oh, no you don't,' I cried.

I was determined not to let her dine and dash, but I had nothing to corral her with this time. The mist shot off away from me, coalesced into a thin, red tendril, and escaped through a crack in the window.

The words that came out of my mouth in that moment went beyond unchristian and all the way to ungodly. There was no keeping that bitch down. I thumped the empty operating table with the butt of my dagger, giving it a fresh divot.

I knelt down by the fallen doctor, her blue apron now coloured red. Her body was limp and unresponsive. Christ. How could I have let this happen? I tailed that body bag to the mortuary to make sure the coroner didn't blab on us, but not like this. I studied the doc's face—her caramel skin now fishbelly white—and craned my neck until our foreheads were almost touching.

'Sorry, Doc, I fucked up.'

It was only then that I got a close look at the wound on her throat and saw fresh bubbles in the blood. She was breathing still. The doc was alive!

I grabbed a thick wad of paper towels from a counter and mashed it to her neck.

'What do I do, what do I do?' I asked myself, one hand applying pressure to the wound, the other searching for something to stitch the hole with.

I was midway through trying to remember if my First Aid training covered patching up slashed throats when I heard a commotion.

Footsteps. Lots of them. Approaching fast.

That meant two things. The first was that there were medical professionals on the way; the kind who could close up a throat laceration, even if they were generally more used to opening them. The second thought that occurred was that I was trespassing on private property, drenched in someone else's blood, and carrying a big fat knife.

I needed to get out of that place, but before I took off, there was one thing left to do. If this little visit was going to be anything less than a total failure, I needed to get rid of some evidence. I snatched the video camera from its tripod and went looking for the slot that held its SIM card. When I couldn't find that, I took the camera in two hands and crushed it to the size of a marble, destroying the card by proxy. There. No more evidence. Vampires were a fiction again.

With that little task out of the way, I tucked my head, cannonballed through the theatre's exterior wall, and made off as fast as my legs would carry me. Another building wrecked. Sometimes I think I've done more damage to this city than the Luftwaffe ever did.

14

'Let me see if I have this correct,' said Vizael, leaning back in his chair and steepling his fingers, 'instead of getting rid of the vampire's body like you were instructed, you allowed her to return from the dead, almost kill someone, and slip your clutches?'

'I'll admit it,' I replied, 'I might not be bowling 300 on this one.'

We were back in the War Room, and so far the debriefing was not going great.

Sat opposite the table from me, Gendith placed her head in her hands and let out a long, plaintive sigh.

Neil gave my hand a comforting squeeze. 'You did your best. And look, now she's alive again, we have our lead back. That's something, right?'

'And how exactly do you propose we find this so-called lead?' spat Gen.

'I don't know,' he replied. 'Maybe we don't even need to find her. What if we cut out the middleman—well, *middlewoman*—and sent a message direct to this Savina lady?'

'A message?' Gen shot back. 'Are you and this vampire in some WhatsApp group that I haven't been invited to?'

I sat up. 'Maybe he's on to something. What about if we sent her the same kind of message she sent us?'

Neil's hand unconsciously went to his chest, feeling the scars beneath the cloth of his t-shirt. 'Like… cut her up with a spell?'

Viz shook his head. 'For us to perform blood magic, the consequences would be dire.'

'How dire are we talking?' I asked.

Viz fixed me with a hard stare. 'Imagine your soul, ripped from your body and subjected to eternal agony. A dreadful suffering that cannot be compared to any pain you have ever experienced.'

'Right then. So maybe no blood magic.'

Neil shot up a hand. 'What if we went big with it and hired a skywriter?' He swept his hand through the air, spelling out a message. 'SAVINA. OUTSIDE THE OLD SALOON. HIGH NOON. That could work, right?'

'Sure,' said Gen. 'Let's give the entire Uncanny world our exact whereabouts. You really are as dumb as a shoe, you know that?'

'Hey, at least he's trying,' I said. 'Not like you two Debbie Downers.'

I rocked back in my chair, lost in thought, then snapped my fingers. 'I've got it! Why don't we just ask God where Savina is?'

'God?'

'Yeah. You know, the guy who runs Heaven?'

Viz placed his forehead on the table. 'I'm sorry, but that has to be the most idiotic idea we've heard yet. Really, quite poor.'

'I fail to see what's wrong with getting the Big Man to weigh in on this thing. We did it once before and that worked out fine.'

'I was almost turned into a vampire and got buried alive,' said Neil, 'so I don't know about *fine*.'

'In any case,' said Viz, attempting to get things back on track, 'the Lord God Almighty is not in the business of granting wishes, so we won't be using him as our personal genie.'

'All right,' I said, folding my arms. 'Fine.'

The four of us wracked our brains for a while after that – so long that the pregnant pause it created almost went full term. Any hope we had of finding Savina was rapidly curdling into crushing disappointment.

'Guys,' said Neil, pointing across the room, 'what's that?'

A trickle of something red and viscous was forming on the floor, emerging from the crack beneath our door. Our magic door. Our magic *one-way* door.

The four of us pushed back our chairs and got vertical.

'That's blood,' I said, pulling my dagger from its spot on the ping pong table and delivering it to my hand.

The tide of burgundy rolled further into the room and began coalescing into a shape like an undiscovered continent.

Gen went for her morning star. Viz drew a slim blade from his walking cane. Neil picked up his oxygen tank and held it like a barbarian's club.

The continent became a puddle, then the puddle became convex, bulging, ascending, becoming something solid.

A person.

A woman.

Blood turned flesh.

The woman waltzed across the room with an air of nonchalance, the dainty clack of her high heels echoing around the War Room. She was petite, pretty, and dressed in a dandelion yellow dress that complimented her silver-blonde coiffure. As she approached, I felt an icy sense of dread that made the hairs on the back of my neck stand to attention, and my teeth itch. The brand on my palm turned retina-searingly bright.

I recognised the woman from the news clipping. There she was. The queen bee. Savina Iscariot herself, strolling into our secret base, bold as brass.

'Oh good,' she purred, 'I see we're quorate.' She spoke with an indeterminate European accent that put her origin somewhere in the region of bad guy land. 'And look, you have a ping pong table. How absolutely darling.'

I turned to Viz. 'How is this happening? Is our address in that Yellow Pages too?'

Savina turned to Neil. 'Sorry about carving you up, my lad, but I had to get the message out there somehow. Besides, using you was cheaper than buying a stamp.'

I stepped between her and Neil, and as I did, the blue flame of my dagger threw Savina's shadow across the room. It was a shadow that cut entirely the wrong way. Something was very wrong with this woman. Something altogether evil.

Savina grinned. No fangs, no demonic-looking skull ridges or blood red eyes, just a nice, pleasant smile set on a face that couldn't have been any smoother if it had been taken to with an industrial sander. What was it with this line of work? Did every woman I ran into have to look like she belonged on the cover of Vogue Magazine?

'She's like the anti-you,' Neil whispered.

'What's that supposed to mean?'

'I'm just saying, she's understated, well-mannered, dresses in bright colours… she's like your perfect villain, your total opposite. You know, from a writer's perspective.' He caught the look I was giving him. 'I'll shut up now.'

'Good idea.'

Vizael aimed his sword at Savina. 'Why did you come here, vampire?'

'Well, since your pup there beat my second in command halfway to death with a Buddha statue, I decided I'd rather like to deal with her personally.'

'I'd like to see you try, mate,' I told her, using a flick of my wrist to turn the hallowed dagger into a hallowed bloody-great-sword.

Savina let out a sing-song laugh. 'You misunderstand. I have no intention of harming you. Well, I did at first, back when I sent you that message, but I've decided it would be a shame to kill you now. I've taken quite a shine to you, Abbey Beckett.'

I did my best not to look rattled as she addressed me by name. 'So, you just popped in to say hello, did you? You're not a bit miffed that I killed your son, or your fuck buddy, or whatever Lauden was to you?'

'Oh, that?' she replied. 'That's all ancient history now. Vampires don't hold their kin in quite the same regard as your kind. Lauden was a means to an end, nothing more. A lusty old Casanova that I used to amass my fortune.'

'And that's all he was to you, eh? A sugar daddy. Or sugar son, I suppose. God, everything is so gross with you lot.'

She laughed again. 'I suppose I did think of Lauden as something more than just a money man. After all, when Judas ordered my kind killed, it was Lauden who helped me on to the steamer and allowed me to escape to Europe. But listen to me go on – you don't need to know any of this. The point is, when I received word that Lauden had died, I felt a certain obligation to the horny old gold digger. He really was quite the charmer, but then you already know that, don't you?' She gave me a wink.

Neil's nose wrinkled. 'What does she mean by that?'

Gen turned and gave me some serious side-eye. 'Yes, what *does* she mean by that?'

'Nothing,' I said, brushing off the notion that I'd been in any way intimate with Lauden, which of course I had. 'She's talking shit, that's all. Trying to rile us up.'

Savina gave me a knowing look, her smile loaded with mischief. 'That's right. Just me being puckish, that's all.'

Viz pounded the butt of his walking stick on the ground. 'If you didn't return to these shores to repay a debt, vampire, why did you come?'

'To say thank you,' Savina replied. 'It took me a moment to come to terms with, but once I looked past my vendetta, I realised your ward here had done me a considerable favour.'

'I did?' I asked, failing to see her logic.

'But of course. With Lauden dead, the last Clansman I cared one iota about is gone, which means I can finally put my plan into action.'

'I'm not going to like this, am I?'

'You set me free, Abbey. Now I have nothing holding me back. No attachments, no sentiments, no reason not to mount my uprising and wipe the Clan from the face of this planet.'

'I stand corrected,' I said, taken by surprise, 'that actually sounds pretty sweet.'

'We do not ally ourselves with vampires,' said Viz, warding Savina off with the tip of his blade. 'Now, begone from this place, foul woman.'

'But I only just got here,' Savina replied, mock hurt. She turned to me. 'Are you going to take orders from this dotard, or are you going to do what you were put here to do, and destroy the Clan for good?'

I recoiled from her like she was trying to feed me a tablespoon of cold shite. 'Are you seriously telling me that you—a vampire—expect me—the Nightstalker—to sack off my friends and join your gang of... busty bloodsuckers?'

'That is exactly what I'm telling you. I have spent decades strategising, growing in strength, making new allies, and now I come here seeking your help. Join me, Abbey. Together we can exterminate Judas and his entire operation.'

'There must be something in your blood, woman. Your boy Lauden had a nutty idea just like that.'

If Savina was bothered by my dismissal of her offer, she didn't show it. She turned to Gen, smooth and serene. 'You've been quiet, angel. What about you? Would you like to join my cause?'

Gen tugged at the chain of her morning star. 'You obviously don't know me very well.'

'Quite the opposite, Gendith. I know you all too well. I know your life, I even know your death.'

I saw Gen's features harden. She took a step towards Savina, but Viz used the flat of his blade to hold her back.

Savina went on, pacing the room like a detective who'd gathered her suspects in the drawing room and was about to yell *J'accuse!* 'Born in Barbados, enslaved in 1692 and brought to the Americas, only to be accused of witchcraft and sentenced to death in the Salem trials. And the real irony? The final kick in the teeth? The witchfinder who condemned you was a vampire; a member of the Judas Clan no less.'

Gen spoke through gritted teeth. 'I repay the Clan for that injustice every day.'

'Yes. And you do it in the name of God. The man who made you an angel. The same man who decided you weren't deserving of your martyrdom after all and sent you here.'

'What is your point?'

'A man enslaved you. A man burned you at the stake. A man stripped you of your wings and spat you back to Earth like a piece of chewed-up gum.' She looked to Viz, then back to Gen. 'My point is this: aren't you tired of submitting to the will of men?'

'This is my duty,' Gen replied, her voice beginning to crack. 'I belong here.'

Savina smiled, warm and kind. 'You've never belonged anywhere, girl. But maybe with us you can.'

Gen had heard enough. Growling, she pushed Viz's blade aside and ran at Savina, ball and chain whirling. The vampire simply rolled her eyes, grabbed Gen by the throat, and launched her through the air like a clay pigeon. The angel bounced off a wall and landed in a painful heap.

'You really are a glutton for punishment, aren't you?' said Savina, tucking an errant strand of hair behind her ear.

I went to give Gendith some backup, but Viz hooked a hand on my shoulder. 'Stay.'

'Get off me,' I demanded.

'She's too strong,' he replied, deadly serious. 'Even though we are three against one, we are still outnumbered.'

Neil held up a hand. 'Um, technically we're four against one, just in case anyone's taking a register.'

Gen managed to make it to her feet. She was dazed and unsteady, weaving about like she was staggering through a dust storm.

'I told you I didn't come here to fight,' said Savina, as much for Gen's sake as mine. 'Now, if you don't mind, I'm going to take my leave and let you consider my offer. Do join the team, girls, we'd love to have you.'

I pulled away from Viz's grip. 'The only place you're going is the morgue,' I told Savina. 'Right after I've murdered you to death.'

'Let her go,' Viz insisted.

'Why should I?'

Savina answered the question, and she did it with a show of strength that made it perfectly apparent just how outgunned we were. It started with a simple clap of her hands – a clap that thumped The Vault like it had been punched in the gut. A deafening shockwave rippled across the War Room that knocked furniture sideways, atomised anything made of glass, and blew apart a three-foot thick, fifteen tonne, reinforced steel vault door. It was a display of magic as impressive as it was devastating.

'That's why,' explained Viz.

I had to lip-read his reply, being as I was half-deaf from the bang.

It was only with the smoke cleared that I realised Savina was no longer with us, having bid us farewell and departed through her exit hole.

Neil and I teetered over to the ruined vault door in a post-concussion haze.

'That's going to need a new lock,' he said.

15

I didn't give Savina's offer any real thought, of course. At least not until I was ready to go to sleep, when her words came marching to the forefront of my mind in Size 12 clodhoppers.

Join me, Abbey.

Join me, Abbey.

Join me, Abbey.

Again and again, over and over, louder and louder.

As ridiculous as it sounded to throw in with a vampire who cut up my boyfriend and went Krakatoa on my home, what if Savina was the key to killing Judas? She could have sliced Neil up like a Christmas turkey instead of just leaving me a note, but she let him live. She could have blown me apart along with that vault door, but the worst I had from that encounter was a ringing in my ears. Would it really be the worst thing in the world to accept a little help? We definitely had the same goal, which sort of put us on the same side. Well, except for the whole *her being a vampire* thing. If we could just overlook that though, at least for a little bit... I mean, surely there was only so much our ragtag gang of plucky misfits could achieve on our own. Three of us—sorry, four, including Neil— against a bible character with an evil army at his back? Fat chance.

But no.

My job was to wipe out the Clan. All of them. Savina might

have resigned from the Judas club, but there was no scrubbing that letter J off her forehead. I couldn't get picky just because she was a "sister". She had to go. First her people, then the rest. I wasn't sure how I was going to do it exactly, but a couple of weeks back I didn't know how to lop off a vampire's head and toe punt it into his mate's face either, and I'd figured that one out just fine.

And on that happy thought, I finally drifted off to sleep. It came like an axe-fall, spiriting me away to a blissful, uninterrupted slumber. At least until Judas showed up.

He came to my bedside, withered and crusty, a thin bag of skin with bones inside. His spine was hunched so badly that I could see the dull shine bouncing from the surface of his mottled scalp. He stood at the foot of my bed, his eyes roaming over my body, which I realised now was on display. The bedsheets were gone, and the only thing I had on was Neil's ratty old Thundercats t-shirt, which I was wearing as a nightdress, hitched up to my thighs. Judas licked his lips, his tongue brown and wet and obscene.

I tried to get away from him, tried to go for my weapon, but I couldn't move. I was paralysed. I couldn't move the rest of my body, but I was able to move my mouth just enough to form a protest. 'I know I'm dreaming, dickhead.'

Judas leaned forward and I heard the creak of his ancient bones. 'How very perceptive of you,' he said, wearing the ghost of a smile.

As I lay on my back, eyes fixed on the vampire master, he transformed, changing from a withered old geezer into a handsome, young man dressed in a sharp black suit.

I offered him a shrug, although I'm pretty sure my shoulders stayed fixed in place. 'That's your dream-demon outfit, is it? No hat, no stripy jumper, no fingertip razors? Bit disappointing.'

'Savina,' he said, arching his back, his breath cold on my face; cold as the grave. 'I see her lingering in your thoughts. So, the rebel is the source of your troubles?' He smirked, his lips like red candy, his fangs like pure white snow.

I kept my cool. 'Except she's your problem too, isn't she?

Unless that was a bomb that went off in your little old boys' club.'

His smirk faded.

'Maybe I should let Savina carry on the good work,' I suggested. 'Let her have her little uprising. Maybe even find out where you're holed up and do you in too.' I tried stabbing a finger at him, but my hand stayed palm-down on the mattress, limp and useless.

'I think not,' Judas replied.

'Oh, I think so,' I contested. 'That woman's got a real boner for you.'

'Savina's rage is boundless, that much is true, but her blood-lust isn't confined to me and my kind. Allow her to live and you will know the truth of this.'

'Yeah, excuse me if I'm not totally sold on your "truth", you low-rent Freddy Krueger.'

Judas straightened up. 'Perhaps a history lesson is in order...'

He waved a hand and the shadows on the wall behind him formed shapes. Moving shapes that became pictures. Pictures that told a story.

I saw Savina. In her hand was a pair of pincers, fresh from a fire, white-hot. As I watched, she approached a man strapped to a chair, his mouth cranked open by some crude, metal implement. Going by their surroundings and what they were wearing, the scene had happened a long time ago. Centuries even. The image was clear as day though as Savina reached into the man's mouth and took his tongue in the jaws of her hot, hot pincers. I tried to close my eyes, tried to turn away, but I had no choice but to watch as Savina yanked the tongue from his mouth like a strip of chewing gum on a hot summer's day.

'This is Savina as she truly is,' said Judas, his voice reverberating in my skull, 'this is the woman I know.'

The picture changed. Another place, another time. I saw a man, lashed to a tree, unable to defend himself as animals chewed on his flesh and pecked at his eyeballs. As the beasts picked him apart, Savina stood by and smiled.

'This is the woman you would let live?' asked Judas. 'This is the woman you would call an ally?'

Again the scene shifted. I saw another man, stretched out on a rack as Savina turned its wheel, forcing his limbs to dislocate from their sockets with gunshot cracks.

Visions of atrocities throughout history, across continents. Savina, waging war on mankind, with a marked emphasis on "man".

'Do you wish to see more?' asked Judas. 'Or do you have the picture?'

'That's enough,' I said, stomach churning, bile clawing its way up my throat.

'No, I do not think you yet understand.' He brought his face in front of mine and offered me a razorblade smile. 'Perhaps this will enlighten you…'

He pulled his face away, showing me the picture show behind him. The show I couldn't help but watch.

A new place, a new time. The surroundings looked modern, but the scene… the scene was nothing less than medieval. A man hung from the ceiling in a complicated cradle, naked, legs spread by a stout length of wood. The cradle was weighted and lowering the man slowly to the ground. At first I wasn't sure why he was screaming exactly, and then I saw it. Beneath the man was a large metal pyramid, its point aimed squarely between his milk-white thighs.

'No,' I heard myself say, 'no, no, no.'

The seat of the cradle had a hole in it, exposing the man's backside to the pyramid's brutal spike.

'Don't do it,' I screamed, as if saying it loud enough could alter history and prevent this torture from happening.

The picture widened and I saw Savina at the crank, lowering the cradle further, inch by agonising inch. The seat continued its descent, and as it did, the man's screaming matched my own.

'Oh God! Help him, someone help him!'

The spike entered him, impaling him, opening him wide, and as it did, Savina laughed.

It was a laugh that turned my whole body into gooseflesh.

16

'Abbey? Abbey, wake up.'

My eyes snapped open. It was Neil, lying next to me, shaking me gently by the shoulder. My heart was pistoning in my chest. I was greased in sweat from head to toe.

'It's okay. You were dreaming, that's all.'

I blinked, and for a moment I saw the man on that pyramid, as though his afterimage had been burned into the backs of my eyelids.

'I'm all right,' I said, pressing the heels of my hands into my eye sockets, trying to rub the picture away. 'I'm all right.'

Neil looked back at me with concern. 'Are you sure?' He put a hand on my forehead. 'Your skin's hot enough to cook an egg on, and your heart's going a mile a minute. Maybe you have a fever or something.'

'I don't have the luxury of getting sick.'

'Okay then, tough stuff,' he replied, smiling. He reached for his breathing respirator, placed it over his mouth, and continued talking, this time in his best Batman villain voice. *'Because only when Gotham is ashes, do you have my permission to die...'*

I hit him with my pillow. 'You bell-end,' I said, laughing. His dumb Bane impression always made me laugh.

He dived at me and I wrestled him for a bit—being extra

careful not to accidentally snap him in half—until finally we met in a tight hug, all tied up in a twist of duvet.

Neil kissed me on the forehead. 'Are you sure you're okay, Abbey?'

I thought about continuing the lie, but the effort was too much. 'Honestly, I don't know. That dream I had… it was more than just a nightmare.'

'What do you mean?'

'I mean, it was a message. Judas was in my head.'

'Are you serious?'

'Yeah. I wasn't *completely* sure the first time, but I'm sure now.'

'There was a "first time"? So you're telling me Judas has paid you a visit before?'

'Yeah.'

'Right then,' he said, grabbing me by the wrist and yanking me out of bed.

'Where are we going?' I asked.

'Where are we going? We're going to get a vampire out of your brain.'

Neil marched me into the War Room like a naughty school girl, and I played along, even though I could have taken his hand off me at any time (not to mention his arm out of its socket).

'Abbey needs your help,' Neil told Vizael, who was sat at his desk reading some dusty old grimoire.

'Is that so?' the old man replied, looking over the rims of his spectacles. 'And how might I assist her?'

'You can start by getting Judas out of her skull.'

Viz turned to me. 'He's back again?'

'What?' Neil sputtered. 'You knew about this?'

I put a hand on Neil's arm. 'Yeah, I kind of told him the first time it happened.'

'But not me?'

'I didn't know it was going to be a repeat visit. Honestly, I thought he'd gone away.'

Neil scrunched up his face. 'We're talking about a bloke who betrayed Jesus, earned the wrath of God, died, then came back from the dead and started making a vampire army. He's not just going away, Abbey.'

'He's right,' said Viz. 'We must sever this connection Judas had with you before it grows any stronger. I should have insisted on it the first time, I was a fool not to.'

'Sounds about right,' said Gendith, entering the room and joining us.

I turned back to Viz. 'When you say "sever", what exactly are you talking about?'

He sat up from his chair and hobbled over to me on his walking stick. 'A spell. A spell to probe the recesses of your unconscious mind and detach you from the vampire's influence.'

'So what you're basically saying is, you want to root around in my noggin and go through my brain's browser history?'

'In a manner of speaking, yes.'

'Pass. Can't I just stick a knitting needle in my ear and get Judas out that way? Honestly, I'd take that over an angel getting a look at the dank shit that goes on in here.' I rapped a knuckle on my temple.

Viz set aside his walking stick and held up his arms. 'Place your head between my hands. I promise, you won't feel a thing.'

'Do as he says,' said Gen. 'So long as Judas has access to your mind, you pose a serious security risk. For all we know, he could be looking out from your eyes as we speak, spying on us.'

Viz stroked his chin whiskers. 'You know, there might just be a way to make this work for us. If I can make the link Judas has with you visible, there's a chance I can follow the trail of that link and discover his physical whereabouts.'

Finding out where Judas was hiding? Now, that was some motivation.

'Okay then, old man, I'm giving you the key to my brain. Just make sure you wipe your feet on the way in, and stay out of any rooms marked Tom Hardy.'

I took a step towards Viz and bobbed my head to let him know I was ready.

He nodded back and placed a hand either side of my head. His skin was warm on my cheeks; comforting. The warmth intensified, growing hotter, but not painfully so. The warmth spread, soaking through my skull, moving inwards, deeper and deeper. My head filled with light; soft and diffuse at first, then brilliant and white; a whiteness that made fresh snow look grey.

Outside of my head, I could hear distant, muffled words. Viz, I assumed. He was talking about something he'd found. Signs of interference. Evidence of Judas' fingerprints.

The light in my head grew brighter still, but not so much that it became overpowering. Despite its intensity, the light never dazzled. Never made me uncomfortable. It reminded me of lying on a sun-kissed beach, looking up at a golden sky through closed eyes.

The light dimmed slightly, as if the sun had been momentarily blotted out by a passing cloud.

And again, darker this time.

Eclipse dark.

Black tendrils appeared in the corners of my vision, crawling across the white like Indian ink dropped into a pail of milk.

'What's happening?'

I said it, but I couldn't hear my words.

The outside world was gone now. Gone completely. I was trapped inside my own head. Trapped in a world of white and black. Then black and white.

The light was losing.

The dark tendrils were spreading, conjoining, blotting out the white until only pin-prick specks remained. Soon, the specks were lost too, vanishing like burned-out stars, until all that was left was blackness, an empty, silent void.

The silence didn't last long. I heard a faraway thrumming. A deadened, panicked sound, like a group of people arguing on the other side of a thick wall. The thrumming grew louder. Closer. More intense. So intense it became deafening.

My eyes snapped open.

I smelled sulphur. There was smoke in the air. Neil and Gen looked back at me with wide, panicked eyes.

Where was Viz?

There he was, across the other side of the War Room, heaped on the floor against the far wall. The trail of lingering smoke snaked between us like an umbilical cord.

'Jesus, are you okay?' I asked, jogging over and crouching down by his side.

The old man's fingertips were burnt. His beard and eyebrows singed. He wore the expression of a man who had tried, and failed, to defuse a bomb.

'What happened?'

'Backfired,' he croaked. 'Judas sensed my influence and retaliated.'

'Are you hurt?' asked Gen.

'Nothing serious,' he replied, groaning and pushing his back to the wall until he was sat upright.

'What about Judas?' I asked. 'Is he still in there?'

'The link has been severed. Judas no longer has a toe-hold in your unconscious mind. Unfortunately, the connection was broken before I could trace its point of origin.'

Gen threw her hands to the sky in frustration. 'So we're no closer to knowing where Judas is hiding?'

'No,' Viz confessed.

I felt my shoulders slump. 'Okay then. Okay. So, what do we do now?'

'I don't know about you guys,' said Neil, scratching his tummy, 'but I could right go for some breakfast.'

17

As soon as we were done having a go at Neil for his misplaced priorities, it was agreed that, actually, we were all quite hungry, and, yes, breakfast seemed like a pretty great idea, all things considered.

Being as The Vault stank like rotten eggs and we all needed a break from the place, we decided to eat out. Despite my protests, Cath's Caff was the group's preferred option, so we headed to Whitechapel in search of a cheap fry up. Run by the titular "Cath", the all-day greasy spoon was a popular meeting spot for the city's less discerning denizens—both civilian and Uncanny—and was considered by many to be a pot of fried treasure at the end of a long, grey rainbow.

Having arrived, the four of us took a corner booth opposite a couple of builders sharing a copy of *The Sun*, and selected some fare from the restaurant's blackboard. Cath took our order, sizing us up through piggy eyes framed with tar-thick mascara. She'd had a purple rinse put in her hair since the last time we'd visited, but the rest of her was just the same; her hatchet face lined with wrinkles that came together at her bullseye mouth, a result of decades spent with a cigarette plugged in her gob.

Our food arrived suspiciously quickly, mine a plate of scrambled eggs on toast, which was so unappetising that I was forced to drown it in ketchup (a mercy killing if ever there was one). We were about to start discussing the Savina situation when something unusual caught my eye. Among the cement-caked labourers and grimy garage workers was a good-looking man dressed in his Sunday best. He wore a tailored black suit and a pencil tie, and was making a beeline for our booth. At first I took him for a vampire, but saw no sign of a letter J on his person. All the same, I reached a hand into my jacket and closed a mitt around the hilt of my dagger.

'Don't look now,' I whispered, 'but we've got company.'

Predictably, Neil turned around in his seat and meerkated over the top of the booth to get a gander. Less predictable, was his reply.

'Eh?' he said. 'I don't see anyone.'

This was particularly surprising, not just because the rest of us could make out the visitor no problem, but because he was now standing right next to us, shooting his cuffs and wearing a wonky smirk.

'Morning,' he chirped.

'Um, hello,' I replied. 'Can we help you?'

'Who are you talking to?' asked Neil, looking left and right.

'Oh, about that,' said the stranger, 'there's a reason he can't see me. Or hear me. It's because I'm a ghost.'

'A ghost?'

'Yup.'

'As in a dead person?'

'Bang on. Snuffed it a while back.' He chuckled to himself. 'Life; it'll kill you.'

Viz and Gen sat there observing, content to let me do the talking for the time being.

I'd met one ghost before, and he hadn't been anywhere near as friendly as this guy. As a matter of fact, he'd been so *unfriendly* that I'd had to feed his semi-corporeal form into the guts of a London Underground escalator (again, it's a long story).

'Please can someone explain what's going on?' said Neil, fed up at being left out of the conversation, yet again.

'Why can't he see you?' I asked the ghost.

'Because he doesn't have The Sight, that's why. Apparently

the rest of you do though, which makes me wonder, what kind of Uncanny are you?'

Vizael leaned forward in his chair. 'Who are you, ghost?'

'The name's Jake Fletcher,' the stranger replied, straightening his tie.

Viz squinted at him. 'Jake? As in short for Jacob?'

'That's right. What of it?'

'May I ask, are you a religious man, Mister Fletcher?'

'It's been a while since I've sat in a pew and belted out a bible banger, if that's what you're asking.'

'Then permit me to refresh your memory and remind you of a story from the Book of Genesis. In it, a man named Jacob is said to have crossed the ford of the Jabbok and wrestled with an angel from dusk until dawn. I was that angel, Jake, short for Jacob. So tell me this, am I going to have to choke-slam you too?'

I studied the ghost's face for a reaction, but if he was rattled at all, he did a good job of hiding it.

'Tell you what, old man,' the ghost replied, 'how about I answer that question with a smack in the mouth?'

Neil flinched as Viz reached for his sword cane. Gen went for her morning star.

'Woah, woah, woah!' I said. 'Easy now.' Everyone froze. Some of the restaurant's other patrons looked over to our booth to see what the commotion was, including a fry cook dressed in a filthy apron that violated any number of health code regulations. I lowered my voice to a whisper. 'Why don't we all take a minute and chill out?'

'I've got a better idea,' said the ghost, 'why don't you tell me why you tried to off my friend, or I'll do worse than wrestle you.'

What the what? 'Listen, mate, unless your friend's a vampire, I had nothing to do with it.'

'She's not a vampire, she's a coroner. Goes by the name of Doctor Anand, and according to my source, you attacked her at her morgue.'

'In that case, your source is full of shit,' I told him. 'I kill vampires, not doctors.' He didn't look convinced, so I showed him the brand on my palm. 'I'm hoping you know what this means?'

He saw the N seared into my flesh. 'Oh, bollocks.'

'Yeah, *oh, bollocks.*'

The ghost's expression hardened. I saw his fists bunch. 'Razor...'

'You what?'

'An eaves I know. He was the one who told me you were on the hook for Anand getting a new neck hole.'

'Sounds like you need a new informant.'

Jake sighed and slotted himself into the booth beside me.

'Shuffle up,' I told Neil.

'Oh cool, is the ghost joining us for breakfast now? That's great. Nothing mental about that.'

Jake looked to Viz, sat opposite the table from him. 'Sorry about that. I tend not to get on with angels.'

'Nor I with ghosts,' Viz replied, 'unless you count the holy ghost.'

The two of them shook hands, which came as a surprise, being as I thought ghosts were supposed to pass through solid objects.

'So then,' I said, 'now we're all chums, why don't you tell us about this friend of yours?'

'Anand? She was the coroner who performed my autopsy.'

Gen pushed her plate away. 'Thank you for that image.'

'Nothing wrong with an old autopsy,' said Jake. 'That's an intimate act, that is. Maybe the most intimate, when you really think about it.'

'Can someone please tell me what the invisible ghost is doing here?' asked Neil, at the end of his tether now.

I turned back to Jake. 'Since you're sticking around, what *are* you doing?'

'Well, being as I came in here all half-cocked, I feel like I owe you a favour.'

'What kind of a favour?' Gen asked, eyes narrowed.

'A bit of information you might be interested in,' he replied, turning to me, 'what with you being the intrepid Nightstalker and all.'

'I'm listening.'

He set his elbows on the table and spoke in hushed tones. 'A bloke showed up at my office the other day, knees knocking, piss-scared. I sussed him for a vamp right away; one of them Judas Clan vamps.'

'What did a vampire want with a ghost?' It sounded like the start of a bad Halloween joke.

'I meet a lot of characters in my line of work, love,' Jake explained. 'I'm a PI. Folks call me the spectral detective. Ring any bells?'

I shook my head. 'Don't take it personally, I've been a bit tied up with the whole vampire apocalypse thing.'

'Fair play. Anyway, this Clan geezer reaches out to me saying he needs help.'

'Your help? I don't get it. Why come to you?'

'Why not?' he said, defensively. 'I can be pretty handy. Ask around. So, this vamp who came to see me… I got the feeling our conversation wasn't strictly on the record. Like he was acting alone, without Clan approval.'

Without Clan approval? Judas must be losing grip of his people if they were seeking help behind his back. Savina really was a force to be reckoned with.

'That's interesting,' I said.

'Got my attention too, but not as much as the vamp's story did. Apparently, some wrong'uns have been knocking off his old muckers by the boatload. Really sticking the boot in. Worst threat the Clan have ever faced, so he tells me. Far worse than anything they've had to deal with from the Nightstalker. His words, not mine.'

Now it was my turn to get defensive. 'Look, I already know all of this, so there's really only one thing I care about: how exactly did your conversation with this vampire end?'

The ghost folded his arms. 'How do you think? I told him to get fucked. I have standards, you know?'

We sat there for a moment staring at each other.

'So,' said Viz, rejoining the conversation, 'where do we go from here?'

Neil held up a hand. 'I know I've only been able to hear half of this little chat, but from what I've picked up, it sounds like the four of us and Mister Ghost have a common enemy. Have I got that right?'

'Yeah,' I said. 'I suppose.'

Technically, we were on the same side. I wanted Savina for cutting up Neil, and the ghost wanted Savina—or one of her soldiers at least—for cutting up his doctor friend. Our motivations matched.

'Tell you what,' said the ghost, unfolding his arms, 'you seem like a nice enough lot, so I'm going to do you a favour. I'm going to let you help me slot the muppet who attacked Anand.'

Gen snorted. 'Help *you*? If anything, you're helping *us*.'

'Not until I get what I want.'

'What's that supposed to mean?' asked Gen.

The ghost smiled and reached inside his jacket.

'Hands where I can see them,' I insisted, pressing the tip of my dagger into the ghost's crotch.

'Easy, girl,' he said, taking a peek under the table. 'Nice weapon, by the way. Enough to make a bloke feel inadequate, that.'

He slowly dipped a hand into his inside pocket and produced a sheaf of black and white photographs, which he spread across the table. The photos were of me and Gen, fleeing Beehive's bath-house, pebble-dashed in blood and brains.

'Oh, that is not a good look,' I said.

'Where did you get these?' Gen demanded.

'The copper you had a barney with—the one with the natty bob and the no-fucking-around attitude—she's a mate of mine.'

I turned to Gen, then back to the ghost. 'We tried to blank her memory but it didn't work. Why was that?'

'Because Kat has The Sight too, that's why. Don't get hung up on it. What matters is that she has copies of these CCTV pictures, and a real hard-on for you two. Now, I can leave her out of this and let her carry on her investigation, which will—believe me—cause you no end of shit, or we can be friends and I can tell her to drop the case and take your faces off the criminal register. So, what's it going to be, ladies and germs? Do we have a deal?'

I discreetly placed the dagger back in its sheath. 'Listen, Casper, you seem like a friendly enough ghost, but this is risky business. You've died once already – why don't you let us do the heavy lifting so it doesn't happen again?'

The phantom cocked an eyebrow. 'Sweetheart, I've literally been to Hell and back. I reckon I can handle a few misbehaving bloodsuckers.'

'This is a specialised area,' said Viz, offering some wisdom. 'Vampires are the Nightstalker's purview. Let Abbey do her work. Do not fear, she will avenge your doctor friend, just as soon as we have located the person responsible for harming her.'

'You mean you don't know where this nutter is?' asked Jake.

'Not exactly, no,' I admitted.

The spectral detective grinned. 'Well then, that's something I can definitely help you with. Finding things is sort of my specialty.'

18

I persuaded the rest of the gang to return to The Vault while I accompanied Jake on an expedition. None of them was particularly thrilled at the notion of me toddling off with a dead man we barely knew, but I assured them I could handle myself. This was a one-person job, and there was plenty of other work they could be getting on with in my absence. After all, someone needed to figure out what exactly we were going to do with Savina once we'd found her. We might be able to corner this cat, but we still had to deal with her claws.

Jake took me on a field trip to King's Cross for reasons he wasn't in a hurry to explain. On the way there, I told him what I knew about Savina, and explained how Anand had come to be caught in the crossfire.

'Bloody vampires,' he said. 'Never did like them. Got a bit of aggro from a couple a while back. Bad bastards.'

I agreed. 'So, this detective stuff, this is this what you do now, since you… you know...?'

'Fell off me perch? Curled up me toes? Yeah. I help out clients and I work off sins from a misspent youth.'

'What does that mean?'

'It means I've got this ledger I need to get the red out of. It's a whole thing.'

'You get a lot of work then?'

'Mate, I'm the busiest dead man since Tupac Shakur.'

I laughed. I was starting to like this guy. 'So what's it like, Jake? Being dead?'

He grinned. 'They say death is the ultimate adventure, but truth be told, I'd take a dirty weekend in Margate any day.'

We strolled on through some smelly back streets until we arrived at a shop front sandwiched between an adult book store and an out-of-business jewellers. Hanging above the establishment's door was a weathered sign, upon which—written in scabby gold paint—was the word Legerdomain.

'What's this then, a shop for ghosts?'

'What would a shop for ghosts sell?'

'I don't know. Ectoplasm? Extra rattly chains?'

'You should probably stop talking.'

'Point taken.'

'This, my dear, sweet girl, is where the magic happens.' He swept a hand theatrically through the air. 'And I say that literally.'

He walked through the shop door without opening it, drifting through a solid object like it wasn't even there. It was comforting in a way. You want your ghosts to be able to do that.

I pushed through the door using the old-fashioned method, and stepped inside, triggering a bell. The decor of the shop was a queasy red colour; walls, ceiling and carpet. Bowed black shelves heaved under dusty magic sets, crystal balls, ventriloquist dummies, and juggling pins.

Sitting behind the counter with her nose buried in a celebrity magazine was a middle-aged woman wearing an unflattering outfit that looked more like a quilt some grandma had stitched together than a dress. A mop of grey hair like a thundercloud hovered over her head. She had the stony, unyielding features of someone who didn't laugh very much, if at all.

Jake made introductions. 'Abbey, I'd like you to meet my good friend, Madame Olena, better known as Jazz Hands.'

The woman looked up from her magazine, perched a pair of violet-lensed spectacles on her nose, and frowned. 'More waifs and strays, Fletcher? Bit young for you, isn't she? Not to mention *alive*.'

'Jazz, this one's not just some bit of fluff, she's the Nightstalker.'

'Well, bully for her,' the woman replied, returning to her magazine.

'Why do they call you Jazz Hands?' I asked.

'*They* don't,' she huffed. '*He* does.'

Jake brought his mouth to my ear. 'On account of the magic,' he said, wiggling his fingers and pantomiming a bit of abracadabra.

'She doesn't seem very friendly,' I whispered back.

'Don't you worry. Just let old Jake turn on the charm spigot and off we go.' He gave me a wink and sidled up to the shop counter. 'So. Turns out I need a favour.'

'When do you ever need anything else?' she sniped.

'Don't be like that, Jazz. What about the other day when I brought you that nice bunch of flowers from my favourite florist?'

'You mean the bunch of flowers you stole from a grave?'

'Aw, come on. What was I supposed to do? You know I have trouble handling money. Like, literally.' He swiped a ghostly hand through the counter to make his point.

The woman continued to read her article, uninterested.

'Pretty please,' Jake pleaded, placing his hands together in prayer.

The woman grunted

'Pretty please with a cherry on top?'

She set down her magazine. 'You're not going to leave me alone, are you?'

'Not a chance.'

The woman sighed and regarded me with hooded eyes. 'What is it the girl wants?'

'What I want,' I said, insinuating myself into their conversation, 'is for you to help me find a killer.'

'Is that so? What kind of a killer?'

'The fanged kind.'

'Not just any kind of vampire either,' Jake interjected. 'The tippy-top of her bloodline.'

'I see.' Her eyes stayed glued to me. 'Come closer then, let me get a look at you.'

I approached the counter feeling more than a little exposed.

'So, you're the Nightstalker, are you? And what's that around your neck?' She stabbed a finger at me.

The pendant Vizael had given me—the one I'd used to follow the trail of magic to the Society of the Black Sun—I had it on still without realising. I have a habit of going to bed wearing my jewellery. Tampons too. If the Clan weren't the end of me, Toxic Shock Syndrome would be the next most likely culprit.

'Give it here,' said the woman, and I handed it over. She held the silver pendant by its long, thin chain and let it spin slowly so she could examine it. 'Good God, woman, what cowboy made this?'

'Don't mind her,' said Jake. 'This is her field, and she can be a bit critical about it. You know how it is when you get a plumber in and they spend half the time they're there rubbishing the work of the last bloke you had in? Same thing.'

Jazz Hands set the pendant down on the counter, her lip curled in disgust. 'I can make this tracking charm work for you,' she said. 'Modify it so you can use it to find your fanged killer. Give it a *signal boost*, as you kids are so fond of saying.'

'Thank you,' I replied.

'Very well then, let us begin.' She closed her eyes, tilted her head back, and cupped her hands over the pendant.

'I'd step back for this bit, if I were you,' Jake warned.

I retreated a few steps as Jazz Hands went to work, chanting in some alien language, her volume rising, words colliding against one another like crashing waves. The room seemed heavy with electricity, and a roaring waterfall of static filled my ears. Ribbons of coloured light escaped from between the woman's fingers, shooting off in every direction, blinding in their intensity, making the air wobble with liquid heat.

Then the light show went out.

Silence.

Stillness.

The room was back to normal.

'My payment, please,' Jazz Hands insisted.

'How much do you want?'

'What do you have?'

I turned out my pockets and found a ruby the size of a walnut. It used to belong to Lauden, before I robbed it. And no, I probably shouldn't have been carrying the thing around with me, but it was just *so shiny*.

'That, uh, should just about cover it,' said the woman, trying to stop her eyes looking quite so wide and hungry.

'Ah, man, this is the last of the stash. I was going to use this thing to buy us an air hockey table.'

She gave me gimme fingers. *Hand it over.*

'Do I at least get change?'

She rummaged around the till and produced a fiver.

'Fine.' I set the ruby down on the counter.

The woman popped the till and dropped it in the drawer before handing me my change and slamming it shut. 'There,' she said, scooping up the pendant and tossing it back to me. 'Caveat emptor.'

The metal was hot to the touch still, which forced me to play a little game of hot potato before the thing was cool enough to put back on.

'Caveat emptor? What is that? The magic word that makes it go?'

'It's Latin, you nincompoop. It means buyer beware.'

I won't lie, that stung. 'This thing had better work,' I grumbled.

'Of course it will. The pendant is now capable of pinpointing your vampire exactly. All you need is to find someone who belongs to her bloodline, smear their blood on it, and the pendant will act as a dowsing rod that leads you to your prey.'

Hmm. I was hoping for a simple dot on a map, but apparently this thing came Batteries Not Included. 'Thanks,' I said, doing my best to mask my disappointment

She sniffed and returned to her magazine, less interested in my vampire vendetta than why Ryan Reynolds was upset at being unfollowed on Instagram by whoever (or whatever) a "Blake Lively" was.

'Right then, thanks for everything,' I said, turning to Jake. 'I'd better be off.'

'I've got nothing on if you want an extra insubstantial hand.'

'Thanks, but you've done more than enough, Jake. It's like Viz said, vampires are my thing.'

He gave me that wonky smile of his and shook my hand. 'All right, Abbey Beckett, good luck, hope you don't end up stone dead.'

'I don't remember telling you my surname.'

'What can I say? Your thing's vampires, mine's being nosey.'

'Fair enough. And you're sure you're all right taking a back-seat on this one?'

'Yeah. I need to have a word with the eaves who almost tricked me into knocking your block off anyway. Just promise me one thing before you go.'

'What's that?'

'When you find this vampire, you deal with her. No trial, no mucking about, just get it done. Understood?'

I remembered what Judas had shown me; visions of Savina's cruelty through the centuries. More than that though, I remembered the look on Beehive's face when she escaped my grasp for the third time. 'Don't you worry. I'm going to batter them all silly.'

He laughed. 'You really hate this lot, don't you?'

'Oh yeah. They're right up there with unicycle owners and people who use the word "entrepreneur" in their twitter bio.'

Jake crossed himself. 'In that case, may God have mercy on their souls.'

19

I arrived back at The Vault, for once not drenched in blood, which was a nice change of pace. The gang were sat in the War Room, peppered around our circular table, each wearing a face like they were stuck in a state of perpetual satellite delay.

'Would I be right in saying you haven't sussed out a way to defeat Savina yet?'

'Let us call it a work in progress,' Vizael replied.

'Well, at least one of us has something.' I slid the pendant across the table like a hockey puck.

'My word,' Viz exclaimed, catching it and jolting upright. 'Who did this?'

'Did what?' asked Neil, squinting at what—to him and the rest of us—looked like the same bit of jewellery I'd been wearing for days.

'Someone has performed a powerful invocation upon this item,' Viz explained, rolling the pendant around in his chubby palm. 'This is the work of a master enchanter.'

'I don't know about that,' I said, 'it needs dipping in vampire blood before it even switches on.'

I explained what Jazz Hands had told me; that the pendant would lead us to Savina only once it had been given a lick of her bloodline's red stuff. 'Question is, how are we meant to get hold of that?'

Gen was the one to answer. 'I have an idea, but you're not going to like it.'

'Try me.'

'We draw out one of Savina's soldiers by using bait.'

'What kind of bait?'

'Your boyfriend.'

'Pardon me?' said Neil. 'Because it sounded like you said you wanted to use me as bait.'

'That is what she said. That's ridiculous, Gen.'

'Yeah, I have to say, I'm not totally wild about it either,' Neil reported.

'What's the matter, boy?' Gen shot back. 'You keep saying you want to be involved in this fight. Well, this is it. This is your chance to be a contribution.'

'Gen, I'm not putting Neil in the firing line just because we don't have any decent ideas.'

'This *is* a decent idea. A practical one too. Think about it; Neil can perform an *actual* function for once.'

'As bait? Why would we even need that? Why not just point the vampire the way we want her to go and jump her when she sets off our trap?' I wasn't exactly sure how any of that would work, but it took Neil out of the equation, and that's all I really cared about.

'A trap doesn't work without a lure. The Clan won't come to us without a reason. Neil can be that reason.'

I turned to Viz for support. 'Will you tell her she's off her nut?'

The old man tented his fingers and sucked in some air. 'It might not be the worst idea. We know Savina's people are killing off the Clan. If we could somehow convince them that Neil was a Clansman...'

'If it's a Clansman you want, why not Carlo?'

'Because they'd smell Carlo a mile off,' Gen replied. 'I can still smell him on my clothes, and it's been days since we visited that storage unit.'

I was beginning to get seriously wound up. 'Tell you what, Gen, if you're so keen on this bait plan, why don't you dangle yourself on the line?'

'Because that would be a waste of our firepower,' she replied. 'I am a capable fighter. That is my specialty. Neil's specialty—as he has proved time and time again—is getting himself in trouble.'

'Thanks…?' replied Neil.

'That's hardly the only thing he's good at,' I argued.

'Really? Then what else?'

'He's… he's… well, he's great at, um…'

Neil held up a hand. 'Let me help you out there before you give yourself an aneurysm. I'll do it.'

'What?'

'I said, I'll do it. I'll be the bait.'

'You're not putting yourself in danger like that,' I told him. 'You'd be chum in the water out there.'

'I'm doing it. It's my choice.'

'No. I'm the Nightstalker, I'm the boss of this little outfit, and I say no.'

'Don't be such a control freak.'

'Don't tell me I'm a control freak! I decide who's a control freak!'

Neil arched an eyebrow.

'Okay, I just heard that, but my point still stands. No being bait.'

'Abbey, I'm going to do this whether you like it or not. Unless of course you have any better ideas?'

There was that pregnant pause again.

I had to admit, deep down, I was impressed at Neil for stepping up like that. Of course, I wasn't exactly chuffed at the idea of dangling him in front of Savina's people like a hot bag of blood, but he'd shown some big, swinging balls, no doubt about it.

It took a lot more convincing to persuade me that Gen's plan had merit, but after a few hours of strenuous debate, we arrived at a strategy that balanced risk and reward in a way I wasn't entirely uncomfortable with. I didn't like it, but then I didn't like the idea of Savina and her band of merry bitches running wild either.

We used an eaves to get a message out there (the reliable kind, not the type who'd fitted Jake up and sent him on a suicide mission). Typically speaking, people pay eaves' to provide them with gossip, but they can be used to disseminate rumours too. Little fun fact for you there.

The message we spread was meant to provide Savina's people with the motivation they needed to walk into our ambush. The location we chose was perfect; a Docklands warehouse, out of the way, nice and private. A few weeks back, before Savina arrived on the scene, we'd discovered that the Clan used the place to host a backroom poker game: a little after-dark gambling den for yuppie vamps to smoke cigars and fritter away their riches. We soon took care of that, and now, having mopped up the blood, we had ourselves the perfect site for a trap. A site that our eaves had told the whole of the Uncanny Kingdom about.

'I hope no one died in this thing,' said Neil, running a finger under his collar.

He was wearing a suit about two sizes too big for him, a suit we'd liberated from a charity shop only hours earlier.

'Apologies, it's the best I could do at short notice,' Viz replied.

If Neil was going to be the bait that tempted Savina's people into this "Clan hideout", he needed to look the part, and a threadbare Thundercats t-shirt wasn't going to cut it.

It was nighttime, and the city was coloured bone-white with moonlight. We let ourselves into the warehouse and shuttered the door behind us. If you want to build a mental picture of the inside of the place, imagine a low-lit scene from any low-budget action movie: pigeons fluttering in the rafters, chains hanging from the ceiling for no good reason, and plenty of water dripping through the roof to give off a nice, eerie ambience. At the far end of the space was a manager's office overlooking the factory floor, accessible via a series of stairways and catwalks. The office lit the warehouse's dark interior like an angler fish's luminous lure.

'That's where we'll place the bait,' said Gen, pointing up at the office.

'Hi,' said Neil, giving her a wave. 'I'm Neil by the way, "the bait".'

Gen ignored him. 'We only have until midnight to lay our trap. Come on.'

We headed upstairs, Neil's oxygen tank clanking as he dragged it up the metal steps.

We followed a catwalk to the manager's office, a decent-sized space that had once been used to oversee a thriving flour mill, but had since been converted into a two-bit casino that smelled of stale sweat and tobacco. Neil took a seat in one of the chairs and slid his tank beneath the table.

'Look at me,' said Neil, 'aren't I just the plumpest, juiciest bait you ever saw?'

Despite his bravado, I could see his knee jittering up and down.

'It's going to be all right,' I told him, and turned to Gen. 'Tell him it's going to be all right.'

Given Gen's notorious lack of people skills, Viz saw fit to talk on her behalf. 'Time is fleeting, and we have yet to discuss our strategy. I recommend we do so as quickly as possible in order to ensure Neil's safety.'

'Okay,' I said, 'hit me with it, Highway to Heaven.'

Viz bobbed his head and went on. 'Now, we know from your previous encounter with Savina's soldiers that they have the ability to turn gaseous, which means we'll have to be especially careful they're not given the chance to escape once they've triggered our ambush. To ensure that doesn't happen, I'll be taking it upon myself to seal off all but one entry point.' Using his walking stick, he pointed through the office window and downstairs to the door we'd used to enter the warehouse. 'The three of us will position ourselves on the shop floor and observe that entrance from a hidden vantage point, while our bait draws their attention up here. Once they're through the door they'll smell blood, see Neil in his suit and go to work.'

'And what about us?'

'The moment our prey steps through that entrance, we will seal it off and take them down before they get anywhere near this floor.'

It seemed like a sound enough plan. 'How do we know how many people Savina will send?'

Gen answered. 'She sent a single soldier to dispatch a hive of high-ranking Clan members. As far as they're concerned, they're coming here to terminate a small group of gamblers. We have every reason to believe we'll be dealing with a lone operative.'

Neil raised a hand. 'And just in case anything does go wrong, do we have a Plan B?

'Yes,' said Gen. 'Don't fuck up Plan A.'

We waited for an hour. Then another. By half-two in the morning, I was seriously starting to doubt whether this Dracula drop-in was going down. The anticipation was killing me. I felt like a dog sat at her master's heels, waiting on him to open a bag of kibble. What happened? Did the word not reach Savina's people, or did we get hoodwinked by an eaves too? What's coming of this world when you can't put your faith in a rat-faced weasel who trades gossip for cash?

I looked up from the unlit factory floor to the manager's office, and saw Neil nodding off in his chair.

'What do you reckon?' I asked Vizael, stifling a yawn. 'Do we call it a day?'

His lips were parted to answer my question, when—

A distant hissing noise.

Gen's head turned on a swivel. 'What is that?'

'Er, guys…' Neil's voice.

My eyes shot to the other end of the factory. Through the glowing rectangle of the office window, I saw Neil spring from his chair. Above him, pouring through a ventilation duct, were two tendrils of red mist. The tendrils snaked down, growing ever-solid, twisting around each other like a double helix.

I dug a knuckle into Viz's arm. 'You said you'd sealed off all the other entrances!'

'I thought I had,' he stammered, glancing back at the "lone" choke point we'd been guarding, as though it would shoulder the blame for him.

For a second I floundered, then my legs came to life and began carrying me in the direction of the danger. I pegged it towards the office, crossing the entirety of the factory floor and sprinting up two flights of steps. I was going like the clappers, but I felt like I was moving in slow motion. Like I was wading through treacle. Every second I wasted was another second Neil was stuck there alone with… whatever or whoever had slipped by us and breached our trap.

I bolted across the catwalk, heart hammering, feet pounding metal like two sacks of wet cement. I shouldered the office door off its hinges and felled it like a drawbridge. My heart almost stopped when I saw what was going on inside.

Neil was laid flat out on his back, pinned to the table by a pair of intruders; two women, identical, crazy-looking. Their hair shot off in every direction, as though it was trying to escape from their heads. Their bodies were thin and wiry, their bare arms covered in spidery blue veins that looked like a madman's Biro scribble. In their hands they carried small, hooked blades; their sharpened edges held disconcertingly close to Neil's groin, which was out in the open. The vampires had pulled his trousers to his ankles, exposing his pale, white flesh from his waist to his socks.

'Do something!' he screamed, wriggling helplessly.

Working on instinct, I snatched my dagger from its sheath and launched it at the vampire holding Neil's feet. She twisted her body to avoid the blade and came away with nothing worse than a nick across her forearm. It was enough to get her attention though.

The vampires hissed liked spritzed cats and released their grip on Neil. What was I facing here? I was counting on Beehive to show up, but instead, I'd been graced with this gruesome twosome. I readied myself for their attack, but by this point Gen and Viz had caught up with me, tipping the odds in my favour. The vampires regarded us for a moment with wild, darting eyes, then made their retreat, transforming into twin plumes of red mist and heading for the ceiling.

'They're getting away,' I shouted, stating the obvious.

It was too late to stop them, even if I were able to somehow wrangle smoke. The tendrils slithered into the ventilation duct and vanished from view.

I tugged my dagger from the wall. 'Come on,' I cried, pogoing on the spot in frustration, 'we have to get after them.'

Viz slumped into a chair and groaned. 'Give it up, Abbey. They're gone.'

'That was our one chance, you doddery old codger! How could you let that happen?

Gen shook her head at him. 'Another mission failed, thanks to you.'

'Mission?' cried Neil, gathering up his trousers. 'What about me?'

He was red-faced, wiping away tears with the cuff of his oversized jacket. He looked like a child, dressed up for a wedding and throwing a tantrum.

I put an arm around his shoulder. 'I'm so sorry, Neil…'

'I almost got castrated!'

'That was my error,' Viz admitted.

'Damn right it was,' Gen agreed.

'No,' said Neil, his eyes boring into me. 'This is on you. None of this would have happened if you hadn't joined up with those two loonies. None of it!'

He said the last so loud that he blew his breathing tube from his nostrils.

'Let me get that,' I said, stooping down to pick it up, but he snatched it away from me.

'And that's another thing,' he said, plugging himself back into his oxygen tank, I wouldn't even have to use this thing if you'd just let me be.'

'Let you be? You mean let you be a vampire?'

'You ever hear of a vampire with cystic fibrosis?' The truth was coming out now. 'I was strong, Abbey. Immortal. Now I'm just a fucking invalid again.'

'You were six feet under!' I cried. 'I saved you!'

'Do I look saved to you?'

Viz and Gendith had retreated to a distance while the two of us tore strips off each other.

'I don't get you, Neil. One minute you're telling me you're

pissed off that I got mixed up in all this, now you're saying you want to be a vampire? What do you want from me?'

'What do I want? I want you to leave me alone.'

'You want to be alone? Fine. Be alone.'

I couldn't argue anymore. It was getting on for four in the morning, and if I didn't get out of that room fast, I was going to put my fist through someone. I spun on my heel and went for the door.

20

There was really only one place to go if you wanted to completely get away from the world at four in the morning, and that was The Beehive.

Lenny, the proprietor, wasn't in possession of a 24-hour drinking licence, but then his pub didn't abide by the laws of the land, nor the laws of physics.

As I passed through the threshold, I felt a familiar, warm tingle as my body punctured the bubble of dampening magic that protected the place. Lenny had installed it years ago as an insurance policy after a couple of warlocks got into a spat about whose round it was, and started slinging fireballs at one another. Now, The Beehive was a safe place, for the most part anyway. Just don't get on the wrong side of Lenny. I once saw a guy ask him for a drinking straw, and he left the place wearing his arse for a hat.

I sat in the corner of the pub, alone, ignoring the rest of the pub's patrons; a motley collection of scoundrels and sinners, ghouls and goblins. The place wasn't for everyone, with its sticky floor, grubby surfaces, and occasional vermin infestations, but I'd sooner drink there surrounded by monsters than prop up a bar at some hipster joint with top-knotted web designers who brine their own pickles.

I was two drinks in and staring into the hypnotising amber of my beer. The dancing eddy of bubbles reminded me of blood cells squirming under a microscope. It was soothing to watch, and drinking the stuff didn't hurt either. By the time I'd polished off my third pint, the tension I'd been feeling had slithered from my brain and was ready to exit gracefully through the soles of my feet.

'Abbey.'

I looked up from my glass to see Gendith towering over me.

'What do you want?' I grunted.

'Same thing as you, to get away from those two.'

'Three,' I corrected. 'It was your plan that almost got Neil killed.'

Gen's eyebrows knitted together. 'Vizael was the one who let us down. The plan was solid, only the execution was flawed.'

She had a point there. The old man really did shit the bed. 'Well, are you going to sit down or are you going to just stand there like a gorgeous giraffe?'

Gen smiled, pulled out a seat, and tucked her long legs under the table. She ordered another round of beers, and Lenny delivered them without a word. The man was a locked box; as taciturn as he was gigantic.

Gen and I supped from our pints. For a while, the two of us didn't speak. I was halfway through my drink before Gen broke the silence.

'That stupid, old man. Of all the angels, why did I have to be assigned to him? Why was I made to study at the feet of that senile fool? I am so tired of doing his bidding. So sick of his incompetence, his senility. He's so out of touch. So antiquated. Shuffling around on his walking stick and smelling like a bingo hall. It's driving me insane. The only reason we're even dealing with a vampire epidemic is because he failed to kill Judas when he had the chance.'

I let out a long whistle. 'Bloody hell, Gen, tell me what you really think.'

'I'm sorry, I've been holding that in for a while.'

'I can tell.' I stifled a burp. 'Gen, I've been meaning to ask, why do you let Viz boss you around?'

'I explained that already. I serve Vizael because I was

instructed to by God, back when I was a new angel, all young, dumb, and full of kumbaya.'

That didn't explain why she continued to do the Big Man's bidding—particularly as He'd been an absent Father ever since—but I let it slide and changed the subject.

'That story Savina mentioned—the one about you being burned in the Salem witch trials—was that true?'

Her face stiffened. 'Yes.'

It was obvious she didn't want to talk about it. I took a pull on my beer. 'So then… um, what's Heaven like?'

'I'm not telling you that.'

'What do you care – they chucked you out, right? Why did they do that anyway? I thought you angels farted rainbows.'

Gen remained closed-mouthed.

'You're a real Chatty Cathy, you know that?'

Gendith finished her drink and placed her palms on the table. 'You've been asking a lot of questions, so why don't you answer one of mine?'

'Go ahead, I'm an open book, ask me anything, anything at all.'

'What exactly do you see in Neil?'

'Anything apart from that.'

Gen snorted. 'I thought so.'

I saw Neil in my mind's eye for a moment, how angry he'd been. I dismissed him with a shake of the head.

'I'm just finding it hard to think about Neil, that's all. Hard to think about men at all, really. Maybe the two of us should just ditch that useless pair of blokes and go it alone. Listen to me, I sound like a right old Lesbo Baggins.'

Gen looked at me, quizzically. 'Do you have a problem with lesbians?'

'What? No, of course not.'

I leaned across the table to her conspiratorially. I had something I'd been holding in for a while too, and I really wanted it off my chest. Gen wasn't my first choice for a confidante, but who else was I meant to unload on? My circle of friends had dilated pretty tight since I became the Nightstalker.

'Can I tell you a secret?' I asked.

'If it's about that horrible tattoo on your thigh, I already know.'

'No, it's not that, and what's wrong with my Edgar Allan Poe tattoo?' I took a breath. 'Listen, back when Neil was out of the picture and Lauden was around… the two of us got kind of close. If you catch my drift.'

I was talking about the vampire who'd turned Neil. The one who'd almost succeeded in turning me too, before I got wise and murdered the bloke.

Gen shrugged. 'You got taken for a ride. So what? It would never have worked anyway… physically, I mean. Vampires are impotent. Something to do with blood flow to the… well, you know.'

'Oh, that's definitely not true,' I replied, way too quickly, trying to stifle the smile that was attempting to force its way across my face.

'How would you know?' Gen asked, regarding me coolly.

'I kind of… well, I sort of, in a way, slept with Lauden. By accident.'

Gen's lips thinned. 'You slept with a vampire? We don't get into bed with monsters, Abbey, I thought that went without saying. Do I need to crochet it on a picture frame so you hang it over your headboard?' She shook her head, flabbergasted. 'So?'

'So what?'

'So how was he?'

She propped her elbows on the table and leaned forward, swaying just a little. Apparently, I wasn't the only one feeling the beer.

I smiled. 'He was gentle. Experienced. Not like some men, rooting around up there like they're looking for a factory reset button.'

Her lips quirked. 'You have a lot of experience?'

'No, the opposite, really. Just a couple before Neil came along.'

She nodded. 'And now you're here, hiding from him in The Beehive. Why?'

'Because I'm fed up with the guy, and this is somewhere I know he can't follow me.'

'Are you hiding, or are you trying to push him away?'

'What do you mean?'

'I mean, is the real reason you're avoiding him because you're worried that your relationship has finally run its course, and that being around him any longer will only confirm that suspicion?'

'Hey, I've got an idea,' I said, clicking my fingers, 'let's get another drink instead of answering that question!'

I drained the last of my beer and waved across the bar to Lenny. 'Shots!'

'Shots?' said Gen, a note of concern in her voice.

'Yeah. You know what they say: when life gives you lemons, ask for salt and tequila.'

Lenny lumbered into view with two short measures and set them down on the table with a grunt.

'Cheers,' I said, and clinked Gen's glass.

Judging by my previous encounters with tequila, this was probably going to end with me throwing up, falling down, and making a puke angel, but I figured what the hell.

'Ladies night!' I said, then drained my glass and slammed it obnoxiously on the table.

I have no idea what time it was when we left that place, but I do remember birdsong and spots of sunlight peeking over the rooftops.

For once, the two of us were as drunk as each other as we weaved our way home, screeching the words to *Ebony and Ivory*. I admired Gen's tottering pins as she ricochetted to and fro on her endless legs; the legs of a thoroughbred dressage horse. We rounded into a side street, and as we banked the corner, she took a sudden veer. The innumerable tequila shots she'd downed sent her tumbling and pinned her to the alley wall, where she laughed like a goon, trying to regain her balance and failing miserably.

'Come on, you big lump, time to go home.' I took her by the hand and attempted to get her in motion, but she stayed rooted to the spot, giggling still.

It was contagious. I chuckled along with her, revelling in the rare sight of Gen enjoying herself. She was laughing so hard I could see her back teeth – a sight I'd only seen once before, and that was only because she was rushing into battle and unleashing a war cry.

I looked at her under the chalky glow of a streetlight that had yet to switch itself off, and stroked some stray hair away from her eyes.

'I must look like a total mess,' she said, grinning back at me.

'Are you serious? You look fucking heart-stopping, Gen. I tell you what, if I was a guy…'

A smile tugged at her perfect, bee-stung lips. 'Yes? What would you do?' She studied me with eyes as blue as glacier run-off.

As we stood there, looking into each other's eyes, something strange happened. I found myself leaning in, bringing my face close to hers, and stranger still, I found her doing the same...

What the hell was going on?

I was about to kiss a girl. I'd never kissed a girl. I'd *thought* about kissing a girl—of course I had, who hadn't?—but to actually go ahead and do it?

'What is this?' I asked, my lips all but brushing hers now. 'I thought you hated me.'

'I don't hate you.'

'Then you've been giving off some seriously mixed signals.'

I thought the two of us were getting on, not getting *it* on. I'd always thought Gen was nice to look at, but not in this way. Not in a lady-boner way. Okay, there had been the odd hair-smelling hug, but that was different. That was friendly. This was… well, I don't know what it was exactly. Was it magic? Had Gen put a spell on me? Lowered my defences with some angel super-roofie?

No.

This wasn't something she was doing, it was something that was just happening. Something that was happening to me *and* Gen, and it had taken us both by surprise. All the times she'd told me to let go of my attachments, all the times we'd fought side-by-side, we'd been blind to what was really happening. The truth was, we'd been developing an attachment for each other.

The love in our love/hate relationship had formed a grain of sand that had polished the hate into a perfect, gleaming pearl. Or at least it felt perfect, right there, the two of us holding on to each other, bathed in lamplight, feeling each other's breath, hot on our skin.

I gave in.

My lips parted, and I felt all the tension between Gen and me released in one explosive moment of passion. Breath shaking, I placed my hand on the back of her head and pulled her quickly to my mouth. Our lips slammed together hard enough to knock the air from my lungs. Two women—an avenging angel and a vampire slayer—snogging in the street. It's fair to say that somewhere in the world there was a nerd with only two wishes left.

My hands worked their way around Gen's body, feeling the crevasse at the small of her back, grazing the supple lines of her flawless physique. In return, her fingertips ran up and down my spine, coaxing shivers out of me, making me feel things I hadn't felt before. The brand crackled and sparked in my hand, electrified by her touch, painting the alleyway neon blue.

Then a third person paid a visit. 'Abbey?'

It was Neil.

Oh, shit.

He must have used The Vault's magic door to get here; stepped out of a shop doorway and snuck up on us, unnoticed. He stood off to one side, shoulders slumped, a wretched, hangdog look on his face.

I pulled away from Gen like a teenager caught with her pants around her ankles. 'Neil, what are you doing?'

'What am *I* doing?' He held up his phone, displaying the app that tracked my mobile. 'You didn't come home, so I wanted to make sure you were okay. Looks like you're doing fine though. Hi, Gen.'

'This isn't a thing,' I said, 'I just got caught up in the moment. We both did. I blame tequila. Why is it even legal, that's my question.'

'Right,' said Neil. 'It's alcohol's fault you're cheating on me. So what, you're gay now?'

'Just because she kissed a woman, doesn't mean she isn't into men,' said Gen.

'What would you know?' Neil spat back.

'More than you do, apparently,' she replied, ominously.

Neil read between the lines. He turned to me. 'Wait. Wait, wait, wait; what's she talking about?'

'Ignore her, she's wasted.'

'Abbey, have there been other men?'

I gulped. 'Neil, you have to understand—'

His eyes wore a glossy, liquid sheen. 'Who was it? When was it?'

'I thought you were dead… I was a mess…'

'No. No fucking way. The vampire? Lauden? You slept with him while I was in a coma?'

'It wasn't like that!'

'Then how was it?'

'Okay, it was like that, but it wasn't something I meant to do.'

His shimmering eyes threatened to unleash tears at any moment. 'Jesus, Abbey. I know things haven't been great between us lately, but I thought we were riding different waves, not different people.'

He turned and began walking away.

'Neil.'

He paused for a second, then continued into the distance.

'Let him go,' said Gen, placing a hand on my shoulder.

I bucked her off. 'Leave me alone.'

Gen backed away, leaving me to stew on my lonesome.

I tasted tequila in the back of my throat—sour, bitter, making me nauseous—and with one violent contraction, the contents of my stomach emerged into the cold morning light.

All in all, a great end to another tip-top day.

Shit.

21

I woke up in my bed with no recollection of how I got there. My head ached and my stomach felt unsettled, but the brand had soaked up the lion's share of the hangover. Neil was nowhere to be seen; just an empty crater in his side of the mattress. I searched the rest of The Vault for him, but from the looks of things, he hadn't returned home after our fight. He'd disabled the share location app on his phone, and when I tried ringing him, all I got was his voicemail.

I told myself that Neil was a big boy, and that he could take care of his own well-being. He knew what was going on out there. He knew to lay low. Just because we were having a spat, didn't mean his neck was on the chopping block. Neil would be fine. He was going to be fine. *Yeah, just keep telling yourself that, Abbey.*

I thought about what had happened the night before. Was the thing I had with Gen something more than a drunken indiscretion? Was I really into women, and only just now coming to terms with it? Had I been suppressing my true feelings all these years, pushing them down, convincing myself I was straight because that's what was expected of me?

I wondered if my relationship with Neil was over. Had I forced him away? Maybe that's the way it was meant to be. Having Neil around only made a difficult job even harder. If there was one thing these last few weeks had taught me, it was that being the Nightstalker wasn't really compatible with a relationship. Maybe, in my heart, I'd been waiting for Neil to leave me. Could kissing Gen have been part of that? Something I did subconsciously to get him out the door? To get him out of this life, and take the target off his back?

My brain needed a rest. I was tired and punchy. I needed to do something with my fists—something to vent my frustration—so I marched to the dojo to take out my anger there. To get out of my head. To make something suffer.

I ripped a punch into the dojo's heavy bag and watched it sway before my eyes. I slugged it again, so hard I thought its chain might snap. I came at it from every direction, assaulting it with flurry of jabs, crosses, hooks, and uppercuts. I carried on punching until I had nothing left. Until I was gasping, breath hissing through my teeth, folded over and gripping my knees for support.

As I stood there, sweat dripping from my skin and splattering on the ground, Neil refused to leave my thoughts. I needed to find him. I needed to tell him I was sorry. To beg him for forgiveness.

'Abbey.' It was Gen.

I straightened up. 'Yeah?'

She looked a little frayed around the edges for last night's drinking, but was doing an impressive job of keeping it together. 'We have a lead on Savina,' she announced. That was it. No mention of our kiss, no apologies, just straight to business.

'What kind of a lead?' I asked.

She held up my dagger. 'You left this next to the toilet last night. I was about to clean it when I saw something on its blade.'

She showed it to me. There was a red stain there.

'Is this what I think it is?'

'Back at the warehouse, you must have drawn blood when you threw it at that vamp.'

'Can we use it?'

'Why don't we find out?'

That settled that then. Things might have been crappy, but I still had a mission to attend to. I'd make peace with Neil, just as soon as I found Savina and put her in the ground.

I threw one last punch at the heavy bag, so hard I broke the thing in half.

At first, nothing happened. Vizael carefully scraped the vampire's blood from the dagger with forensic precision, but when he applied it to the pendant as instructed, it had zero effect.

'What's wrong?' I asked. 'Is there something wrong with the thing? Did we get ripped off?'

'No,' Viz replied. 'From what I can deduce, the device takes a while to return a result. We need only wait.'

'For how long?'

'Until sundown.'

Ugh. That was hours away. All dressed up and no one to kill.

Viz placed the pendant in the centre of the War Room table and we waited. For hours, we waited, until finally the thing came to life. At first it skittered on the spot, then off it shot, so fast I only just managed to snatch its chain before it raced over the edge of the table. I held on, the pendant tugging at me as if it were being pulled on by an invisible hand.

'Where's it telling us to go?' I asked.

'Let's see,' replied Vizael. He took the pendant between his hands, closed his eyes, and uttered a short incantation. I felt a brief, staticky fizz of magic that made my skin tingle. Viz opened his eyes and turned to me. 'According to the tracking charm, Savina is located in a building a few miles South West of here called Pandora's Box.'

'Never heard of it,' I replied.

'I have,' said Gendith. 'It's a lesbian club in Vauxhall… or so I've heard.'

I cocked an eyebrow at her. 'Moving on… are we ready for this? To go up against Savina, I mean?'

Viz tipped his head from left to right. 'If we were able to take her by surprise, with all three of us attacking at once, we might, *might*, be able to overcome her.'

'How do we sneak up on her?'

'The portal,' said Gen, pointing to our magic door. 'I'm… familiar with the location. We could use the door to bypass the building's security and come up right under Savina's nose.'

That thing really was paying for itself. 'Good enough for me. Right then, let's suit up and get going.'

We had one last pow-wow, gathered our weapons, and headed for the portal.

'Pandora's Box it is,' said Gen, placing a mitt on the door handle.

She turned it, expecting the door to open out into the night-club, but instead, something else happened. The air in the room rippled and I felt a sensation like a plane depressurising.

Gen was gone.

She hadn't stepped through the portal, she'd simply vanished. One second she was there, stood right in front of me, the next she was no more.

'Uh, where did she go?' I asked Viz.

He looked back at me, wide-eyed. 'I cannot say.'

The moment she tried opening that door, she'd been erased from existence. Cut from the movie. I was about to really start panicking when I heard a small, pinched sound, not unlike a mouse squeaking.

'What is that?'

'It's coming from down there,' Viz replied, pointing to the ground.

There was something down there. Something tiny. I took it for an insect at first, but it was more vertical than horizontal. I dropped to my haunches to get a better look. It definitely wasn't an insect. It was a person.

'Gen?'

There she was, perfectly proportioned still, but about the size of a Jelly Bean. 'What happened?' I just about heard her say. 'Why are you so huge?'

'Take a look around,' I said. 'We're not big, you're *small*.'

Viz lowered himself to the floor and inspected tiny Gen

through his reading glasses. 'This is Savina's work,' he said. 'She used our door once already when she mounted her home invasion; she must have found her way back inside the portal and laid a hex. A magical trap,' Viz explained. 'A trap that is triggered by the proximity of an unwanted presence.'

'You mean us?'

He nodded. 'Hexes can be used to inflict all manner of harm: wounds, bad luck, physical defects… I recently heard of a detective in Blackpool who was rendered invisible by a particularly powerful one.'

'Can we focus, please?' Gen squeaked. 'How do we get rid of the thing?'

Viz scratched his chin. 'There are only two ways. Either we convince the person who cast the hex to remove it—'

'Not going to happen.'

'—or we kill the caster and break the curse that way.'

'I've got a question,' I said. 'If Savina really wanted to hurt us, why didn't that hex go off like a landmine and blow us all to bits?'

'That is a good question,' Viz replied.

'I'll tell you. It's because she doesn't want to kill us.'

'Then what is she after?' asked Gen.

'For us to confront her. And I say we give her what she wants.'

'But we're a man down,' said tiny Gen. 'The odds were against us before, but even a surprise attack won't work against Savina now. She's just too strong.'

'We can take her.'

'How? What are we supposed to do?'

I stroked the top of her teeny head with my finger. 'Tell you what, why don't we start by getting you some crayons and a colouring book?'

She hammered her fists against my fingertip, which hurt about as much as a fly landing on me. 'Have you cracked, woman? This is no time for jokes!'

'That would be a lot easier to take seriously if you didn't sound like you were sucking helium.'

'I swear to God, girl, little or not, I will beat you.'

I cupped my hand to my ear. 'Sorry, Gen, you're not coming through. Can you send me a hex message?'

'Damn you.'

I laughed, but I was the only one enjoying myself.

Viz eyed me with concern. 'This is serious, Abbey. Take a look at the scoreboard; can't you tell we're losing? Why are you so jolly?'

I scooped Gen up in my palm. 'Because I have a plan.'

22

The portal delivered me and Viz into the guts of Pandora's Box, spitting us out through one of the nightclub's interior doors.

'This must be the place,' I shouted, fighting to make my voice heard over the club's pumping techno.

The place was a riot of colour. The walls were covered in neon graffiti depicting plucked eyeballs, lightning bolts, and a snake that wound along an entire corridor and disappeared into the dance floor. Nearby, a diesel dyke in bike leathers chatted with a tomboy wearing a neck tattoo that made her look like she was being strangled by art. The tomboy had ears that tapered at the top, and a forked tongue that flashed from her mouth as she spoke. Her abnormal features weren't just body mods either, the woman was demonic. Pandora's Box wasn't just a lesbian club, it was a lesbian club for the Uncanny.

'Oi, you,' barked an unknown voice. We turned to find a muscular, troll-like creature with green skin, a shaved head and a ring through her septum. She wore a Security laminate pinned to the front of her bomber jacket. 'What were you doing in there?' She stabbed a finger at Viz, and then at the door we'd arrived through.

According to the sign, the portal had ejected us from the women's toilets. It wasn't a good look for the old man.

'It's cool,' I replied, answering on Viz's behalf. 'She's transitioning.'

The bouncer looked Viz up and down, nostrils flared, seemingly unconvinced. Apparently, demons were welcome in this place, just not the patriarchy. 'Where are your hand stamps?' she demanded.

'Hand stamps?' I asked, innocently.

'Yeah. The ones that show me you paid to get in here. The ones that show me you didn't sneak by the front desk while I was out smoking a fag.'

It's important for the yanks among you—particularly given the context of the situation—to understand that the bouncer was using British slang there. Got that? Cool, let's move on.

'I don't have a stamp,' I said, unfurling my right hand, 'unless this one counts…'

The troll saw the letter N branded on my palm. She backed off a couple of steps, a nervous bulge travelling up and down her throat.

'Oh, so you know what this is, do you? I asked.

The bouncer nodded.

'Great,' I said, bunching my fists. 'Now, are you going get out of my face?'

The bouncer moved aside, back pressed to the wall.

'Thank you.'

I led Viz down the corridor, through a pair of double doors, and into the main dance hall. The music inside was loud as thunder; so loud I could feel it in my guts. Revellers with hyped-up faces danced like they'd forgotten how to stand still, throwing shapes, flailing their limbs, banging their heads. My eyes scanned the club looking for Savina as we pushed our way through the crowd, parting a bacchanalian sea. My eyes glided over a snake-hipped sylph with a Ziggy Stardust tan who danced like a stray cat in heat. Over a glamorous lipstick lesbian with lots of flesh on show, and a figure to soap cars with. Over an athletic woman in equestrian clothing, spanking a dance partner with a riding crop. The club had something for everyone. A flavour for every taste.

Far from offending my delicate sensibilities, I actually found myself quite taken by the place. Okay, the music needed some work, but these were definitely my kind of people. Misfits. Outcasts. People who wouldn't look twice at a girl for showing up for a night out dressed in cargo trousers and a Joy Division t-shirt. The last time I'd been convinced to go clubbing, for a work colleague's hen party, I'd had a godawful night. I showed up wearing my usual ensemble—chipped black nail varnish, back-combed hair, the same t-shirt I had on now—and got bawled at for it. Hollered at in the toilets by the hen. Called a dirty goth by a coked-up, spray-tanned girl with massive eyebrows and so much highlighter on her face that she looked like Groucho Marx fallen into a rock polisher. This place was different though. This was a place I could be me. Too bad I was about go 9/11 on the joint.

Having threaded our way to the other side of the dance floor, I saw a private booth occupied by four beautiful women drinking bottle service. Compared to the rest of the club's patrons, this lot looked practically regal. If Savina was here like the pendant said she was, I felt sure these were the people she'd be hanging with. Still, no matter which angle I looked at them from, none of the women was her.

Then again…

As the music from the dance floor reached a fever pitch, a strobe fell across the booth, casting four long, flickering shadows across the ground, one of which travelled in a different direction to the rest.

Savina.

I remembered her visit to The Vault; how the light from my dagger had thrown a shadow off her that defied all rational thinking.

'There she is,' I said.

The woman sipped from a martini, her black hair lying over one shoulder of her sequined red dress.

'Are you sure?' Viz replied, not quite seeing it.

'Positive. I don't know what she's doing to disguise herself, but that's her.'

Viz wasted no time. He drew his sword from his cane with a metallic *shing*, raised it above his head, and let fly a war cry. 'In the name of the Father, the Son and the... holy moley, what is that?'

The walls were moving, or more accurately, the graffiti on them was moving. The painted snake, which circled the club entirely, had come to life and was peeling from its moorings. The woman in the red dress—who had dropped the facade and now wore Savina's face—held her arms high, her hands frothing with black mana. The serpent was three-dimensional now, and slithering across the dance floor, leading the club's revellers to scream and stampede for the fire exits. I went to draw my dagger, but the snake was too fast, darting in our direction and coiling itself around us, pinning our arms to our sides. I tried to wriggle free, but the more I struggled, the tighter the snake contracted. I felt a tremendous pain in my chest as one of my ribs gave in and popped with a sound so loud I heard it over the music.

'That's enough,' said Savina.

The snake ceased its tightening and pointed its head at me, hissing and drooling venom.

I could see now that the rest of her party had reverted to their true forms too. Beehive was there with her black and gold talons, plus the two witchy-looking vamps we'd chased off from the warehouse.

Savina waved a hand and the music shut off, filling the room with a lingering, heavy silence. She *click-clacked* over to us on her high heels and brought her face close to mine. It was the kind of face that belonged on an oil painting. Old, wise eyes stared back at me; pale, almost transparent.

'Let's talk, shall we?' she said, more as a demand than a suggestion.

'Okay, we can talk,' I wheezed, my cracked rib grinding against my insides as I forced out the words. 'Why don't you start by saying what you want with me?'

Savina grinned. 'What I want it for us to be on the same side.'

I thought back to the slaughter at the old boys' club, then on to Jake's story about the Clansman who came to his office, begging for help. 'Why would you need my help?' I asked. 'You seem to be cleaning up pretty well out there without me.'

'Yes, but with you we can do so much more.'

She held up a hand and a slim vial filled with red liquid appeared in it.

'What's that?' I asked.

'Don't you recognise it? It's yours.'

'Bullshit.'

Her eyes glittered. 'You weren't the only one to pay a visit to Lauden's mansion. I went there too, after you'd killed him and looted the place, and you know what I found? There, among the remains of my kin, I discovered this; your blood. The blood of the Nightstalker.'

'So what?' I said, trying to shrug and failing. I twisted my neck to look to Viz. His expression was grave.

Savina went on. 'I took the blood back to my laboratory and examined it. Experimented with it. Attempted many things.'

'Like what?'

'I tested its viability for cloning, to see if I could use it to produce a Nightstalker of my own. Nothing. I tried to manufacture a poison with it; a toxin to kill all vampires with a pair of XY chromosomes. Still nothing. Finally, I tried fusing it with a sample of my own blood, and you know what I found? I found a future.'

The only thing I was finding was confusion. 'Is this mad scientist shit leading anywhere in particular?'

'Very much so. You see, I discovered that the blood of the Nightstalker unlocks a potential I thought impossible. The potential to create progeny.'

'More vamps, you mean?' I looked to her companions – to the other vampires she'd sired. 'But you could already do that.'

'Once, yes, sparingly, but over the centuries, the well dried up.'

'Wait, are you telling me this is it? That there are only four of you? Like, in total?'

Savina nodded. I couldn't believe it. I'd been charging around town, busting my hump, and all for a gang of chicks who couldn't make up a five-a-side football team.

'So now you see why I need your help?' said Savina. 'The only way we will triumph against the Clan is by multiplying, and we need you to do that. With enough of your blood, we can cure our faulty DNA and build an army.'

'Here's the thing though,' I replied, 'I don't really want to give you my blood. I'm quite keen on the stuff, you see?'

Beehive made her way over, circling me, tracing her lethal talons across my skin. 'Let me take it from her,' she snarled. 'Let me drain her dry.'

'No,' Savina ordered. She turned to me, all smiles. 'We don't need all of your blood, Abbey, just a measure at a time until we have what we require.'

'And then what? You destroy the Clan and pick up where Judas left off?'

She laughed. 'I have no interest in kicking down the doors of Heaven, and I certainly bear God no ill will. I haven't had sight of Him in my lifetime, so why would I hold a grudge? No, my objective is entirely my own. All I want is to wipe out all men on Earth. Just that one little thing.'

'You monster!' growled Vizael, squirming beneath a smooth column of armoured muscle.

'Quiet, old man, the women are talking.' Savina waved a hand and the snake shifted its grip to cover the angel's mouth, leaving him breathing through his nostrils, red-faced and eyes bulging.

So, Savina didn't just want the Clan dead, she wanted all men dead? This vendetta of hers was so much bigger than getting revenge on Judas. And to think I actually toyed with the idea of joining up with this nut bar. I'm telling you, you really need to read the small print with these villainous master plans.

'Men are old news,' said Savina. 'History. We vampires don't need sperm to breed, so their kind are surplus to requirements.'

'Yeah, I kind of got that you weren't keen on blokes when you carved up my boyfriend.'

'I told you, my plans have changed. Now I want you by my side; Gendith too, once I've removed my hex and she steps out of whatever matchbox she's living in.' Her lips pursed. 'Your friend Neil though, he will have to go.'

It seemed Savina's offer was pitched somewhere between a valentine and a kick in the fanny. 'Oh, so the only snag to joining your little club is that I have to watch my boyfriend die? Is that all?'

'Come on, love,' said Savina. 'You can't smash the patriarchy without breaking a few men.'

This bitch was off her rocker. 'Look, thanks for the invitation and everything, but I'm going to take a pass.'

'Why? Ask yourself, what have men ever brought us but bloodshed?'

'That's a bit rich coming from a vampire.'

Savina continued, undaunted. 'I have lived through centuries of mankind's mistakes, patiently waiting for women to take their place on the stage, but I can wait no more. Being prim and proper will do us no good. Unless we rise up and take charge, men will destroy this world. It's time for a revolution.'

'A revolution? You're talking about killing half the population.'

'I'm talking about cutting out a cancer.'

Beehive came at me, spitting acid. 'We're wasting our time,' she told Savina. 'She's not going to fall in line.'

'Is that right, Abbey? Do you refuse to join us still?'

'Too right I do.'

'Very well then.' She nodded to Beehive, who broke out in a broad smile before circling around me to get to Viz. 'Kill the old man.'

'With pleasure,' Beehive replied, bringing her thumbnail to his throat and drawing a bead of blood.

'Stop!' I cried.

Savina held out a hand. 'Stand down,' she ordered her second, and Beehive reluctantly removed her claw from the soft flesh of Viz's throat.

'I'll join your gang if that's what you want, okay? Just don't hurt him.'

'Oh, you would have anyway, one way or another,' Savina replied, grinning like a split watermelon. 'Welcome aboard, Abbey.'

She clicked her fingers, and the world turned blacker than a goth wedding.

23

Turns out I was right when I said mad scientist before. Compared to the Clan's slick, antiseptic facilities, Savina's lair was a regular Frankenstein's laboratory.

When I opened my eyes, I found myself manacled to the wall of an antiquated chemistry workshop that belonged to another century. I jerked my head from side to side, searching for Vizael, but he was nowhere to be seen. I pulled against my bonds until my wrists bled, but the chains holding my wrists were an inch thick at least. I scanned the room, which was dominated by a large wooden bench, generously populated with flasks, beakers and retorts. Jars of organs and dissected animal parts preserved in formaldehyde lined the walls, along with a dusty blackboard filled with equations I had no hope of understanding. The only thing missing was a Tesla coil and one of those rabbit-ear antenna things with the lightning arcing up them.

'You're awake.' Savina swept into the room like a cold wind, shortly followed by her three companions.

I instinctively went to summon my dagger, but when I tried to call it to my hand, nothing happened.

'Sorry about that,' said Savina. 'I took the precaution of having you frisked. Quite thoroughly in fact.'

Damn.

'So this is where you guys live, huh?' I asked.

'Yes. Why, what were you expecting?'

'I dunno. A big spider's web? The inside of a giant, hollowed-out skull? Maybe a haunted gingerbread house?'

'Very droll.'

Much as I was trying to make light of the situation, I knew I was in trouble, particularly with Viz out of the picture. 'Where is he?' I asked.

'The angel? With us, unharmed.'

She pointed to a black and white monitor sat on a shelf among the grisly collection of mason jars. The monitor looked incongruous set against the rest of the room's archaic decor, like a digital wristwatch on the arm of an actor in a gladiator movie. Its screen showed the inside of a small, unfurnished chamber; a prison cell, occupied by Viz. Rather ominously, the image then switched to a camera in another cell; this one empty except for a single metal bedstead. My cell, I was betting.

'It used to be an operating theatre,' Savina explained, 'this place we're in now.' She circled the room as she talked, as if addressing a student. 'Picture it: sawdust on the floor to soak up the blood, men in frock coats, stiff and stinking of pus, a place where people died in agony. But no more. Now this humble theatre will bring life to a dying world. It will be the seat of a great rebirth. A cradle for a new civilisation.'

'That's great and everything,' I said, 'but why am I shackled to the wall? I thought we were all on the same team now.'

'You think me daft? I know your allegiance hasn't been won yet, Abbey. Given time though, I believe we will be friends.'

She nodded to the wild-haired twins, who wheeled over a trolley supporting a large metal machine decorated with tubes, pumps and pistons, all activated by a central hand crank. Atop the device, shaped like a Martian's head, was a large glass bulb. From the sides of the machine, the twins drew two slim rubber hoses, each of which was tipped with a brass needle long enough to puncture one of my arms and go through to the other side.

'If this is how you make friends, Savina, I'd hate to get on your wrong side.'

'You needn't fear, I have no intention of doing you harm today.' I'd have believed her a lot more if her sentence wasn't immediately followed by a cold needle piercing my skin and slipping into a vein at the crook of my elbow. 'I want you to consider this a symbolic gesture, Abbey,' she said, as she rolled up a sleeve and the other twin placed a needle in her arm.

Beehive stepped forward and worked the machine's crank, activating its pistons and drawing our blood up the tubes and into the glass bulb, where the thick, scarlet snakes met and comingled, forming a mixture that sizzled ominously.

'This is the true beginning of our partnership,' said Savina. 'My blood and your blood. Alchemy.'

I watched the blood bubble and pop, then go still. It was as if one half of the solution had triumphed over the over, and I was fairly certain mine hadn't come out the victor.

'We have a long way to go, you and me,' said Savina, 'but I believe, in time, that you will come around to my way of thinking.'

'And if I don't?'

Creases formed at the corners of her eyes. 'I admire your strength of will, girl—I truly do—but my admiration will only stretch so far.' She nodded at one of the twins, who plucked the needle from my arm with all the care of a magician snatching a tablecloth from under a crowded buffet. 'For the time being, I will leave you alone to think; to consider my offer properly. After that, you will be returned here, and we will continue our work in earnest. Whether you have any blood left in you at the end of it is entirely up to you.'

I couldn't let Savina hook me up to that machine again. One more spell on the pump and she'd have all the blood she needed to start her revolution. The four of them alone had succeeded in putting a dent in the Clan's operation big enough to cause a mutiny. If they were allowed to multiply, who knew how quickly they'd finish what they started and move on to their endgame: the extinction of all men.

'Now, go and think over my proposal. You have until the sunrise to decide whether you want to join me, or whether you'd prefer to be drained to a lifeless husk.'

'No option C?'

Beehive unshackled me from the wall, jacked an arm up

behind my back, and marched me from the room. I was led down a series of featureless corridors, too weak from blood loss to fight back, and knowing that even if I did—without my weapon—Beehive would get the better of me.

We moved into an area of the hospital lined with unsanitary cells containing threadbare padded walls and wicked-looking restraints. A madhouse. The kind where "problem" people were dumped by callous families, only to be subjected to bizarre treatments and gawped at by sadists who paid money to watch their suffering.

We passed a cell to my right, and as we did, I was able to snatch a glimpse through a small hatch in its door.

'Viz?'

'Abbey?'

The old man rushed to the door and pressed his face against the bars, but the moment we made eye contact, I was whisked away and shoved into a cell of my own, the one from the security monitor.

The room contained a rusted metal bedstead covered by a paper-thin mattress. Attached to the bedstead were four thick, leather restraints, strong enough to pin a gorilla.

'Lie down,' Beehive ordered.

I looked at the bed, then back to her. 'Aren't you at least going to buy me a drink first?'

She didn't crack.

'Fine,' I said, and lowered myself on to the bed.

Beehive strapped me down, starfish style, and as she did, I got a sudden flashback of Savina, working the wheel of a torture rack, tearing a man's limbs from their roots.

'Sleep well, princess,' said Beehive, stroking my cheek with the back of a shellacked fingernail, before stepping outside, slamming the cell door, and leaving me alone under a heavy, suffocating darkness.

It was a night riddled with fitful dreams.

I saw a darkening sun sinking into the London smog. Saw feral women, tearing through the street with teeth as sharp as knives; predators, taking down innocents like they were pack animals. I saw the gutters of London running red with blood. Saw corpses, piled high like death camp photos, only rendered in gruesome, Hammer Horror Technicolor.

I was woken by a beam of sunlight lancing through the window in my cell door, bright as a shaft of gold.

'Wakey wakey eggs and bakey,' Beehive's voice, accompanied by the teeth-jarring rattle of metal against metal; the sound of my dagger being drawn along the bars of the cell.

'Oh, you want this?' she asked, daring me to use my connection with the blade to snatch it from her.

We both knew there was no point. Even with the weapon in my hand, I was still immobilised.

She unlocked the cell door, let herself inside, and took a seat beside me. 'Well?' she said, twirling my dagger between her fingers teasingly. 'Will you be joining our merry little gang?'

My silence told her everything she needed to know.

A smile spread across her face and I saw that her fangs were on show. 'That's the answer I was looking for. Just between us two girls, I knew you'd never go for it. Savina was mad to think you were capable of seeing the bigger picture.'

On the outside I remained expressionless, but on the inside I was ALL CAPS.

'Look at you,' she went on. 'An absent father, a scumbag boss, a runaway boyfriend, and still you're beholden to men. Aren't you tired of it, Abbey? Haven't you had enough of living at the nexus of powerful and exploited?'

I kept my mouth shut, but Beehive didn't care. The question was a rhetorical one.

She leaned in a little closer. 'This is where it ends for you, Nightstalker, but before Savina gets her blood, I'm going to have myself a taste. God knows, I've earned it.'

Her head craned to my neck and I felt the needles of her fangs graze my jugular.

At the exact same time, she felt the fingers of my right hand clamp down on the hair at the back of her head and yank her away from me. I gave her just enough time to see the unbuckled leather strap dangling over the edge of the bedstead, then twisted her head a full 360.

Vertebrae burst through the skin of her scrawny neck as her head cranked all the way round, spitting an arc of blood that covered all four walls.

'Yowsers,' I said, pushing her body to the floor and unbuckling the rest of my straps. 'That's going to be a closed casket.'

There'd be no second chances for Beehive this time. No turning into gas and whiffing out of a window. No unlikely resurrections. Just a busted up body laying on the ground, one leg twitching in a pool of her own piss. Finally. Man, I was getting some real blue balls there.

I scooped up my dagger and felt its comforting weight in my hand.

A certain ghost I knew was going to be very happy with the way that went down.

'Bloodsuckers beware,' I purred.

Okay, so you're probably wondering how I pulled that trick off, right? I mean, it was looking pretty grim there, wasn't it? Me, tied down, defenceless, about to be dragged away to die a shabby little death at the hands of a superior enemy. Hopeless, you might say, and yet that was kind of the point.

You see, I figured something out right after Gen got shrunk by that hex. I figured out that the only way we were going to beat Savina was by letting her think she'd already won. That's why I went to her at that nightclub, outnumbered, and knowing full well I'd get captured. I knew she had no intention of killing me—at least not right away—and that she'd be sure to take me to her lair to gloat about her victory. It was a move right out of the supervillain playbook.

Okay, I hear you say, *that explains how you found your way into the lion's den, but how did you manage to get your hand out of that strap, Abbey?*

Simple. I used my head. Literally.

'How much longer do I have to stay in here?' asked Gen.

'Just for a little bit, I replied, putting a finger to the side of my head like I was using an earpiece, which in a way, I was.

Tiny Gen, the size of a Jelly Bean, was lodged in my ear canal. Savina had assured me I was frisked thoroughly when she brought me into her den, but I'm happy to report that she failed to order the full cavity search. Thanks to that oversight, Gen was able to wriggle out of my ear and undo one of the straps securing me to the bed, before climbing back in and waiting until our jailer returned, none the wiser.

'It's the safest place for you,' I told Gen. 'Besides, I thought you'd like the idea of sitting inside my head giving me instructions like you're my conscience.'

'I'd like it a good deal more if it wasn't so filthy in here. Would it kill you to use an ear bud from time to time? Really.'

'Yeah, I'll get right on that,' I replied, 'just as soon as I've figured out how to single-handedly take down three triple-hard vampires on their own turf.'

I cast a glance about the cell, and for the first time, in an upper corner of the room, noticed the security camera that fed into the monitor in Savina's laboratory. I'd forgotten about that.

'Oops,' I said.

'What?' asked Gen.

'I think we're about to have company,' I replied, pointing to the camera.

'Wonderful,' she sighed. 'Got any more great ideas?'

I looked down at my feet and saw Beehive, splayed out on the ground.

'Yeah, I think I might do,' I said, and hurled the dagger at the camera, turning it into junk.

A couple of minutes later. Heavy footfalls, two sets of them, coming my way.

The cell door was flung open, and I watched from my hiding place as the twin vampires burst inside, their twitching hands crackling with black juju. They saw Beehive's body face-down on the floor and rocked back on their heels.

'That bitch,' one of them growled.

'Come on, we have to get after her,' said the other, heading back out the door.

'No,' replied the first vamp, her nose sifting the air. 'She's still in here.'

I held my breath and stayed as still as possible, my heartbeat hammering in my ears.

'But there's nowhere to hide,' said the vampire at the door.

'There's one place,' the other replied.

She aimed a finger at the only item of furniture in the room; the rusted bedstead with its malnourished mattress.

With no further discussion necessary, the twins turned in the direction of the bed and aimed open palms at its underside. A current shot through their arms and tore through their hands, exploding in a torrent of iridescent darkness that blew the bed to pieces and torched the person hidden beneath it right down to their bones.

The twins cackled as they reached down and dragged me out from under the remains of the bed.

Well, not *me* exactly.

'Wait,' said the vampire who'd sniffed me out. 'This isn't her.'

No, it wasn't.

The body they were hanging on to—the one that wasn't wearing any clothes and had a missing scalp—that body belonged to Beehive. The person they thought they'd just cremated was elsewhere. That person—*this person*—was lying face-down on the ground behind them wearing Beehive's outfit, not to mention her impressive coiffure, perched on top of her head and glued down by blood.

'Say goodnight,' I said, right before I extended the dagger to sword and took both of their heads with one cut.

I dropped the scalp on the floor next to Beehive's bones, headed out of the room, and kicked down Vizael's cell door.

'Told you I had a plan,' I said, as a fleshy glob of blood-matted hair that wasn't mine bounced off my shoulder and landed at his feet.

24

My Nightstalker vision picked out Savina's catwalk silhouette no problem. We found her in the building's library; a large, dusty space furnished with rows of bookshelves laid out neatly on a tiled chessboard floor. The books were thick, leather-bound tomes that gave off that distinctive, almond odour unique to old, yellowed paper.

Savina turned to greet Viz and I. 'You found your way out of your cell?' she said, impressed. 'How?'

I opened my left hand and showed her tiny Gen, sat on my palm.

'Oh, that is clever,' said Savina, quite giddy. 'Well, look at you! Brains and beauty. It's so rare to see riches concealed behind the pretty painting.'

'I thought you'd be a little more upset,' I replied. 'You do get that I killed all of your children, right? I mean, killed them dead. Dead as shit.'

'But I can make new children now. Thanks to you.'

She did that thing that vampires do when they're suddenly across the other side of the room, despite you not having seen them bridge the distance. One second we were having a guarded, arm's length conversation, the next she was right on top of me, or more accurately, right on top of Viz. She held the old man's head between her hands, gripping him like a vice.

'Wow,' I remarked. 'You're a nippy whippet.'

'Thank you.'

'Obviously, I'm going to have to kill you though.'

I took a step towards her and she squeezed, making Viz scream.

'I wouldn't recommend it,' she said. 'Not unless you want to get painted blue with angel blood.'

'Are you okay, Viz?'

He was held too tight to nod, but he managed to spit the word *yes* through gritted teeth.

'You really do care for this daft old goat, don't you?' said Savina, genuinely perplexed. 'And what about you, little lady?' she asked Gen, who stood on my palm spinning the world's tiniest morning star. 'Aren't you tired of taking orders from a man?'

'I take my orders from God,' she squeaked back.

'Ha! God! The ultimate man!' She gave Viz's skull a squeeze as her shoulders wracked with mirth, making him hiss with pain. 'God cast you down to this plane centuries ago and hasn't spoken to you since. What make you think you're doing His bidding?'

It wasn't an unreasonable question. I had to ask myself, why was Gen so loyal to the cause? For centuries, men had done nothing but persecute the woman. Why not take Savina's offer?

Savina tightened her grip on the old man, making him scream.

'Stop!' I said. It was the best I had. The brand made me fast, but not fast enough to cover the distance to Savina before she popped Viz's head.

'The angel's mission is over,' Savina replied. 'It's time he was reunited with his God.'

'Please don't.'

'You need this, Abbey. You both do. Killing this man will set you free, just like you killing Lauden freed me.'

I expected Gen to object, but she stayed quiet. She'd done little else but argue with Viz since I'd known them. Every step of the way he'd let her down; passing her over for the Nightstalker role, shouting down her ideas. Had Gen finally had enough of the old man holding her back? By joining Savina, she could claw back some of the power Viz had denied her. She could be a queen.

'Don't think of it as killing him,' said Savina, 'think of it as sending him home. Ending his banishment. You should think of this as a favour.'

'Look,' I said, 'the world's a messed up place—I get that—but the only way we're going to solve anything is by working together. Women and men. The world doesn't need any more hatred. We're full up. We're not going to solve a punch with another punch.'

Savina sighed deeply. 'And what of you, Gendith? Do you agree with the Nightstalker? The girl who stole your mantle, who buried you in her own shadow?'

Gendith went slack, her miniature weapon dangling by her side.

'Say the word, Gendith, and I will remove the hex and return you to your natural size. Cast your vote—put your faith in me—and together we will transform this world.'

Gen looked to me, then to Viz. 'Just because I've been wronged by men, doesn't mean half a species has to die for it. My pain doesn't give me the right to take away people's brothers. Their husbands. Their fathers. I've seen this madness before. I've seen discrimination in all of its forms, and this is no different. No one person is more apt to follow Satan than another. We are all of us sinners. The serpent speaks to us all, and right now, he has your ear the loudest.'

It was a good speech, though knocked down a notch or two by the squeaky pitch it was delivered in.

Savina shook her head despondently. 'Very well then,' she said, and tilted her head back to look at me. 'If I cannot have your allegiance, I will settle for your blood.'

A snarl rippled over her lips and a bolt of black lightning shot between her palms, lighting up Viz's head and sending his body into spasms.

She let go and he slumped to the ground, a smoking corpse.

25

I felt like a trapdoor had opened beneath me.

I ran at Savina, my sword cleaving the air. For a moment, I thought she'd turn into a mist to escape me, but that wasn't the transformation she was going for.

Savina's features ran like melting wax. Muscles and connective tissue dissolved. Flesh was resculpted, giving way to bone, which fired out of her liquefied skin in spurs and horns until it looked as though she were wearing her skeleton on the outside. Savina was a beast, more animal than woman, but not any kind of animal you'd see at the zoo.

The transformation stopped me in my tracks.

'Such a shame,' she growled, her voice like two rough stones being ground together. 'We could have been friends.'

She came at me with bone claws ending in wicked points. I lashed out at her with my blade, but it glanced harmlessly off of her chitinous body. I tried again, but the armour was too tough, sending a shockwave through the blade that exploded in my shoulder like dynamite.

Gen leapt from my free hand and hit the ground running. I wasn't sure what her endgame was, but whatever it was, it had to beat standing on the spot and getting clawed to ribbons by an inside-out vampire, so I headed off in pursuit.

As I burst through the exit to the library and into the corridor beyond, I saw the walls either side of me ripple, like a wave across a pond. Just as she'd done in Pandora's Box, Savina was using her magic to make the building come alive.

Stone arms burst from the walls, thrusting out at me as I hurtled down the corridor. It was like running through a forest of fists. The monster mitts battered me left and right, one jarring connection following the next, beating me senseless. I managed to carry myself to the end of the hallway using momentum and sheer force of will, but I staggered out wearing so many lumps I looked like the complete braille collection of *Game of Thrones*.

I didn't stand a chance against Savina, and I knew it. Gen was no good to me, and Viz was… oh, God, Viz was dead. The man who'd made me what I was, who taught me how to fight, was lying flat on the ground next door, smoke pouring from his ears. I was nothing without him. I was no Chosen One. I was boring old Abbey Beckett, an ordinary girl with a Styrofoam life. Not a fighter, not a hero, just a weak twenty-something layabout with no prospects and a body so skinny I could fall through my own arsehole.

I ran, but I didn't get far. Savina appeared in front of me and delivered a punch to my gut that wrung the air from my lungs and left me folded in half on the floor. I staggered to my feet, my breathing strained, but no sooner had I got up than Savina hit me again. The ground lurched away from me and I landed painfully on my tailbone.

Once again, I managed to get upright, slower still this time. I went to swing my sword at Savina, but realised too late that it wasn't in my hand, and ended up punching her with my bare fist. Pain bled into my knuckles, and I gripped my wrist as if to stop it invading the rest of me.

From the corner of my eye, I spotted the sword, and recalled it to my hand. The brand flared hot and bright, and I heard blood pumping in my head like an EDM song, right before the drop.

Stand and fight.

That's what the brand told me.

Put up your fists and slay the vampire.

But this was no ordinary vampire. This was a vampire Judas had sired personally, and if there was one thing Savina had taught me, it was that the female of the species was more deadly than the male.

A claw tore across my upper arm, shredding flesh and cutting me to the bone. My legs turned weak and bloodless. My brain was full of cotton wool.

I had to buy myself time. Time to heal. Time to figure out a way to defend myself.

I sidestepped Savina and ran some more.

'There's nowhere for you to go, Abbey,' I heard her call after me. 'You're sealed in tight.'

I bounced off a wall as I fled, striping it red. Blood pattered noisily on the floor behind me, the wound wasn't healing quickly enough. I looked down and saw the tread of my Doc Martens had left waffle shapes in the red puddle at my feet. I was leaving a breadcrumb trail for Savina to follow.

A trail.

I rounded a corner and arrived in the laboratory, back where I started.

'Make sure you leave me some of that blood,' called Savina, her voice drawing closer. 'Don't make me have to scoop it all up off the floor.'

The wound she'd given me had healed up and stopped gushing now, but my shoes had tracked the blood all the way across the laboratory floor. Savina entered the room, her eyes following the bloody footprints to their completion; a spot behind the lab bench, behind the bubbling test tubes and the coils of twisting glass.

'I do so hate to see women suffer,' she said. 'Women already get hurt so much in this world.'

I heard her bony feet crossing the lab's stone floor, clopping like a demon's hooves. She rounded the bench, claws poised, ready to finish what she'd started and tear me apart. Except all she found at the end of the breadcrumb trail, sat in a puddle of blood, was a pair of discarded shoes.

'Blood for Blood, you miserable bitch!' I screamed, as I leapt out from behind Savina's blood suction machine, a hose in each hand.

Before she could turn around to defend herself, I rammed the needles into each of her ear holes.

Shunk.

I was hoping that jamming eight combined inches of brass into Savina's brainpan and whirling them about like I was whisking a bowl of eggs would be enough to put her down, but she wasn't done yet.

She bucked against me like a prize bronco, kicking back violently, desperate to throw me off. She almost managed to disengage herself as she forced her body upright and slammed me against the workbench, but I clung on, stubbornly refusing to let go.

I dragged her towards the suction machine and attempted to get a hand to the crank that activated the thing, but the moment I loosened my grip on her, she almost succeeded in hurling me over her shoulder. My heel connected with the machine as I was jerked into the air, toppling it sideways and shattering its glass bulb on the floor. I stayed stuck to Savina, hanging on like a limpet, holding the needles in place and praying that she ran out of steam before I did.

She threw herself backwards, hammering me into a wall. I felt something explode in my stomach and realised I'd been elbowed, only not in any conventional way.

A sharp, curved bone protruded from Savina's elbow, slick with blood. My blood.

She launched her other elbow into my gut and I felt it pierce the skin and slip inside. She toppled and we both hit the floor, still entwined. Every fibre of my being told me to let go—to roll away and gather my strength—but I knew that the moment I did, Savina would rip those needles from her ears and be on top again. I had to hold on. Just for a little longer.

The blood gushing from my stomach was so thick and copious that it practically glued me to the floor now. I felt hollow. Spent. My grip began to give.

Then I saw something.

There on the ground, right by my eyeball, less than an inch high.

Gendith.

'Keep fighting,' she said, then turned and ran.

I felt a slice of adrenalin rip through my body, and came alive like a hand grenade. I wrapped my biceps around Savina as tight as I could, pinning her arms to her sides, feeling my heart beating fiercely against the sturdy bone of her back. She wriggled, scuttling about on the stone floor like a cockroach running from the light.

Gen slalomed broken glass to arrive at the toppled pump, and scaled the side of the machine to reach its crank. It didn't seem possible that a person her size would be able to work the thing, but she surprised me by wrapping both arms around its handle and pushing. With a mighty heave, the crank began to move, and Gen powered after it like a barbarian turning a giant slave wheel.

The syringes plugged into Savina's ears twitched as the pump came to life, sucking out her vital fluids in a grisly reverse transfusion. A scream tore through her like a dentist drill against a glass bottle. I clung on, keeping her arms bound tight about her and locking my fingers together to prevent her escape.

'Keep pumping!' I yelled, and Gendith pushed and pushed with all her might.

I heard a crack and felt Savina's armoured hide give. An arm snapped in two under my grip, then another. I expected the vampire to scream all the louder for it, but she was quiet now. Her whole body had turned egg shell thin. There was a sound like a burst of gunshot from a distant firing squad as her brittle body collapsed completely, then turned to dust.

I rolled on to my back, muscles burning, feeling like my whole body was having a heart attack.

'Are you just going to lie there?'

Gen blotted out the light, towering over me on her impossibly long, giraffe legs.

'You got embiggened!' I gasped.

She reached down, to hug me I thought, but instead tugged me unceremoniously to my feet. 'No time for that.'

She marched me out of the lab, past a trail of my own blood, back to the library.

'Help him,' she demanded, pointing at Vizael's body.

'Help him?' I dropped to my knees and put my hands on his

neck. He was warm still, but rapidly cooling. He had no pulse, no heartbeat, and we'd been away from him for five minutes at least. 'It's no use, we're too late.'

'Just try,' Gen cried, her voice charged with fear.

Panic gripped me and my brain went into overdrive as I tried desperately to recall my First Aid training.

What do we do with a person who isn't breathing?

CPR.

I interlocked my fingers, placed the heel of my left hand in the centre of his chest and used my body weight to start making compressions.

'Come on, old man,' I said, rocking back and forth, begging him to rejoin the land of the living.

It was no good though. I knew that before I'd begun. He'd be brain dead by now, even if I could get his heart started. The old man was gone, and there was no getting him back.

I felt a tingle in my hand and an arc of blue light zapped from my palm and connected with Viz's chest, no bigger than the spark from a stun gun. In response, his leg shot up and kicked the air.

'What the hell was that?' I asked, pulling back in surprise.

'The Lazarus hand!' Gen replied.

'The what?'

'The divine spark. The power to revive the dead.'

'You mean that thing Viz told me about? The hearty starty power?'

'Yes!'

I remembered what Viz had said to me: that I hadn't learned the full extent of my powers, and that one day I'd be able to jump start dead people, provided they weren't too messed up. How messed up was Viz, I wondered.

'Well, go on then,' Gen shrieked. 'Use the brand to revive him.'

'I don't know how; I haven't learned how to do that yet.'

'Then what better time to start?'

Fuck it. I had no clue what I was doing, but what did I have to lose? I placed my hand brand-down on the old man's chest and said a silent prayer.

Nothing.

Not a sausage.

'Are you serious?' I said, casting my eyes to the heavens. 'You're going to muck me about now?'

I pressed my brand harder into Viz's sternum, eyes squeezed tight, trying to summon the precious spark that would return him to us.

Nothing.

'Come on, what are you waiting for?' cried Gen.

'I'm trying as hard as I can!' I shot back.

I ripped open Viz's shirt and pressed my flesh to his, hard enough to leave the white imprint of an N in the meat of his chest. I gave it everything I had, grinding my teeth, concentrating so hard it made my head throb.

The brand sparked like a defibrillator and spat a current through Viz that lifted his whole body off the ground. Blue light danced beneath his skin, coursing around his body, lighting him up like a live wire. I felt the hand of the universe, working through my hand.

Viz gasped and broke into a great barking cough.

He was alive! I brought him back. I fixed a broken angel.

'What happened?' he wheezed, his chest heaving up and down.

Gen collapsed and wrapped her arms around him, tears spilling down her face. 'You doddering old fool.'

And with that, I let out a breath I didn't even know I'd been holding.

26

'You wanted to talk,' said Gen, taking a slug of her beer. 'So talk.'

Vizael was back at The Vault, recuperating still while the two of us shared a booth at The Beehive.

Across the bar I saw a woman with a writhing head of snakes instead of hair. 'Check her out,' I said, leaning over the table and nudging Gen's elbow, 'do you reckon the rug matches the drapes?'

'Stop changing the subject,' Gen replied. 'Why are we here?'

I'd been dreading this, but she was right. I'd brought us to the pub to address the elephant in the room, so address it I would.

'Okay, here goes,' I sighed. 'We need to talk about what happened last time we came here. When we snogged.'

'Keep your voice down, will you?' she hissed, her eyes darting about the salon.

'Gen, there's a wizard over there playing darts with his brain. I'm thinking that hearing about us kissing won't be the most outrageous thing that happens here tonight.'

Gen sunk into her seat and folded her arms. 'Well? Go ahead then, say your piece.'

'Don't be like that. Work with me here.'

'What do you want me to say?'

'I don't know! Christ, I'm so muddled up right now. I didn't know I could be attracted to women, Gen. Not like that. I thought I was straight.'

Her ice-chip eyes searched my face. 'And now you think otherwise?'

'I guess. I kissed a girl, didn't I, and I would have gone further than that if… well, if we hadn't been interrupted.'

'You were drunk. We both were.'

'I knew what I was doing,' I replied, taking a gulp of my beer.

Gen nodded, whether in agreement or just to move the conversation on, I couldn't be sure. 'What about Neil?' she asked.

'I haven't really thought that much about Neil, to be honest.'

'Will you let him go?' she asked, bluntly.

It felt weird getting into the nitty-gritty of my long-term relationship with a woman I'd only recently been physical with, but the need to spill my guts outweighed that discomfort. 'We've been together a long time, me and Neil. I always thought we'd go the distance. Assumed it, anyway. I told myself I wasn't going to be part of failed relationship like my parents were.'

'Just because something runs its course, doesn't mean it's a failure.'

I downed my pint. 'Tell me the truth, did God kick you out of Heaven because you're gay?'

'You're changing the subject again.'

'I want to know.'

She polished off her beer. 'He did, but this was back when He was stricter about that sort of behaviour. I'm given to believe He's calmed down considerably since then.'

'Couldn't you complain?'

'There's no fair employment tribunal in Heaven.'

I patted the back of her hand. 'And here you are now, stuck down here with the rest of us. You and me.'

'Me and you. So what do we do about this? About... us?' I went to answer, but Gen accidentally cut in on me with a follow-up question. 'Sorry,' she said, 'you go first.'

'Okay, here's what I'm thinking,' I replied. 'I like you, Gen. I like you more than I knew I could like a woman, but this thing between us… it can't work. We have a job to do out there, and I wouldn't be able to do my part if I was with you that way. You get that, don't you?'

'Yes,' she replied, stony-faced. 'I get that.'

'Okay then, glad to hear it. Now, what were you going to say?'

Gen looked away. 'Same thing. The two of us need to keep it professional. Strictly business.'

I could tell just from her expression that what she'd really meant to say was headed in a different direction altogether. Balls. As if killing vampires wasn't complicated enough.

Thamesmead. I stared up at a twelve-storey block of flats; the monolithic granite tombstone that memorialised my old life, before I got drawn into all this mess. The sky above was a great black ceiling that stubbornly refused to offer so much as a pinprick of light. I shivered, but only because I was cold, not out of fear. It's funny, I used to worry about walking alone in that estate after dark, now I worried for the well-being of anyone stupid enough to cross my path with bad intentions.

I stepped inside the tower block's echoing lobby and made my way up the stairs, knowing full well the lift would be out of order. Visit *The Guardian* and you'll find articles written by boojie middle-class types defending Thamesmead's architecture—waxing lyrical about the sparse beauty of its brutalist design—but let me tell you, those articles are written from a long, long way away.

And yet, to me, Thamesmead still held a special place in my heart. Yes, it smelled like a festival toilet, yes it looked like a prison block that had inexplicably expanded and spread across an entire borough, but I still had an affection for the place. Call me institutionalised, but when I looked out of my window across that concrete hellscape, I saw home.

'Abbey?'

An elderly man in a disheveled duffle coat stood a couple of steps up from me, passing down the stairs in the opposite direction. It was Mister Munford, my curtain-twitching neighbour from across the hall.

'You've been quiet,' he said, for once not wearing his trademarked sneer. 'Haven't heard a peep from you in weeks.'

No surprise there. I hadn't had much use for my old flat since I got mixed up with angels and bloodsuckers. The only reason the place hadn't been re-occupied was because my rent was paid up three months in advance.

'Just being a considerate neighbour,' I said, putting on a smile.

'Well then,' he said, wearing an expression that was somehow both impressed and deeply circumspect, 'keep it up.'

He carried on down the stairs, eyes trained on me until he rounded a corner and disappeared from sight.

I sighed and carried on up the steps, hiking the last few flights to the ninth floor.

My flat was just as I left it; same mildew smell, same neighbour kid squalling through the walls, same sparsely furnished, Travelodge aesthetic. The only thing different was the dust, which covered everything in a thin grey film. I ran a fingertip along Neil's writing desk, drawing a line, then another, then one more until I had a letter N in front of me. Not an N for Nightstalker. An N for Neil.

I was hanging my coat on the back of his chair when I heard a rattle of keys, and the front door swung open. There he was, as if drawn by magic, as if the initial I'd sketched on his desk was part of some summoning spell.

'Hi, Neil.'

He stood in the door frame uncertainly, an oxygen tank propped by his side... an almost-empty oxygen tank. I knew he'd have to stock up soon, and seeing as he obviously had no intention of returning to The Vault for a refill, that made this place his next most likely option. I wasn't expecting him quite this soon though, and his sudden appearance threw me off kilter.

'Aren't you going to come in?' I stammered.

He stood there for a moment, frozen to the spot, then cast his eyes to the ground and dragged his trolley inside. I followed him as he trudged to the lounge and took a seat on the sofa.

'It's good to see you,' I said, managing to strike a chord that was both chipper and apologetic, though of course not apologetic enough. Not for what I'd done.

He looked back at me, his face as still as a billboard model, perfectly content to let me do the talking.

I slumped down in the armchair opposite him. 'Okay, here it is. I'm sorry. I'm *so sorry*. What happened with Gen—what happened with Lauden—that isn't who I am. You know me, Neil. You've known me half my life and you have to understand that I'd never do anything to hurt you. It's this job, this war I'm fighting, it's turned my brain into a rubber ball, bouncing all over the place. Making me do things I never would have done before.'

He continued to look on as my thoughts unravelled, his expression unreadable.

I carried on, speaking from the heart, words slipping off my tongue without forethought. 'Look, just because my whole life's changed, doesn't mean I don't have room for you. I need you, Neil. You're the only normal thing I have left. Please don't give up on me.'

All the while, Neil just sat there, staring at me blankly.

I shuffled forward in my chair. 'Well, aren't you going to say anything? You must have things you want to say to me.'

For a few seconds, he did nothing, then his shoulders started to hitch. At first I thought he was about to cry, but that wasn't it.

He was laughing.

Head back and cackling.

Something was wrong. Something was horribly wrong.

When Neil looked back at me, I saw a glowing letter J stamped on his forehead.

'Hello, Abbey,' said Judas.

Was I dreaming? No. The details were too crisp. Too lifelike. Judas had taken hold of my boyfriend.

'You?' was all I managed to say.

'I came here to say thank you,' he replied, the amber light of his eyes shining through Neil's. 'For killing the rebel, Savina. Your silly little vendetta has done me a great service, girl.' He climbed to his feet and took a step in my direction. I instinctively drew my dagger before I realised the futility of it. I couldn't use the thing. Not on Neil. 'I had that woman hunted across four continents,' Judas went on, 'I lied to my people, told them that she was dead, but it took you to really do the deed, Abbey. Thank you for my victory, and for giving me this vessel.'

'I didn't give you anything.'

'Oh, no. Oh no, no, no. When I first made acquaintance with this boy, his conviction was rock-solid. I visited him every night, whispering in his ear, trying to turn him to my side, but he would not be swayed. Would not hear of it. No matter how hard I tried, every sunrise, the honeyed words I poured into his ear would evaporate with the morning dew.'

I felt a knot in my stomach. The dagger weighed heavy in my hand. Just the thought of Judas in Neil's head was enough to make me feel sick.

'Try as I might, I could not sink my hooks into your beau,' said Judas. 'Even when the cracks between you began to show, I could not find purchase. Not until you cheated on him. It took *you* to drive the wedge. To corrupt him. After that, he came to me willingly. All I had to do was show him a place to go. A place he was welcome. A place he could serve a purpose.'

I should never have let Neil out of my sight. Judas had established a link to me that let him visit my dreams, why hadn't I counted on him doing the same with Neil? Lauden's blood had once flowed in his veins. Lauden's blood was Judas' blood. I should have known the vampire master would be in Neil's head too. I thought back to Neil's behaviour, before it all went wrong between us: the sleepwalking, the late night talking, the mood swings. The clues were all there if I'd only opened my eyes.

'You're right,' I told Judas. 'It's my fault you got to Neil. But that doesn't mean I can't fight for him now.'

I stepped into the lounge doorway, cutting off the room's only exit.

'What do you think you're doing?' asked Judas.

'This isn't the first time Neil's been turned,' I replied. 'I've broken your influence before and I'll do it again. I might have given you Savina, but I'm not giving you this. Neil comes home with me.'

Judas dragged the corners of Neil's mouth up into a rictus grin. 'No. I'm afraid he won't be joining you. You see, Neil is about to perform an important function. The first useful function of his entire, miserable existence.'

I gripped the hilt of my dagger. 'Oh, yeah? And what's that?'

Judas removed the breathing tube from Neil's nostrils and stepped away from his oxygen tank.

'What are you doing?' I asked, my voice tinged with panic.

Judas raised Neil's arms in the air, crucifix-style, and began walking him backwards towards the window.

'No, stop!' My legs pedalled after him, but not fast enough.

Crash.

The window came apart in a thousand glittering fragments.

Time seemed to stop as Neil tipped through the shattered opening and hung suspended in the air, surrounded by a swarm of freeze-framed glass.

Then time started up again.

'No!'

I saw a foot slip out of view, and Neil was gone.

Silence—a horrible, sinking silence that seemed to drag for an eternity—then a cold howl as the numbness left me and I felt wind whipping against my bare arms and face, snatching at my hair, filling my ears with its annihilating roar. My whole body shaking, I willed myself towards the window, one halting step at a time. My teeth bit into my lip hard enough to draw blood. My head was chaos.

He wasn't dead. He couldn't be dead. He'd have snagged something on the way down. Been caught by a neighbour's balcony. Landed in that pile of rubbish that someone had fly tipped down below; the one Mister Munford had been complaining about for months, and still hadn't been collected.

I crumpled to the ground, hugging the carpet as I edged over to the shattered window, and dipped my head to stare into the abyss.

Nine storeys below, face-down in a pool of pale lamplight, lay Neil.

Shattered.

A colour that looked almost black crept out from him like a blooming flower.

There would be no last-minute rescue this time.

No magic strong enough to bring him back.

Neil was gone.

And with that, my whole world broke into pieces.

To Be Continued…

LEAVE A REVIEW

Reviews are gold to indie authors, so if you've enjoyed this book, please consider visiting the site you purchased it from and leaving a quick review.

BECOME AN INSIDER

Sign up and receive **FREE UNCANNY KINGDOM BOOKS**. Also, be the **FIRST** to hear about **NEW RELEASES** and **SPECIAL OFFERS** in the **UNCANNY KINGDOM** universe. Just visit:

WWW.UNCANNYKINGDOM.COM

MORE STORIES SET IN THE UNCANNY KINGDOM

The Hexed Detective Series

Hexed Detective

Fatal Moon

Night Terrors

The London Coven Series

Familiar Magic

Nightmare Realm

Deadly Portent

The Spectral Detective Series

Spectral Detective

Corpse Reviver

Twice Damned

The Dark Lakes Series

Magic Eater

Blood Stones

Past Sins

Strange Stories

Apocalypse Hill

37048667R00334

Printed in Great Britain
by Amazon